全新！NＥＷ GEPT 全民英檢

除語言中心委員會、郭文興、許秀芬——著

中級 聽力&閱讀 題庫解析

新制修訂版

全書MP3一次下載

9789864541584.zip

「iOS系統請升級至iOS 13後再行下載，
此為大型檔案，建議使用WIFI連線下載，以免佔用流量，
並確認連線狀況，以利下載順暢。」

CONTENTS

目錄

NEW GEPT 全新全民英檢中級
聽力&閱讀題庫解析 [新制修定版]

全民英語能力分級檢定測驗的問與答

　　財團法人語言訓練中心（LTTC）自 2000 年全民英檢（General English Proficiency Test, GEPT）推出至今，持續進行該測驗可信度及有效度的研究，以期使測驗品質最佳化。

　　因此，自 2021 年一月起，GEPT 調整部分初級、中級及中高級的聽讀測驗題數與題型內容，並提供成績回饋服務。另一方面，此次調整主要目的是要反映 108 年國民教育新課綱以「素養」及「學習導向評量（Learning Oriented Assessment）」為中心的教育理念，希望可以透過適當的測驗內容與成績回饋，有效促進國人的英語溝通能力。而調整後的題型與內容將更貼近日常生活，且更能符合各階段英文學習的歷程。透過適當的測驗內容與回饋，使學生更有效率地學習與應用。

Q 2021 年起，中級測驗的聽力與閱讀（初試）在題數與題型上有何不同？

中級的聽力及閱讀測驗皆有改變題型，調整的部分如下：

聽力測驗：

調整前	調整後
■ 第一部分 看圖辨義 15 題 ■ 第二部分 問答 15 題 ■ 第三部分 簡短對話 15 題 共 45 題	■ 第一部分 看圖辨義 5 題 ■ 第二部分 問答 10 題 ■ 第三部分 簡短對話 10 題 ■ 第四部分 簡短談話 10 題 共 35 題

調整重點：

1. 第三部分「簡短對話」增加圖表題。

2. 新增第四部分「簡短談話」，部份的題目包含圖表。

閱讀測驗：

調整前	調整後
■ 第一部分 詞彙與結構 15 題 ■ 第二部分 段落填空 10 題 ■ 第三部分 閱讀理解 15 題 共 40 題	■ 第一部分 詞彙 10 題 ■ 第二部分 段落填空 10 題 ■ 第三部分 閱讀理解 15 題 共 35 題

調整重點：

1. 第一部分「詞彙與結構」，改成「詞彙」。

2. 第二部分「段落填空」增加選項為句子或子句類型。

3. 第三部分「閱讀理解」增加多文本、圖片類型。

Q 考生可申請單項合格證書

另外，證書核發也有新制，除了現在已經有的「聽讀證書」與「聽讀說寫證書」外，也可以申請口說或寫作的單項合格證書，方便考生證明自己的英語強項，更有利升學、求職。

Q 本項測驗在目的及性質方面有何特色？

整體而言，有四項特色：

（1）本測驗的對象包含在校學生及一般社會人士，測驗目的在評量一般英語能力（general English proficiency），命題不侷限於特定領域或教材；

（2）整套系統共分五級—初級（Elementary）、中級（Intermediate）、中高級（High-Intermediate）、高級（Advanced）、優級（Superior）—根據各階段英語學習者的特質及需求，分別設計題型及命題內容，考生可依能力選擇適當等級報考；

（3）各級測驗均重視聽、說、讀、寫四種能力的評量；

（4）本測驗係「標準參照測驗」（criterion-referenced test），每級訂有明確的能力指標，考生只要通過所報考級數即可取得該級的合格證書。

Q 本測驗既包含聽、說、讀、寫四項，各項測驗方式為何？

聽力及閱讀測驗採選擇題方式，口說及寫作測驗則採非選擇題方式，每級依能力指標設計題型。以中級為例，聽力部分含 35 題，作答時間約 30 分鐘；閱讀部分含 35 題，作答時間 45 分鐘；寫作

部分含中翻英、引導寫作，作答時間 40 分鐘；口說測驗採錄音方式進行，作答時間約 15 分鐘。

Q 何謂 GEPT 聽診室 — 個人化成績服務？

「GEPT 聽診室」成績服務，提供考生個人化強弱項診斷回饋和實用的學習建議，更好的是，考生在收到成績單的一個月內即可自行上網免費閱覽下載，非常便利。其中的內容包括：

1. 能力指標的達成率—以圖示呈現您（考生）當次考試的能力表現。
2. 強弱項解析與說明—以例題說明各項能力指標的具體意義。
3. 學習指引—下一階段的學習方法與策略建議。
4. 字彙與句型—統計考生該次考試表現中，統整尚未掌握的關鍵字彙與句型。

Q 英檢中級的聽力需要達到什麼程度及其運用範圍為何？

中級考生須具備基礎英文能力，並能理解與使用淺易的日常用語，其參考單字範圍以「教育部基礎 2000-5000 字」為主，而聽力測驗考生必須聽出這 5000 字以內的詞彙，並能聽懂母語人士語速慢且清晰的對話，並能聽懂一般會話。透過視覺輔助，理解人、事、時、地、物的簡單描述，例如簡單的問路與方向指示。考生應能大致聽懂日常生活相關的對話，例如簡短的公共場所廣播、體育賽事、天氣狀況播報、電話留言、廣告等。

PRELUDE

Q 英檢中級的閱讀需要達到什麼程度及其運用範圍為何？

閱讀測驗考生必須可以認出並理解 5000 個單字以內，與個人生活、家庭、朋友及學校生活相關的基本詞彙與用語。並能閱讀短文／故事／私人信件／廣告／傳單／簡介及使用說明等。考生應能掌握短文主旨與部分細節、釐清上下文關係與短文結構，並整合與歸納兩篇文本的多項訊息。

Q 英檢中級初試的通過標準為何？

級數	測驗項目	通過標準
中級	聽力測驗 閱讀測驗	兩項測驗成績總和達 160 分，且其中任何一項成績不得低於 72 分。

Q 這項測驗各級命題方向為何？考生應如何準備？

全民英檢在設計各級的命題方向時，均曾參考目前各級英語教育之課程大綱，同時也廣泛搜集相關教材進行內容分析，以求命題內容能符合國內各級英語教育的需求。同時，為了這項測驗的內容能反應本土的生活經驗與特色，因此命題內容力求生活化，並包含流行話題及時事。

由於這項測驗並未針對特定領域或教材命題，考生應無需特別準備。但因各級測驗均包含聽、說、讀、寫四部分，而目前國內英語教育仍偏重讀與寫，因此考生必須平日加強聽、說訓練，同時多接觸英語媒體（如報章雜誌、廣播、電視、電影等），以求在測驗時有較好的表現。

Q 通過「全民英檢」合格標準者是否取得合格證書？又合格證書有何用途或效力？

是的，通過「全民英檢」合格標準者將頒給證書。以目前初步的規畫，全民英檢測驗之合格證明書能成為民眾求學或就業的重要依據，同時各級學校也可利用本測驗做為學習成果檢定及教學改進的參考。

Q 國中、高中學生若無國民身分證，如何報考？

國中生未請領身分證者，可使用印有相片之健保 IC 卡替代；高中生以上中華民國國民請使用國民身份證正面。外籍人士需備有效期限內之台灣居留證影本。

Q 初試與複試一定在同一考區嗎？

測驗中心原則上儘量會安排在同一地區，但初試、複試借用的考區不盡相同，故複試的考場一律由測驗中心安排。

Q 請問合格證書的有效期限只有兩年嗎？

合格證書並無有效期限，而是成績紀錄保存兩年，意即兩年內的成績單，如因故遺失，可申請補發。成績單申請費用 100 元，證書 300 元，申請表格備索。

Q 複試是否在一天內結束？

不一定，視考生人數而定，確定的時間以複試准考證所載之測驗時間為準。

Q 報考全民英檢是否有年齡、學歷的限制？

除國小生外。本測驗適合台灣地區之英語學習者報考。

Q 合格之標準為何？

初試兩項測驗成績總和達 160 分，且其中任一項成績不低於 72 分者，複試成績除初級寫作為 70 分，其餘級數的寫作、口說測驗都 80 分以上才算通過，可獲核發合格證書。

Q 初試通過，複試未通過，下一次是否還需要再考一次初試？

初試通過者，可於二年內單獨報考複試未通過項目。

★關於「全民英語能力分級檢定測驗」之內容及相關問題請洽：

財團法人語言訓練測驗中心

中心地址：106台北市辛亥路二段170號（台灣大學校總區內）

郵政信箱：台北郵政第 23-41號信箱

電話：(02)2362-6385-7

傳真：(02)2367-1944

辦公日：週一至週五（週六、日及政府機構放假日不上班）

辦公時間：上午八點至十二點、下午一點至五點

全民英檢中級

第一回 初試 聽力測驗

本測驗分四部份，全為四選一之選擇題，共 35 題，作答時間約 30 分鐘。

第一部分　看圖辨義

共 5 題，試題冊上有數幅圖畫，每一圖畫有 1~3 個描述該圖的題目，每題請聽錄音播出每題以及四個英語敘述之後，選出與所看到的圖畫最相符的一個答案。每題只播出一遍。

例題：（看）

（聽） Look at the picture.
What does the woman want
the boy to do?
A. Pick up the rubbish.
B. Tie his shoelaces.
C. Carry her luggage.
D. Hail a cab.

正確答案為 A。

聽力測驗第一部分自本頁開始。

A:　Question 1

B:　Question 2 and 3

C: Question 4

D: Question 5

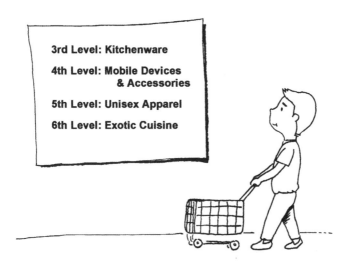

第二部分　問答

　　共 10 題，每題請聽光碟放音機播出一英語問句或直述句之後，從試題冊上 A、B、C、D 四個回答或回應中，選出一個最適合者作答。每題只播出一遍。

例：　（聽）　What happened to your feet?
　　　（看）　A. They were too hungry.
　　　　　　　B. I got a new pair.
　　　　　　　C. My new shoes are too small.
　　　　　　　D. These are not mine.

正確答案為 C。

6. A. Why not have a garage sale?
   B. I can do it in an hour.
   C. We can look for a shorter controller one.
   D. Maybe the line is busy. alert.

7. A. You should believe it, shouldn't you?
   B. They could handle it, couldn't they?
   C. We can't predict everything, can we?
   D. It won't be taught, will it?

8. A. He hasn't finished it yet.
   B. I did it first thing in the morning.
   C. The report is in my drawer.
   D. There is no Internet connection.

9. A. Please pack it first.
   B. It's famous for its maple leaves.
   C. You can't be serious.
   D. By air or by sea?

10. A. You bet. I love the art gallery.
    B. Spare me. I have lost count.
    C. Maybe. About 400 meters or so.
    D. Oh dear. I forgot where I keep it.

11. A. I'm into fantasy and romance.
    B. I'm usually gentle and polite.
    C. I think you should head south.
    D. I believe writing is not an easy task.

12. A. It's cool. I travelled there by bus.
    B. It's great. Thai food is terrific.
    C. It's sad. They tied the elephants to trees.
    D. It's insane. Nobody follows the rules.

13. A. Nice to meet you, too.
    B. We are vegetarians.
    C. I'll do it right away.
    D. We need more information.

14. A. What an unfortunate accident!
    B. Please put on the safety belt.
    C. Excuse me for a moment.
    D. I agree that it was a kind gesture.

15. A. No. I can't find it here.
    B. Yes. It was really distressing.
    C. No. I think it is a great movie.
    D. Yes. It's important to be on time.

第三部分　簡短對話

共 10 題，每題請聽光碟放音機播出一段對話及一個相關的問題後，從試題冊上 A、B、C、D 四個選項中選出一個最適合者作答。每段對話及問題只播出一遍。

例：　(聽)　(Man)　　　Did you happen to see my earphones?
　　　　　　　　　　　I remember leaving them in the drawer.
　　　　　　(Woman)　Did you search your briefcase?
　　　　　　(Man)　　　I did but they are not there. Wait a second. Oh.
　　　　　　　　　　　They are right here in my pocket.

　　　　　　Question:　Where are the man's earphones?

　　(看)　A.　The woman's pocket.
　　　　　B.　Briefcase.
　　　　　C.　The man's pocket.
　　　　　D.　Drawer.

正確答案為 C。

16. A. At a hospital.
　　B. In an auditorium.
　　C. At a theme park.
　　D. In a restaurant.

17. A. The buildings in Italy.
　　B. The people in Italy.
　　C. The traditional festivals in Italy.
　　D. The pop culture in Italy.

18. A. Tips for an interview.
　　B. Answers to an exam.
　　C. Good hygiene habits.
　　D. A live performance.

19. A. The woman misunderstood him.
　　B. The woman had a good reason.
　　C. The woman left something undone.
　　D. The woman didn't know where the bank is.

20. A. Give the man an envelope.
　　B. Fill in some information.
　　C. Come back again tomorrow morning.
　　D. Send the man an email.

16

21. A. A chef.
    B. A waiter.
    C. A pilot.
    D. A secretary.

22. A. He should park the vehicle for at least an hour.
    B. He should find out where his car is first.
    C. He shouldn't violate traffic regulations.
    D. He shouldn't blame the woman for his bad luck.

23. A. On a cargo train.
    B. On an airplane.
    C. In a textile factory.
    D. In a repair garage.

24.

Date	Event
2/10	Workshop: How to use scented candles to relax
2/11	Seminar: How to build eco-friendly environment
2/12	No Meat Banquet

A. The workshop of scented candles.
B. The seminar of eco-friendly environment.
C. No Meat Banquet.
D. None of these events she will go.

25.

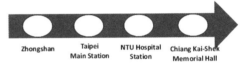

TO Xiangshan

Zhongshan　Taipei Main Station　NTU Hospital Station　Chiang Kai-Shek Memorial Hall

A. Zhongshan Station.
B. Taipei Main Station.
C. NTU Hospital Station.
D. Chiang Kai-Shek Memorial Hall Station.

共 10 題，每題請聽光碟放音機播出一段談話及一個相關的問題後，從試題冊上 A、B、C、D 四個選項中選出一個最適合者作答。每段談話及問題只播出一遍。

例：　　　(聽)　　Good morning, everyone. Please come over here and take these registration forms. Then, go back to your seats. This is the workshop on APP design. The lecturer of this workshop is an engineer from SBE Software. He has excellent experience in designing smartphone applications. Before you fill in the forms, please look through the forms carefully. If you have any questions, I will answer you later.

Question:　　What might the listeners do, after they read through the registration forms?

(看)　　A. Leave the forms on the desks.
　　　　B. Pay the registration fee.
　　　　C. Ask the speaker some questions.
　　　　D. Go to another location.

正確答案為 C。

26. A. Charge her a late fee.
　　B. Freeze her bank account.
　　C. Increase her interest rate.
　　D. Cancel her credit card membership.

27. A. The happy feeling.
　　B. The excited feeling.
　　C. The angry feeling.
　　D. The lonely feeling.

28. A. Bring their umbrellas.
    B. Use the sunscreen cream.
    C. Wear some sweaters.
    D. Don't go out.

29. A. Talk on the cellphones.
    B. Take pictures with the flashes.
    C. Touch the sculptures.
    D. Watch the painting.

30. A. Place the tree in their yard.
    B. Give the tree to their parents.
    C. Put the gifts under the tree.
    D. Burn the tree to get warm.

31. A. 800 calories.
    B. 700 calories.
    C. 600 calories.
    D. 500 calories.

32. A. A free screen.
    B. A free key board.
    C. A free anti-virus software.
    D. A free speaker.

33. A. In an amusement park.
    B. In a factory.
    C. In a market.
    D. In a campus.

34.

South Airline BOARDING PASS
Name of passenger: Lillian Song
Flight NO: 675C   Class: Y
From: New Delhi   To: Los Angeles
Date: 10/20/2022   Seat: 33A
GATE: 22
BOARDING TIME: 08:30

    A. 08:25
    B. 08:30
    C. 08:35
    D. 08:40

35.

Identification Card
Name: Andy Wang
Date of Birth: 07/22/1998
Identification NO: AW128537229

    A. He will see the sea animals in the zoo.
    B. He can't play roller coaster because it's still in maintenance.
    C. He will get 20 percent discount when he goes to the park.
    D. He can't eat many kinds of food in the park.

— 結束 —

第一回 初試 閱讀測驗

本測驗分三部分，全為四選一的選擇題，共 35 題，作答時間為 45 分鐘。

第一部分：詞彙

本部分共 10 題，每題有一個空格。請就試題冊上的四個選項中選出最適合題意的字或詞作答。

1. A survey questionnaire was given to the candidates to _____ their strengths and weaknesses before a second round of interviews were scheduled.
   A. integrate
   B. orientate
   C. evaluate
   D. mutate

2. Being out of a job for several months, the young man was _____ for any kind of work that would enable him to cover his rent and other expenses.
   A. desperate
   B. aspired
   C. outrageous
   D. eligible

3. The simple story of a farm girl, who took part in a talent show, was blown out of _____ after being circulated through the Internet for a few months.
   A. revolution
   B. configuration
   C. proportion
   D. imitation

4. The man whose wife was suffering from cancer decided to put an end to her _____ by giving her an overdose of sleeping pills.
   A. ailment
   B. misery
   C. disease
   D. recovery

5. To everyone's disbelief, the defending champions were _____ in the first round of the tournament.
   A. destroyed
   B. eliminated
   C. compromised
   D. violated

6. Despite repeated _____ to put out the fire, it could not be brought under control and it spread to other parts of the forest within a few hours.
   A. constructions
   B. phenomena
   C. attempts
   D. forecasts

7. The president's speech was temporarily _____ when someone threw a shoe onto the stage, which only missed the president's head by a few inches.
   A. recommended
   B. classified
   C. interrupted
   D. abstained

8. The burglar pretended _____ and insisted that he entered the wrong house because he was drunk.
   A. acknowledgement
   B. ignorance
   C. detention
   D. behavior

9. You could have called me to tell that you wouldn't be able to make it to the party. I was the only girl without a dance partner. How _____!
   A. wonderful
   B. embarrassing
   C. lovely
   D. careful

10. Never _____ what you can do today till tomorrow. Tomorrow has its own troubles.
    A. put away
    B. put on
    C. put off
    D. put out

第二部分：段落填空

共 10 題，包括二個段落，每個段落各含 5 個空格。請由試題冊上四個選項中選出最適合題意的字或詞作答。

Questions 11-15

In recent years, an increasing number of people have opted to include more vegetables in their daily diet out of health ___(11)___ . The key to a healthy vegetarian diet — like any diet — is to enjoy a variety of foods. No single food can provide all the nutrition your body needs. The more ___(12)___ your diet is, the more challenging it can be to get all the ___(13)___ you need. A vegan diet, for example, eliminates natural food sources of vitamin B-12, as well as milk products, which are good sources of calcium. With a little planning, however, you can be sure that your diet includes everything your body needs. A food pyramid can be a helpful tool. The vegetarian pyramid outlines food groups and food choices that, ___(14)___ , form the foundation of a healthy vegetarian diet. Some people follow a semi-vegetarian diet — also known as a flexitarian diet — which is ___(15)___ a plant-based diet but includes meat, dairy, eggs, poultry and fish on occasion or in small quantities.

11. A. measurements
    B. principles
    C. considerations
    D. responsibilities

12. A. productive
    B. restrictive
    C. objective
    D. constructive

13. A. substances
    B. elements
    C. ingredients
    D. nutrients

14. A. in spite of the tasteless food
    B. if eaten in the right quantities
    C. when given the best solution
    D. in addition to the recipe

15. A. inevitably
    B. primarily
    C. consequently
    D. completely

Questions 16-20

The Harry Potter film series made Leavesden its home for more than ten years. As the books were still being ___(16)___ while the films were being made, the production crew saved many of the iconic sets, props and costumes that were created especially for the films - ___(17)___. Once filming wrapped on *Harry Potter and the Deathly Hallows - Part 2* in 2010, the production crew was left with a treasure trove of thousands of intricate and ___(18)___ artifacts, many of which wouldn't ___(19)___ on a typical production. The team behind Warner Bros. Studio Tour London - The Making of Harry Potter wanted to preserve and showcase these iconic props, costumes and sets so that Harry Potter fans could experience the magic of filmmaking ___(20)___, and on 31st March 2012, the Studio Tour opened its doors.

16. A. distributed
 B. sacrificed
 C. repudiated
 D. concluded

17. A. although the investors did not want to fund this project
 B. so that the film production company will sell these products
 C. just in case they were ever needed later on in the series
 D. because the fans would like to bid these precious products

18. A. made-beautiful
 B. made-beautifully
 C. beautifully-made
 D. beautiful-made

19. A. save
 B. be saving
 C. have saved
 D. have been saved

20. A. first-hand
 B. second-hand
 C. handful
 D. hands-on

　　本部分共 15 題，包括 5 個題組，每個題組含 1 至 2 篇短文，與數個相關的四選一的選擇題。請由試題冊上的選項中選出最適合者作答。

Questions 21-23

DANGER

This restricted area allows staff only.

This area contains dangerous chemical materials.

Staff must wear protective gear.

Trespassers will be charged with mischief

and could be fined up to 5,000 NTD.

21. What is the purpose of this sign?
    A. To prevent unauthorized people from entering
    B. To provide sightseeing information
    C. To collect tax for the government
    D. To conduct a chemical experiment

22. People who sneak into the area without permission will _____.
    A. be given a reward
    B. be fined a sum of money
    C. be beaten by security
    D. be hired by the company

23. Where might you see this warning sign?
    A. In front of a shopping mall
    B. By a dangerous river which runs extremely fast
    C. Outside a nuclear plant
    D. On a street with heavy traffic

Yummy Cake House

Do you enjoy having delicious and unforgettable cakes? Yummy Cake House is the number one bakery in town. Our chef now develops a brand new menu for all of our customers. Her new cakes will satisfy all the customer's stomachs. She can also customize the birthday cakes for our clients. Come to our cake house now and enjoy the delicious cakes.

Macrons	**NT 60**
Cupcake	**NT 70**
Fruit tart	**NT 120**
Tiramisu cake	**NT 120**
Strawberry cake	**NT 150**

Opening hours:
Monday to Friday, 10:30 A.M. to 9:00 P.M.
Saturday, 10:00 A.M. to 8:00 P.M.

VIP members can have 10% off discounts of all the items.

24. What is this advertisement for?

   A. A new barbershop.

   B. A new bakery.

   C. A new cloth shop.

   D. A new grocery store.

25. What information CANNOT be found in the advertisement?

   A. The prices of the products.

   B. The opening hours of the shop.

   C. VIP's discounts bonus.

   D. The location of the shop.

26. Mrs. Smith is the VIP member of Yummy Cake house. How many discount can she have?

   A. 40%

   B. 30%

   C. 20%

   D. 10%

40-year-old Martin, who lived alone, had worked for his stepfather's car rental business after he graduated from high school. He found his interest in landscape gardening and worked his way up from apprentice to master. But in April last year he lost his job when the firm downsized. He unsuccessfully applied for 40 posts over the next three months – and most of these applications went ignored because he was 'undercut' on wages by younger and less experienced candidates. Martin died 24 hours after visiting his local job where he was only offered a 'follow-up' appointment.

Speaking yesterday after an inquest into his death, Martin's stepfather described how the aspiring gardener "hated" going to his local job center, saying: "Many people go in with a sense of self-worth – they really do want a job – but come out feeling demoralized and put down. In the last months of his life, Martin became a statistic to other people. He was a statistic by being out of work, a statistic when he went into the Job Centre and now he is a statistic by killing himself."

Martin was highly independent and he never claimed any social benefits in his life. He got nothing off the government and was proud not to. There was enough money left in his bank to cover his monthly expenses for a full year. The reason he could not accept a gardening job with a lower pay was that he felt it was not a reflection of his talent, skills and more importantly, his self-worth as an individual.

27. Why was Martin out of work?
    A. He lacked the necessary experience.
    B. He decided to further his studies.
    C. He was fired by his stepfather.
    D. He was laid off by his company.

28. What happened when Martin tried to seek help from the local job center?
    A. He felt more depressed after every visit.
    B. He rejected over 40 job offers.
    C. He was told to arrange an appointment with a doctor.
    D. He had to learn statistics and other subjects.

29. What can be said about the local job center?
    A. It is impersonal.
    B. It is efficient.
    C. It is understaffed.
    D. It is corrupted.

Animal Rights supporters oppose zoos because cages and cramped enclosures at zoos deprive animals of the opportunity to satisfy their most basic needs. The zoo community regards the animals it keeps as commodities, and animals are regularly bought, sold, borrowed, and traded without any regard for established relationships. Zoos breed animals because the presence of babies draws zoo visitors and boosts revenue. But the animals' fate is often bleak once they outgrow their "cuteness." And some zoos still import animals from the wild.

In general, zoos and wildlife parks preclude or severely restrict natural behavior, such as flying, swimming, running, hunting, climbing, scavenging, foraging, digging, exploring, and selecting a partner. The physical and mental frustrations of captivity often lead to abnormal, neurotic, and even self-destructive behavior, such as incessant pacing, swaying, head-bobbing, bar-biting, and self-mutilation. Proponents of zoos like to claim that zoos protect species from extinction—seemingly a noble goal. However, wild-animal parks and zoos almost always favor large and charismatic animals which draw large crowds of visitors, but they neglect less popular species that also need to be protected. Most animals in zoos are not endangered, and while confining animals to zoos keeps them alive, it does nothing to protect wild populations and their habitats.

30. What is the main argument against locking wild animals in zoos?
   A. Zoos abuse and cause death to many animals.
   B. Zoos treat wild animals in an inhumane manner.
   C. Zoos make money by helping animals to reproduce.
   D. Zoos purchase wild animals in danger of extinction.

31. Why is the writer concerned about the fate of 'zoo-born' animals?
   A. They are likely to be attacked by other species.
   B. They are likely to hurt themselves in an enclosed area.
   C. They are likely to be neglected once they are fully grown.
   D. They are likely to attract more visitors to the zoo.

32. Which of the following is NOT a consequence caused by a loss of freedom?
   A. Wild mood swings
   B. Compulsive behavior
   C. Self-inflicted wounds
   D. Enriched lifestyle

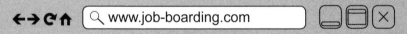

www.job-boarding.com

Job Description: Marketing Manager

Natural Beauty Cosmetic is an international brand. Our company aims at producing natural makeup products. We're looking for a creative and versatile marketer who will be responsible for the growth of our sales figures.

Responsibilities

- Develop strategies and tactics to promote our company's products
- Build the relationship with social media influencers to promote our company
- Oversee and approve marketing materials, such as website banner, product cover
- Produce eye-catching content for our website, social media

Requirements

- Master's degree in Business Administration
- Managerial skills and experience
- Social media posts writing skills
- Interpersonal skills and out-going personality

If you're interested in this position, please send your resume to human resource director, Ellie Green (ellie. g@naturalbeauty.com).

To:	ellie.g@naturalbeauty.com
From:	jeff.chen@hotmail.com
Subject:	Marketing Manager Application
Attachment:	Jeff Chen-resume.pdf

Dear Ms. Green,

I'm Jeff Chen. I found your company's advertisement on the job boards website. In response to your advertisement, I am interested in applying for the Marketing Manager position as offered. I believe my qualification below meets the requirement.

- Master degree in Business Administration in H.S University
- 5-year managing experience at SFY Advertisement
- Budget reviewing skills
- Advertisement writing skills

I am an out-going person. I have a good relationship with all my clients and colleagues. I am very persistent and determined in achieving a challenging and rewarding career.

A copy of my resume can be found in the attachments. There is also a brief introduction to my educational background and previous job experience. I would be honored to be allowed to discuss more details of my contribution. I look forward to hearing from you.

Sincerely yours,
Jeff Chen

33. How did the applicant probably find out about this job offer?
    A. He contacted the Marketing Manager.
    B. He read the ad on the website.
    C. He went to the company in person.
    D. We can't tell from the letter.

34. Which of the following is NOT stated as part of the job requirement?
    A. Ability to get along well with people
    B. Fluency in another language apart from mother tongue
    C. Budget reviewing skills
    D. Related educational background

35. Which statement best fits Jeff Chen's description of himself?
    A. He is dedicated and enthusiastic.
    B. He is humble and shy.
    C. He is proud and arrogant.
    D. He is talkative and greedy.

—結束—

初試 聽力測驗 解析

第一部分 / 看圖辨義

Q1

For question one, please look at picture A.

What is the woman doing?
這位女子在做什麼？

A. She is drawing a portrait.
B. She is giving a speech.
C. She is taking a nap.
D. She is practicing yoga.

A. 她正在畫一張人物像。
B. 她正在發表一場演說。
C. 她正在打盹。
D. 她正在練習瑜珈。

詳解　　　　　　　　　　　　　　　　　　　　　**答案：D**

　　圖片中若只有單一人物，在聽題目前就要先注意該人物的特徵，有可能是人物的服裝、配件或動作。本題可以看到一個女子正在做瑜珈，因此題目有可能是跟瑜珈有關係的問題。題目是在問女子是在做什麼，因此選項 D 為答案。

補充說明

　　隨著不同的運動或活動，前面會使用不一樣的動詞，最常使用的動詞是 play / go / practice / do，但什麼時候要用 play / go / practice / do 呢？其實是有跡可循的。通常如果是競技型的團隊運動，例如籃球則用 play（play basketball），若是個人做的活動，而且該項活動的字尾是 -ing，則用 go，例如釣魚是 go fishing，若活動的字尾不是 -ing，則用 practice 或 do，例如本題中的 practice yoga。但如果我們做的是一些健身運動，例如做伏地挺身，則只用 do（do push up）。

第 1 回

第 2 回

第 3 回

第 4 回

第 5 回

第 6 回

Q2

For question two and three, please look at picture B.

What's the girl in the last row doing?
最後一排的女孩在做什麼？

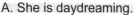

A. She is daydreaming.
B. She is taking notes.
C. She is dozing off.
D. She is performing on stage.

A. 她正在做白日夢。
B. 她正在作筆記。
C. 她正在打瞌睡。
D. 她正在舞臺上表演。

詳解　　　　　　　　　　　　　　　　　　　答案：A

　　在圖片題中，老師在上課，坐在最後一排的女孩卻在做白日夢，幻想自己當歌星。學生是否認真？女孩未來想當什麼等？這些題目屬於初級的常見題型，中級的題目應該較有難度。題目問的是女孩在做什麼。做白日夢的英文剛剛好和中文直翻相同，所以正確答案為 A。

＜補充說明＞

　　夢遊的英文則不能直接用中文翻譯，夢遊的英文說法是 sleepwalking（在睡覺時走路）。

Q3

For question 3, please look at picture B again.

What's the boy in the last row doing?
最後一排的男孩在做什麼？

A. He is listening to the teacher.
B. He is using his cell phone.
C. He is taking notes.
D. He is answering the teacher.

A. 他在聽老師說話。
B. 他在用他的手機。
C. 他在做筆記。
D. 他正在回答老師。

詳解　　　　　　　　　　　　　　　　　　　答案：C

　　在圖片題中，老師在上課，坐在最後一排的男生在做筆記，認真聽課。題目問的是最後一排的男生在做什麼，所以正確答案為 C。

Q4

For question four, please look at picture C.

Which description best fits the picture?
哪一項描述最適合這張圖？

A. The ox is in the third position.　　A. 牛在第三個位置。
B. The rooster takes up the last position.　　B. 雞占據最後一個位置。
C. The dragon comes after the rabbit.　　C. 龍排在兔子之後
D. The goat is before the horse.　　D. 羊排在馬之前。

詳解　　　　　　　　　　　　　　　　　　　　　**答案：C**

　圖片題出現華人的十二生肖，即便沒有把十二種動物的順序記熟也無妨，只需要在聽到選項後判斷是否正確。牛在圖中排名第二，選項 A 是錯誤的。最後一個生肖是豬不是雞，選項 B 也是錯誤的。龍排名第五，兔子排名第四，龍排在兔子之後的敘述是正確的，正確答案為 C。羊排在馬之後，選項 D 並不正確。

補充說明

　向外國人解釋十二生肖時可以這麼說：
This is the Chinese horoscope. I was born in the year of the Tiger.
這是華人的十二生肖，我屬虎。
It is similar to the zodiac signs.　這跟星座很相似。

Q5

For question five, please look at picture D.

Which level should the man go to if he wants to purchase some ties?
如果這個男子想要購買一些領帶，他應該去哪一層樓？

A. Level 3　　　　　　　　　A. 三樓
B. Level 4　　　　　　　　　B. 四樓
C. Level 5　　　　　　　　　C. 五樓
D. Level 6　　　　　　　　　D. 六樓

詳解　　　　　　　　　　　　　　　　　　　　　**答案：C**

　這個圖片是大賣場的指示牌，看懂指示牌上的單字是第一個關鍵。第二個關鍵則是聽出題目在問什麼，題目中提到這一名男子想要購買一些領帶，因此

選項 A 三樓廚房用具（Kitchenware）不可能是答案。選項 B 四樓賣的是手機和配件（Mobile Devices & Accessories），應該沒在賣領帶。選項 C 五樓剛好有領帶，Unisex 指的是「中性或兩性適用」，而 Apparel 指的是「衣服」，所以 C 是正確答案。選項 D 則是異國料理（Exotic Cuisine），是餐廳，所以也不可能賣領帶。

〈補充說明〉

千萬別把 exotic 跟 erotic 搞混，erotic 的意思是色情的。

第1回

第2回

第3回

第4回

第5回

第6回

Q6

What are we going to do with all this stuff we no longer need?

我們要怎麼樣處置所有這些我們已經不需要的東西？

A. Why not have a garage sale?
B. I can do it in an hour.
C. We can look for a shorter one.
D. Maybe the line is busy.

A. 何不來場舊物拍賣會？
B. 我可以在一小時後完成它。
C. 我們可以找一個更短的。
D. 也許正在忙線中。

詳解

答案：A

聽到 What... going to do 就可以知道題目在問「要做什麼事」，所以答案應該是提議要做某件事情，因此答案為 A。選項 B 是重複題目 do 藉以混淆的選項，選項 C 則是利用與 stuff 有關的相關詞語 shorter one 來設置陷阱的選項。

補充說明

garage sale 是一種把家裡面不用的東西，放在自家的車庫、庭院等地方，對外拍賣的「家庭式拍賣會」。在台灣很少見，但在國外卻是很常見的拍賣模式。所以人在國外時，看到 garage sale 的招牌，不妨進去看看有沒有什麼便宜好撿。

Q7

I thought the weather forecast said it will be sunny today.

我以為天氣預報說今天會是晴天。

A. You should believe it, shouldn't you?
B. They could handle it, couldn't they?
C. We can't predict everything, can we?
D. It won't be taught, will it?

A. 你應該相信氣象預測，不是嗎？
B. 他們可以應付的，不是嗎？
C. 我們不能預測所有的事，對嗎？
D. 這個不會被教到，對嗎？

詳解

答案：C

I thought 在口語中經常出現，意思是「我以為⋯」，用 I thought 表示目前的情況跟「我以為⋯」的情況完全不同。「我以為天氣預報說今天將會是晴

天」並不是指聽者聽錯，而是在懷疑消息的可靠性。把以上句子理解為「天氣預報不是說今天將會是晴天嗎？」，就能理解現在並不是晴天。當對方這麼說，最適合的回應是「我們不能預測所有的事，對嗎？」，答案為 C。

<補充說明>

I thought you are not coming. 我以為你不會來。（現在你卻來了）

第 1 回
第 2 回
第 3 回
第 4 回
第 5 回
第 6 回

Q8

Have you faxed the report to Mr. Anderson?
你已經把報告傳真給 Anderson 先生了嗎？

A. He hasn't finished it yet.
B. I did it first thing in the morning.
C. The report is in my drawer.
D. There is no Internet connection.

A. 他還沒完成。
B. 我早上第一件事就是辦這個。
C. 這份報告在我的抽屜裡。
D. 沒有網路連結。

詳解

答案：B

　　這是在職場上會被問到的問題，問的人應該是老闆或上司，回答的人應該是員工或下屬。老闆問的是之前交代的事情是否已經完成，「這份報告在我的抽屜裡」是「報告在哪裡」的回答，因此選項 C 是答非所問。而傳真用的是電話號碼，不需要網路連結，選項 D 也是錯的。正確答案為 B，表示老闆交代的事情早已經完成了。

Q9

Excuse me. I need to send this package to Canada.
不好意思。我需要把這個包裹寄到加拿大。

A. Please pack it first.
B. It's famous for its maple leaves.
C. You can't be serious.
D. By air or by sea?

A. 請先把它包起來。
B. 加拿大以楓葉聞名。
C. 你不是說真的吧？
D. 空運還是海運？

詳解

答案：D

　　從問題可推斷，說話者應該是在郵局，聽者則是郵局員工。身為郵局員工，當客人說「我需要把這個包裹寄到加拿大」，最為合理的回應是「請問您要用空運還是海運？」答案為 D。聽到 package 而猜選項 A 的 pack，是不合理的。package（包裹）是已經包好的，不應該說「請先把它包起來。」

express 是快遞郵件，美國最知名的快遞服務之一為 Federal Express，而美國最知名的信用卡之一為 American Express。

Q10

Do you keep track of your calories on a daily basis?
你有持續記錄每天的卡路里攝取量嗎？

A. You bet. I love the art gallery.
B. Spare me. I have lost count.
C. Maybe. About 400 meters or so.
D. Oh dear. I forgot where I keep it.

A. 這還用說。我很愛畫廊。
B. 饒了我吧。我已經算到忘記了。
C. 或許。大約 400 公尺左右。
D. 糟了。我忘了我放在哪裡。

詳解　　　　　　　　　　　　　　　　　　　答案：B

　　卡路里（calories）跟維他命（vitamin）一樣，都是直接從英文音譯的單字。當別人問這個問題時，最合理的答案為 B。選項 A 是陷阱，若把 calories 聽成 gallery，就有可能被誤導，而選了錯誤的選項。

|單字片語| on a daily basis 每天 / on a weekly basis 一週一次 / on a regular basis 固定期間

Q11

What kinds of movie do you prefer to watch?
你比較喜歡看什麼類型的電影？

A. I'm into fantasy and romance.
B. I'm usually gentle and polite.
C. I think you should head south.
D. I believe writing is not an easy task.

A. 我很迷奇幻片跟愛情片。
B. 我通常很溫柔、有禮貌。
C. 我認為你應該往南走。
D. 我認為寫作不是件容易的事。

詳解　　　　　　　　　　　　　　　　　　　答案：A

　　對方問電影的種類，合理的答案為 A. fantasy and romance（奇幻跟愛情）。電影的種類除了奇幻跟愛情外，還有動作片（action）、搞笑喜劇（comedy）、驚悚片（thriller）等等。紀錄片則是（documentary）。

　　很投入很熱衷於某件事的英文是「into something」，例句：
He's really into yoga and all that. 他真的很熱衷瑜珈那些活動。（除了瑜珈的運動，還有打坐之類的活動。）

第 1 回
第 2 回
第 3 回
第 4 回
第 5 回
第 6 回

Q12

How is the traffic in Thailand?
泰國的交通如何呢？

A. It's cool. I travelled there by bus.
B. It's great. Thai food is terrific.
C. It's sad. They tied the elephants to trees.
D. It's insane. Nobody follows the rules.

A. 很涼爽。我坐公車去的。
B. 很棒。泰國料理很讚。
C. 令人難過。他們把象綁在樹邊
D. 很瘋狂。沒有人遵守規則。

詳解　　　　　　　　　　　　　　　　　　　　　**答案：D**

　　「泰國的交通」如何指的是交通的狀況，最為合理的答案為 D，指出那裡的交通一團亂，非常瘋狂，因為沒有人遵守交通規則。當然，這是比較誇張的說法，回答者應該剛從泰國回來，對那裡的交通狀況感到有些不可思議。

〈補充說明〉

　　是「有理性的」，insane 是「沒有理性的，瘋狂的」，名詞為 insanity。之前在美國和台灣造成轟動的 Jeremy Lin（林書豪熱潮），美國人結合「林 Lin」跟 insanity 這個字，來形容「林來瘋 Linsanity」的現象。

Q13

Please inform the others that the meeting will start in five minutes.
請通知其他人，會議將在五分鐘後開始。

A. Nice to meet you, too.
B. We are vegetarians.
C. I'll do it right away.
D. We need more information.

A. 我也很高興認識你。
B. 我們是素食者。
C. 我馬上去辦。
D. 我們需要更多資訊。

詳解　　　　　　　　　　　　　　　　　　　　　**答案：C**

　　這是在工作上會遇到的英文對話，說話者應該是主管或上司，回答者則是下屬，最合理的回應是「我馬上去辦」，答案為 C。

|單字片語| inform [ɪnˈfɔrm] 通知 / information [ˌɪnfəˈmeʃən] 消息；資訊

Q14

Will the owner of vehicle number AZ2649 kindly move your car away?
車牌號碼 AZ2649 的車主，能請您好心地把您的車子移開嗎？

A. What an unfortunate accident!
B. Please put on the safety belt.
C. Excuse me for a moment.
D. I agree that it was a kind gesture.

A. 真是不幸的意外！
B. 請繫好安全帶。
C. 抱歉我失陪一下。
D. 我同意那是一個友善的手勢。

詳解　　　　　　　　　　　　　　　　　　　　　　　　**答案：C**

　　車子被吊車拖走在外國也是常見的景象，當車主聽到這個廣播時，最適當的回應是「抱歉我失陪一下」，因此答案為 C。在一些社交場合，需要接電話或上廁所都可以說 Excuse me for a moment. 不需要特別說明必須暫時離開的原因。

Q15

Did you hear about the tragic accident?
你聽到關於那場悲慘的意外了嗎？

A. No. I can't find it here.
B. Yes. It was really distressing.
C. No. I think it is a great movie.
D. Yes. It's important to be on time.

A. 沒有。我在這裡找不到。
B. 是的。真是令人悲傷。
C. 沒有。我認為是一部好電影。
D. 是的。準時是很重要的。

詳解　　　　　　　　　　　　　　　　　　　　　　　　**答案：B**

　　對於悲慘的意外或其他不幸事件，可用 It was really distressing.（真是令人悲傷。）回應，表示感同身受，所以答案是 B。其他比較常見的回應是 I'm sorry to hear that.（聽到這個消息真是令人難過。）

Q16

M: Please turn off all mobile devices as it will disturb the others.
　　請關掉所有的行動裝置，因為會打擾到其他人。

W: May I switch it to silent mode?　我可以切換到靜音模式嗎？

M: As long as it doesn't interrupt my lecture.　只要不妨礙到我授課就好。

Q: Where might this conversation take place?
這段對話可能是在哪裡發生？

A. At a hospital.
B. In an auditorium.
C. At a theme park.
D. In a restaurant.

A. 在一家醫院。
B. 在一個講堂。
C. 在一座主題樂園。
D. 在一間餐廳。

詳解　　　　　　　　　　　　　　　　　　　　　　　　　答案：B

　　在聽題目前，光看選項就可以猜到題目應該是跟「地點」有關，所以要注意聽與地點有關、或是暗示這段對話所在地點的部分。對話中男子提到 lecture，顯然對話的場所是適合授課、演講的地方，因此 B 是正確答案。

補充說明

　　手機的聲音模式通常可以分為「一般」、「震動」、「靜音」三種，英文會怎麼說呢？「一般模式」英文是 Normal Mode，「震動」是 Vibrate Mode，「靜音」是 Silent Mode，下次可以將自己的手機轉換成英文來看看。

Q17

W: You won't believe it. Rome is such a spectacular city.
　　你不會相信，羅馬是如此雄偉壯觀的城市。

M: What's so unique about it?　它有什麼獨一無二的地方？

W: The ancient architecture. They have been around for thousands of yerars.
　　古代的建築。它們已經有幾千年的歷史了。

Q: What impressed the woman so much?
讓這位女子如此印象深刻的是什麼？

A. The buildings in Italy.
B. The people in Italy.
C. The traditional festivals in Italy.
D. The pop culture in Italy.

A. 義大利的建築。
B. 義大利的人。
C. 義大利的傳統節慶。
D. 義大利的流行文化。

詳解 答案：A

　　選項有義大利的建築、人民、節慶和文化，共同的地方就是義大利的「什麼」，所以聽取對話的重點就在這裡，但若只專注想聽到 Italy 這個字，考生可能就會因為在對話中沒聽到這個字而開始慌張，進而找不到答案，而忽略了 Rome（羅馬）其實是義大利的一個城市，這也是題目設陷阱的一個方法。從對話 architecture（建築）可判斷令這位女子印象深刻的是當地的建築，答案為 A。

|單字片語| architect [ˈɑrkəˌtɛkt] 建築師 / architecture [ˈɑrkəˌtɛktʃə] 建築，建築風格

Q18

W: Remember to maintain eye contact and smile.
　　記得要保持眼神交流和笑容。

M: I'm so nervous. Do you think I will get the position I want? There's only one vacancy.
　　我好緊張。你認為我會得到我想要的職位嗎？只有一個空缺。

W: Just put up a good show and worry about that later. Here are some questions.　　就先好好表現，那個我們之後再來操心。這裡有一些問題。

Q: What is the woman talking about?
這位女子在談論的事情是什麼？

A. Tips for an interview.
B. Answers to an exam.
C. Good hygiene habits.
D. A live performance.

A. 面試的一些建議。
B. 考試的答案。
C. 良好的衛生習慣。
D. 一場現場演出。

詳解 答案：A

　　四個選項的單字都不同，其實比較容易作答。每個選項的關鍵詞等於一個情境，在聽對話時只需要判斷對話的情境，不用擔心有陷阱。從 position（職位）和 vacancy（空缺），可知道說話者在談論找工作的事情，答案為 A。

第 1 回

第 2 回

第 3 回

第 4 回

第 5 回

第 6 回

Q19

M: Have you settled the payments to the suppliers?
你已經把款項付給供應商了嗎？

W: I was about to do it but the bank has closed.
我正要去做這件事，但是銀行已經關門了。

M: This is the first and the last time you give me an excuse. Do you understand?　這是你第一次也是最後一次給我找藉口。你明白嗎？

Q: Why is the man angry?　為何這位男子會生氣？

A. The woman misunderstood him.
B. The woman had a good reason.
C. The woman left something undone.
D. The woman didn't know where the bank is.

A. 女子誤會他了。
B. 女子有一個好理由。
C. 女子有些事沒做。
D. 女子不知道銀行在哪裡。

詳解

答案：C

選項有四個可能的情況，從男子一句「這是你第一次也是最後一次給我找藉口」，可得知女子沒有把事情做好。was about to do it 是指「正要去做這件事的時候」，但是發生了狀況沒有把事情做好，答案為 C。

補充說明

雖然這題是聽力考題，也可以拿來當口說的素材。was about to do it 是口語中常用的說法，非常實用，例如：I was about to call you.（我正要打電話給你。）

Q20

W: When will the package arrive if I mail it today?
如果我今天寄出去的話，包裹什麼時候會到？

M: If you use express mail, it might get there as early as tomorrow morning.
如果你用快捷郵件的話，最早可能明天早上就會到那裡。

W: Great! May I have an envelope, please?
太棒了！可以請你給我一個信封嗎？

Q: What will the woman probably do next?
接下來這位女子可能會做什麼？

A. Give the man an envelope.	A. 給那位男子一個信封。
B. Fill in some information.	B. 填寫一些資料。
C. Come back again tomorrow morning.	C. 明天早上再回來。
D. Send the man an email.	D. 發電子郵件給那位男子。

詳解   答案：B

　　這類 probably do next（接下來可能會做什麼）的題型要特別注意，因為可能會出現陷阱題。首先，要聽清楚接下來會做什麼的到底是男子還是女子。從對話中可推斷，說話者在郵局，男子是郵局櫃檯人員，而女子是一般民眾。試題問接下來這位女子應該會做什麼，拿信封出來是男子的工作，所以選項 A 是陷阱。男子把信封交給女子，女子接下來應該會做的是填寫一些資料，答案為 B。

|單字片語| **fill in** 填寫 / **fill up** 裝滿（加油）/ **fill with** 充滿，裝著

Q21

M: Good evening, ma'am. Do you have a reservation?
夫人，晚安。請問您有訂位嗎？

W: I'm afraid not. Don't you have an empty table over there?
沒有。那裡不是有張空著的桌子嗎？

M: My apologies. Those seats are reserved by another guest. The estimated waiting time is about a half hour or so. Would you like to leave your name and contact number?
不好意思。那些座位被另一位客人預訂了。估計的等待時間是半個小時左右。您想要留下姓名和聯絡電話嗎？

Q: What is the man's occupation?
這位男子的職業是什麼？

A. A chef.	A. 廚師。
B. A waiter.	B. 服務生。
C. A pilot.	C. 飛行員。
D. A secretary.	D. 祕書。

詳解　　　　　　　　　　　　　　　　　　　　**答案：B**

　　光看選項就知道題目要問的是說話者的職業，不過也不能掉以輕心，必須確認試題問的是男子還是女子的職業。從關鍵詞 reservation（訂位），empty table（空著的桌子）和 waiting time（等待時間），可判斷對話的情境是在餐廳。雖然廚師也在餐廳，不過在門口接待客人的是服務生，答案為 B。

＜補充說明＞

　　打電話到餐廳預約可以這麼說：
I would like to reserve a table for four.　我想要預約一桌四人的座位。

Q22

W:　Don't you know it's illegal to park your vehicle here?
　　你不知道把車子停在這裡是違法的嗎？

M:　It's just for a few minutes. I can't be so unlucky, can I?
　　只是幾分鐘而已。我不會這麼倒楣，對吧？

W:　Fine. Don't blame me when you don't see your car out here later.
　　好啊。等一下當你出來時看不到你的車子可別怪我。

Q:　What is the woman trying to tell the man?
這位女子想要告訴這位男子什麼？

A. He should park the vehicle for at least an hour.
A. 他應該把車子停至少一個小時。

B. He should find out where his car is first.
B. 他應該先知道他的車子在什麼地方。

C. He shouldn't violate traffic regulations.
C. 他不應該違反交通規則。

D. He shouldn't blame the woman for his bad luck.
D. 他不應該因運氣不好怪這位女子。

詳解　　　　　　　　　　　　　　　　　　　　**答案：C**

　　日常對話的時候往往都有言外之意，有些對話可以直接理解，但有些對話必須從旁推敲，才能明白對方的意思。這位女子想要告訴男子的是，男子若因為車子違規停放被拖走的話不要怪她，意思是請這位男子不要違規停車，答案為 C。

|單字片語| **violate** ['vaɪə,let] 違反，侵犯 / **violent** ['vaɪələnt] 暴力的

Q23

M: Attention all passengers. I will demonstrate how to use the safety vest now.

所有乘客請注意。現在我會示範如何使用救生衣。

W: Where is it located? 它放在哪裡呢？

M: It's right beneath your seat. I will show you how to use it in case there is an emergency.

就在您座位的下方。我會告訴您，以防萬一有緊急狀況時，要如何使用。

Q: Where could this conversation have taken place?
這段對話可能是在什麼地方發生的？

A. On a cargo train.　　　　　A. 在運送貨物的火車。
B. On an airplane.　　　　　　B. 在飛機上。
C. In a textile factory.　　　　C. 在紡織品工廠。
D. In a repair garage.　　　　D. 在汽車維修廠。

詳解　　　　　　　　　　　　　　　　　　　　答案：B

　　這題看到選項就能知道這題要問的是對話發生的地方。從關鍵詞 passengers（乘客）和 seat（座位），可推斷說話者在某種大眾交通工具上。火車應該不會掉進水裡，不需要救生衣（safety vest），答案為 B。

Q24

Date 日期	Event 活動
2/10	Workshop: How to use scented candles to relax 工作坊：如何使用香氛蠟燭來放鬆
2/11	Seminar: How to build eco-friendly environment 研討會：如何建立環保的環境
2/12	No Meat Banquet 無肉宴會

W: Hey, Shawn. I will attend the seminar on February 11th. People will discuss the environmental issues in the meeting. Do you want to join me? 嘿，Shawn。我將會參加 2 月 11 日的研討會。大家會在會議上討論環境議題。你要跟我一起參加嗎？

第 1 回
第 2 回
第 3 回
第 4 回
第 5 回
第 6 回

M: Oh, I'm afraid I can't go with you. I will take a day off on that day. I need to take my mom to see the doctor. 喔，我恐怕不能和你去那場研討會。我會在那天請一天假，我需要帶我媽媽去看醫生。

W: I see. I will get you a handout of the seminar for you. 知道了。我會幫你拿一份研討會的講義。

Q: Look at the schedule. Which event will the woman attend?
請看行程表，這位女子將會參加哪一場活動？

A. The workshop of scented candles.   A. 香氛蠟燭的工作坊。
B. The seminar of eco-friendly environment.   B. 環保環境的研討會。
C. No Meat Banquet.   C. 無肉宴會。
D. None of these events she will go.   D. 她都不會參加這些活動。

詳解

    在對話中，女子提到她要參加的研討會日期是 2 月 11 日，並且提到會議中會談論環保相關的議題，再對照行程表可知答案為 B。

答案：B

Q25

TO Xiangshan

Zhongshan   Taipei Main Station   NTU Hospital   Chiang Kai-Shek Memorial Hall

M: Excuse me, miss. Do you know how to transfer to the blue line? 小姐，不好意思。你知道怎麼轉乘到藍線嗎？

W: We are at the red lines. According to this map, you can go to the platform which is to Xiangshan, and transfer to the blue line at Taipei Main Station. 我們現在在紅線上，根據這張地圖，你可以走到往象山的月台，並在台北車站轉乘到藍線。

M: Thank you for helping me. Have a nice day. 謝謝你幫助我，祝你有美好的一天。

Q: Look at the map. Which station might the man and woman be at?
請看這張地圖，男子和女子可能在哪一個車站？

A. Zhongshan Station
B. Taipei Main Station
C. NTU Hospital Station
D. Chiang Kai-Shek Memorial Hall Station

A. 中山站
B. 臺北車站
C. 臺大醫院站
D. 中正紀念堂站

詳解

答案：A

題目詢問男子與女子目前可能在哪一站，從對話中可知他們還沒到台北車站，再從地圖可以看到台北車站的前一站是中山站，答案為 A。

第四部分 / 簡短談話

Q26

M: Hello, Miss Carson. This is Marshall Jackson from the GNE Bank. I'm calling to tell you that you haven't pay your credit card bill on March 5th. According to the credit card terms, your interest rate will increase to 15%, if your payment becomes 30 days past due. Please contact me, once you receive this voicemail. Thank you.

Carson 小姐，您好。我是 GNE 銀行的 Marshall Jackson。我打來要告知您，您在 3 月 5 日尚未繳納信用卡帳單。根據信用卡的條款，如果您超過 30 天尚未付款，您的利率將會上升至 15%。一旦您收到這則語音訊息，請和我聯絡，謝謝您。

Q: What will the bank do, if Miss Carson does not pay the bill for over 30 days?
如果 Carson 小姐超過 30 日未付清帳單，銀行將會做什麼？

A. Charge her a late fee.	A. 向她收取遲繳費用。
B. Freeze her bank account.	B. 凍結她的銀行帳戶。
C. Increase her interest rate.	C. 增加她的利率。
D. Cancel her credit card membership.	D. 取消她的信用卡會員資格。

詳解　　　　　　　　　　　　　　　　　　　　　　**答案：C**

題目詢問如果超過 30 日未付清帳單會有什麼後果，因此關鍵詞是 30 days，獨白提到「如果超過 30 天尚未付款，利率將會上升至 15%」，而符合的敘述是 increase her interest rate，答案為 C。

Q27

W: Welcome back to our show, Music Holiday. The last song was Jeremy Jones' "Lonely Island." Jeremy Jones composed the music and wrote the lyrics by himself. He expressed his lonely feelings through the lyrics. After releasing his latest album, this song has stayed on the charts for over a month. It seems that many people felt the same way when they listened to the song. Later, our show will discuss loneliness in this cyber era.

歡迎回到我們的節目「Music Holiday」。上一首歌是 Jeremy Jones 的「Lonely Island」。Jeremy Jones 自己作曲、作詞。他透過歌詞來傳達他

寂寞的感受。在他發行最新專輯之後，這首歌已經蟬聯在榜上超過一個月。似乎很多人在聽到這首歌時，都有相同的感受。接下來，我們的節目會討論數位時代的孤獨。

Q: What feeling did people have, after they listened to the song Lonely Island?

人們聽到 Lonely Island 之後，會有什麼感覺？

A. The happy feeling.　　　　　　A. 高興的感受。
B. The excited feeling.　　　　　　B. 興奮的感受。
C. The angry feeling.　　　　　　C. 生氣的感受。
D. The lonely feeling.　　　　　　D. 寂寞的感受。

【詳解】　　　　　　　　　　　　　　　　　　　　【答案：D】

　　題目詢問人們聽完 Lonely Island 會有什麼感覺，因此要注意談話中的關鍵詞 feeling、Lonely Island，而獨白談到帶給這首歌給人們寂寞的感受，答案為 D。

Q28

M: Next is the weather forecast. Now, let's see tomorrow's weather. In Greenland city, the temperature will be 22 to 25 degree Celcius. It might rain tomorrow, so don't forget to bring umbrella. The weather in Carmel City will be sunny and windy. The temperature will be 25 to 28 degree Celcius. Please remember to use the sunscreen cream when going out. That's the weather report for tomorrow. Thank you.

接下來是天氣預報。現在，我們來看明天的天氣。Greenland 市的氣溫是攝氏 22 到 25 度，明天可能會下雨，所以不要忘記帶雨傘。Carmel 市的天氣則是晴朗、風大，氣溫是攝氏 25 到 28 度，請記得在外出時擦防曬乳。這是明天的天氣報導，謝謝您。

Q: What should people do if they live in Carmel City?

如果人們住在 Carmel 市，他們應該怎麼做？

A. Bring their umbrellas.　　　　　A. 攜帶他們的雨傘。
B. Use the sunscreen cream.　　　B. 擦防曬乳。
C. Wear some sweaters.　　　　　C. 穿一些毛衣。
D. Don't go out.　　　　　　　　D. 不要出門。

第 1 回
第 2 回
第 3 回
第 4 回
第 5 回
第 6 回

詳解　　　　　　　　　　　　　　　　　　　**答案：B**

　　題目詢問住在 Carmel 市的人們應該做什麼事情，因此要注意的關鍵詞是 Carmel City，而獨白提到「Carmel 市的氣溫是攝氏 25 到 28 度，請記得在出門時擦防曬乳」，答案為 B。

Q29

W: Visitors have to follow the rules in the art museum. First, do not touch the paintings, the antiques, and the sculptures. Second, please do not take pictures with a flash. That might hurt the artwork. Third, do not eat or drink in the exhibition area. Fourth, do not talk on the phone in the exhibition area. Thanks for your cooperation.

訪客在美術館必須遵守幾項規則。第一，請勿觸摸畫作、古物及雕刻品。第二，請不要開閃光燈拍照，那樣可能會傷害藝術品。第三，請不要在展覽區域飲食。第四，請不要在展覽區域講電話。感謝您的配合。

Q: What can visitors do when they are in the art museum?
訪客可以在美術館做什麼？

A. Talk on the cellphones.　　　　　A. 講電話。
B. Take pictures with the flashes.　　B. 開閃光燈拍照。
C. Touch the sculptures.　　　　　　C. 觸摸雕刻品。
D. Watch the paintings.　　　　　　 D. 觀賞畫作。

詳解　　　　　　　　　　　　　　　　　　　**答案：D**

　　獨白提到訪客在美術館不能做的事情，分別是：觸摸展覽品、開閃光燈拍照、飲食、講電話，但沒有提到不能觀賞畫作，因此正確答案是 D。

Q30

M: The closer Christmas gets, the higher the price of the Christmas trees goes. Many people will go to Christmas tree farms to buy trees. According to a customer, Johnny, he said that his family tradition was to buy a Christmas tree and place it beside the fireplace inside the house. His family members would decorate the tree and place the gifts under the tree. That's how they celebrated Christmas.

聖誕節越接近，聖誕樹的價格就越高，許多人會去聖誕樹農場買樹。根據一位顧客 Johnny，他表示他家的傳統是買一棵聖誕樹，並且放置在他家的火爐邊。他的家庭成員會裝飾聖誕樹，並把禮物放在樹下。這是他們慶祝聖誕節的方式。

Q: What will Johnny's family members do after they buy the Christmas tree?
在 Johnny 的家庭成員買聖誕樹後，將會做什麼？

A. Place the tree in their yard.	A. 在庭院放置樹。
B. Give the tree to their parents.	B. 把樹交給他們的父母。
C. Put the gifts under the trees.	C. 把禮物放在樹下。
D. Burn the tree to get warm.	D. 燃燒樹來取暖。

詳解

答案：C

　　題目詢問 Johnny 的家庭成員買樹之後會怎麼做，因此要注意的關鍵詞是 "family members" 和 "Christmas trees"，而獨白提到「他的家庭成員會裝飾聖誕樹，並把禮物放在樹下」，而符合敘述的選項為 B。

Q31

W: Do you have a hard time losing weight? Do you have difficulty maintaining your healthy body? Healthy Diet Restaurant has made a completely new diet meal to help our customer to stay fit. Every diet meal is around 500 calories. We have also lowered the fat intake of every meal. If you're looking for a healthier diet, please dial 2232-5674 to get more information.

您很難減重嗎？您很難維持健康的身體嗎？健康飲食餐廳已經做了全新的節食餐來幫助我們的顧客保持苗條。每份節食餐在 500 大卡左右，我們也降低每份餐點的脂肪攝取。如果您在找更健康的飲食，請撥打 2232-5674 以獲得更多資訊。

Q: How many calories does a meal have?
一份餐有多少大卡？

A. 800 calories.	A. 800 大卡。
B. 700 calories.	B. 700 大卡。
C. 600 calories.	C. 600 大卡。
D. 500 calories.	D. 500 大卡。

詳解

答案：D

　　題目詢問一份餐點有多少大卡，因此要注意的關鍵詞是 meal 和 calories，而獨白提到「每個節食餐已經控制在 500 大卡左右」，因此符合敘述的選項為 D。

第 1 回
第 2 回
第 3 回
第 4 回
第 5 回
第 6 回

Q32

M: Hello, Mr. Simpson. This is Carter Wester from Good Price PC. The computer you ordered last week has arrived at our retail store. Also, your purchase was over 10,000 dollars, so you can get free anti-virus software. We will install the software on your new computer. Please come to our store at Nelson West road at your convenience. Our opening hours are 10:30-20:30 from Monday to Saturday. Thank you.

Simpson 先生您好，我是 Good Price 電腦的 Carter Wester。我來電要通知您，您上週訂購的電腦已經送達到我們的零售門市。此外，您的消費超過一萬元，所以您可以獲得免費防毒軟體。我們會在您的新電腦安裝這個軟體。請您在方便的時間前往我們在 Nelson 西路的門市。我們的營業時間是週一至週五 10:30 到 20:30。謝謝您。

Q: **What will Mr. Simpson get from his purchase at Good Price PC?**
Simpson 先生在 Good Price 電腦的消費中會得到什麼？

A. A free screen.
B. A free key board.
C. A free anti-virus software.
D. A free speaker.

A. 免費的螢幕。
B. 免費的鍵盤。
C. 免費的防毒軟體。
D. 免費的喇叭。

詳解　　　　　　　　　　　　　　　　　　　　　　　　　答案：C

　　題目詢問 Simpson 先生在消費中會得到什麼，因此要注意的關鍵詞是 purchase 和 get，而獨白提到「您的消費超過一萬元，所以您可以獲得免費防毒軟體」，因此符合敘述的選項為 C。

Q33

W: Hi, everyone. I'm Annie, your tour guide. Before we start our tour, I would like to introduce the route we'll use today. First, we'll go to the K area, where the Science department is. Then, we'll go to the R area, which is the location of the student cafeteria. Finally, we'll go to Center Square. Our college dean will give a speech to you there.

大家好，我是你們的導遊 Annie。在我們開始我們的遊覽之前，我想介紹一下我們今天會走的路線。首先，我們會去 K 區，那裡是科學部門的所在地。接著，我們會去 R 區，也就是學生自助餐廳的地點。最後，我們會去中央廣場，我們的大學教務長會在那裡為你們演講。

Q: **Where might the listeners be?**
聽者可能會在哪裡呢？

A. In an amusement park.	A. 遊樂園。
B. In a factory.	B. 工廠。
C. In a market.	C. 市場。
D. In a campus.	D. 校園。

詳解 　　　　　　　　　　　　　　　　　　　　　　答案：D

　　題目詢問聽者可能在哪裡，而這題要聽完整段獨白才能作答。首先獨白提到「會去 R 區，學生自助餐廳的地點」，最後又提到「大學教務長會在中央廣場演講」，可以推測聽者是在校園裡，答案為 D。

Q34

South Airline BOARDING PASS
Name of passenger: Lillian Song
Flight NO: 675C　　Class: Y
From: New Delhi　　To: Los Angeles
Date: 10/20/2022　　Seat: 33A
GATE: 22
BOARDING TIME: 08:30

南方航空　登機證
旅客姓名：Lillian Song
班機號碼：675C　　艙等：Y
起飛地：新德里　　目的地：洛杉磯
日期：10/20/2022　　座位：33A
登機門：22
登機時間：08:30

M:　Good morning passengers. This is the pre-boarding announcement for flight 675C to Los Angeles. We are now inviting the passengers of class Y. Please have your boarding pass and passport ready. Flight 675C is boarding at gate 22. Don't forget your personal belongings.

Thanks for your cooperation.

各位旅客早安，這是往洛杉磯班機 675C 的登機前廣播，我們現在請艙等 Y 的旅客在此刻開始登機。請準備好您的登機證和護照。675C 班機在 22 號登機門登機。請別忘了您的隨身行李。謝謝您的合作。

Q: Look at the boarding pass. What time will Lillian Song board the airplane?
請看這張登機證，Lillian Song 會在幾點登機呢？

A: 08:25.
B: 08:30.
C: 08:35.
D: 08:40.

詳解　　　　　　　　　　　　　　　　　　　　　　　答案：B

　　題目詢問 Lillian Song 會在幾點登機，這題要看登機證上的資訊並聽到關鍵詞 class Y 才能作答。首先獨白提到「現在請艙等 Y 的旅客在此刻開始登機」，而 Lillian Song 的登機證上的時間顯示登機時間是 08:30，答案為 B。

Q35

Identification Card

Name: Andy Wang
Date of Birth: 07/22/1998
Identification NO: AW128537229

身分證

姓名：Andy Wang
出生日期：07/22/1998
身分證字號：AW128537229

W: Welcome to Wonderful Paradise. This amusement park has 4 main areas. The Space Planet area has the biggest roller coaster in the country. The Joyful Theater has all the wonderful shows in the world. The Adventure Explorer area has the most exciting games. The Happy Zoo has the cutest land animals. Visitors who have 2, 5, or 7 in their identification numbers will get a 20 percent discount when they visit the park.

歡迎來到完美天堂。這個遊樂園有四個主要區域。太空星球區全國最大的雲霄飛車。歡喜劇院有世界上所有最棒的表演。冒險探險家區有最刺激的遊戲。快樂動物園有最可愛的陸地動物。遊客的身份證字號有 2、5、7，入園可享八折優惠。

Q: Look at the identification card. What can Andy Wang get when he goes to the park?
請看身分證，請問 Andy Wang 來遊樂園時可以得到什麼？

A. He will see the sea animals in the zoo.

A. 他會在動物園看到海洋動物。

B. He can't play roller coaster because it's still in maintenance.

B. 他不能玩雲霄飛車，因為還在維修。

C. He will get 20 percent discount when he goes to the park.

C. 他入園時會享有八折的優惠。

D. He can't eat many kinds of food in the park.

D. 他在園區不能吃到很多種食物。

詳解　　　　　　　　　　　　　　　　　　　　　　　　　　　**答案：C**

題目詢問 Andy Wang 入園時可以獲得什麼，而這題要看身分證上的資訊並聽到最後一句才能作答。獨白提到「遊客身份證字號有 2、5、7，在十月入園可享八折優惠」，而 Andy Wang 的身分證號碼剛好有這三個數字，因此符合敘述的選項為 C。

第一回

初試 閱讀測驗 解析

第一部分／詞彙和結構

Q1

A survey questionnaire was given to the candidates to
_____ their strengths and weaknesses before a second
round of interviews were scheduled.

在第二輪面試被安排之前，求職者都得到一份問卷調查以便評估他們的優
缺點。

A. integrate
B. orientate
C. evaluate
D. mutate

詳解　　　　　　　　　　　　　　　　　　　　　　**答案：C**

　　這題考的是單字，若選項的單字都看得懂，就能從試題的關鍵詞 strengths
and weaknesses（優缺點），知道答案是 evaluate（評估）。和 evaluate 相近的
單字還有 assess（評估）、gauge（估計）、determine（測定）。

|單字片語| **integrate** [ˋɪntəˌgret] 整合／**orientate** [ˋorɪɛnˌtet] 融入；適應環境
　　　　　mutate [ˋmjutet] 突變；變種

Q2

Being out of a job for several months, the young man was
_____ for any kind of work that would enable him to cover
his rent and other expenses.

失業了好幾個月，那個年輕人迫切需要能夠讓他支付房租和其他開銷的任
何工作。

A. desperate
B. aspired
C. outrageous
D. eligible

詳解　　　　　　　　　　　　　　　　　　　　　　**答案：A**

　　從選項判斷，這題考的是單字。從句子中的 out of a job（失業）和 cover
his rent（支付房租）這兩個重要訊息，可判斷這名男子非常需要工作，答案為

A。desperate 的意思很多，可以用來形容某人窮途潦倒，也可以說某人迫切需要某個東西。aspire 是動詞「渴望、追求」的意思，若作為被動式 was aspired 變成男子是「被渴望、追求的」與題意不符。

例句

People would do anything when they are **desperate**.
人們在走投無路的時候任何事情都做得出來。
Out of **desperation**, she called her ex-boyfriend for help.
迫於無奈，她打電話向前任男友求救。

I單字片語I **aspire** [ə'spaɪr] 渴望，追求 / **outrageous** [aut'redʒəs] 駭人聽聞的；令人震怒的
eligible ['ɛlɪdʒəbl] 有資格的

Q3

The simple story of a farm girl, who took part in a talent show, was blown out of _____ after being circulated through the Internet for a few months.
農村女孩參加才藝表演的單純故事，在網路上流傳了幾個月後被誇大到不成比例。

A. revolution
B. configuration
C. proportion
D. imitation

詳解　　　　　　　　　　　　　　　　　　　　　　　　　　答案：C

　　四個選項都是不同的名詞，理解單字的意思和用法是非常重要的。proportion 的意思是「比例；等分」，blown out of proportion 是常見的用法，意思是某件事情被放大到不成比例，被過度誇大。

I單字片語I **revolution** [ˌrɛvə'luʃən] 革命；公轉 / **configuration** [kənˌfɪgjə'reʃən] 輪廓，構造
imitation [ˌɪmə'teʃən] 仿製品

Q4

The man whose wife was suffering from cancer decided to put an end to her _____ by giving her an overdose of sleeping pills.
妻子患有癌症的那個男人決定藉由給妻子過量的安眠藥來結束她的痛苦。

A. ailment
B. misery
C. disease
D. recovery

第 1 回
第 2 回
第 3 回
第 4 回
第 5 回
第 6 回

詳解

這題考的不只是單字，還加上搭配詞的用法，選項中有三個負面的單字，可是只有選項 B 可以跟 put an end to（結束）一起搭配，答案為 B。recovery 是「復原」，因此「結束復原」是不合理的。

|單字片語| **ailment** [ˈelmənt] 疾病；不適 / **misery** [ˈmɪzərɪ] 痛苦；苦難
disease [dɪˈziz] 疾病；詛咒 / **recovery** [rɪˈkʌvərɪ] 恢復；復原

〈補充說明〉

除了單字的意思，單字之間的搭配也很重要。例如： on the road to recovery（逐漸康復），a minor ailment（小病痛），a contagious disease（傳染病）。

Q5

To everyone's disbelief, the defending champions were _____ in the first round of the tournament.

讓每個人都無法置信的事情是，衛冕冠軍在錦標賽的第一輪就被淘汰了。

A. destroyed
B. eliminated
C. compromised
D. violated

詳解

答案：B

從 disbelief 可猜測事情的發展出乎意料，defending champions（衛冕冠軍）在錦標賽的第一輪就被淘汰是出乎意料的事情，答案為 B。

|單字片語| **destroy** [dɪˈstrɔɪ] 摧毀，消滅 / **compromise** [ˈkɑmprəˌmaɪz] 妥協；受威脅
violate [ˈvaɪəˌlet] 違反，侵犯

Q6

Despite repeated _____ to put out the fire, it could not be brought under control and it spread to other parts of the forest within a few hours.

儘管反覆嘗試撲滅大火，火勢還是無法控制，並在幾個小時內蔓延到森林的其他地方。

A. constructions
B. phenomena
C. attempts
D. forecasts

詳解

答案：C

這題要從句意來看才能判斷空格中要填入的名詞，整句的句意是「儘管反覆…要去撲滅大火，火勢還是無法控制，蔓延到森林其他地方」，因此從選項來看只有 attempts 的後面才可以接上 to put out the fire，因此答案為 C。

l單字片語l **attempts** [ə'tɛmpt] 試圖；企圖 / **put out** 撲滅 / **construction** [kən'strʌkʃən] 建造
phenomena [fə'namənə] 現象 / **forecast** ['for,kæst] 預測，預報

Q7

The president's speech was temporarily _____ when someone threw a shoe onto the stage, which only missed the president's head by a few inches.

當有人朝臺上丟擲鞋子時，總統的演講被暫時中斷，那隻鞋子只差幾吋就會打中總統的頭。

A. recommended   B. classified

C. interrupted   D. abstained

詳解　　　　　　　　　　　　　　　　　　　　　　　　答案：C

　　題目指出總統在演講時有人朝臺上丟鞋子，照常理推斷，總統的演講應該會被中斷，答案為 C。

l單字片語l **recommend** [,rɛkə'mɛnd] 推薦 / **classify** ['klæsə,faɪ] 分類
abstain [əb'sten] 棄權

Q8

The burglar pretended _____ and insisted that he entered the wrong house because he was drunk.

這名竊賊假裝什麼都不知道，並堅持自己是因為喝醉了才進錯房子。

A. acknowledgement   B. ignorance

C. detention   D. behavior

詳解　　　　　　　　　　　　　　　　　　　　　　　　答案：B

　　學習英文除了要有豐富的單字量，還必須知道不同的單字可以如何運用。很多時候，光靠字典的中文定義是不夠的。ignorance 是 ignore 的名詞，ignore 是「不理，不顧」，而 ignorance 是「無知，愚昧」。然而，光知道 ignorance 「無知」並沒有幫助，還需要明白 pretended ignorance 的用法。pretended 是「假裝」，而 pretended ignorance 是「裝傻，裝做不知道」。

l單字片語l **acknowledgement** [ək'nalɪdʒmənt] 致謝；確認 / **detention** [dɪ'tɛnʃən] 拘留；滯留
behavior [bɪ'hevjə] 行為

第 1 回

第 2 回

第 3 回

第 4 回

第 5 回

第 6 回

Q9

You could have called me to tell that you wouldn't be able to make it to the party. I was the only girl without a dance partner. How _____!

你大可以打電話告訴我，你不能來參加派對。我是唯一一個沒有舞伴的女生。真是丟臉！

A. wonderful
B. embarrassing
C. lovely
D. careful

詳解   答案：B

　　You could have called me 是英文的過去假設語氣，按照以上句子的情境可以看出，說話者在抱怨對方沒有打電話通知她，使她變成唯一沒有舞伴的女生，因此答案為 B。

例句

You **could have** told me you would be late.
你大可以告訴我你會遲到。
You **might have** told me but I couldn't remember.
你或許告訴過我，但是我想不起來。
You **must have** told me but I forgot.
你一定告訴過我，但是我忘了。

Q10

Never _____ what you can do today till tomorrow. Tomorrow has its own troubles.

千萬不要把今天可以做的事拖延到明天。明天自有明天的煩惱。

A. put away
B. put on
C. put off
D. put out

詳解   答案：C

　　從選項可看出，這題考的是動詞片語。動詞片語非常難學，因為加了介系詞的動詞，所表達的意思通常和動詞原來的意思完全不同。 put off 是「拖延；延後」，Never put off what you can do today till tomorrow. 的意思是「今日事、今日畢」。

I單字片語I **put away** 把…放到一邊 / **put on** 穿上，戴上
　　　　　put out 撲滅，澆熄 / **put up with** 忍受

Questions 11-15

In recent years, an increasing number of people have opted to include more vegetables in their daily diet out of health (11) considerations. The key to a healthy vegetarian diet — like any diet — is to enjoy a variety of foods. No single food can provide all the nutrition your body needs. The more (12) restrictive your diet is, the more challenging it can be to get all the (13) nutrients you need. A vegan diet, for example, eliminates natural food sources of vitamin B-12, as well as milk products, which are good sources of calcium. With a little planning, however, you can be sure that your diet includes everything your body needs. A food pyramid can be a helpful tool. The vegetarian pyramid outlines food groups and food choices that, (14) if eaten in the right quantities, form the foundation of a healthy vegetarian diet. Some people follow a semi-vegetarian diet — also known as a flexitarian diet — which is (15) primarily a plant-based diet but includes meat, dairy, eggs, poultry and fish on occasion or in small quantities.

近幾年來，越來越多人因為健康考量，已經選擇在他們的日常飲食中包含更多的蔬菜。如同任何飲食方法，健康的素食飲食的關鍵是享受各式各樣的食物。沒有單一的食物可提供身體所需要的所有營養。你的飲食越受限制，想要得到你所有需要的養分就越有挑戰性。例如純素飲食，排除了有維他命 B-12 的天然食物來源，與鈣質絕佳來源的乳製品。然而，只要稍微規劃，就能確保你的飲食中包含所有身體所需要的東西。食物金字塔可以是非常有幫助的工具。素食餐飲的金字塔大略列出食物的組別和選擇，若攝取正確的份量，能夠形成健康素食飲食的基礎。有些人遵循半素食的飲食，也稱為彈性素食飲食，主要是以植物為主的飲食，不過偶爾或少量包含肉類、乳製品、蛋類、雞鴨和魚肉。

Q11

A. measurements   B. principles
C. considerations   D. responsibilities

 詳解   答案：C

空格處前面指出於健康⋯（out of health...），因此最合理的答案為 C，指出自於健康考量，答案為 C。

第 1 回

第 2 回

第 3 回

第 4 回

第 5 回

第 6 回

<補充說明>

其他選項的搭配有：
According to actual measurements,（根據實際測量）
In accordance with the principles,（按照原則）
Out of a sense of responsibility,（出自於一種責任感）

|單字片語| **measurement** [ˋmɛʒəmənt] 測量 / **principle** [ˋprɪnsəpl] 原則
responsibility [rɪ,spɑnsəˋbɪlətɪ] 責任

Q12

A. productive
B. restrictive
C. objective
D. constructive

〔詳解〕　　　　　　　　　　　　　　　　　　　　　　　　　答案：B

　　這題的困難之處是要從整句的意思去判斷，不能只看關鍵詞。The more...
the more... 是寫作中常見的句型，意思是「越…越加…」。前半句和後半句互相
呼應，前者是正面的，後者也必須是正面的。短文中，後半句用的是 the more
challenging（更有挑戰性）因此前半句必須也是負面的，答案為 B。

<補充說明>

　　challenge 是「挑戰」，有挑戰性的應該算好事，為什麼會是負面的呢？
challenge 除了「挑戰」，也有「困難」的意思。在西方國家，為了避免歧視身
障人士，類似 disabled（有缺陷）和 handicapped（有殘疾）的詞彙必須改為
physically challenged，意思是在肢體上受到挑戰、有困難的。

|單字片語| **productive** [prəˋdʌktɪv] 有生產力的 / **objective** [əbˋdʒɛktɪv] 客觀的
constructive [kənˋstrʌktɪv] 有建設性的

Q13

A. substances
B. elements
C. ingredients
D. nutrients

〔詳解〕　　　　　　　　　　　　　　　　　　　　　　　　　答案：D

　　短文中提到，飲食越受限制，想要得到所有需要的…就更加有困難。從飲
食中能取得的，自然是 nutrients（養分；營養），答案為 D。ingredients 是指烹
飪所用的食材，食材不一定是營養的東西。

|單字片語| **substance** [ˋsʌbstəns] 物質 / **element** [ˋɛləmənt] 元素
ingredient [ɪnˋgridɪənt] 食材；材料

Q14

A. in spite of the tasteless food
B. if eaten in the right quantities
C. when given the best solution
D. in addition to the recipe

(詳解) 答案：A

　　此題要依據前後句來判斷，前句提到「素食餐飲金字塔大略列出食物的組別和選擇」，而後句則提到「能夠形成健康素食飲食的基礎」，可以看到只有選項 B 才能填入空格，其他選項皆不符合，答案為 B。

|單字片語| **tasteless** ['testlɪs] 沒味道的 / **quantity** ['kwɑntətɪ] 分量 / **solution** [sə'luʃən] 解決
　　　　recipe ['rɛsəpɪ] 食譜

Q15

A. inevitably　　　　　　　B. primarily
C. consequently　　　　　　D. completely

(詳解) 答案：B

　　有彈性的飲食，主要（primarily）是以植物為主的飲食，但是也可以加入少量的肉類，並非完全都是蔬菜，答案為 B。

|單字片語| **inevitably** [ɪn'ɛvətəblɪ] 無可避免地 / **consequently** ['kɑnsə‚kwɛntlɪ] 因此
　　　　completely [kəm'plitlɪ] 完全地

Questions 16-20

　　The Harry Potter film series made Leavesden its home for more than ten years. As the books were still being (16) distributed while the films were being made, the production crew saved many of the iconic sets, props and costumes that were created especially for the films – (17) just in case they were ever needed later on in the series. Once filming wrapped on *Harry Potter and the Deathly Hallows - Part 2* in 2010, the production crew was left with a treasure trove of thousands of intricate and (18) beautifully-made artifacts, many of which wouldn't (19) have been saved on a typical production. The team behind Warner Bros. Studio Tour London - The Making of Harry Potter wanted to preserve and showcase these iconic props, costumes and sets so that Harry Potter fans could experience the magic of filmmaking (20) first-hand, and on 31st March 2012, the Studio Tour opened its doors.

第 1 回
第 2 回
第 3 回
第 4 回
第 5 回
第 6 回

哈利・波特系列電影以利維斯登為大本營已經超過十年。由於書本發行的同時，電影版本也正在拍攝，劇組人員保存了很多特別為拍攝電影所製作的，具有代表性的場景、道具和服裝，以免日後的續集需要用到。在 2010 年，一旦《哈利波特－死神的聖物 2》完成拍攝後，劇組人員被留下有數以千計寶貴且設計精巧又精美的手工藝品，多數的物品都是一般電影拍攝中不會被保留的。倫敦華納兄弟工作室之旅－哈利・波特的幕後團隊，想要保留並展現這些具有代表性的道具、服裝和場景，以便讓哈利・波特的粉絲能夠第一手體驗到電影拍攝的魅力，在 2012 年 3 月 31 日，攝影棚遊覽正式開張。

Q16

A. distributed
C. repudiated

B. sacrificed
D. concluded

詳解

答案：A

空格處的句子是指「哈利・波特系列小說暢銷全球，這些書會被發行到世界各地」，答案為 A。

|單字片語| **sacrifice** [`sækrə,faɪs] 犧牲 / **repudiate** [rɪ`pjudɪ,et] 否認
conclude [kən`klud] 作出結論

Q17

A. although the investors did not want to fund this project
B. so that the film production company will sell these products
C. just in case they were ever needed later on in the series
D. because the fans would like to bid these precious products

詳解

答案：C

此題要依據前後句來判斷，前句提到「劇組人員保存了很多特別為拍攝電影所製作的，具有代表性的場景、道具和服裝」，而後面的段落也提到留下的物品用在什麼用途，可以看到選項 C 才能符合敘述，其他選項皆不符合，答案為 C。

|單字片語| **investor** [ɪn`vɛstə] 投資者 / **fund** [fʌnd] 資金 / **in case** 假如
later on 後來；以後 / **bid** [bɪd] 出價；投標

Q18

A. made-beautiful   B. made-beautifully

C. beautifully-made   D. beautiful-made

詳解   **答案：C**

　　這是高中會教到特定用法，副詞加過去分詞形成一個形容詞。除了 beautifully-made（做得很美的），還有 well-done（做得很好的），brightly-colored（顏色鮮豔的），highly-prized（高度評價的）。此外，handmade 是「手工製成的」，manmade 是「人造的」。

Q19

A. save   B. be saving

C. have saved   D. have been saved

詳解   **答案：D**

　　這題是文法題，主詞是 artifacts（手工藝品），手工藝品是物品，不會主動做出「保存」的動作，因此選項 A、B 和 C 都是錯誤的。手工藝品是「被保存」下來的，答案為 D。

Q20

A. first-hand   B. second-hand

C. handful   D. hands-on

詳解   **答案：A**

　　看空格應該是要填入修飾動詞 experience 的副詞，所以形容詞的選項 C、D 就可以先刪除。雖然英文和中文的文化不同，但有些時候某些概念和邏輯不謀而合。「二手的」是別人用過的，「第一手的」指的是優先、直接，英文也有相似的語感，experience... first-hand（親自體驗），答案為 A。

例句

Used books are also called **second-hand** books.   用過的書也稱為二手書。

He has a **handful** of problems to deal with.   他有好幾個問題要處理。

Hands-on-experience is more important than theory.

親手實際操作的經驗比理論重要。

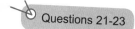

第三部分 / 閱讀理解

Questions 21-23

DANGER

This restricted area allows staff only.
This area contains dangerous chemical materials.
Staff must wear protective gear.
Trespassers will be charged with mischief
and could be fined up to 5,000 NTD.

危險

管制地帶只允許工作人員進入。
本區域存有危險化學材料。
工作人員必須穿戴保護裝備。
侵入者將控以損害行為
並最高可處新台幣 5,000 元的罰鍰。

|單字片語| **restricted** [rɪˈstrɪktɪd] 受限制的 / **chemical** [ˈkɛmɪkl] 化學的
protective [prəˈtɛktɪv]保護的 / **trespasser** [ˈtrɛspəsə] 侵入者
charge [tʃɑrdʒ] 控告 / **mischief** [ˈmɪstʃɪf] 損害；惡作劇

Q21

What is the purpose of this sign?
這個警示牌的目的是什麼？

A. To prevent unauthorized people from entering　為防止閒雜人等進入。
B. To provide sightseeing information　為提供觀光資訊。
C. To collect tax for the government　為政府收取稅金。
D. To conduct a chemical experiment　為進行化學試驗。

詳解　　　　　　　　　　　　　　　　　　　　　　　答案：A

　　從警示牌的許多關鍵詞如 restricted area（限制區）、trespassers（侵入者），都可得知答案為 A，此警示牌為防止閒雜人等進入限制區。

Q22

People who sneak into the area without permission will _____.

擅自溜進這個區域的人會…。

A. be given a reward　獲得一筆獎金
B. be fined a sum of money　被罰款
C. be beaten by security　被警衛毆打
D. be hired by the company　被公司僱用

詳解　　　　　　　　　　　　　　　　　　　　　答案：B

permission 是「允許」，警示牌很清楚的表示擅闖禁區者可處罰款最高新台幣五千元，答案為 B。

Q23

Where might you see this warning sign?

你可能會在什麼地方看到這個警告標示？

A. In front of a shopping mall　在購物中心前面
B. By a dangerous river which runs extremely fast
　　在水流湍急的危險河流邊
C. Outside a laboratory　在實驗室外面
D. On a street with heavy traffic　在交通繁忙的街道上

詳解　　　　　　　　　　　　　　　　　　　　　答案：C

警示牌寫著：This area contains dangerous chemical materials.（本地區存有危險材料。）按常理判斷，選項中最有可能的是在實驗室外面，答案為 C。

Questions 24-26

Yummy Cake House

Do you enjoy having delicious and unforgettable cakes? Yummy Cake House is the number one bakery in town. Our chef now develops a brand new menu for all of our customers. Her new cakes will satisfy all the customer's stomachs. She can also customize the birthday cakes for our clients. Come to our cake house now and enjoy the delicious cakes.

Macrons	**NT 60**
Cupcake	**NT 70**
Fruit tart	**NT 120**
Tiramisu cake	**NT 120**
Strawberry cake	**NT 150**

Opening hours:
Monday to Friday, 10:30 A.M. to 9:00 P.M.
Saturday, 10:00 A.M. to 8:00 P.M.

VIP members can have 10% off discounts of all the items.

第1回
第2回
第3回
第4回
第5回
第6回

Yummy 蛋糕屋

　　你很享受吃美味又令人難忘的蛋糕嗎？Yummy 蛋糕屋是市區首屈一指的烘培坊，我們的主廚現在為我們所有的顧客開發出一套全新菜單，她新的蛋糕將會滿足所有顧客的胃口，她也能為我們的客戶客製生日蛋糕。現在就來我們的蛋糕屋並享用美味的蛋糕。

馬卡龍	60 元
杯子蛋糕	70 元
水果塔	120 元
提拉米蘇蛋糕	120 元
草莓蛋糕	150 元

營業時間：
週一至週五，上午 10:30 至 晚上 9:00
週六，上午 10:00 至晚上 8:00

VIP 會員可享全品項 9 折優惠。

Q24

What is this advertisement for?

這一則廣告是關於什麼？

    A. A new barbershop. 一間新開的理髮店。

    B. A new bakery. 一間新開的烘焙坊。

    C. A new cloth shop. 一間新開的服飾店。

    D. A new grocery store. 一間新開的雜貨店。

〔詳解〕   〔答案：B〕

    廣告的標題就寫著 Yummy Cake House，可知道這是與烘焙食物相關的商店，而下一段也寫下 "Yummy Cake House is the number one bakery in town." ，因此答案為 B。

Q25

What information CANNOT be found in the advertisement?

哪一項資訊無法在這則廣告被找到？

    A. The prices of the products. 商品的價格。

    B. The opening hours of the shop. 商店的營業時間。

    C. VIP's discounts bonus. VIP 的折扣優惠。

    D. The location of the shop. 商店的地點。

〔詳解〕   〔答案：D〕

    題目詢問哪一項資訊沒有在廣告內，內文可以看到商品的價錢，因此選項 A 是可知的。商店的營業時間也可以找到，因此選項 B 是可知的。VIP 的折扣優惠是 9 折，因此選項 C 是可知的。而廣告中沒有顯示商店的地址，答案為 D。

Q26

Mrs. Smith is the VIP member of Yummy Cake house. How many discount can she have?

Smith 太太是 Yummy 蛋糕屋的 VIP 會員，她可以享有多少的折扣？

    A. 40% 六折。

    B. 30% 七折。

    C. 20% 八折。

    D. 10% 九折。

第 1 回
第 2 回
第 3 回
第 4 回
第 5 回
第 6 回

詳解

題目詢問 VIP 會員會享有多少的折扣，而廣告內文的最後一句寫 "VIP members can have 10% off discounts of all the items"，可知優惠是打九折，答案為 D。

Questions 27-30

40-year-old Martin, who lived alone, had worked for his stepfather's car rental business after he graduated from high school. He found his interest in landscape gardening and worked his way up from apprentice to master. But in April last year he lost his job when the firm downsized. He unsuccessfully applied for 40 posts over the next three months – and most of these applications went ignored because he was 'undercut' on wages by younger and less experienced candidates. Martin died 24 hours after visiting his local job where he was only offered a 'follow-up' appointment.

四十歲的 Martin 自己一個人住，他從高中畢業後，曾經在繼父的出租車公司上班。他發現自己對園藝造景的興趣，並從學徒一路往上當到師傅。但是去年四月公司裁員，讓他失去工作。在之後的三個月他申請了四十個工作卻沒有成功，大部份的工作申請都被忽視，因為經驗比他少的年輕人選在工資上「削價競爭」。他去了當地的就業中心，只是被告知「後續的」會面，在二十四小時後，Martin 過世了。

Speaking yesterday after an inquest into his death, Martin's stepfather described how the aspiring gardener "hated" going to his local job center, saying: "Many people go in with a sense of self-worth – they really do want a job – but come out feeling demoralized and put down. In the last months of his life, Martin became a statistic to other people. He was a statistic by being out of work, a statistic when he went into the Job Centre and now he is a statistic by killing himself."

昨天在調查 Martin 死亡的審訊中，Martin 的繼父提到這位有志氣的園藝愛好者「痛恨」到當地就業中心去，他說：「許多人進去的時候都懷著一種自我價值—他們真的要找工作—可是他們出來後完全洩氣並被打擊了。在 Martin 生命中的最後這幾個月，他被人當作是一種統計數字。因為失業他成為一項數字，到就業中心他也是一種統計數字，現在他自殺了，他還是一項統計數字。」

Martin was highly independent and he never claimed any social benefits in his life. He got nothing off the government and was proud not to. There was enough money left in his bank to cover his monthly expenses for a full year. The reason he could not accept a gardening job with a lower pay was that he felt it was not a reflection of his talent, skills and more importantly, his self-worth as an individual.

Martin 非常的獨立，而他一生中從來沒有領取任何社會福利。他沒有從政府那裡得到什麼，而且以此為榮。他的銀行裡有足夠的錢，可以維持他的每月開支長達一年。他無法接受薪資比較低的園藝工作的原因，是他認為太低的薪資不能反應他的才華和技能，更重要的是他身為一個人的自我價值。

Q27

Why was Martin out of work?
為什麼 Martin 會沒有工作？

A. He lacked the necessary experience.　他缺乏必需的經驗。
B. He decided to further his studies.　他決定要去進修學業。
C. He was fired by his stepfather.　他被他的繼父開除。
D. He was laid off by his company.　他被公司裁員。

┌─ 詳解 ─┐　　　　　　　　　　　　　　　　　　　　　　　　答案：D

Martin 是園藝造景的師傅，他非常有經驗，選項 A 是錯誤的。短文中並沒有提到他要去深造，選項 B 也是錯誤的。Martin 從高中畢業後，先在繼父的公司上班，後來發現自己的興趣才離開，並不是被繼父開除，選項 C 是錯誤的。Martin 是因為公司裁減員工人數（downsized）而被裁退的，答案為 D。

|單字片語| **lay off** 裁員 / **downsize** [ˈdaʊnˈsaɪz] 裁員
retrench [rɪˈtrɛntʃ] 刪減 / **cut cost** 降低成本

Q28

What happened when Martin tried to seek help from the local job center?
當 Martin 到當地就業中心尋求協助時發生了什麼事？

A. He felt more depressed after visit.　他去了之後更加憂鬱。
B. He rejected over 40 job offers.　他拒絕了超過 40 份工作機會。
C. He was told to arrange an appointment with a doctor.
　　他被告知要安排和醫生見面。
D. He had to learn statistics and other subjects.
　　他必須學習統計學和其他科目。

第 1 回
第 2 回
第 3 回
第 4 回
第 5 回
第 6 回

詳解

答案：A

　　根據 Martin 的繼父所說的，Martin 去了就業中心出來後覺得 demoralized（洩氣；意志消沉），可想而知，去就業中心後的失望讓他感到更加憂鬱，答案為 A。

|單字片語| **morale** [məˋræl] 士氣 / **moral** [ˋmɔrəl] 道德；有道德的
　　　　 depression [dɪˋprɛʃən] 憂鬱；蕭條

What can be said about the local job center?
可以如何形容當地的就業中心？

A. It is impersonal.　那個地方很冷漠。
B. It is efficient.　那個地方很有效率。
C. It is understaffed.　那個地方人手不足。
D. It is corrupted.　那個地方很腐敗。

詳解

答案：A

　　Martin 的繼父認為，當地的就業中心把去找工作的人都當作統計數字，非常的冷漠，答案為 A。

|單字片語| **personal** [ˋpɝsn̩l] 個人的，私人的 / **impersonal** [ɪmˋpɝsn̩l] 冷淡的
　　　　 personality [͵pɝsn̩ˋælətɪ] 個性 / **personalize** [ˋpɝsn̩l͵aɪz] 使人格化

Questions 30-32

　　Animal Rights supporters oppose zoos because cages and cramped enclosures at zoos deprive animals of the opportunity to satisfy their most basic needs. The zoo community regards the animals it keeps as commodities, and animals are regularly bought, sold, borrowed, and traded without any regard for established relationships. Zoos breed animals because the presence of babies draws zoo visitors and boosts revenue. But the animals' fate is often bleak once they outgrow their "cuteness." And some zoos still import animals from the wild.

　　動物權利支持者反對動物園，因為動物園的籠子和狹小的圈地剝奪動物滿足其基本需求的機會。動物園團體把其所飼養的動物當作商品，動物經常被買、賣、借用和交換，完全不考慮到動物之間已經建立起來的感情。動物園繁殖動物是因為動物寶寶的出現能吸引訪客並增加收入。但是，一旦這些動物長大了便不

再「可愛」，牠們的命運往往是淒涼的，而且有些動物園依然進口野生動物。

In general, zoos and wildlife parks preclude or severely restrict natural behavior, such as flying, swimming, running, hunting, climbing, scavenging, foraging, digging, exploring, and selecting a partner. The physical and mental frustrations of captivity often lead to abnormal, neurotic, and even self-destructive behavior, such as incessant pacing, swaying, head-bobbing, bar-biting, and self-mutilation. Proponents of zoos like to claim that zoos protect species from extinction—seemingly a noble goal. However, wild-animal parks and zoos almost always favor large and charismatic animals which draw large crowds of visitors, but they neglect less popular species that also need to be protected. Most animals in zoos are not endangered, and while confining animals to zoos keeps them alive, it does nothing to protect wild populations and their habitats.

一般來說，動物園和野生動物園防止或嚴格約束動物的自然行為，例如：飛行、游泳、奔跑、狩獵、攀爬、搜尋、覓食、挖掘、探索還有尋找伴侶。能力被囚禁而在身體上和精神上造成的挫折感，時常導致異常、神經質、甚至自我毀滅的行為，例如：不停徘徊、左右擺動、頭部晃動、咬籠子的鐵條還有自殘。動物園的擁護者喜歡去聲稱動物園可以保護物種，避免他們絕種—這似乎是偉大高尚的目標。然而，野生動物園區和動物園幾乎總是偏好吸引大批遊客的大型、有魅力的動物，但他們忽略也需要被保護卻較不受歡迎的動物。大部分在動物園裡的動物沒有瀕臨絕種的危機，儘管將動物限制在動物園內能讓牠們存活，但對於保護野生動物總數和牠們的棲息地卻沒有作用。

What is the main argument against locking wild animals in zoos?
對於反對把野生動物關在動物園的主要論點是什麼？

A. Zoos abuse and cause death to many animals.
動物園虐待並造成許多動物的死亡。
B. Zoos treat wild animals in an inhumane manner.
動物園以不人道的方式對待動物。
C. Zoos make money by helping animals to reproduce.
動物園藉由幫助動物繁殖來賺錢。
D. Zoos purchase wild animals in danger of extinction.

動物園購買瀕臨絕種的野生動物。

詳解　　　　　　　　　　　　　　　　　　　　答案：B

　　文中反對把野生動物關在動物園的主要論點是，動物園以不人道的方式對待動物，例如以狹小的空間囚禁動物，還有限制牠們的自然行為，答案為 B。

Q31

Why is the writer concerned about the fate of 'zoo-born' animals?

為什麼作者擔心動物在「動物園出生」的命運？

A. They are likely to be attacked by other species.
　　牠們可能會遭受其他物種的動物攻擊。

B. They are likely to hurt themselves in an enclosed area.
　　牠們可能會在圈養的區域傷害自己。

C. They are likely to be neglected once they are fully grown.
　　一旦牠們完全長大後，牠們可能會被忽略。

D. They are likely to attract more visitors to the zoo.
　　牠們可能會吸引更多訪客到動物園。

詳解　　　　　　　　　　　　　　　　　　　　答案：C

　　根據作者的敘述，動物園把動物寶寶當搖錢樹，一旦這些動物長大，沒那麼可愛，也無法吸引遊客時，他們可能會遭到冷落，答案為 C。

Q32

Which of the following is NOT a consequence caused by a loss of freedom?

以下哪一項不是失去自由的後果？

A. Wild mood swings　情緒的極大波動

B. Compulsive behavior　強迫行為

C. Self-inflicted wounds　自我造成的傷害

D. Enriched lifestyle　更加豐富的生活方式

詳解　　　　　　　　　　　　　　　　　　　　答案：D

　　失去自由的後果應該是負面的敘述，而選項中只有 D 是正面的敘述，答案為 D。

第 1 回
第 2 回
第 3 回
第 4 回
第 5 回
第 6 回

← → ⟳ ⌂ 🔍 www.job-boarding.com

Job Description: Marketing Manager

Natural Beauty Cosmetic is an international brand. Our company aims at producing natural makeup products. We're looking for a creative and versatile marketer who will be responsible for the growth of our sales figures.

Responsibilities
- Develop strategies and tactics to promote our company's products
- Build the relationship with social media influencers to promote our company
- Oversee and approve marketing materials, such as website banner, product cover
- Produce eye-catching content for our website, social media

Requirements
- Master's degree in Business Administration
- Managerial skills and experience
- Social media posts writing skills
- Interpersonal skills and out-going personality

If you're interested in this position, please send your resume to human resource director, Ellie Green (ellie.g@naturalbeauty.com).

To:	ellie.g@naturalbeauty.com
From:	jeff.chen@hotmail.com
Subject:	Marketing Manager Application
Attachment:	Jeff Chen-resume.pdf

Dear Ms. Green,

I'm Jeff Chen. I found your company's advertisement on the job boards website. In response to your advertisement, I am interested in applying for the Marketing Manager position as offered. I believe my qualification below meets the requirement.

- Master degree in Business Administration in H.S University
- 5-year managing experience at SFY Advertisement
- Budget reviewing skills
- Advertisement writing skills

I am an out-going person. I have a good relationship with all my clients and colleagues. I am very persistent and determined in achieving a challenging and rewarding career.

A copy of my resume can be found in the attachments. There is also a brief introduction to my educational background and previous job experience. I would be honored to be allowed to discuss more details of my contribution. I look forward to hearing from you.

Sincerely yours,
Jeff Chen

工作敘述：行銷經理

自然美彩妝是一個國際品牌，我們的公司旨在生產天然的彩妝產品。我們正在找尋有創意且具備多種技能的行銷人才，將會負責我們銷售數字的成長。

職務
- 發展戰略及策略以推廣公司商品
- 與網路紅人建立關係以推廣公司
- 監督並批准行銷素材，例如網站橫幅、產品包裝
- 為網站和社群媒體創造引人注目的內容

必要條件
- 企業管理碩士學位
- 管理技能和經驗
- 社群媒體貼文寫作技巧
- 人際關係技巧和外向性格

如果您對這個職缺有興趣，請寄您的履歷給人事部主管 Ellie Green（ellie.g@naturalbeauty.com）。

第1回
第2回
第3回
第4回
第5回
第6回

收件人：	ellie.g@naturalbeauty.com
寄件人：	jeff.chen@hotmail.com
主旨：	行銷經理申請
附件：	Jeff Chen- 履歷表 .pdf

Green 小姐您好：

　　我是 Jeff Chen，我在工作公告網站上看到貴公司的廣告。為回應貴公司廣告，我有興趣申請貴公司提供的行銷經理一職。我相信我下列的資格符合必要條件。

- ·H.S. 大學企業管理碩士學位
- ·在 SFY 廣告五年的管理經驗
- ·預算審查技能
- ·廣告寫作技能

　　我是外向的人，我和我所有的客戶和同事都有良好的關係。我是對達成挑戰和有益的職業非常堅持不懈和果斷。

　　我的履歷表副本可以在附件中找到。也有我的教育背景和之前工作經歷的簡短介紹。我會很榮幸被允許討論我更多的貢獻。我期待能聽到您的回音。

誠摯地
Jeff Chen

Q33

How did the applicant probably find out about this job offer?
申請者應該是如何得知這份職缺的？

A. He contacted the Marketing Manager. 他聯絡了行銷經理。
B. He read the ad on the website. 他讀了網站上的廣告。
C. He went to the company in person. 他親自到公司去。
D. We can't tell from the letter. 從信中我們無法得知。

信中提到申請者是回應該公司的廣告（in response to your advertisement），申請者最有可能在工作公告廣告看到徵人啟事，答案為 B。

Q34

Which of the following is NOT stated as part of the job requirement?

以下哪一項並不是工作需求的一部分？

A. Ability to get along well with people　和人們相處的能力

B. Fluency in another language apart from mother tongue
　　除母語外另一個語言的流利度

C. Budget reviewing skills　預算審查技能

D. Related education background　相關的教育背景

具備人際手腕（interpersonal skills）表示要有和人們相處的能力，選項 A 是工作需求的一部分。選項 C 中的預算審查技能（budget reviewing skills），也是其中一項要求。商業管理碩士學位（Master's degree in Business Administration）相關的教育背景的選項 D 也是不可或缺的能力，唯有選項 B 中的另一個語言的流利度（fluency in another language）並不是必要的條件。

Q35

Which statement best fits Jeff Chen's description of himself?

哪一個敘述最符合 Jeff Chen 對自己的描述？

A. He is dedicated and enthusiastic.　他很投入也很有熱忱。

B. He is humble and shy.　他很謙虛也很害羞。

C. He is proud and arrogant.　他很驕傲也很自大。

D. He is talkative and greedy.　他很多話也很貪心。

Jeff Chen 對自己的描述是他能和別人相處（relate well to people），工作態度堅持並有決心（persistent and determined），答案為 A。

全民英檢中級

第二回 初試 聽力測驗

本測驗分四部份，全為四選一之選擇題，共 35 題，作答時間約 30 分鐘。

第一部分 看圖辨義

共 5 題，試題冊上有數幅圖畫，每一圖畫有 1~3 個描述該圖的題目，每題請聽錄音播出每題以及四個英語敘述之後，選出與所看到的圖畫最相符的一個答案。每題只播出一遍。

例題：（看）

（聽） Look at the picture.
What does the woman want the boy to do?
A. Pick up the rubbish.
B. Tie his shoelaces.
C. Carry her luggage.
D. Hail a cab.

正確答案為 A。

聽力測驗第一部分自本頁開始。

A: Question 1

B: Question 2

C: <u>Question 3</u>

Mr. Jefferson's daily schedule
7~8 am : Morning rounds.
8~12 am : Follow up on patients.
12~1 pm : Lunch Break.
1~3 pm : Surgery.
3~5 pm : Paperwork.

D: <u>Question 4-5</u>

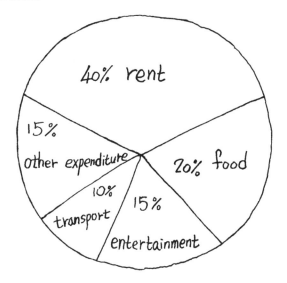

共 10 題，每題請聽光碟放音機播出一英語問句或直述句之後，從試題冊上 A、B、C、D 四個回答或回應中，選出一個最適合者作答。每題只播出一遍。

例： （聽） What happened to your feet?
　　（看）　A.　They were too hungry.
　　　　　　B.　I got a new pair.
　　　　　　C.　My new shoes are too small.
　　　　　　D.　These are not mine.

正確答案為 C。

6. A. We are not allowed to park here.
　 B. I can't help it. I am too nervous.
　 C. Don't you think they are too short?
　 D. Who has a hammer?

7. A. This is already the largest.
　 B. The size doesn't fit.
　 C. We will invite each other.
　 D. I'm afraid you have to purchase it.

8. A. Is this the first time you are here?
　 B. How will you get here?
　 C. Why do you choose this job?
　 D. When did you brush your teeth?

9. A. Kids are not for sale.
　 B. The doctor is not available.
　 C. Admission for children is free.
　 D. Math is a tough subject.

10. A. I hope there will be more.
　　B. I usually report to my boss.
　　C. I'll correct them immediately.
　　D. I'll type quietly next time.

11. A. Yes, and he is really getting old.
    B. Yes, and he needs to send it out by today.
    C. Yes, and he said he will give me a ride.
    D. Yes, and he was banned from driving.

12. A. My appetite is pretty small.
    B. Medium will do just fine.
    C. I would prefer a large one.
    D. You did a great job.

13. A. I can't believe what you just said.
    B. I can't eat beans.
    C. I can't continue living like this.
    D. I can't find the time.

14. A. Did she hurt herself?
    B. How could she do something so stupid?
    C. When did she become so strong?
    D. Hasn't she done enough shopping?

15. A. I just watched a funny one.
    B. I don't think I want to sell it.
    C. I think you shouldn't watch too much TV.
    D. I have to admit that I am camera-shy.

請 翻 頁 ⇨

第三部分　簡短對話

　　共 10 題，每題請聽光碟放音機播出一段對話及一個相關的問題後，從試題冊上 A、B、C、D 四個選項中選出一個最適合者作答。每段對話及問題只播出一遍。

例：（聽）　（Man）　　Did you happen to see my earphones?
　　　　　　　　　　　I remember leaving them in the drawer.
　　　　（Woman）　Did you search your briefcase?
　　　　（Man）　　I did but they are not there. Wait a second.
　　　　　　　　　　　Oh. They are right here in my pocket.

　　　　Question:　　Where are the man's earphones?

　（看）　A.　The woman's pocket.
　　　　　B.　Briefcase.
　　　　　C.　The man's pocket.
　　　　　D.　Drawer.

正確答案為 C。

16. A. She doesn't want to part with so much money.
　　 B. She doesn't want to make a purchase on the Internet.
　　 C. She doesn't want to spend any money.
　　 D. She doesn't want to steal anything.

17. A. Call a veterinarian.
　　 B. Prepare a shopping list.
　　 C. Visit the pharmacy.
　　 D. Take some medicine.

18. A. The woman shares the room with the man.
　　 B. The woman rents a room.
　　 C. The woman's laptop needs to be fixed.
　　 D. The woman is pleased with her landlord.

19. A. They are having an interview.
　　 B. They are bargaining over prices.
　　 C. They are arranging for a meeting.
　　 D. They are discussing about health issues.

20. A. In a bank.
    B. In a travel agency.
    C. In a clothing store.
    D. In an auditorium.

21. A. The woman agrees with the man.
    B. The woman is a strong supporter of the writer.
    C. The man received negative comments.
    D. The man is not affected by the bad reviews.

22. A. The man should be careful.
    B. The man should give it a try.
    C. The man should play it safe.
    D. The man should eat something else.

23. A. No, she is going mountain climbing by herself.
    B. No, she will invite the man to her house.
    C. Yes, but she also wants to go out with christopher.
    D. Yes, but she doesn't want to exercise under the sun.

24.

Sports Club

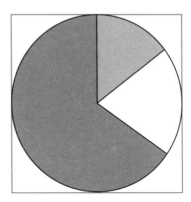

    A. The table tennis club
    B. The basketball club
    C. The softball club
    D. The baseball club

25.

Notes
Beach & SPA package: skincare and picnicking
Voyage package: diving and cooking classes
Nature package: hiking and mountain food barbecue
Luxury package: best pool view and kitchen

    A. Beach & SPA package
    B. Voyage package
    C. Nature package
    D. Luxury package

共 10 題，每題請聽光碟放音機播出一段談話及一個相關的問題後，從試題冊上 A、B、C、D 四個選項中選出一個最適合者作答。每段談話及問題只播出一遍。

例：　　　　(聽)　　　Good morning, everyone. Please come over here and take these registration forms. Then, go back to your seats. This is the workshop on APP design. The lecturer of this workshop is an engineer from SBE Software. He has excellent experience in designing smartphone applications. Before you fill in the forms, please look through the forms carefully. If you have any questions, I will answer you later.

Question:　　What might the listeners do, after they read through the registration forms?

(看)　　　A. Leave the forms on the desks.
B. Pay the registration fee.
C. Ask the speaker some questions.
D. Go to another location.

正確答案為 C。

26. A. In a movie theater.
    B. In a studio.
    C. In a lecture hall.
    D. In an award ceremony.

27. A. A flight accident.
    B. A road accident.
    C. A flood accident.
    D. A sports accident.

28. A. Talk to another staff member.
    B. Check his message.
    C. Go back to his office.
    D. Leave a voicemail.

29. A. Sauces.
    B. Milk.
    C. Cereals.
    D. Peanut oils.

30. A. A driver left his twins in a hot car.
    B. A driver texted his friend while driving.
    C. A driver moved over for an ambulance.
    D. A driver applied makeup while driving.

31. A. Composition.
    B. Statistics.
    C. Biology experiment.
    D. Economics analysis.

32. A. YouTube.
    B. Facebook.
    C. Twitter.
    D. LinkedIn.

33. A. Repairing a brake.
    B. Fixing a tire.
    C. Renting a bike.
    D. Hanging a bell.

34.

2020-2021 Student Council Election Result

Candidates	Votes	Percentages
Ella Jones	26	32.5%
Chloe Smith	27	33.8%
Ivy Taylor	13	16.3%
Ethan Brown	14	17.4%

    A. Ella Jones.
    B. Ethan Brown.
    C. Chloe Smith.
    D. Ivy Taylor.

35.

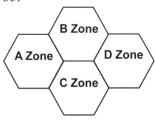

A Zone: Tropical Area
B Zone: Desert Area
C Zone: Aquarium
D Zone: Bird World

    A. A zone.
    B. B zone.
    C. C zone.
    D. D zone.

—結束—

第二回 初試 閱讀測驗

本測驗分三部分，全為四選一的選擇題，共 35 題，作答時間為 45 分鐘。

第一部分：詞彙
　　共 10 題，每題有一個空格。請由試題冊上的四個選項中選出最適合題意的字或詞作答。

1. We will have to determine if the drugs are effective. _____, a surgery might be the last option available.
   A. However
   B. Therefore
   C. Otherwise
   D. In addition

2. College life is unlike high school, the hours are more _____ as students are allowed to select optional courses according to their preferences.
   A. flexible
   B. sustainable
   C. eligible
   D. predictable

3. Cases of dengue fever have been on the rise during the summer, and we have to take all the necessary precautions to prevent mosquitoes from _____.
   A. stinging
   B. circulating
   C. breeding
   D. trading

4. Being a/an _____ fan of Stephen King, Sandra collected every book by the author and has read through most of them more than once.
   A. loyal
   B. casual
   C. appropriate
   D. ignorant

5. Mr. Andrews has retired and he is now _____ to helping the needy.
   A. hasty
   B. joyful
   C. included
   D. devoted

6. There was a fierce debate on whether the rainforest should be _____ or not. Environmentalists argue that the rainforest is the habitat of a few endangered species.
   A. deserved
   B. reserved
   C. conversed
   D. preserved

7. Since that close _____ with death, Mr. Grisham has adopted a whole new perspective of life. He has learned not to take his health for granted.
   A. encounter
   B. intensity
   C. attraction
   D. offence

8. Many people, _____ age, sex or race, volunteered to join the peaceful demonstration in support of the non-smoking campaign.
   A. even though
   B. regardless of
   C. provided that
   D. insofar as

9. Mrs. Wang was heartbroken when her son demanded that she stop _____ in his life now that he is an adult capable of making his own decisions.
   A. interfering
   B. participating
   C. existing
   D. delegating

10. A psychiatrist is a doctor who has the authority to prescribe drugs whereas a _____ is not in the position to do likewise.
    A. therapist
    B. pharmacist
    C. psychologist
    D. archaeologist

第二部分：段落填空

共 10 題，包括二個段落，每個段落各含 5 個空格。請由試題冊上四個選項中選出最適合題意的字或詞作答。

Questions 11-15

The Vatican City, one of the ___(11)___ sacred places in Christendom, is a testimony of its great history as a spiritual fortress. A unique collection of artistic and architectural masterpieces lies ___(12)___ the boundaries of this small state, which is ___(13)___, the world's smallest sovereign state that encompasses an area of a mere 0.44 square km. It sits proudly atop the low-lying Vatican hill a few hundred meters west of the Tiber. Centered on the domed bulk of St Peter's Basilica, it boasts some of Italy's most celebrated masterpieces, many housed in the ___(14)___ Vatican Museums. You'll need at least a morning to ___(15)___. The highlight is the Michelangelo-decorated Sistine Chapel, but there's enough art on display to keep you busy for years.

11. A. more
    B. most
    C. many
    D. much

12. A. between
    B. along
    C. within
    D. without

13. A. as usual
    B. as long as
    C. as a matter of fact
    D. as soon as possible

14. A. magnificent
    B. ridiculous
    C. average
    D. ordinary

15. A. make do with the artwork
    B. do away with the tradition
    C. have to do with some artists
    D. do justice to the Vatican Museum

Questions 16-20

With wear gear technology being the talk of the town for months, a wide ___(16)___ of smartwatches is on parade at the IFA electronics trade show in Berlin. Google's software for smartwatches, Android Wear, will start appearing as a companion accessory on a range of devices from various ___(17)___ this autumn, and this year's IFA electronics trade show is expected to be packed with rival models. Google Wear is a new platform, an overhaul of Google's Android smartwatch software, which simplifies the user experience by cutting out all ___(18)___ the essential features. For users, the pertinent question is whether Android Wear is worth investing in, and ditching a perfectly adequate watch for. As a matter of facts, ___(19)___, to prove that having notifications on the wrist instead of the smartphone is worth ___(20)___ £150-200 on. However, for those not inundated with email, messages and social media, it might take more time to convince them.

16. A. variety
    B. example
    C. margin
    D. option

17. A. consumers
    B. supporters
    C. manufacturers
    D. instructors

18. A. yet
    B. while
    C. only
    D. but

19. A. Google Watch hasn't attracted to many customers
    B. Android Wear has appealed to the mass market
    C. Google Watch needs to lower its price
    D. Smart watch didn't have so many functions

20. A. spend
    B. to spend
    C. spending
    D. to be spent

第三部分：閱讀理解

　　本部分共 15 題，包括 5 個題組，每個題組含 1 至 2 篇短文，與數個相關的四選一的選擇題。請由試題冊上的選項中選出最適合者作答。

Questions 21-22

　　Search engine optimization (SEO) is the art of creating Web pages that will rank high in search engine returns. SEO is accomplished by optimizing certain sections or "elements" in the computer programming language known as HTML. These sections encoded in the HTML of any given webpage are specifically read by search engines and, depending on the level of optimization, can create a greater likelihood of free referral traffic. In other words, your web address has a better chance of appearing on the first page of a search browser, which in turn increases the likelihood of people clicking on the link to your website.

　　There are several methods and opinions about how a web page should be optimized, and much will depend on the type of site, its content, purpose and competition, if relevant. But in general search engine optimization relies heavily on the proper use of keywords and key-phrases that describe the site's content. That is why programmers try to cram as many keywords as possible when describing the site's product, services or content.

21. Where would you probably find this passage?
    A. In a classified ad
    B. In a business journal
    C. In a fashion magazine
    D. In a legal document

22. Who is more likely to take advantage of the principles behind SEO?
    A. A student who surfs the Net frequently
    B. A teacher who wants to create online worksheets
    C. A restaurant operator who needs to hire a chef
    D. A resort owner who needs to attract more visitors

Should students wear uniforms to school? Supporters of uniforms claim they can increase school safety. Uniforms allow staff to quickly identify people who do not belong on campus and limit the ways that gangs can infiltrate into schools. In 1994, Long Beach United School District in California began requiring uniforms with the hopes of improving safety. Just five years later, the overall crime rate in the district was down 91 percent. Specifically, sex offenses dropped 96 percent and number of incidents of vandalism had decreased by 69 percent.

When all students are dressed alike, economic and social barriers between students are reduced. There is no peer pressure to wear expensive clothes or bullying of those who can't afford designer labels. Children have one less distraction, as they do not have to concern themselves with what others are wearing.Common dress can also make students feel like they belong to the school community, increase pride and even improve attendance. A 2012 study by the University of Houston of 160 publics, urban schools, found that student attendance increased after schools began making the wearing of uniforms compulsory. Supporters of school uniforms often cite increased academic achievement as a main reason to adopt such a policy. While there are some testimonies from individuals to support this claim, overall, studies yielded inconclusive results and there is no clear evidence that wearing uniforms lead to better academic achievement.

23. In what ways do school uniforms help to make schools a safer place?
    A. By slowing traffic when students in uniform leave the school
    B. By unifying all students with a specific dress code
    C. By keeping out strangers with harmful intent
    D. By cooperation with police in uniform

24. How may the wearing of uniforms help to bring about harmony in a school?
    A. Students see themselves as equals who are a part of the school
    B. Students protect those who wear the same type of clothes
    C. Students express their personal identity with accessories
    D. Students believe that they face a common enemy

25. Which of the following is NOT one of the benefits of implementing school uniforms?
    A. A lower crime rate in the neighborhood
    B. Fostering a sense of belonging
    C. Better than expected academic results
    D. Increase in student attendance

This document is automatically generated.
Please do not respond to this mail.

QQ AIRWAYS E-TICKET ITINERARY AND RECEIPT ABN 16 009 661 901
International customers require this document for immigration, customs, airport security checks and duty purchases.
Australian and New Zealand domestic customers should carry this document at all times during travel and produce it when required.
All customers should retain a copy for their records.

Travel Details for:
Customer Name: Peter Wu
Booking Ref: 4O89B3
E-ticket No.: 081 2419240070
Issued by: QQ AIRWAYS-34382331-TAIPEI
Date: 12 MAR 22

Your itinerary and travel details:

QQ AIRWAYS:	QQ330	Economy Class	Confirmed
Depart: 15 APR 22		TAIPEI	2255
Arrive: 16 APR 22		BRISBANE	0955
Baggage Allowance: 20 Kilo.			

QQ   AIRWAYS: Q329   Economy Class   Confirmed
        Depart: 22 APR 22   BRISBANE   2245
        Arrive: 23 APR 22   TAIPEI   0525
    Departs From: Terminal 1
    Arrives at: Terminal 2
    Baggage Allowance: 20 Kilo.

26. Who is the sender of this email?
    A. The president of QQ Airways
    B. The customer of QQ Airways
    C. Mr. Wu
    D. No one. It is sent by the company's automation system.

27. What can you tell from the information above?
    A. Mr. Wu will reply to confirm the ticket.
    B. Mr. Wu is an Australian.
    C. Mr. Wu is employed by QQ Airways.
    D. Mr. Wu will not be in Taipei for about a week.

28. When might the passenger make a reservation?
    A. In May 2015
    B. In April 2015
    C. A month in advance
    D. A week before departure

City Museum

Operating Hours:
- Open to the public from 9:00 a.m. to 5:00 p.m.
- No entry after 3:30 p.m.
- Closed on Mondays and the day following a public holiday.

Fees:
- Normal Ticket: NT$90
- Discount Ticket: NT$60
- Eligibility for Discount Tickets:
  1. Teachers or military and police personnel (appropriate identification required)
  2. Students (with valid student card)
  3. Group purchase of 25 tickets or more

- Free Entry:
  1. Physically challenged persons (with certification)
  2. Seniors at the age of sixty years old and above (with ID card)
  3. Low income households (with certification from Kaohsiung City Government)

Regulations:
- No entry for children under five years of age
- No food or drinks
- No pets allowed
- No photography

Other:
- For wheelchairs, brochures or other services, please inquire at the Information Desk.
- Tel:886-7-2136521 ext.:5000

29. On which day will the city museum be closed?
    A. On Saturday
    B. On Sunday
    C. On a public holiday
    D. On the second of January

30. Who can purchase a ticket at a lower price?
    A. Someone who is fifty years old
    B. Someone who is seventy years old
    C. Someone who has young children
    D. Someone who works as a sailor in the navy

31. Which of the following behavior is a violation of museum rules?
    A. Having low income
    B. Completing a challenge
    C. Taking pictures of the paintings
    D. Purchasing a discount ticket

Questions 32-35 are based on the information provided in the following table and passage.

🎵 Musical Instruments courses at the High Music Studio

Musical Instruments	Description	Times
Guitar	Playing the guitar demands strong finger motor skills, so you will develop strength in your finger muscles. You may play the guitar while sitting or standing.	Monday 5 p.m. – 6 p.m. Wednesday 6 p.m. – 7 p.m. Friday 7 p.m. – 8 p.m.
French horn	When playing the French horn, you need to have a big hand to grasp the horn. Once you can produce a nice and characteristic sound, you will enjoy the pleasure. When you play the French horn, you are free to sit or stand.	Tuesday 6 p.m. – 7 p.m. Wednesday 6 p.m. – 7 p.m. Friday 6 p.m. – 7 p.m.
Piano	Playing the piano requires not just high finger skills, but moderate arm strength and endurance to hit the keys. You also need to use the strength of your foot and leg to pedal. You can sharpen your small muscles by piano playing.	Monday 6 p.m. – 7 p.m. Tuesday 7 p.m. – 8 p.m. Thursday 6 p.m. – 7 p.m. Friday 5 p.m. – 6 p.m.
Drums	Playing the drum is an activity of the entire body. You will use the muscle groups in your upper body to deliver power. Hitting a drum or holding drum sticks does not require finger skills.	Wednesday 5 p.m. – 6 p.m. Thursday 5 p.m. – 6 p.m. Saturday 5 p.m. – 6 p.m.

I'm reading an article in *Parents and Kids Monthly Magazine*. I am surprised to know that there is a lot to know when choosing a musical instrument for children. Everyone knows that music soothes our souls, but it is surprising that music can also shape and strengthen our brains. Learning a musical instrument allows people to nourish their brains. At the same time, many cognitive and physical parts of their bodies may be enhanced.

Learning to play a musical instrument is a great challenge, but it does have physical health benefits. Some instruments help children strengthen fine motor skills. Some help children build balance and coordination. Fine motor skills are the ability to carry out movements using the small muscles of our hands and wrists, like finger skills. Balance and coordination are two important capacities in the physical development of children, like whole-body activities.

Knowing the strengths and weaknesses of your children can help you and your kids select the best suiting their needs.

32. According to the second passage, which of the following statements is NOT mentioned?
    A. Learning musical instruments may benefit the brain.
    B. Learning musical instruments is a good way to enhance physical health.
    C. Learning musical instruments may improve memory ability.
    D. Learning musical instruments can calm the soul.

33. Joanna would like to sign up for a course for her child, but her child has developmental delays. Which class would be more appropriate for Joanna's child?
   A. The guitar course.
   B. The French horn course.
   C. The piano course.
   D. The drums course.

34. Martin has basketball evening training on Tuesdays, Thursdays, and Fridays. If he enrolls in a French horn course, when should he go?
   A. Wednesday 5 p.m. – 6 p.m.
   B. Wednesday 6 p.m. – 7 p.m.
   C. Monday 5 p.m. – 6 p.m.
   D. Monday 6 p.m. – 7 p.m.

35. Which musical instrument can improve the strength of the fingers and the legs?
   A. The guitar.
   B. The French horn.
   C. The piano.
   D. The drums.

—結束—

第 1 回
第 2 回
第 3 回
第 4 回
第 5 回
第 6 回

第二回

初試 聽力測驗 解析

第一部分 / 看圖辨義

Q1

For question one, please look at picture A.

What's the matter with the man at the door?
在門口的男子怎麼了？

A. He had a drop too much.
B. He went into the women's room.
C. He doesn't have his boarding pass.
D. He is inappropriately dressed for the occasion.

A. 他喝了太多酒。
B. 他進入了女廁。
C. 他沒有登機證。
D. 他的穿著對這個場合並不適當。

詳解　　　　　　　　　　　　　　　　　　　　**答案：D**

　　圖片題中背景為飯店的高級雞尾酒舞會，其他嘉賓穿著燕尾服和晚禮服，唯獨在門口的男子身穿 T恤和短褲，一臉錯愕的模樣。從圖片可判斷，男子的穿著不適當於這種場合，正確答案為 D。

〈補充說明〉

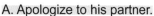

What's the special occasion today?　今天是什麼特別的場合？

Q2

For question two, please look at picture B.

What should the man do?
這位男子應該怎麼做？

A. Apologize to his partner.
B. Pretend that nothing happened.
C. Offer to give the lady a ride.
D. Request the woman to kneel down.

A. 向他的舞伴道歉。
B. 假裝什麼都沒發生。
C. 提供送女子一程。
D. 要求女子跪下。

　　圖片題中一位男子跟女伴在跳舞，男子不小心踩到女伴的腳，他接下來應該做的是向他的舞伴道歉，正確答案為 A。

Q3

For question three, please look at picture C.

What is on Mr. Jefferson schedule right after lunch?

Mr. Jefferson 午餐過後的行程是什麼？

Mr. Jefferson's daily schedule
7~8 am : Morning rounds
8~12am : Follow up on patients
12~1 pm : Lunch Break
1~3 pm : Surgery.
3~5 pm : Paperwork.

A. Check on patients.
B. Perform an operation.
C. Handle administration tasks.
D. Empty time slot for recreation.

A. 查看病患。
B. 動手術。
C. 處理行政事務。
D. 空出一段時間來休閒。

　　從 Mr. Jefferson 的每日行程（daily schedule）可得知，午餐之後要動一個手術，所以正確答案是 B。聽力考試中主要是測試關鍵詞，也可說是考單字。只要知道 surgery 和 operation 是同樣的意思，就能輕鬆解題。

|單字片語| **morning rounds** 晨間巡房 / **follow up on patients** 病患複診
　　　　lunch break 午餐時間 / **surgery** [ˈsɝdʒərɪ] 手術 / **paperwork** [ˈpepə͵wɝk] 文書工作

Q4

For questions four and five, please look at picture D.

What accounts for almost half of Janet's monthly budget?

哪一項支出占用 Janet 每月的預算將近一半？

40% rent
15% other expenditure
20% food
10% transport
15% entertainment

A. Rent.
B. Food.
C. Entertainment.
D. Transport.

A. 房租。
B. 食物。
C. 娛樂。
D. 交通。

　　從圓餅圖可看出，房租占用了 Janet 每月預算的 40%，將近一半，正確答案為 A。

第 1 回
第 2 回
第 3 回
第 4 回
第 5 回
第 6 回

<補充說明>

　　half 是「一半」，用在時間的話則是 30 分鐘的意思。a quarter 是「四分之一」也就是 25%，用於時間的話是 15 分鐘。此外，「三分之一」的英文是 one-third，「三分之二」是 two-thirds，三分之二被視為複數。

Q5

For question five, please look at picture D again.

What can we tell from the chart?
從這張統計圖中可以看出什麼？

A. Janet spends most of her money on enjoyment.
B. Janet doesn't manage to save any money at all.
C. Transport takes up less than 5% of Janet's budget.
D. Food adds up to exactly a quarter of Janet's budget.

A. Janet 大部分的錢都花在享受上。
B. Janet 完全沒辦法存到錢。
C. 交通占用 Janet 的預算少於 5%。
D. 食物總加起來正好是 Janet 預算的四分之一。

[詳解]

[答案：B]

　　Janet 每月花 15% 在娛樂，享受並不是最大的支出，選項 A 是錯誤的。交通費用是 10%，選項 C 也是錯誤的。食物方面的費用是 20%，四分之一是 25%，選項 D 還是錯的。把 Janet 的所有支出加在一起，總開支是月薪的百分之一百（40+20+15+10+15= 100），也就是說，Janet 每個月都沒存到錢，正確答案為 B。

Q6

Could you stop biting your nails?
你可以不要再咬指甲嗎？

A. We are not allowed to park here.	A. 我們不被允許在這裡停車。
B. I can't help it. I am too nervous.	B. 我控制不了。我太緊張了。
C. Don't you think they are too short?	C. 你不認為他們太短了嗎？
D. Who has a hammer?	D. 誰有鐵鎚？

詳解   **答案：B**

有些人在很緊張的情況下會咬指甲，因此符合敘述的答案為 B。

〈補充說明〉

在文法上必須注意，I can't help + N/V-ing 跟 I can't help but + V 的區別，前者必須加動名詞，而後者必須加原形動詞。I can't help feeling nervous.（我沒辦法不感到緊張。）I can't help but feel nervous.（我沒辦法不感到緊張。）這兩句意思是一樣的。

Q7

Is an extra battery included in the deal?
一顆額外的電池有包含在這項買賣裡嗎？

A. This is already the largest.	A. 這已經是最大的了。
B. The size doesn't fit.	B. 尺寸不符合。
C. We will invite each other.	C. 我們會邀請彼此。
D. I'm afraid you have to purchase it.	D. 恐怕您必須購買。

詳解   **答案：D**

在聽題目前先看完選項是考聽力的基本訣竅，從題目的 A、B、D 三個選項大概可以猜出題目跟買賣東西有關。在買手機時，或許會送一顆副廠的備用電池，不過原廠的第二顆電池通常要自費購買，回答以上問題最為恰當的答案是 D。

|單字片語| include [ɪnˈklud] 包括，包含 / inclusive [ɪnˈklusɪv] 包含的
exclude [ɪkˈklud] 不包括 / exclusive [ɪkˈsklusɪv] 獨家的

第 1 回
第 2 回
第 3 回
第 4 回
第 5 回
第 6 回

Q8

I want to make an appointment with the dentist.
我想要跟牙醫預約門診。

A. Is this the first time you are here?
B. How will you get here?
C. Why do you choose this job?
D. When did you brush your teeth?

A. 你是第一次來這裡嗎？
B. 你會如何過來這裡？
C. 你為什麼選擇這份工作？
D. 你是什麼時候的刷牙？

詳解

答案：A

　　從語句中可判斷，說話者想要預約看門診。回答這個問題的人應該是診所的護士或服務人員，最為合理的答案是 A。雖然 brush（刷牙）跟 dentist（牙醫）這兩個單字有關連性，卻不可能是服務人員問求診者的問題，而且診所的服務人員也不太會詢問求診者的交通方式，因此其他選項是錯誤的。

補充說明

　　跟醫生或大人物預約用 make an appointment，餐廳訂位和預訂飯店房間則是用 make a reservation。

Q9

We need two adult tickets and one for my four-year-old daughter.
我們需要兩張成人票還有一張給我四歲大的女兒的票。

A. Kids are not for sale.
B. The doctor is not available.
C. Admission for children is free.
D. Math is a tough subject.

A. 小孩子不出售。
B. 醫生現在沒空。
C. 兒童入場免費。
D. 數學是很難的科目。

詳解

答案：C

　　以上說話內容應該是在售票處，回應者是售票人員，最適合的答案為 C。選項 D 是屬於搞笑的回答，不能出現在以上對話情境。

補充說明

　　精品和服飾會出現 Sale 的單字，表示「特價」。出售房子用 For Sale，房屋出租用 For Rent。Sales 的意思是「銷售額」和「業績」，雖然中文常說「某某人是 Sales」把 Sales 當成「銷售員」理解，但那是錯的，要說 salesman 或 saleswoman。

Q10

There are quite a few typing errors in your report.
你的報告裡頭有好幾個錯字。

A. I hope there will be more.
B. I usually report to my boss.
C. I'll correct them immediately.
D. I'll type quietly next time.

A. 我希望會有更多。
B. 我通常向老闆回報。
C. 我會立刻更正。
D. 我下次會安靜地打字。

詳解

答案：C

　　說話者應該是老師或上司，而當自己的過失被對方點出，最合理的回應是 C。

Q11

David got himself a brand new car.
David 為自己買了一台全新的車子。

A. Yes, and he is really getting old.
B. Yes, and he needs to send it out by today.
C. Yes, and he said he will give me a ride.
D. Yes, and he was banned from driving.

A. 是的，而且他真的變老了。
B. 是，而且他需要在今天寄出去。
C. 是，而且他說會載我去兜風。
D. 是的，而且他被禁止開車。

詳解

答案：C

　　這類題目屬於兩個朋友之間的對話，談論的話題是另一個人。有個叫 David 的朋友買了新車，最適當的回應是「是的，他買了新車而且他將會載我去兜風」，答案為 C。

補充說明

　　take... for a ride 可從字面上理解，開車載某人去兜風，但也有另一層含意，就是欺騙別人的意思。例句：I trusted him with my money but he took me for a ride.（我信任他並把錢交給他，可是他卻欺騙我。）

第 1 回
第 2 回
第 3 回
第 4 回
第 5 回
第 6 回

Q12

How would you like your steak done, sir?
先生，請問您的牛排要幾分熟？

A. My appetite is pretty small.
B. Medium will do just fine.
C. I would prefer a large one.
D. You did a great job.

A. 我的胃口挺小的。
B. 五分熟剛剛好。
C. 我比較喜歡大的。
D. 你做得很好。

詳解　　　　　　　　　　　　　　　　　　　　　　**答案：B**

　　先看到的四個選項，只有選項 D 可能跟吃的沒有什麼關係，所以可先推測題目可能是跟吃的有關。這是在牛排餐館常聽到的問題，服務生問客人牛排要幾分熟，答案為 B。

|單字片語| **well done** 全熟；做得好 / **medium** [ˈmidɪəm] 五分熟
　　　　　medium-raw 三分熟 / **raw** [rɔ] 生的

Q13

Have you ever been to a concert?
你去過演唱會嗎？

A. I can't believe what you just said.
B. I can't eat beans.
C. I can't continue living like this.
D. I can't find the time.

A. 我無法相信你剛剛說的話。
B. 我不能吃豆子。
C. 我不能繼續這樣生活下去。
D. 我抽不出時間。

詳解　　　　　　　　　　　　　　　　　　　　　　**答案：D**

　　當對方問「你去過演唱會嗎？」不一定要用「去過」或「沒去過」回答。可以直接說明沒有去過的原因，選項 D 最為合理，是正確答案。

Q14

Margaret was caught for shoplifting yesterday.
Margaret 昨天因為在商店裡偷竊被抓了。

A. Did she hurt herself?
B. How could she do something so stupid?
C. When did she become so strong?
D. Hasn't she done enough shopping?

A. 她有弄傷自己嗎？
B. 她為何做出如此愚蠢的事？
C. 她什麼時候變得如此強壯？
D. 她買東西還買不夠嗎？

詳解

不管是聽、說、讀或寫的能力，都建立在單字的基礎上。對話時單字更是關鍵，若不知道 shoplifting 是「偷竊」的意思，就很容易被誤導。偷竊是錯誤也是愚蠢的行為，所以答案為 B。

|單字片語| **shoplifting** [`ʃɑp,lɪftɪŋ] 偷竊 / **lift** [lɪft] 舉起；電梯

Q15

Why don't you make a video about yourself and put it on YouTube?

你為何不錄製自己的影片，然後放在 YouTube 上呢？

A. I just watched a funny one.　　　　　A. 我剛剛看了一個好笑的。
B. I don't think I want to sell it.　　　　B. 我不想要賣掉它。
C. I think you shouldn't watch too much TV.　C. 我認為你不應該看太多電視。
D. I have to admit that I am camera-shy.　D. 我必須承認我害怕面對鏡頭。

詳解

答案：D

回應對方的建議，最合適的答案為 D。若只聽 video 跟 YouTube，會以為可以選擇選項 A，但分析整句的意思會發現，選項 A 並沒有問答對方的問題。對方建議你為何不錄製自己的影片然後放在 YouTube 上，最適當的回覆是「我害怕面對鏡頭」。

第 1 回
第 2 回
第 3 回
第 4 回
第 5 回
第 6 回

第三部分 / 簡短對話

Q16

W: Are you sure it's worth it? Shouldn't we compare the prices first?
你確定這個值得？我們不是應該先比較價格嗎？

M: I have done some research on the Net. At this price, it is a steal!
我在網路上做過一些研究了。以這個價格來說，簡直就是賺到了！

W: I don't feel good about it. We're talking a big sum here.
我覺得這樣不好，我們在說的是一大筆錢。

Q: What is the woman's concern?
這位女子擔憂的是什麼？

A. She doesn't want to part with so much money.
A. 她不想花這麼多錢。

B. She doesn't want to make a purchase on the Internet.
B. 她不想在網路上購物。

C. She doesn't want to spend any money.
C. 她不想花任何錢。

D. She doesn't want to steal anything.
D. 她不想偷任何東西。

詳解　　　　　　　　　　　　　　　　　　　　　　　　　　　　　答案：A

　　從對話中可得知，女子並不是不想花錢，只是要在買之前貨比三家。既然要比較價格，表示已經有花錢的心理準備，選項 C 是錯誤的。sum 是「總數」，a big sum 是一大筆，雖然沒有直接提到 money，女子所影射的當然是一大筆錢，答案為 A。

補充說明

　　It is a steal 是一句俚語，意思是「撿到便宜」，並不是偷東西的意思，也可以說 It is a bargain。

Q17

M: Gosh! I think I need some aspirin. This headache is killing me.
天啊！我想我需要一些阿斯匹林。我的頭快疼死了。

W: We ran out of drug supplies a long time ago. Make a list and I will go get them.　我們早就沒有藥了。寫張清單，然後我會去買。

M: Thanks. Let's see what we need.　謝謝。讓我們看看需要什麼。

Q: What will the woman probably do next?
接下來這位女子可能會做什麼？

A. Call a veterinarian.　　　　　　A. 打電話給獸醫。
B. Prepare a shopping list.　　　　B. 準備購物清單。
C. Visit the pharmacy.　　　　　　C. 去一趟藥房。
D. Take some medicine.　　　　　　D. 吃一些藥。

詳解　　　　　　　　　　　　　　　　　　　　　　　　　　**答案：C**

　　四個選項分別為四件要做的事情，而且四個選項有一些關聯，必須注意聽對話內容，才能作答。在對話中，寫張清單是男子會做的事，因此選項 B 是錯誤的。接下來這位女子應該會做的，是拿著清單去買男子需要的止痛藥和其他醫療用品，答案為 C。

│單字片語│ **pharmacy** [ˈfɑrməsɪ] 藥房 / **drugstore** [ˈdrʌɡˌstor] 藥房
　　　　　　dispensary [dɪˈspɛnsərɪ] 藥房

Q18

W: Oh no. Water is leaking. I had better put my laptop away.
　　糟了。漏水了。我最好趕快把筆電收起來。

M: You should get your landlord to fix the problem.
　　你應該請你的房東來解決這個問題。

W: I have tried it many times. She keeps saying OK, but she never does anything about it.　　我試過很多次了。她一直說好，但什麼都沒做。

Q: What can we tell from the conversation?
從這段對話中可以知道什麼？

A. The woman shares the room with the man.　A. 這位女子跟男子共用一個房間。
B. The woman rents a room.　　　　　　　　　B. 這位女子租房間。
C. The woman's laptop needs to be fixed.　　C. 這位女子的筆電需要修理。
D. The woman is pleased with her landlord.　D. 這位女子對房東很滿意。

詳解　　　　　　　　　　　　　　　　　　　　　　　　　　**答案：B**

　　男子用「你的房東」，表示兩個人並沒有住在一起，選項 A 是錯誤的。房子漏水，不過說話者並沒有說水滴到電腦，也沒有說電腦壞了，選項 C 也是錯誤的。這位女房客向房東反應了很多次，可是房東還是沒有把漏水的問題處理好，所以選項 D 不可能是答案。若沒有學過 landlord（房東）這個單字，依照對話內容，也能利用「排除法」選出正確答案 B。

│單字片語│ **landlord** [ˈlændˌlord] 房東 / **landlady** [ˈlændˌledɪ] 女房東 / **tenant** [ˈtɛnənt] 房客

Q19

M: Your basic pay will be 25,000 NT dollars, health care and insurance included. 你的底薪是兩萬五，包含健保和勞保。

W: When can I expect a raise? This salary is a little on the low side. 我何時可以預期加薪？這份薪水有一點低。

M: We will adjust your pay after three months. Is that acceptable? 我們會在三個月後調整你的薪資。這樣可以接受嗎？

Q: What are the speakers doing?
說話者在做什麼？

A. They are having an interview.　　A. 他們在進行工作面試。
B. They are bargaining over prices.　B. 他們為了價錢在討價還價。
C. They are arranging for a meeting.　C. 他們在籌備會議。
D. They are discussing about health issues. D. 他們在談論健康議題。

詳解　　　　　　　　　　　　　　　　答案：A

從對話中的關鍵詞 pay（薪水）和 raise（加薪）可判斷兩人正在談論工作的酬勞，這樣的對話內容應該是在面試的時候進行，答案為 A。薪水和價格是不同的概念，25,000 指的是薪資而非商品的價格，選項 B 是錯的。

|單字片語| **pay** [pe] 待遇；薪資 / **salary** [ˈsælərɪ] 薪水
　　　　wages [ˈwedʒɪs] 工資 / **bonus** [ˈbonəs] 獎金

Q20

W: I need to go to Europe. What is the exchange rate for the Euro? 我需要去歐洲。歐元的匯率是多少？

M: Currently it is one Euro for 41.5 NT dollars. How much would you like to change? 目前是一歐元兌換 41.5 元新台幣。您需要兌換多少？

W: Thirty thousand NT dollars. Thank you. 三萬元新台幣。謝謝。

Q: Where are the speakers most likely?
說話者最有可能在什麼地方？

A. In a bank.　　　　　　A. 在銀行。
B. In a travel agency.　　B. 在旅行社。
C. In a clothing store.　　C. 在服飾店。
D. In an auditorium.　　　D. 在大禮堂。

　　光從選項可判斷，題目應該是問「什麼地點」，而這題問的是說話者所在的地點。而這位女子要兌換外幣，所在地點顯然是銀行，答案為 A。

|單字片語| **Euro** [ˈjʊro] 歐元 / **Greenback** [ˈɡrin,bæk] 美元紙幣
Swiss Franc 瑞士法郎 / **Yen** [jɛn] 日圓

Q21

M: I bought every single novel written by this author. He has a great sense of humor.　我買了這位作家的每一本小說。他很有幽默感。

W: But the reviews given by some readers are rather negative.
不過有些讀者給的評語挺負面的。

M: You can't believe everything on the Internet. Some people like to criticize others for the sake of criticizing.
你不能相信網路上的一切。有些人就是為了批評而批評他人。

Q: What is true about the conversation?
關於這段對話，什麼是真的？

A. The woman agrees with the man.
B. The woman is a strong supporter of the writer.
C. The man received negative comments.
D. The man is not affected by the bad reviews.

A. 女子同意男子的說法。
B. 女子是那位作家的死忠支持者。
C. 男子收到了負面的評語。
D. 男子不受負面的書評影響。

　　對話中的女子提出 but（但是）還有 negative（負面）這兩個關鍵詞，表示不認同男子的看法，選項 A 是錯誤的。作家的支持者是說話的男子，而不是女子，因此選項 B 是陷阱。收到了一些負面的評語的對象是兩人在談論的作家，並非正在說話的男子，因此選項 C 是錯誤的。男子說「有些人就是為了批評而批評他人」，表示這些批評不影響他，答案為 D。

Q22

W: And now for the final touch. A little chili to improve your appetite.
現在來個最後的動作。用一點辣椒來增進你的胃口。

M: Just a second. I don't fancy spicy food.　等等，我不喜歡吃辣的食物。

W: Come on. A little chili won't hurt.　拜託，一點點辣椒不會怎樣。

Q: What does the woman mean?
這位女子的意思是什麼？

A. The man should be careful.
B. The man should give it a try.
C. The man should play it safe.
D. The man should eat something else.

A. 這位男子應該小心謹慎。
B. 這位男子應該試一試。
C. 這位男子應該保險一點。
D. 這位男子應該吃點別的。

詳解

答案：B

　　學習任何語言除了學習單字和文法，也要學習文化。英文有自己獨特的文化，有時候不能光從字面上理解。當外國人說某事情 won't hurt，意思並不是你不會受傷，而是這件事對你不會有太大的影響。這位女子的意思是，吃一點辣的不會怎樣，要男子勇敢嘗試，答案為 B。

補充說明

　　play it safe 的意思是為確保安全起見，還是不要冒險。

Q23

M: Let's go rock climbing this weekend. I have already invited Christopher.
這個週末我們去攀岩吧。我已經邀請 Christopher 了。

W: Count me out unless it is indoors.
除非是在室內，不然不要把我算在內。

M: I remember they do have that facility in the gym.
我記得健身房內有那種設施。

Q: Will the woman go out with the man?
這位女子會跟男子出去嗎？

A. No, she is going mountain climbing by herself.
B. No, she will invite the man to her house.
C. Yes, but she also wants to go out with Christopher.
D. Yes, but she doesn't want to exercise under the sun.

A. 不，她會自己去爬山。
B. 不，她會邀請男子到她家去。
C. 是的，但是她也想跟 Christopher 出去。
D. 是的，但是她不想在太陽下做運動。

從 unless（除非）這個從屬子句連接詞，可以知道這位女子提出了某個條件，除非符合她提出的條件，否則她不會答應。而她的條件是必須在室內，表示她不想曬太陽，答案為 D。

|單字片語| **Count me in.** 算我一份。 / **Count me out.** 我不要參與。

Q24

Sports Club 運動社團

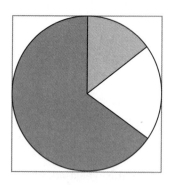

M: I don't know which club I should sign up for.
　　我不知道我應該參加哪個社團。

W: Why? I remember you are fond of softball, right?
　　為什麼？我記得你喜歡壘球，對嗎？

M: Yes, but there are only three clubs in my school, not counting that one. At first, I planned to be in the table tennis club, but there are only a few members. Now, I am thinking to register for the baseball club.
　　是的，但是我的學校只有三種社團，不包括那一個。起初，我打算加入桌球社，但社團裡只有一些社員。現在，我正在考慮要登記棒球社。

W: Don't you think there are too many members? How about going to the basketball club? 你不認為社員太多嗎？參加籃球社怎麼樣？

M: But I am not tall enough. Besides, I am bad at it.
　　但是我不夠高。此外，我不擅長打籃球。

W: You're right. You should play to your strengths.
　　你說的沒錯。你應該發揮自己的優勢。

第 1 回

第 2 回

第 3 回

第 4 回

第 5 回

第 6 回

Q: Look at the pie chart. What does the largest section refer to?
請看圓餅圖，最大的部分指的是什麼？

A. The table tennis club
B. The basketball club
C. The softball club
D. The baseball club

A. 桌球社
B. 籃球社
C. 壘球社
D. 棒球社

詳解

答案：D

　　雖然圖表題看起來有些複雜，卻是日常生活中經常看得到的資訊，掌握圖表資訊是答題關鍵。在聽到題目前，從圓餅圖和選項可以猜測題目跟運動社團相關，所以，聆聽時要注意聽各個社團可能對應在圓餅圖上的位置。雖然整段對話並沒有直接表達各個社團的人數，但是從 there isn't that kind of club、only a few、too many members，可以知道，分別是指壘球社、桌球社和棒球社，整合以上的資訊，可以推論出，男子不擅長的是籃球社。題目問的是圓餅圖中佔最大的部份是男子認為人數太多的是「棒球社」，答案為 D。

Q25

Notes

Beach & SPA package: skincare and picnicking
Voyage package: diving and cooking classes
Nature package: hiking and mountain food barbecue
Luxury package: best pool view and kitchen

筆記

海灘和水療組合：護膚和野餐

航海組合：潛水和烹飪課

自然組合：健行和山地食物燒烤

豪華組合：最佳的泳池景觀和廚房

W: Honey, I've got some honeymoon packages. Any thoughts on that?
親愛的，我拿到了一些蜜月組合。有什麼想法嗎？

M: Hmm, since we both like to cook, cooking together on our honeymoon is going to be a great memory.　嗯，因為我們倆都喜歡做

飯，所以蜜月時一起烹飪會是一個美好的回憶。

W: That's why I picked out these packages. The problem is I can't come to a final decision.

這就是為什麼我挑選了這些組合。問題是我無法做出最後的決定。

M: Well, don't forget that savings are still required. And you get seasick easily. 好吧，別忘記節省仍然是需要的。而且你容易會暈船。

W: That's true. Maybe it is better not to stay on board a ship.

這是真的。也許最好不要待在船上。

M: Great! It will be a unique and special honeymoon.

太好了！這將會是一個獨一無二又特別的蜜月。

Q: Look at the notes. Which package will the speaker most likely choose?

請看筆記。說話者最有可能會選擇哪一個組合？

A. Beach & SPA package　　　A. 海灘和水療組合
B. Voyage package　　　　　　B. 航海組合
C. Nature package　　　　　　C. 自然組合
D. Luxury package　　　　　　D. 豪華組合

詳解　　　　　　　　　　　　　　　　　　　　　　　　　答案：C

　　這一題在聽到敘述前，從筆記和選項可以猜測題目跟旅行組合相關，所以，聆聽時要注意整筆記上四種旅行組合的個別資訊，才能知道說話者最後選擇的旅行組合。在男子提到 cooking together 時，就可以先刪除未包含烹煮活動的 Beach & SPA package。接著男子又提到 savings are still required. And you get seasick easily.，就可以刪去 Luxury package 和 Voyage package。從兩人的對話搭配筆記資訊，可以推論出，Nature package 最符合他們的需求，答案為 C。

第 1 回
第 2 回
第 3 回
第 4 回
第 5 回
第 6 回

Q26

M: Not only an outstanding actor, but Matthew McConaughey is also an inspiring speaker. In several of his best movies, he delivered passionate speeches at critical points. In addition to the big screen, McConaughey has given several motivational and insightful speeches based on his own personal experiences. Now, let's applaud our speaker loud and clear.

不僅是一位傑出的演員，馬修・麥康納（Matthew McConaughey）也是一位鼓舞人心的演講者。在幾部他的最佳電影中，他在關鍵的時刻發表了熱情洋溢的演講。除了大螢幕，麥康納還以自己的親身經歷，發表了一些激勵人心且具深刻見解的演講。現在，讓我們給演講者大聲而清晰的掌聲。

Q: **Where would you most likely hear this talk?**
你最可能在哪裡聽到這段談話？

A. In a movie theater.
B. In a studio.
C. In a lecture hall.
D. In an award ceremony.

A. 在電影院。
B. 在工作室。
C. 在演講廳。
D. 在頒獎典禮。

詳解　　　　　　　　　　　　　　　　　　　　　　　　　　　　　　答案：C

　　在聽到題目前，從選項可以猜測可能和四種不同的場所有關，因此聽敘述時要注意說話者提到與「地點」相關的內容。從說話者的第一句 Matthew McConaughey is also an inspiring speaker. 以及最後一句 Now, let's applaud our speaker loud and clear. 可以知道，說話者正在向聽眾介紹演講者，答案為C。

|單字片語| **outstanding** [ˋaʊtˋstændɪŋ] 傑出的 / **motivational** [͵motəˋveʃənəl] 激發積極性的
insightful [ˋɪn͵saɪtfəl] 有深刻見解的

Q27

W: Welcome to News Today, this is the late-night edition. Kobe Bryant and his 13-year-old daughter, along with six other passengers, died in an accident. This crash occurred due to the pilot having poor visibility because of cloudy condition. As news of his death broke out, Twitter was quickly flooded with sorrow, and many of his fans refused to believe this shocking news.

歡迎收看《今日新聞》，這是深夜節目。科比・布萊恩特和他的 13 歲女兒以及其他六名乘客在這場事故中身亡。發生墜機是因為在濃雲中飛行員

123

的能見度很差。當他過世的消息突然發生時，推特迅速湧入悲傷，他的許多粉絲無法相信這一則令人震驚的消息。

Q: What kind of accident was reported?
什麼樣的事故被報導了？

A. A flight accident.	A. 一起飛行事故。
B. A road accident.	B. 一起道路事故。
C. A flood accident.	C. 一起洪水事故。
D. A sports accident.	D. 一起運動事故。

詳解　　　　　　　　　　　　　　　　　　　　　　　　　**答案：A**

　　在聽到題目前，從選項可以猜測可能和四種不同的意外事故有關，因此聽敘述時要注意說話者所說與事故相關的內容。從 This crash occurred due to the pilot having poor visibility in a thick cloud. 可以知道，發生墜落的原因是在濃雲中飛行員的能見度很差。由此可知，這是一起飛行事故，答案為 A。

|單字片語| visibility [ˌvɪzəˈbɪlətɪ] 能見度 / **break out** 突然發生

Q28

M: Hi! You have reached the office of HIGH TECH. Our entire staff is currently engaged in assisting other callers. We understand how precious your time is, and instead of keeping you waiting, we'll make sure to call you back. Please leave a brief message with all your contact details. We will get back to you within two business hours. Thanks!

您好！您已經連繫到 HIGH TECH 辦公室。我們全體員工目前正在努力協助其他的來電者。我們了解您的時間有多麼寶貴，我們一定會給您回電，而不是讓您一直等待。請留下簡短訊息和您所有的聯繫細節。我們將在兩個工作小時內與您聯繫。謝謝！

Q: What would the caller probably do next?
來電者接下來可能會做什麼呢？

A. Talk to another staff member.	A. 與另一位工作人員交談。
B. Check his message.	B. 檢查他的留言。
C. Go back to his office.	C. 回到他的辦公室。
D. Leave a voicemail.	D. 留下語音訊息。

詳解　　　　　　　　　　　　　　　　　　　　　　　　　**答案：D**

　　聽到題目前先閱讀選項，可以猜測可能是四種與工作連繫相關的行動。所

以，聆聽時要注意與行動相關的資訊。從這則電話語音中，instead of keeping you waiting, we'll make sure to call you back. 可以知道來電者並無法立即進行直接電話上的對話。下一句 Please leave a brief message with all your contact details. 清楚說明語音訊息希望來電者做的後續動作。由此可知，答案為 D。

Q29

W: Good afternoon. GOOD MART Shoppers! Don't miss our in-store special on dairy products. Check out aisle ten and stock up today! Now, we have a limited bonus for you. The best deals on oils and sauces are available for the upcoming hour. The offer ends at 5 pm and is restricted to stock on hand.

午安。GOOD MART 的顧客！不要錯過我們店內特製的乳製品。今天到第十排走道看看，並立即選購！現在，我們為您提供限時的優惠。在接下來的一個小時中，油和調味醬都有最佳優惠。優惠在下午5點截止，限量供應。

Q: Which items are not promoted?
哪一種品項並未被促銷？

A. Sauces.
B. Milk.
C. Cereals.
D. Peanut oils.

A. 調味醬。
B. 牛奶。
C. 麥片。
D. 花生油。

詳解　　　　　　　　　　　　　　　　　　　　　　　　**答案：C**

　　在聽到題目前，從選項可以猜測敘述和食物相關。所以，聆聽時要注意四種食物在廣播內容中出現的情況。從說話者的廣播訊息中，Don't miss our in-store special on dairy products. 可知乳製品有特惠，因此選項 B 牛奶可刪除。接著 The best deals on oils and sauces are available for the upcoming hour. 可知油和調味醬也有優惠，故選項 A 和 D 可刪除。由此可以知道，只有選項 C 麥片並未被提到的，答案為 C。

|單字片語| **stock up** 貯備

Q30

M: Here's a brief overview of the new traffic and driving-related laws. First, the use of an electronic device while driving, even in hands-free mode, is prohibited. Another new law protects children left unattended in vehicles. Finally, drivers are required to slow down or change lanes on approaching a stationary emergency vehicle with emergency lights.

以下簡要概述與交通和駕駛相關的新法規。首先，禁止在駕駛時使用電子
設備，即使在免持模式的情況下。另一條新法規是保護被留在交通工具中
無人照管的兒童。最後，駕駛被要求在接近有緊急燈號的靜止緊急車輛
時，放慢或改變車道。

Q: Which driving behavior is not indicated in the report?
這則報導中未指出哪一種駕駛行為？

A. A driver left his twins in a hot car.

B. A driver texted his friend while driving.

C. A driver moved over for an ambulance.

D. A driver applied makeup while driving.

A. 一名駕駛把雙胞胎獨自
留在一輛很熱的車上。

B. 一名駕駛在開車時，傳
訊息給他的朋友。

C. 一名駕駛禮讓救護車。

D. 一名駕駛在行駛時化妝。

詳解

答案：D

　　這是一段交通安全法規的宣導廣播，四個選項都是駕駛行為，要注意各個
行為在廣播中出現的狀況。選項 B 是違反廣播中的在駕駛中禁止使用電子裝置
（the use of an electronic device while driving is prohibited）。選項 A 是違反廣播
中保護被留在交通工具中無人照管的兒童（protects children left unattended in
vehicles）。選項 C 是遵守廣播中接近緊急燈號的靜止車輛要放慢或變換車道
（slow down or change lanes on the approaching a stationary emergency vehicle with
emergency lights）。由此可知，選項 D 未在敘述中被提及，答案為 D。

|單字片語| **overview** [ˈovəˌvju] 概要 / **unattended** [ˌʌnəˈtɛndɪd] 沒人照顧的
stationary [ˈsteʃənˌɛrɪ] 不動的

Q31

W: Qualified students can monitor their comprehension of a text by summarizing their reading. Even if you have absolutely memorized all the facts in it, you may not be sure whether you have learned it. It is thus important to practice writing a one- or two-sentence summary for each paragraph once you have read it.

符合資格的學生可以透過總結閱讀來檢視他們對文本的理解。即使假設你
完全記住文本的所有事實，也可能不確定自己是否已經學會它了。因此，
重要的是，一旦你閱讀過每個段落，就練習寫出一句或兩句的總結。

第 1 回
第 2 回
第 3 回
第 4 回
第 5 回
第 6 回

Q: Which class is the speaker teaching?
說話者正在教授的是哪一類課程？

A. Composition.
B. Statistics.
C. Biology experiment.
D. Economics analysis.

A. 寫作。
B. 統計。
C. 生物學實驗。
D. 經濟學分析。

詳解　　　　　　　　　　　　　　　　　　　　　　　**答案：A**

　　這題是一段教學時的談話，由四個選項可以知道是分別為不同科目課程，聽敘述時要注意關鍵字詞。說話者的教學內容第一句提到 Qualified students can monitor their comprehension of a text by summarizing their reading.，可以知道教學的內容與寫作訓練相關，答案為 A。

Q32

M: This survey includes more than 450 social media users. The most interesting finding, however, is that LinkedIn is the best platform for this poll, even over Facebook, Twitter, and YouTube. This is due to the fact that most of the respondents are professionals, which can twist the results.

這項調查包含超過 450 個社群媒體用戶。然而，最有趣的發現是，LinkedIn 是此次民意調查中的最佳平台，甚至在 Facebook、Twitter 和 YouTube 之上。這個事實是因為大多數受訪者都是專業人士，這可能會使結果偏差。

Q: Which social media is the top platform in the survey?
此次調查中的最佳平台是哪一個社群媒體？

A. YouTube
B. Facebook.
C. Twitter.
D. LinkedIn.

A. YouTube。
B. 臉書。
C. 推特。
D. 領英。

詳解　　　　　　　　　　　　　　　　　　　　　　　**答案：D**

　　在這題中，四個選項均為社群媒體，聽敘述時僅需注意四個社群媒體出現的關鍵句，聽到題目後就可以知道答案。說話者的談話提到此次民意調查的最佳平台是領英（The most interesting finding, however, is that LinkedIn is the best platform for this poll.），答案為 D。

Q33

W: Before checking out your U-Bike, there are four things you should do. Firstly, please check whether the tires are filled with air. Secondly, please check whether the brakes are working. Thirdly, please check whether the bell is working. Lastly, please adjust the seat. If there are any problems, you may rotate the seat around and leave it hanging.

在租借您的微笑單車之前,有四件您應該做的事。首先,請檢查輪胎是否是硬的且充飽氣。其次,請檢查煞車是否是有作用的。第三,請檢查鈴鐺是否可以發出響音。最後,請調整座椅。如果以上任何一部份故障,您可以旋轉座椅並使其懸空。

Q: What is the listener doing?
聽者正在做什麼?

A. Repairing a brake.	A. 修理剎車。
B. Fixing a tire.	B. 修理一個輪胎。
C. Renting a bike.	C. 租一輛單車。
D. Hanging a bell.	D. 掛一個鈴鐺。

詳解

答案:C

　　在這則談話說明中,四個選項均和單車有關,因此,聽敘述時需注意所述內容的目的,才能選出答案。從說話者的第一句話,Before checking out your U-Bike, there are four things you should do. 可以知道聽者正在租借 U-Bike 微笑單車,答案為 C。

Q34

2020-2021 Student Council Election Result
2020-2021 學生會選舉結果

Candidates 候選人	Votes 得票數	Percentages 百分比
Ella Jones	26	32.5%
Chloe Smith	27	33.8%
Ivy Taylor	13	16.3%
Ethan Brown	14	17.4%

M: After five days of campaigning, the result of the 2020-2021 Student Council election was finally released. That was such an extraordinary outcome! As much as I know that all the candidates

第 1 回

第 2 回

第 3 回

第 4 回

第 5 回

第 6 回

ran very hard for president, I still feel bad about the result. She devoted her time to the rights of students. What caused her to lose so many votes? I assume she took her eye off the ball.

經過五天的競選活動，2020-2021 年學生會選舉的結果最終發布了。那真是一個意想不到的結果！據我所知，所有候選人都為會長競選非常投入，但我仍然對這個結果感到難過。她把時間投注在學生的權利上。是什麼原因使她輸了這麼多票？我猜想是她忽略了主要的目標。

Q: Whom does the speaker talk about?
說話者在談論誰？

A. Ella Jones.
B. Ethan Brown.
C. Chloe Smith.
D. Ivy Taylor.

詳解　　　　　　　　　　　　　　　　　　　　　　　答案：D

　　在聽到題目前，從圖表和選項可以猜測題目跟候選人相關，因此聽敘述時要注意聽各個候選人的細節，從最後二句 What caused her to lose so many votes? I assume she took her eye off the ball. 可以知道，說話者談論的人是女性、得票相當低。圖表中所見的較低票二人是 Ivy Taylor 和 Ethan Brown，而 Ethan Brown 是男性。可以推論出，談話者所談論的候選人是 Ivy Taylor，答案為 D。

|單字片語| **extraordinary** [ɪkˋstrɔrdṇˏɛrɪ] 非凡的 / **devote** [dɪˋvot] 將…奉獻
take one's eyes off the ball 不留神

Q35

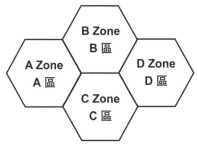

A Zone: Tropical Area
A 區：熱帶地區
B Zone: Desert Area
B 區：沙漠地區
C Zone: Aquarium
C 區：水族館
D Zone: Bird World
D 區：鳥類世界

W: Welcome to the Amazing Zoo, one of the five best zoos in the world. This area was built by imitating the warmest and steamiest climate zone on the planet. The wildlife species in this region are highly adapted to a specific climate. When the visitors observe and hear the land animals in the copies of forest landscapes, they can also experience the smell of various animals and plants.

歡迎來到美妙動物園，這是世界上五個其中一個最好的動物園。這個區域是模擬地球上最溫暖且最潮濕的氣候帶所建造成的。在這個地區的野生物種非常適應這種特定的氣候。當遊客在這個模擬森林景觀中觀賞並聆聽這些陸地動物時，他們還可以體驗到各種各樣動植物的氣味。

Q: **Which zone does the speaker introduce?**
說話者介紹的是哪一區？

A. A zone.	A. A 區。
B. B zone.	B. B 區。
C. C zone.	C. C 區。
D. D zone.	D. D 區。

詳解

答案：A

從圖表和選項可以猜測題目會跟動物園內的區域相關，因此聽敘述時要注意各區域的個別資訊，才能知道說話者是介紹哪一區。說話者提到該區域是模仿地球上最溫暖和最潮濕的氣候帶所建造成的（This area was built by imitating the warmest and steamiest climate zone）。而選項 B 只有熱，並沒有潮濕。最後一句 When the visitors observe and hear land animals... 就可以該區域的動物為陸上動物。可以推論出說話者介紹的是熱帶地區，答案為 A。

第 1 回

第 2 回

第 3 回

第 4 回

第 5 回

第 6 回

第二回

初試 閱讀測驗 解析

第一部分 / 詞彙

Q1

We will have to determine if the drugs are effective. _____, a surgery might be the last option available.

我們將必須確認藥物是否有效，否則，動手術可能是最後的選擇。

A. However
B. Therefore
C. Otherwise
D. In addition

詳解　　　　　　　　　　　　　　　　　　　　**答案：C**

　　這題考的是連接詞，從上一句的 if the drugs are effective（藥物是否有效），可從中判斷如果無效的話，會出現某種後果。如果無效的話等同於「否則」，答案為 C。

例句

The drugs are effective. **However**, a surgery is still recommended.
藥物有效。然而，還是建議動手術。
The drugs are effective. **Therefore**, a surgery is not required.
藥物有效。因此，手術並不需要。
The drugs are effective. **In addition**, regular exercise is recommended.
藥物有效。此外，也建議定期運動。

Q2

College life is unlike high school, the hours are more ____ as students are allowed to select optional courses according to their preferences.

大學生活不像高中，上課時間比較有彈性，因為學生可以根據自己的偏好來選擇選修課程。

A. flexible
B. sustainable
C. eligible
D. predictable

從 optional（可選擇的）這個關鍵詞，可以判斷大學生的上課時間比較有彈性，答案為 A。

│單字片語│ **sustainable** [sə'stenəbl] 可持續的 / **eligible** ['ɛlɪdʒəbl] 有資格的 **predictable** [prɪ'dɪktəbl] 可預測的

Q3

Cases of dengue fever have been on the rise during the summer, and we have to take all the necessary precautions to prevent mosquitoes from _____.

登革熱的案例在夏天期間已經上升不少，我們必須採取所有必要的措施以避免蚊子滋生。

A. stinging
B. circulating
C. breeding
D. trading

從 mosquitoes（蚊子）fever（發燒）和 prevent（避免）等關鍵詞，可知道答案是防止蚊子繁殖，因此答案為 C。流傳和散佈（circulate）用在謠言或傳聞，不能表達防止蚊子散佈。

│單字片語│ **sting** [stɪŋ] 叮咬 / **circulate** ['sɜkjə,let] 流傳；散佈 / **trade** [tred] 貿易，交易

Q4

Being a/an _____ fan of Stephen King, Sandra collected every book by the author and has read through most of them more than once.

身為 Stephen King 的忠實粉絲，Sandra 收藏了這位作家的每一本書，而且大部分都至少讀過一遍。

A. loyal
B. casual
C. appropriate
D. ignorant

fan 是「歌迷，球迷，粉絲」的意思，形容死忠的粉絲可以用 loyal（忠心的），ardent（熱衷的），或 diehard（死硬的）。從 Sandra 收藏了這位作家每一本書可判斷，她是 Stephen King 忠實的粉絲，答案為 A。

第 1 回
第 2 回
第 3 回
第 4 回
第 5 回
第 6 回

<補充說明>

以下為各種對某件事有熱忱的人的敘述：an avid reader（一個愛看書的讀者），a fervent supporter（一個熱情的支持者）， a zealous follower（一個有熱忱的跟隨者）。

|單字片語| casual [ˈkæʒʊəl] 隨便的，漠不關心的 / appropriate [əˈproprɪ͵et] 適當的
ignorant [ˈɪgnərənt] 無知的；不知道的

Q5

Mr. Andrews has retired and he is now _____ to helping the needy.

Andrews 先生已經退休了，而他現在全心奉獻在幫助有需要的人。

A. hasty
B. joyful
C. included
D. devoted

詳解　　　　　　　　　　　　　　　　　　　　　　　　答案：D

這題要考的是形容詞的字義，從選項中可知只有選項 D devoted 才是正確答案。「全心全意於某件事」可以用 be devoted to， be dedicated to 或 be committed to，而值得注意的是，be devoted to 的 to 是介系詞，介系詞後面必須加 N/V-ing。

<補充說明>

以下為後面要加 V-ing 的片語：be used to V-ing（已習慣某件事），look forward to V-ing（期待某件事），when it comes to V-ing（當提到某件事）。

|單字片語| hasty [ˈhestɪ] 匆忙的 / joyful [ˈdʒɔɪfəl] 高興的
included [ɪnˈkludɪd] 被包括的 / devoted [dɪˈvotɪd] 專心致志的

Q6

There was a fierce debate on whether the rainforest should be _____ or not. Environmentalists argue that the rainforest is the habitat of a few endangered species.

關於雨林是否應該被保存有一場很激烈的辯論。環保人士主張雨林是一些瀕臨絕種動物的棲息地。

A. deserved
B. reserved
C. converse
D. preserved

詳解　　　　　　　　　　　　　　　　　　　　　　　　答案：D

從 rainforest（雨林），environmentalists（環保人士），habitat（棲息地）

和 endangered species（瀕臨絕種的動物）這些關鍵詞，可斷定辯論（debate）的議題是雨林是否要被保存（preserved），答案為 D。

|單字片語| **deserved** [dɪˈzɜvd] 應得的 / **reserved** [rɪˈzɜvd] 預留的
converse [kənˈvɜs] 相反的

Q7

Since that close _____ with death, Mr. Grisham has adopted a whole new perspective of life. He has learned not to take his health for granted.

自從那次跟死亡擦身而過，Grisham 先生已經採取了全新的人生觀點。他已經學會不要把健康當做理所當然的。

A. encounter
B. intensity
C. attraction
D. offense

詳解   答案：A

    語言是活生生的，單字的用法也很靈活。close 除了動詞「關」的意思，還有形容詞「接近的」的意思。很接近的遇到死亡（close encounter with death），就是和死亡擦身而過，差一點就沒命的意思。

〈補充說明〉

    take... for granted 的意思是「把事情當做理所當然」，其中也暗示某人身在福中不知福，不懂得珍惜。奉勸別人要懂得珍惜可以說：Don't take things for granted.

|單字片語| **intensity** [ɪnˈtɛnsətɪ] 強烈 / **attraction** [əˈtrækʃən] 吸引力
offence [əˈfɛns] 犯規；罪行

Q8

Many people, _____ age, sex or race, volunteered to join the peaceful demonstration in support of the non-smoking campaign.

許多人，無論年齡、性別或種族，都自願參加支持禁菸運動的和平示威。

A. even though
B. regardless of
C. provided that
D. insofar as

詳解   答案：B

    這題考的是連接詞以及詞彙，如果不知道意思就沒辦法運用。題目提到年齡、性別或種族都自願參加，合理的連接詞是「無論，不管」年齡、性別或種族，都自願參加支持反吸菸運動的和平示威，答案為 B。

第 1 回
第 2 回
第 3 回
第 4 回
第 5 回
第 6 回

例句

Many people volunteered for the job **even though** they won't get paid.
多數人自願要做這份工作，即使他們不會得到薪水。
People will take the job **provided that** they are well-paid.
人們會要這份工作，前提是付給他們優渥的薪水。
Insofar as pay is concerned, Americans are less willing to discuss it openly.
至於薪水方面，美國人比較不願意公開討論。

Q9

Mrs. Wang was heartbroken when her son demanded that she stop _____ in his life now because he is an adult capable of making his own decisions.

當兒子要求她現在不要再干涉他的生活時，王太太感到心碎，因為他現在是成年人，有能力自己做決定。

A. interfering
B. participating
C. existing
D. delegating

詳解 答案：A

　　這題考的是動名詞的詞彙，關鍵詞是 stop（停止）和 life（生活），合理的詞語搭配是停止干涉或介入別人的生活。

〈補充說明〉

　　stop 要理解為「別再…」，有助於理解這句的文法。stop eating 是「別再吃」，表示某人正在吃，或一直以來有吃某種食物的習慣。stop to eat 則是「停下來去吃個東西」，表示這個人還沒吃。
　　You should stop eating fast food. 你應該別再吃速食。
　　Let's stop to eat some fast food. 我們停下來，去吃點速食吧。

|單字片語| **participate** [pɑrˈtɪsə,pet] 參與 / **exist** [ɪgˈzɪst] 存在
　　　delegate [ˈdɛlə,get] 委派

Q10

A psychiatrist is a doctor who has the authority to prescribe drugs whereas a _____ is not in the position to do likewise.

精神科醫生是有權力開處方藥的醫生，而心理學家則沒有職務能這麼做。

A. therapist
B. pharmacist
C. psychologist
D. archaeologist

psychologist（心理學家）可能是博士或教授，專門對人類的心理做研究，然而他們並不是醫生，只能輔導不能開藥。psychiatrist 的中文字義是「精神科醫生」，可是有時人們不喜歡說自己有精神方面的疾病，所以也會翻譯為心理醫生。雖然 archaeologist（考古學家）也沒有開藥的權力，但選擇時也要合乎句意，因此 C 是最好的答案。

|單字片語| **therapist** [ˈθɛrəpɪst] 治療師 / **pharmacist** [ˈfɑrməsɪst] 藥劑師
　　　　 archaeologist [ˌɑrkɪˈɑlədʒɪst] 考古學家

第二部分 / 段落填空

Questions 11-15

The Vatican City, one of the (11) most sacred places in Christendom, is a testimony of its great history as a spiritual fortress. A unique collection of artistic and architectural masterpieces lies (12) within the boundaries of this small state, which is (13) as a matter of fact, the world's smallest sovereign state that encompasses an area of a mere 0.44 square km. It sits proudly atop the low-lying Vatican hill a few hundred meters west of the Tiber. Centered on the domed bulk of St Peter's Basilica, it boasts some of Italy's most celebrated masterpieces, many housed in the (14) magnificent Vatican Museums. You'll need at least a morning to (15) do justice to the Vatican Museums. The highlight is the Michelangelo-decorated Sistine Chapel, but there's enough art on display to keep you busy for years.

梵諦岡是基督教世界中其中一個最為神聖的地方，它是這座城市作為精神堡壘的偉大歷史證明。獨一無二的藝術和建築名作收藏聚集在這個小國的邊境內，而事實上該國是世界上最小的獨立國家，其面積僅有 0.44 平方公里。它傲然坐落於低緩的梵諦岡山丘，就在台伯河西邊數百公尺處。以聖彼得大教堂的大圓頂為中心，它以一些義大利最為著名的作品為傲，許多都珍藏在壯麗的梵蒂岡博物館內。你至少需要一個早上的時間，來充分參觀梵諦岡博物館。最精彩的部分是由米開朗基羅所佈置的西斯汀教堂，不過那裡展示的藝術品多到能夠讓你忙著欣賞好幾年。

Q11

A. more　　　　　　　　B. most

C. many　　　　　　　　D. much

詳解　　　　　　　　　　　　　　　　　　　　　　**答案：B**

　　雖然在文法上 one of the most 和 one of the many 都是正確的，其所表達的意思卻不同。one of the most 強調「其中一個最為…的」，而 one of the many 說明是「眾多…的其中一個」。這篇短文描述梵諦岡城，從 spiritual fortress（精神堡壘）這個關鍵詞，可得知它是其中一個最為神聖的地方。

例句

Sony is one of the **many** popular cellphone makers in the market.
Sony 是市場上眾多受歡迎的手機製造商之一。
Apple is one of the **most** popular cellphone makers in the market.
Apple 是市場上最受歡迎的手機製造商之一。

Q12

A. between　　　　　　　B. along

C. within　　　　　　　　D. without

詳解　　　　　　　　　　　　　　　　　　　　　　**答案：C**

　　梵諦岡城的面積不大，不過在其境內聚集了獨一無二的藝術和建築名作的珍藏，boundaries 是「邊界」，within the boundaries 是「邊境內」。可把 within 理解成 inside，意思雖然跟 in 相似，用法上卻不同。in 只是「在…裡面」，within 和 inside 有「之內；內在」的意思。

例句

The answer can be found **within** your heart.　這個答案能在你的內心找到。
This device will be installed **in** your heart.　這個裝置將會安裝在你的心臟裡面。

Q13

A. as usual　　　　　　　B. as long as

C. as a matter of fact　　　D. as soon as possible

詳解　　　　　　　　　　　　　　　　　　　　　　**答案：C**

　　身為世界上最小的國家，梵諦岡所涵蓋的面積非常小，這是一項客觀的事實，答案為 C。

He is late again **as usual**. 他如同往常一樣遲到了。
I don't mind waiting **as long as** I have something to do.
只要我有事情做，我不介意等待。
Can you finish reading the book **as soon as possible**? 你可以儘快看完那本書嗎？

Q14

A. magnificent   B. ridiculous
C. average   D. ordinary

詳解   答案：A

　　梵諦岡是天主教的精神堡壘，其教堂和博物館內收藏了價值連城的藝術品，可以推測出其建築也是金碧輝煌、壯麗無比，所以答案為 A. magnificent（壯麗的）。

|單字片語| **ridiculous** [rɪˋdɪkjələs] 荒謬的 / **average** [ˋævərɪdʒ] 平均的
　　　　 ordinary [ˋɔrdn͵ɛrɪ] 普通的

Q15

A. make do with the artwork   B. do away with the tradition
C. have to do with some artists   D. do justice to the Vatican Museum

詳解   答案：D

　　這題要看前後文才能選出空格處的答案，前句提到「你將必須花一個早上的時間」，而後句提到「最精彩的部分是…」，從選項推測出答案為 D。justice 是「正義」，正義也可理解為公平，這裡的用法是到梵諦岡博物館一遊，如果走馬看花很快地走完，會對不起裡頭的珍藏品，對這些歷史文物不公平。

例句

We ran out of honey. You will just have to **make do with** some brown sugar.
我們沒有蜂蜜了。你只好將就一點，用一些黑糖湊合一下吧。
Let's us **do away with** all the formalities. 讓我們除去所有形式上的禮節。
This case **had to do with** this woman. 這個案件和這位女子有關係。

Questions 16-20

　　With wear gear technology being the talk of the town for months, a wide (16) variety of smartwatches is on parade at the IFA electronics trade show in Berlin. Google's software for smartwatches, Android Wear, will start appearing as a companion accessory on a range of devices from various (17) manufacturers this autumn, and this year's IFA electronics trade show is expected to be packed with rival models. Google Wear is a new platform, an overhaul of Google's Android smartwatch software, which simplifies the user experience by cutting out all (18) but the essential features. For users, the pertinent question is whether Android Wear is worth investing in, and ditching a perfectly adequate watch for. As the matter of facts, (19) Android Wear has appealed to the mass market, to prove that having notifications on the wrist instead of the smartphone is worth (20) spending £150-200 on. However, for those not inundated with email, messages and social media, it might take more time to convince them.

第 1 回
第 2 回
第 3 回
第 4 回
第 5 回
第 6 回

　　隨著穿戴式科技成為了這幾個月來的熱門話題，許多種類的智慧型手錶會在這次的柏林 IFA 電子貿易展展出。Google 的智慧型手錶軟體，Android Wear，在這個秋季將以穿戴配件的形態開始出現在不同製造商各式各樣的裝置上，而今年的 IFA 電子貿易展預期會湧入許多競爭對手的機型。Google Wear 是新平台，是 Google 的智慧型手錶軟體的全面改造，它透過去除掉其他不必要的功能，只留下必要功能的方式，簡化了使用者的體驗。對使用者來說，直接相關的問題是 Android Wear 是否值得投資，是否值得拋棄完美合乎需求的手錶。事實上，Android Wear 已經吸引大眾市場，以證明值得花 150 到 200 英鎊，讓簡訊通知在手錶上收到而不是在智慧手機上。然而，對於那些沒有被電子郵件、簡訊和社群媒體淹沒的人而言，或許要說服他們需要更多的時間。

 Q16

A. variety
B. example
C. margin
D. option

詳解　　　　　　　　　　　　　　　　　　　　　　　答案：A

　　從 trade show（貿易展覽）這個關鍵詞，可猜測出有各式各樣的智慧型手錶被展出，a wide variety of（各式各樣的都有）。而「各式各樣」的說法很多，例如：a full array of，a whole series of 和 a wide range of。

|單字片語| **example** [ɪɡˋzæmpl] 例子 / **margin** [ˋmɑrdʒɪn] 邊緣；差距 / **option** [ˋɑpʃən] 選擇

Q17

A. consumers

B. supporters

C. manufacturers

D. instructors

詳解　答案：C

在展覽會場展出的穿戴式科技的裝置（devices），按照常理是由製造商（manufacturers）提供的，答案為 C。

|單字片語| consumer [kənˈsumə] 消費者 / supporter [səˈportə] 支持者
instructor [ɪnˈstrʌktə] 教師；指導者

Q18

A. yet

B. while

C. only

D. but

詳解　答案：D

連接詞和單字一樣，意思不只一個。在國中時學到 but 是「但是」的意思，屬於連接詞的用法，不過 but 也有「除了…以外」的意思，屬於介系詞的用法。而空格處那句的句意是指「Google Wear 去除掉其他不必要的功能（cutting out all），只留下必要的功能（the essential features）。」

Q19

A. Google Watch hasn't attracted to many customers

B. Android Wear has appealed to the mass market

C. Google Watch needs to lower its price

D. Smart Watch didn't have so many functions

詳解　答案：B

這題要看前後句來判斷空格處應該填入的選項，空格的前句提到「智慧型手錶是否值得使用者拋棄現有的手錶」，而後句寫「以證明值得花錢，讓簡訊通知在手錶上收到而不是在手機上」，因此可以看出智慧型手錶已經吸引到大眾市場了，答案為 B。appeal 和 attract 的意思都是「吸引」，「某事物很吸引某人」用 appeal to，「某人被吸引」用 attracted by。此外，appeal 還有「上訴」的意思。例如：He was sentenced to life imprisonment but he has the right to appeal.（他被判終身監禁，但是他有權力上訴。）

|單字片語| appeal [əˈpil] 對…有吸引力；上訴 / function [ˈfʌŋkʃən] 功能

Q20

A. spend   B. to spend

C. spending   D. to be spent

詳解

答案：C

　　worth（值得⋯）必須用 V-ing 動名詞，這是多益、托福還有研究所喜歡考的概念。我們也可以說 worth trying（值得一試），worth doing（值得去做），worth reading（值得一讀）。而動名詞的定義是當作名詞使用的動詞，動名詞就是名詞。worth（值得）後面也可以加名詞。worth trying 和 worth a try 的意思是一樣的。

第三部分／ **閱讀理解**

Questions 21-22

　　Search engine optimization (SEO) is the art of creating Web pages that will rank high in search engine returns. SEO is accomplished by optimizing certain sections or "elements" in the computer programming language known as HTML. These sections encoded in the HTML of any given webpage are specifically read by search engines and, depending on the level of optimization, can create a greater likelihood of free referral traffic. In other words, your web address has a better chance of appearing on the first page of a search browser, which in turn increases the likelihood of people clicking on the link to your website.

　　搜尋引擎最佳化（SEO）是能創造在搜尋引擎回報中讓網頁高居前位的技術。SEO 是藉由最佳化稱為電腦程式語言（即 HTML）中的特定區塊或「元素」來達成的。編碼在任何給定網頁 HTML 中的區塊，會被搜尋引擎特別讀取，依照最佳化的程度，這些區塊可以創造免費推薦連結流量的更大可能性。換句話說，你的網址有更多機會出現在搜尋引擎瀏覽器的第一頁，作為回報，這會增加人們點選你的網站連結的可能性。

　　There are several methods and opinions about how a web page should be optimized, and much will depend on the type of site, its content, purpose and competition, if relevant. But in general search engine optimization relies heavily on the proper use of keywords and key-phrases that describe the site's content. That is why programmers

第 1 回
第 2 回
第 3 回
第 4 回
第 5 回
第 6 回

try to cram as many keywords as possible when describing the site's product, services or content.

關於應該如何最佳化一個網頁有幾個方法與見解，其中有很大的部分取決於網站的種類、內容、目的，以及競爭對手，若有相關的話。不過一般來說，搜尋引擎最佳化十分依賴描述網站內容的適當使用關鍵字或關鍵詞。這就是為什麼程式設計師在描述網站的產品、服務和內容時，試著盡可能地塞入更多的關鍵字。

Q21

Where would you probably find this passage?
你可能會在哪裡看到這篇文章？

A. In a classified ad　在分類廣告
B. In a business journal　在商業刊物
C. In a fashion magazine　在流行雜誌
D. In a legal document　在法律文件

詳解　　　　　　　　　　　　　　　　　　　　　　　　答案：B

這篇文章所敘述的搜尋引擎最佳化（SEO）和網頁有關，文章提到網頁的內容和服務所包含的關鍵字對 SEO 的影響，可見這些網頁是商業性質的，所以這篇文章應該會在出現在商業刊物裡，答案為 B。

Q22

Who is more likely to take advantage of the principles behind SEO?
誰比較有可能利用 SEO 背後的原則？

A. A student who surfs the Net frequently　一個經常上網的學生
B. A teacher who wants to create online worksheets
　　一個想要製造線上作業表的老師
C. A restaurant operator who needs to hire a chef
　　一個想要聘請廚師的餐廳業者
D. A resort owner who needs to attract more visitors
　　一個想要吸引更多遊客的渡假村業者

詳解　　　　　　　　　　　　　　　　　　　　　　　　答案：D

利用 SEO 的人必須要有自己的網站，想藉由 SEO 背後的原則增加網站的曝光率及瀏覽人數。經常上網的學生不需要 SEO，老師製造線上作業表應該是

給現有的學生，不是為了做生意，也不需要 SEO。想要聘請廚師的餐廳業者，可以在網路上的人力銀行刊登廣告，不需要為此特地增加網頁的瀏覽人數。渡假村業者想要吸引更多訪客，就必須讓更多人知道這個渡假村的存在，當人們在網路搜尋引擎輸入「渡假、旅遊、觀光」等關鍵詞，業者的網址出現在第一頁有助於引導訪客遊覽渡假村的網站，讓業者做到更多的生意，合理答案應為 D。

Questions 23-25

Should students wear uniforms to school? Supporters of uniforms claim they can increase school safety. Uniforms allow staff to quickly identify people who do not belong on campus and limit the ways that gangs can infiltrate into schools. In 1994, Long Beach United School District in California began requiring uniforms with the hopes of improving safety. Just five years later, the overall crime rate in the district was down 91 percent. Specifically, sex offenses dropped 96 percent and number of incidents of vandalism had decreased by 69 percent.

學生應該穿制服去上學嗎？支持穿制服的人宣稱制服能夠提高校園安全。制服讓學校職員可以快速辨認不屬於校園的人，並且能限制幫派滲入學校的方式。1994 年，加州的長灘聯合學區開始要求學生穿制服，希望能改善校園安全。短短的五年後，該區的總體犯罪率下降了百分之九十一。明確來說，性侵案件減少了百分之九十六，而肆意破壞公物的案件也少了百分之六十九。

When all students are dressed alike, economic and social barriers between students are reduced. There is no peer pressure to wear expensive clothes or bullying of those who can't afford designer labels. Children have one less distraction, as they do not have to concern themselves with what others are wearing. Common dress can also make students feel like they belong to the school community, increase pride and even improve attendance. A 2012 study by the University of Houston of 160 public, urban schools, found that student attendance increased after schools began making the wearing of uniforms compulsory. Supporters of school uniforms often cite increased academic achievement as a main reason to adopt such a policy. While there are some testimonies from individuals to support this claim, overall, studies yielded inconclusive results and there is no clear evidence that wearing uniforms lead to better academic achievement.

第 1 回
第 2 回
第 3 回
第 4 回
第 5 回
第 6 回

當所有學生都穿著一致，學生之間在經濟上和社會上的隔閡會減少。不會有穿昂貴衣服的同儕壓力，那些負擔不起設計師品牌的學生也不會被霸凌。孩子們少了一件讓他們分心的事情，因為他們不必擔心別人的穿著。統一的服裝也會讓學生覺得他們屬於學校團體，增加自豪感、甚至改善出席率。一篇 2012 年由休斯頓大學針對 160 所公立、市區學校所做的研究，發現在學校強制學生必須穿制服之後，學生的出席率增加了。支持穿學校制服的人經常引用「穿制服有助於提升學術成就」，當作主要理由來實施這項政策。儘管有些來自個人的證詞支持這樣的主張，整體而言，這些研究得出非決定性的結果，而且沒有明確的證據指出穿制服能導致更優秀的學術成就。

In what ways do school uniforms help to make schools a safer place?
學校制服在什麼方面能讓學校變成一個更安全的地方？

A. By slowing traffic when students in uniform leave the school
   藉由在穿制服的學生離開學校時，讓交通流量慢下來
B. By unifying all students with a specific dress code
   藉由一項特定的服裝規定，讓所有學生團結起來
C. By keeping out strangers with harmful intent
   藉由阻隔有不良意圖的陌生人
D. By cooperation with police in uniform 藉由跟穿制服的警察合作

詳解　　　　　　　　　　　　　　　　　　　　　　答案：C

　　文章提到讓學生穿制服能有效辨認出不屬於校園的人（identify people who do not belong on campus），特別是幫派（gang），因此藉由穿制服阻隔有不良意圖的陌生人，讓學校變成更安全的地方，答案為 C。

I單字片語I gang up 聯合起來 / gangster [ˈɡæŋstə] 歹徒；流氓

How may the wearing of uniforms help to bring about harmony in a school?
穿制服如何能幫助促進校園和諧？

A. Students see themselves as equals who are a part of the school.
   學生把自己視為平等的，是學校的一部分。

B. Students protect those who wear the same type of clothes.
   學生保護那些穿同樣類型衣服的人。
C. Students express their personal identity with accessories.
   學生用配件來表達個人的身分。
D. Students believe that they face a common enemy.
   學生相信他們面對共同的敵人。

詳解　　　　　　　　　　　　　　　　　　　　　　　　答案：A

　　根據文章的陳述，當所有學生都穿同樣的制服，經濟上和社會上的隔閡會
減少（economic and social barriers between students are reduced）。這麼一來，學
生會覺得自己屬於（belong）學校，對學校會產生歸屬感（a sense of
belonging），並把自己視為學校的一分子，答案為 A。

Q25

Which of the following is NOT one of the benefits of implementing school uniforms?
以下哪一個不是實施學校制服其中一項好處？

A. A lower crime rate in the neighborhood　社區的犯罪率比較低
B. Fostering a sense of belonging　培養一種歸屬感
C. Better than expected academic results　比預期的學術成績更好
D. Increase in student attendance　提升學生的出席率

詳解　　　　　　　　　　　　　　　　　　　　　　　　答案：C

　　實施制服的好處包括降低總體的犯罪率、提升學生的出席率的部分，文章
中都有明確的數據證實。學生穿制服到學校有助於培養一種歸屬感，文章中也
有敘述。至於穿制服對學術成績有沒有正面的影響，作者在文末提到研究得出
非決定性的結果（studies yielded inconclusive results），而且沒有明確的證據
（there is no clear evidence）指出穿制服能導致更優秀的學術成績，因此選項 C
不是實施學校制服的好處，答案為 C。

Questions 26-28

This document is automatically generated.
Please do not respond to this mail.

QQ AIRWAYS E-TICKET ITINERARY AND RECEIPT ABN 16 009 661 901
International customers require this document for immigration, customs,

第 1 回
第 2 回
第 3 回
第 4 回
第 5 回
第 6 回

airport security checks and duty purchases.
Australian and New Zealand domestic customers should carry this
document at all times during travel and produce it when required.
All customers should retain a copy for their records.

Travel Details for:
Customer Name: Peter Wu
Booking Ref: 4O89B3
E-ticket No.: 081 2419240070
Issued by: QQ AIRWAYS-34382331-TAIPEI
Date: 12 MAR 22

Your itinerary and travel details:

QQ AIRWAYS:	QQ330	Economy Class	Confirmed
Depart:	15 APR 22	TAIPEI	2255
Arrive:	16 APR 22	BRISBANE	0955
Baggage Allowance: 20 Kilo.			

QQ AIRWAYS:	Q329	Economy Class	Confirmed
Depart:	22 APR 22	BRISBANE	2245
Arrive:	23 APR 22	TAIPEI	0525
Departs From: Terminal 1			
Arrives at: Terminal 2			
Baggage Allowance: 20 Kilo.			

這份文件是自動產生，請勿回覆這封郵件。

QQ 航空電子機票、行程和收據 ABN 16 009 661 901
國際顧客需要這份文件辦理出入境、通過海關和機場安全檢查，以及免稅商店購
物也需要出示這份文件。
澳洲和紐西蘭國內顧客應該在旅途中隨時隨身攜帶此文件，並在需要時出示。所
有顧客應該保留一份副本作為紀錄。

旅遊細節：
顧客姓名：PETER WU
訂購編號：4O89B3
電子機票編號：081 2419240070

發行機構：QQ 航空公司-34382331-台北
日期：2022 年 3 月 12 日

您的行程和旅遊細節：

QQ 航　　空：QQ330 班機　　　　經　濟　艙　確　　認
　　出　　境：2022 年 4 月 15 日　台　　　北　　2255
　　入　　境：2022 年 4 月 16 日　布里斯本　　0955
　　行李限重：20 公斤

QQ 航　　空：QQ329 班機　　　　經　濟　艙　確　　認
　　出　　境：2022 年 4 月 22 日　布里斯本　　2245
　　入　　境：2022 年 4 月 23 日　台　　　北　　0525
　　出　　境：第一航廈
　　入　　境：第二航廈
　　行李限重：20 公斤

|單字片語| **document** [ˋdɑkjəmənt] 文件 / **itinerary** [ɑɪˋtɪnəˏrɛrɪ] 行程 / **receipt** [rɪˋsit] 收據 **immigration** [ˏɪməˋgreʃən] 移民（入境） / **customs** [ˋkʌstəmz] 海關 **domestic** [dəˋmɛstɪk] 國內的；家庭的 / **retain** [rɪˋten] 保留 / **detail** [ˋditel] 細節 **confirm** [kənˋfɝm] 確認 / **cancel** [ˋkænsl] 取消 / **delay** [dɪˋle] 耽誤 **terminal** [ˋtɝmənl] 總站；航廈

Q26

Who is the sender of this email?
誰是這封電子郵件的寄件人？

    A. The president of QQ Airways　　QQ 航空的總裁
    B. The customer of QQ Airways　　QQ 航空的顧客
    C. Mr. Wu　　吳先生
    D. No one. It is sent by the company's automation system.
    　　沒人。這是公司的電腦自動系統發出的。

詳解　　　　　　　　　　　　　　　　　　　　　　　**答案：D**

　　從這份文件是電腦自動發送的（This document is automatically generated），可得知這封電子郵件是公司的電腦自動系統所發出的，答案為 D。

第 1 回
第 2 回
第 3 回
第 4 回
第 5 回
第 6 回

What can you tell from the information above?
你可以從以上的資訊中得知什麼？

    A. Mr. Wu will reply to confirm the ticket.　吳先生將會回覆以便確認機票。
    B. Mr. Wu is an Australian.　吳先生是澳洲人。
    C. Mr. Wu is employed by QQ Airways.　吳先生受聘於 QQ 航空。
    D. Mr. Wu will not be in Taipei for about a week.
       吳先生將會有大概一個星期不在台北。

【詳解】　　　　　　　　　　　　　　　　　　　　　　　　　　答案：D
　　這份文件已經確認了（confirmed），也是乘客的收據（receipt），吳先生不需要回覆。從文中無法判斷吳先生是否為澳洲人。文中也沒提到吳先生是 QQ 航空公司的員工。從機票上的日期判斷，可得知吳先生於 2022 年 4 月 15 日至 2022 年 4 月 21 日，大約一個星期的時間人在澳洲，不會在台北，答案為 D。

When might the passenger make a reservation?
這位乘客可能是在何時預訂機票的？

    A. In May 2022　2022 年 5 月
    B. In April 2022　2022 年 4 月
    C. A month in advance　提前一個月
    D. A week before departure　離境前一週

【詳解】　　　　　　　　　　　　　　　　　　　　　　　　　　答案：C
　　從訂購資料（Booking Ref）中的日期（Date）可得知，乘客在 2022 年 3 月 12 日，也就是提前一個月的時間就已經訂票，答案為 C。

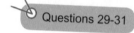

City Museum

Operating Hours:
• Open to the public from 9:00 a.m. to 5:00 p.m.
• No entry after 3:30 p.m.
• Closed on Mondays and the day following a public holiday.

Fees:
- Normal Ticket: NT$90
- Discount Ticket: NT$60
- Eligibility for Discount Tickets:
  1. Teachers or military and police personnel (appropriate identification required)
  2. Students (with valid student card)
  3. Group purchase of 25 tickets or more

- Free Entry:
  1. Physically challenged persons (with certification)
  2. Seniors at the age of sixty years old and above (with ID card)
  3. Low income households (with certification from Kaohsiung City Government)

Regulations:
- No entry for children under five years of age
- No food or drinks
- No pets allowed
- No photography

Other:
- For wheelchairs, brochures or other services, please inquire at the Information Desk.
- Tel:886-7-2136521 ext.:5000

市立博物館

開放時間：
- 上午九點至下午五點對外開放
- 下午三點三十分後不對外開放
- 星期一和國定假日的隔天休息

入館門票：
- 全票：新台幣九十元
- 優待票：新台幣六十元

第1回
第2回
第3回
第4回
第5回
第6回

• 符合下列條件者可購買優待票：
  1. 教師和軍警人員（請出示適當的證件）
  2. 學生（請出示有效的學生證）
  3. 二十五人以上團體購票

• 免費入場：
  1. 身障人士（請出示身心障礙手冊）
  2. 六十歲（含）以上的年長者（請出示身份證件）
  3. 低收入戶（請出示高雄市政府核發之證明文件）

規定：
• 五歲以下的孩童禁止進入
• 禁止攜帶飲料、食物
• 禁止攜帶寵物
• 禁止攝影

其他：
• 需要輪椅、導覽手冊或其他服務，請洽服務台。
• 電話：886-7-2136521 分機：5000

|單字片語| **eligibility** [ɛlɪdʒəˈbɪlətɪ] 資格 / **military** [ˈmɪlə,tɛrɪ] 軍隊
personnel [ˌpɜsṇˈɛl] 人員 / **identification** [aɪ,dɛntəfəˈkeʃən] 身分
physically challenged 身體上不便者 / **senior** [ˈsinjə] 年長者
inquire [ɪnˈkwaɪr] 詢問

On which day will the city museum be closed?
博物館在哪一天會休息？

A. On Saturday.　在星期六。
B. On Sunday.　在星期天。
C. On a public holiday.　在國定假日。
D. On the second of January.　在一月二日。

詳解　　　　　　　　　　　　　　　　　　　　　　答案：D

　　博物館在星期一和國定假日的隔天閉館（Closed on Mondays and the day following a public holiday.）一月一日元旦為國定假日，博物館於隔天閉館，也就是一月二日。

Q30

Who can purchase a ticket at a lower price?

誰可以用比較低的價格來購票？

    A. Someone who is fifty years old　年滿五十歲的人

    B. Someone who is seventy years old　年滿七十歲的人

    C. Someone who has young children　有帶小孩的人

    D. Someone who works as a sailor in the navy　在海軍當水手的人

> **詳解**　　　　　　　　　　　　　　　　　　　　　　**答案：D**
>
> 　　文中提到軍公教可享有優待價，在海軍當水手的人被視為國防人員（military personnel），可以用折扣的價格購票，答案為 D。七十歲可免費入場，因此無須購票。

 Q31

Which of the following behavior is a violation of museum rules?

下列哪一種行為違反了博物館的規定？

    A. Having low income　擁有低收入

    B. Completing a challenge　完成一項挑戰

    C. Taking pictures of the paintings　拍畫像

    D. Purchasing a discount ticket　購買優待票

> **詳解**　　　　　　　　　　　　　　　　　　　　　　**答案：C**
>
> 　　博物館規定館內不可攝影（No photography），用相機拍畫像違反了博物館的規定，答案為 C。

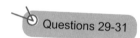

Musical Instruments courses at the High Music Studio

Musical Instruments	Description	Times
Guitar	Playing the guitar demands strong finger motor skills, so you will develop strength in your finger muscles. You may play the guitar while sitting or standing.	Monday 5 p.m. – 6 p.m. Wednesday 6 p.m. – 7 p.m. Friday 7 p.m. – 8 p.m.
French horn	When playing the French horn, you need to have a big hand to grasp the horn. Once you can produce a nice and characteristic sound, you will enjoy the pleasure. When you play the French horn, you are free to sit or stand.	Tuesday 6 p.m. – 7 p.m. Wednesday 6 p.m. – 7 p.m. Friday 6 p.m. – 7 p.m.
Piano	Playing the piano requires not just high finger skills, but moderate arm strength and endurance to hit the keys. You also need to use the strength of your foot and leg to pedal. You can sharpen your small muscles by piano playing.	Monday 6 p.m. – 7 p.m. Tuesday 7 p.m. – 8 p.m. Thursday 6 p.m. – 7 p.m. Friday 5 p.m. – 6 p.m.
Drums	Playing the drum is an activity of the entire body. You will use the muscle groups in your upper body to deliver power. Hitting a drum or holding drum sticks does not require finger skills.	Wednesday 5 p.m. – 6 p.m. Thursday 5 p.m. – 6 p.m. Saturday 5 p.m. – 6 p.m.

High 音樂工作室的樂器課程

樂器	課程敘述	上課時間
吉他	彈奏吉他需要強大的手指運動技巧,因此你將會增強手指肌肉的力量。你可能在坐著或站著的同時彈吉他。	星期一下午 5 點 – 6 點 星期三下午 6 點 – 7 點 星期五下午 7 點 – 8 點
法國號	在演奏法國號時,你需要一隻大手才能握住法國號。一旦你能發出優美、有魅力的聲音,便能享受到樂趣。演奏法國號時,你可以隨意坐著或站立。	星期二下午 6 點 – 7 點 星期三下午 6 點 – 7 點 星期五下午 6 點 – 7 點
鋼琴	彈奏鋼琴不僅需要高階的手指技巧,而且還需要適度的手臂力量和耐力來按琴鍵。你也需要使用腳和腿的力量來踩踏板。透過彈奏鋼琴,你可以鍛煉小肌肉。	星期一下午 6 點 – 7 點 星期二下午 7 點 – 8 點 星期四下午 6 點 – 7 點 星期五下午 5 點 – 6 點
鼓	演奏鼓是個全身的活動。你將會使用上半身的肌肉群來傳送力量。打擊鼓或握住鼓棒則不需要手指技巧。	星期三下午 5 點 – 6 點 星期四下午 5 點 – 6 點 星期六下午 5 點 – 6 點

第 1 回
第 2 回
第 3 回
第 4 回
第 5 回
第 6 回

I'm reading an article in *Parents and Kids Monthly Magazine*. I am surprised to know that there is a lot to know when choosing a musical instrument for children. Everyone knows that music soothes our souls, but it is surprising that music can also shape and strengthen our brains. Learning a musical instrument allows people to nourish their brains. At the same time, many cognitive and physical parts of their bodies may be enhanced.

Learning to play a musical instrument is a great challenge, but it does have physical health benefits. Some instruments help children strengthen fine motor skills. Some help children build balance and coordination. Fine motor skills are the ability to carry out movements using the small muscles of our hands and wrists, like finger skills. Balance and coordination are two important capacities in the physical development of children, like whole-body activities.

Knowing the strengths and weaknesses of your children can help you and your kids select the best suiting their needs.

第1回
第2回
第3回
第4回
第5回
第6回

http://www.comments.com/henry-Jinks

　　我正在閱讀《父母與孩子月刊》上的一篇文章。我很驚訝地知道，為兒童選擇樂器是一門大學問。每個人都知道音樂可以撫慰我們的靈魂，但是令人驚訝的是音樂也可以塑造並強化我們的大腦。學習一種樂器可以使人們滋養自己的大腦。同時，可能增進許多他們的認知和身體部位。

　　學習彈奏樂器是一個很大的挑戰，但這的確對身體健康有好處。有些樂器幫助孩子強化精細運動技能。有些樂器則幫助孩子建立平衡和協調。精細運動技能是指使用我們的手部和手腕的小肌肉進行運動，例如：手指技能。平衡和協調是兒童身體發育的兩項重要能力，像是全身活動。

　　了解孩子的長處和弱點可以幫助你和孩子們選擇出最適合他們需求的樂器。

|單字片語| **characteristic** [ˌkærəktəˈrɪstɪk] 特有的 / **moderate** [ˈmɑdərɪt] 溫和的
endurance [ɪnˈdjʊrəns] 耐力 / **pedal** [ˈpɛdl] 踏板 / **coordination** [koˈɔrdnˌeʃən] 協調

According to the second passage, which of the following statements is NOT mentioned?
根據第二篇文章，下列哪一項敘述未被提及？

A. Learning musical instruments may benefit the brain.
　　學習樂器可能對大腦有益處。

B. Learning musical instruments is a good way to enhance physical health.
　　學習樂器是個提升身體健康的一個好方法。

C. Learning musical instruments may improve memory ability.
　　學習樂器可能會提升記憶力。

D. Learning musical instruments can calm the soul.
　　學習樂器可以使心靈平靜。

詳解　　　　　　　　　　　　　　　　　　　　**答案：C**

　　這題的內容與樂器相關，四個選項都是學習樂器的好處，因此針對短文分辨出文中哪一些描述與學習樂器的好處有關，就能快速找出關鍵句。第二篇文

章第一段 Everyone knows that music soothe our souls, but it is surprising that music can also shape and strengthen our brains.，以及第二段 Learning to play a musical instrument is a great challenge, but it does have physical health benefits.，皆提到學樂器的好處由此可知，選項 C（學習樂器可能會提高記憶力）並沒有被提及，答案為 C。

Q33

Joanna would like to sign up for a course for her child, but her child has developmental delays. Which class would be more appropriate for Joanna's child?

Joanna 想為她的孩子報名一門課程，但是她的孩子發育遲緩。哪一個課程較適合 Joanna 的孩子？

A. The guitar course.　吉他課程。
B. The French horn course.　法國號課程。
C. The piano course.　鋼琴課程。
D. The drums course.　鼓樂課程。

詳解　　　　　　　　　　　　　　　　　　　　　　　　　　　**答案：D**

　　這題需整合表格和短文的內容才能找到答案，因此要先針對短文分辨出文中哪一些內容描述與發育遲緩有關，就能快速地在第一篇表格中找出關鍵答案。短文第二段最後一句提到 Balance and coordination are two important capacities in the physical development of children, like whole-body activities，可知全身的運動有益於兒童身體的發育。對應到表格中，吉他、法國號、鋼琴都未談到全身活動，而鼓樂課程的第一句 Playing the drum is an activity of the entire body.，說明鼓樂課程是一種全身的活動，答案為 D。

Q34

Martin has basketball evening training on Tuesdays, Thursdays, and Fridays. If he enrolls in a French horn course, when should he go?

Martin 在星期二、星期四和星期五有籃球晚間訓練。如果他參加法國號課程，他應該什麼時候去？

A. Wednesday 5 p.m. – 6 p.m.　星期三下午 5 點 – 6 點
B. Wednesday 6 p.m. – 7 p.m.　星期三下午 6 點 – 7 點
C. Monday 5 p.m. – 6 p.m.　星期一下午 5 點 – 6 點
D. Monday 6 p.m. – 7 p.m.　星期一下午 6 點 – 7 點

第 1 回
第 2 回
第 3 回
第 4 回
第 5 回
第 6 回

詳解

　　這題要看第一篇的表格才能作答，而選項都是課程時間，因此要先針對法國號的課程時間，再對應 Martin 的時間，就能快速地找出答案。表格中法國號的課程時間為星期二、星期三、星期五下午，而 Martin 的籃球訓練時間是星期二、星期四和星期五。由此可知，他在星期三下午可以去上課。而表格內的法國號的課程時間是星期三下午 6 點 – 7 點，答案為 B。

Q35

Which musical instrument can improve the strength of the fingers and the legs?

哪一種樂器能夠改善手指和雙腿的力量？

A. The guitar.　吉他。
B. The French horn.　法國號。
C. The piano.　鋼琴。
D. The drums.　鼓。

詳解

　　這題要看第一篇的表格才能作答，而選項都是樂器。故針對各個樂器的課程描述，就能快速地找出與手指和腿部力量有關的課程。表格中鋼琴課程描述提到 Playing the piano requires not just high finger skills... You also need to use the strength of your foot and leg to pedal，答案為 C。

全民英檢中級

第三回 初試 聽力測驗

本測驗分四部份，全為四選一之選擇題，共 35 題，作答時間約 30 分鐘。

第一部分　看圖辨義

　　共 5 題，試題冊上有數幅圖畫，每一圖畫有 1~3 個描述該圖的題目，每題請聽錄音播出每題以及四個英語敘述之後，選出與所看到的圖畫最相符的一個答案。每題只播出一遍。

例題：（看）

（聽）Look at the picture.
What does the woman want
the boy to do?
A. Pick up the rubbish.
B. Tie his shoelaces.
C. Carry her luggage.
D. Hail a cab.

正確答案為 A。

聽力測驗第一部分自本頁開始。

A:　Question 1

B:　Question 2

C: Question 3

D: Question 4-5

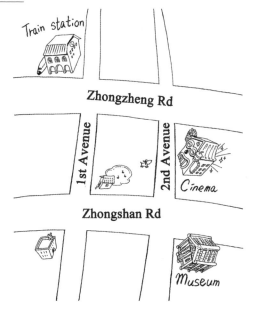

第二部分：問答

共 10 題，每題請聽光碟放音機播出一英語問句或直述句之後，從試題冊上 A、B、C、D 四個回答或回應中，選出一個最適合者作答。每題只播出一遍。

例： （聽） What happened to your feet?
　　 （看） A. They were too hungry.
　　　　　 B. I got a new pair.
　　　　　 C. My new shoes are too small.
　　　　　 D. These are not mine.

正確答案為 C。

6. A. No way.
　 B. Not again.
　 C. Anytime.
　 D. All the time.

7. A. Sure. May I borrow your phone?
　 B. Sure. When should I do it?
　 C. Sure. Why don't you do it yourself?
　 D. Sure. How come she is calling you?

8. A. What are we waiting for?
　 B. How could you do that?
　 C. Be my guest!
　 D. What a shame!

9. A. I am not a British.
　 B. I am not in England now.
　 C. I am not up to it.
　 D. I am not against it.

10. A. I will do it whether she likes it or not.
　 B. I hope she gets well before the exams.
　 C. I am sure she will come up with something.
　 D. I believe we can expect fair weather.

11. A. I promise I won't do it again.
    B. I will get distracted.
    C. I think three is even better.
    D. I suppose it's cheaper that way.

12. A. I told you they can live for a long time.
    B. It's such a pity.
    C. They must be worth a small fortune.
    D. We need to get her a birthday present.

13. A. It is never too late to say sorry.
    B. I suppose you have to pay a fine.
    C. Someone told me the car is his.
    D. Maybe you should ride a bike.

14. A. Both players are talented.
    B. White goes well with any color.
    C. It's no big deal.
    D. Let's keep this between ourselves.

15. A. Have a seat over here.
    B. That's the only one left.
    C. Let's go over it again.
    D. You had better think twice before you quit.

第三部分　簡短對話

共 10 題，每題請聽光碟放音機播出一段對話及一個相關的問題後，從試題冊上 A、B、C、D 四個選項中選出一個最適合者作答。每段對話及問題只播出一遍。

例： (聽)　(Man)　　　Did you happen to see my earphones?
　　　　　　　　　　　I remember leaving them in the drawer.
　　　　　(Woman)　　Did you search your briefcase?
　　　　　(Man)　　　I did but they are not there. Wait a second. Oh.
　　　　　　　　　　　They are right here in my pocket.

　　　　　Question:　　Where are the man's earphones?

　　(看)　A.　The woman's pocket.
　　　　　B.　Briefcase.
　　　　　C.　The man's pocket.
　　　　　D.　Drawer.

正確答案為 C。

16. A. He should use the air-conditioner the whole night.
　　B. He should learn to appreciate what he has.
　　C. He should try to stay young and healthy.
　　D. He shouldn't use the air-conditioner at all.

17. A. Let her take care of his belongings.
　　B. Pay for the items before leaving the store.
　　C. Leave the things he wants to buy with her.
　　D. Take the merchandise to the bathroom.

18. A. She is a guide.
    B. She is an accountant.
    C. She is a diplomat.
    D. She is an interior designer.

19. A. He needs more time to
       finish his work.
    B. He received a strange
       email.
    C. He's a little absent-minded
       this morning.
    D. He has a poor sense of
       humor.

20. A. Doing aerobics.
    B. Having an operation.
    C. Applying makeup.
    D. Taking a first aid course.

21. A. The man's future
       profession.
    B. The man's college life.
    C. The man's qualifications.
    D. The man's health condition.

22. A. Send the woman to the
       hospital.
    B. Give the woman a massage.
    C. Take the woman home.
    D. Help the woman fix her car.

23. A. A marriage counselor.
    B. A fitness instructor.
    C. A publicity officer.
    D. A travel agent.

24.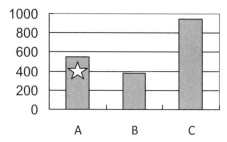

    A. The floods.
    B. The thunderstorms.
    C. The volcano eruption.
    D. The tornadoes.

25.

Movie Schedule

Arch (Sci-fi)	09:05 – 10:55
Competitor (Animated)	11:05 – 13:05
Leopard (Action)	13:05 – 15:05
The Horizon (Horror)	15:15 – 17:05

    A. Arch.
    B. Competitor.
    C. Leopard.
    D. The Horizon.

共 10 題，每題請聽光碟放音機播出一段談話及一個相關的問題後，從試題冊上 A、B、C、D 四個選項中選出一個最適合者作答。每段談話及問題只播出一遍。

例：　　　　(聽)　　　　Good morning, everyone. Please come over here and take these registration forms. Then, go back to your seats. This is the workshop on APP design. The lecturer of this workshop is an engineer from SBE Software. He has excellent experience in designing smartphone applications. Before you fill in the forms, please look through the forms carefully. If you have any questions, I will answer you later.

Question:　　What might the listeners do, after they read through the registration forms?

(看)　　　　A. Leave the forms on the desks.
　　　　　　B. Pay the registration fee.
　　　　　　C. Ask the speaker some questions.
　　　　　　D. Go to another location.

正確答案為 C。

26. A. New doctors.
　　B. New researchers.
　　C. New residents.
　　D. New hosts.

27. A. A mall anniversary sale.
　　B. A beach birthday party.
　　C. An outdoor flea market.
　　D. A soccer match.

28. A. To share the good news.
　　B. To accept an offer.
　　C. To deliver advice.
　　D. To request assistance.

29. A. To educate people about reducing air pressure.
    B. To force people put on an oxygen mask.
    C. To guide people on how to use an oxygen mask.
    D. To request people to assist others.

30. A. Watch TV programs.
    B. Seek safe cover.
    C. Find television sets.
    D. Cover the alarm.

31. A. Combine water and the pasta.
    B. Mix together the pasta with tomatoes.
    C. Place a rack in the pressure cooker.
    D. Set the time of cooking.

32. A. A GPS watch.
    B. A fancy watch.
    C. A workout class.
    D. A fitness tracker.

33. A. A person who is screwing something.
    B. A person who is raising something.
    C. A person who is fixing something.
    D. A person who is sewing something.

34.

March

Sun.	
Mon.	1 Online market meeting
Tue.	2 Product marketing promotion
Wed.	3 Market research survey
Thu.	4 Visit the North Market
Fri.	5 Visit the Nice Market
Sat.	6

A. Product marketing promotion.
B. Market research survey.
C. Visit the North Market.
D. Visit the Nice Market.

35.

A. North street.
B. Main street.
C. South street.
D. Park Ave. East.

第三回 初試 閱讀測驗

本測驗分三部分，全為四選一的選擇題，共 35 題，作答時間為 45 分鐘。

第一部分：詞彙

共 10 題，每題有一個空格。請由試題冊上的四個選項中選出最適合題意的字或詞作答。

1. He can't even walk properly when he is drunk, _____ drive.
   A. let alone
   B. save for
   C. apart from
   D. inasmuch as

2. It was after years of _____ research that the drug was made available to the public.
   A. conducive
   B. extensive
   C. productive
   D. subjective

3. Traffic congestions have become a common scene as a new underground train _____ is being constructed.
   A. permission
   B. foundation
   C. terminal
   D. landscape

4. Someone with a good command of English who is also _____ in another foreign language such as French or German is more suited for this position.
   A. encouraging
   B. competitive
   C. reasonable
   D. fluent

5. Please note that the deadline for the essay competition is this Friday. Late _____ will not be entertained.
   A. fragments
   B. entries
   C. emergencies
   D. drawbacks

6. The Statue of Liberty was given to the United States by France and it is a _____ of freedom.
   A. bribery
   B. refuge
   C. fountain
   D. symbol

7. According to doctors, exercising on a/an _____ basis is the most effective way to lose weight.
   A. occasional
   B. particular
   C. regular
   D. nominal

8. Law enforcement officers are required to _____ orders without any sympathy or fear.
   A. modify
   B. execute
   C. withhold
   D. abandon

9. The patient's condition _____ within such a short span of time that his family feared for the worst.
   A. worsened
   B. exhausted
   C. alleviated
   D. improved

10. My mom _____ the luggage to double-check if we have everything we need for the trip.
   A. went on
   B. went into
   C. went around
   D. went through

第二部分：段落填空

共 10 題，包括二個段落，每個段落各含 5 個空格。請由試題冊上四個選項中選出最適合題意的字或詞作答。

Questions 11-15

Could some of the world's ancient civilizations ___(11)___ aliens instead of humans? That would explain the high level of sophisticated technology they possessed thousands of years ago. If such an assumption is plausible, there is more reason to believe that aliens used to ___(12)___ on earth. A lot of rumors have been circulated online concerning the highly classified government facility known as Area 51. Area 51 might just be a normal military site and it might not. However, so far there is not a single piece of solid evidence to ___(13)___ the suspicions. Many believed that there is more than meets the eye since the US government refused to discuss the matter on numerous ___(14)___ . The base has long been a very closely-guarded secret, with lots of "trespassers will be shot" signs around the base itself and a large no-fly zone surrounding it. ___(15)___ , the base allegedly features elaborate underground labs and hidden tunnels.

11. A. seem to be
    B. claim to be
    C. happen to be
    D. occur to be

12. A. exhibit
    B. explain
    C. exist
    D. explode

13. A. contrast
    B. control
    C. condemn
    D. confirm

14. A. situations
    B. conditions
    C. occasions
    D. interpretations

15. A. According to conspiracy
       theorists
    B. In spite of archeologists'
       denial
    C. Due to the architect's
       reports
    D. Through the astrologist's
       prediction

Questions 16-20

E-books may never replace paper books completely, but they make up a significant portion of book sales and appear ___(16)___ to become the primary way to read. E-books offer a number of advantages for readers that lead us to wonder why people are still buying paper books. First and foremost, e-books do not ___(17)___ resources to print and distribute. Books in print consume paper, ink and time, while e-books are available for download through publishers directly via Internet. ___(18)___, they cost only a fraction of printed books, sometimes as low as one-tenth of the listed price of paperbacks. Another huge plus of e-books is weight and space. E-books are weightless and they do not take up any physical space. Furthermore, e-books allow readers to bookmark pages and highlight words, sentences and paragraphs the way we are ___(19)___ when using paper books. Having said all that, old habits die hard and ultimately, the choice between an e-book or paper book ___(20)___.

16. A. appointed
    B. refused
    C. tolerated
    D. destined

17. A. exploit
    B. consume
    C. replenish
    D. abuse

18. A. As a result
    B. To sum up
    C. On the contrary
    D. In a way

19. A. dependent on
    B. frightened of
    C. accustomed to
    D. satisfied with

20. A. may depend on personal preference
    B. doesn't have something to do with the marketing target
    C. can stand in for publisher's profits
    D. should carry out the government's expectation

第三部分：閱讀理解

本部分共 15 題，包括 5 個題組，每個題組含 1 至 2 篇短文，與數個相關的四選一的選擇題。請由試題冊上的選項中選出最適合者作答。

Questions 21-22

Time for Talent Time?

Forget about TV reality shows such as the American Idol because not everyone can be an overnight success. Many schools, camps, and organizations hold talent shows every year because they are fun, involve the community, and give students a chance to show off their special skills.

Turn your Talent Show into a Fund-Raiser. Sell T-shirts, food, glow bracelets, etc. Sell advertising for the printed program and sponsor banners to be prominently posted near the stage. Sell tickets for admission. Sell flowers, ribbons, or other gifts supporters are likely to give to the performers. Record the performance and sell DVDs to both participants and audience.

We specialized in designing and manufacturing the products mentioned above. Call our toll-free number at 0800-543-3388. If the event does not make a profit, we charge nothing for our service.

21. Who might be the writer of this passage?
    A. A school principal
    B. A talent scout
    C. A music instructor
    D. A business owner

22. The following statements describe the benefits of organizing a Talent Time Contest EXCEPT statement _____.
    A. teenagers are mostly in favor of such events
    B. students have an opportunity to showcase their talent
    C. teachers need to sponsor the event
    D. schools can invite residents in the neighborhood

Randy's Kitchen

Dinner Specials

Premium Steak ································NT $550

Pork Chop·······························NT $500

Fish Sandwich ·····························NT $480

Sweet & Sour Pork ·······················NT $450

Fresh Salad ····························NT $380

Super Hamburger ·······················NT $320

Desserts

Apple Pie ································NT $120

Cheesecake ·······························NT $110

Ice Cream ·······························NT $100

Drinks

Coffee ································NT $120

Juice·································NT $100

Fruit Tea·································NT $90

※Set Dinner: Enjoy a main course, dessert, and beverage of your choice for only NT $699.

※Get a 5% discount when you like our Facebook fan page.

Note: 10% service charge not included in prices shown above. No reservation in advance, all customers will be seated on a first-come-first-served basis.

23. Sophia would like to order the premium steak, ice cream and a cup of coffee. Should she opt for the set dinner?
    A. Yes, they cost the same amount of money.
    B. Yes, it is less expensive that way.
    C. No, she will pay more either way.
    D. No, she will pay less if she orders them separately.

24. According to the menu, which statement is NOT true?
    A. You can get an extra discount by accessing to the Internet.
    B. "Fruit Tea" is the cheapest one in the menu.
    C. "Apple Pie" costs as much as "Coffee".
    D. You can order lamb here.

25. How can you ensure that you have a seat in the restaurant?
    A. Make a reservation in advance.
    B. Be there as early as possible.
    C. Call the manager to make arrangements.
    D. Support the restaurant's online fan page.

Dutch people are very friendly and tolerant on the whole, yet they often keep their distance from strangers. Once you are in the conversation with the Dutch, you will find that they are helpful. In general, Dutch people are pleasant but at the same time they can be very straightforward and frank, some people would say blunt. Sometimes you might feel that they make you lose face, which is a taboo in Asian societies. Please remember that it is not done on purpose to hurt people but it is rather a form of honesty and truthfulness. When going out to a restaurant with the Dutch, we have to keep in mind that the Dutch are very pragmatic. Even if you happen to be a lady invited to dinner by a Dutch man, do not expect a man to foot the bill. Many female foreigners were confused and offended, when Dutch men asked the waiter to split the bill into two. This habit is known as "going Dutch".

Time is not a fluid concept for the Dutch, but rather something fixed. Therefore, being on time is very important for them. When you have an appointment, please remember to be on time. If for any reasons you cannot be on time for the appointment, you have to inform them in advance. Making an appointment before meeting somebody is almost compulsory, otherwise you will waste your time by getting the answer that they cannot see you because they don't have an appointment with you. Instead of getting upset or angry if you cannot make an appointment at short notice, you should realize that the Dutch often make plans months in advance.

26. What do you need to be aware of when speaking to Dutch friends?
    A. They might criticize you in public.
    B. They might ask you for a favor.
    C. They might keep something from you.
    D. They might make fun of you.

27. What does it mean to "go Dutch"?
    A. Women have to fork out the money.
    B. Men will settle the bill.
    C. Each person has to pay for his or her meal.
    D. The restaurant will offer a 50 percent discount.

28. Which of the following actions is considered unacceptable to the Dutch people?
    A. Making comments about your Dutch friends' weaknesses
    B. Asking for your Dutch friends' schedules for the months ahead
    C. Refusing to pay for more than your share in a restaurant
    D. Knocking on their doors with a cake without warning

Fashion trends come and go and clothes can easily go out of style quickly. Today, the most popular designer stores online and offline showcase Asian fashion in casual wear, formal wear as well as office wear for men and women. Asians as well as Westerners are interested in purchasing these clothes due to lively colors, creative designs and low prices. Garments made in Asia used to be associated with inferior quality but that has changed over the years.

With Korean dramas taking Asian markets by storm, Korean fashion has replaced the Japanese as the most popular choice in the fashion industry. Korean designers design fashionable clothes that appeal to all classes and with Korean idols showing off these trendy and glamorous clothes on Korean dramas, it is no wonder that sales have gone through the roof. There is also no denying that the fabrics used are of good quality and taste.

The best way to source out the latest fashion wear is by browsing the internet and finding out details about styles, fashion and latest trends. Several online stores offer clothing from any part of the world. It helps to spend time going through the photos and finding something that appeals to your sense of taste. Many stores offer huge discounts and free delivery if bulk purchases are made. This makes the entire process even more affordable especially when one has a budget to consider.

29. Westerners prefer Asian fashion for the following reasons
EXCEPT _____ .
A. Asian fashion is more affordable
B. Asian fashion is colorful
C. Asian fashion uses cheaper materials
D. Asian fashion puts more ideas into designing

30. What accounts for the rising popularity of Korean fashion?
A. The subsidy provided by the Korean government.
B. The unique winter wear fabric used by Korean fashion designers.
C. The low-cost marketing strategies adopted by Korean online stores.
D. The success of Korean soap operas.

31. You might be able to enjoy the benefits of a free delivery if _____ .
A. you spend enough time browsing
B. you place a large order
C. you find what suits your taste
D. you have a limited budget

Questions 32-35 are based on the information provided in the following two e-mails.

To:	service@hitech.com
From:	chris099@gmail.com
Subject:	About the product problems

To whom it may concern,

I spent NT$16,000 buying one Hitech tablet with built-in wi-fi on your official site two weeks ago. I also purchased a monthly wireless Internet connection plan for NT$1000 per month. Because it was a pre-paid plan which provided a 10 GB data plan via the Hitech Mobile connection, I had paid in advance for 12 months of service.

I am complaining because when I watch movies on Netflix, the quality of video streaming is restricted to the standard definition. As soon as I learned of this issue, I contacted a customer service representative at your company. I was told that I had to pay $1,599 per month to obtain a high-speed plan. I am highly disappointed with your product and service, so I would like a written statement explaining what you will do with respect to my complaint.

Seriously, I look forward to hearing from you as soon as possible to deal with my problem. The copies of my receipt are enclosed.

Yours sincerely,
Chris Chen

To:	chris099@gmail.com
From:	service@hitech.com
Subject:	Re: About the product problems

Dear Mr. Chen,

Thank you for your email. We are serious about customer satisfaction. First, we would like to apologize for your inconvenience and disappointment that you've been suffered.

We provide several data options that would meet the needs of all consumers. Having checked your current data usage, I noticed that you are a heavy Internet user. No wonder the 10 GB data plan is not suitable for you. That is why our service agent suggested that you could purchase the unlimited data plan. It provides no speed restrictions, no usage limits, and no extra costs.

The unlimited data home Internet package is another option that you can use. It streams a great number of videos and keeps your family connected. Starting at NT $5,999 per month for a family of four lines or NT $4,699 for a family of three, you can also get a free upgrade to a Netflix HD subscription.

Finally, we are truly hoping to serve you better in the future. Please contact the customer service department at 5431-9855 with any questions or assistance.

Best regards,
Michael White
Customer Service Director

32. Why did Chris Chen write the email?
    A. He was disappointed with the limitations in the data plan.
    B. He complained about the function of his new tablet.
    C. He was furious with the behavior of a service agent.
    D. He wished to return his new tablet.

33. Which of the following statements is true in relation to the response of Michael White?
    A. He admitted that the customer service representative failed to provide adequate service.
    B. He gave Chris a refund because the quality of the video streaming was limited.
    C. He provided an additional plan for Chris.
    D. He asked Chris to alter his data plan right away.

34. What kind of data plan did the customer service representative propose to Chris?
    A. An unlimited data home Internet package for three lines.
    B. An unlimited data home Internet package for four lines.
    C. An unlimited data plan.
    D. A 10 GB data plan.

35. How much money did Chris pay when he bought the tablet along with the data plan?
    A. NT$ 16,000.
    B. NT$ 17,000.
    C. NT$ 24,000.
    D. NT$ 28,000.

—結束—

初試 聽力測驗 解析

第 1 回
第 2 回
第 3 回
第 4 回
第 5 回
第 6 回

第一部分 / 看圖辨義

Q

For question one, please look at picture A.

Which bin should the boy put the books in?
男孩應該把書本放進哪一個桶子裡？

A. Bin One.	A. 桶子一。
B. Bin Two.	B. 桶子二。
C. Bin Three.	C. 桶子三。
D. Bin Four.	D. 桶子四。

詳解　　　　　　　　　　　　　　　　　　　　　答案：B

　　在圖片中，男孩手中拿著的應該是畫課本，是可以資源回收再利用的紙張，正確答案為 B。

|單字片語| **leftovers** [ˋlɛft͵ovɚ] 廚餘 / **recyclable** [rɪˋsaɪkləbl] 可回收利用的
　　　　radioactive [͵redɪoˋæktɪv] 有放射性的 / **radiation** [͵redɪˋeʃən] 輻射

Q2

For question two, please look at picture B.

What might the man be telling the woman?
這位男子可能正在對女子說什麼？

A. I can take you for a ride in this car.	A. 我可以用這部車載你去兜風。
B. It ran out of gas.	B. 它（車子）的汽油用完了。
C. There's something wrong with the engine.	C. 引擎出了點問題。
D. You put too much water in it.	D. 你放太多水在裡面了。

詳解　　　　　　　　　　　　　　　　　　　　　答案：C

　　圖片的背景是在汽車維修廠裡，維修員和女車主站在車子旁說話。可以看

到車子的引擎蓋打開，車子下有一攤黑油，可能是引擎有問題，最合理的答案為 C。

<補充說明>

除了說明事情出了問題，something wrong 也可用來形容某人出了狀況。例如：Is there something wrong?（有問題嗎？）、There's something wrong with her today.（她今天有點不對勁。）

Q3

For question three, please look at picture C.

Which of the following statements is correct?
下列敘述哪一個是正確的？

Brand X $22,000　Brand Y $20,000　Brand Z $18,000

A. All the phones cost the same.
B. The price of Brand Y is the lowest.
C. Brand X is much cheaper than Brand Y.
D. Brand Z is the least expensive of all.

A. 所有的電話價格都一樣。
B. 品牌 Y 的價格最低。
C. 品牌 X 比品牌 Y 便宜得多。
D. 品牌 Z 是最不貴的。

詳解　　　　　　　　　　　　　　　　　　　　　　　　答案：D

類似這樣的題目作答時要非常小心，每個選項都要聽清楚，而且必須邊聽邊確認是否與圖片中的資料吻合。選項 A 指出所有的電話價格都一樣，顯然是錯誤的。選項 B 指出品牌 Y 的價錢最低也是錯的，因為最低價格的是品牌 Z。選項 C 指出品牌 X 比品牌 Y 便宜，這也是錯誤的資訊。選項 D 指出品牌 Z 是最不貴的，也就是說最便宜，正確答案為 D。

<補充說明>

為什麼最便宜的英文要說成最不貴呢？其實外國人也很愛面子。說某件商品便宜，似乎表示自己喜歡撿便宜，也代表商品的品質較低，因此外國人喜歡用比較婉轉的方式表達。例如：This is less expensive.（這個比較不貴。）、This is more affordable.（這個比較負擔得起。）、This is better value for money.（這個比較物超所值。）

第 1 回
第 2 回
第 3 回
第 4 回
第 5 回
第 6 回

Q4

For questions four and five, please look at picture D.

Samuel just got off the train. How can he get to the theater?

Samuel 剛從下火車，他要如何到電影院呢？

A. Go down Zhongzheng Road and turn right at 1st Avenue.

B. Go down Zhongzheng Road and turn right at 2nd Avenue.

C. Go down Zhongzheng Road and turn left at 1st Avenue.

D. Go down Zhongzheng Road and turn left at 2nd Avenue.

A. 中正路直走，然後在第一大道右轉。

B. 中正路直走，然後在第二大道右轉。

C. 中正路直走，然後在第一大道左轉。

D. 中正路直走，然後在第二大道左轉。

詳解　　　　　　　　　　　　　　　　　答案：B

　　「電影院」的英文除了 cinema 還有 theater，兩者可以通用。圖片中，要到戲院可由中正路直走然後在第二大道右轉，正確答案為 B。若不確定方向應該是右轉還是左轉，可將考卷轉過來，從中正路直走的話，往下應是右轉。

Q5

For question five, please refer to picture D again.

Which of the following descriptions is true?

以下哪一項描述是正確的？

A. The museum is at the corner of Zhongzheng Road and 1st Avenue.

B. The museum is at the corner of Zhongshan Road and 1st Avenue.

C. The museum is at the corner of Zhongzheng Road and 2nd Avenue.

D. The museum is at the corner of Zhongshan Road and 2nd Avenue.

A. 博物館在中正路和第一大道的轉角。

B. 博物館在中山路和第一大道的轉角。

C. 博物館在中正路和第二大道的轉角。

D. 博物館在中山路和第二大道的轉角。

詳解　　　　　　　　　　　　　　　　　答案：D

　　這題要聽每個選項才能作答。在圖片中，博物館位在右下角，於中山路和第二大道的轉角，正確答案為 D。

第二部分 問答

Q6

I really appreciate what you did for me.
我很感謝你為我所做的一切。

A. No way.
B. Not again.
C. Anytime.
D. All the time.

A. 不可能。
B. 不會再來一次吧。
C. 隨時都可以。
D. 每次都這樣。

詳解　　　　　　　　　　　　　　　　　答案：C

　　日常對話中，除了直接的問句，適當的回應也是很重要的。當對方表示很感謝你，最適合的回應是 Anytime（隨時都可以），答案為 C。Anytime 表示沒問題，下次還是很樂意幫忙你的意思。

補充說明

　　表示不客氣的英文還有：Don't mention it. It's my pleasure.（沒什麼，這是我的榮幸。）

Q7

Can you remind me to give my mom a call?
你可以提醒我打電話給我媽媽嗎？

A. Sure. May I borrow your phone?
B. Sure. When should I do it?
C. Sure. Why don't you do it yourself?
D. Sure. How come she is calling you?

A. 當然可以。你的電話可以借我嗎？
B. 當然可以。我該何時提醒你呢？
C. 當然可以。你為何不自己來？
D. 當然可以。她為何打電話給你？

詳解　　　　　　　　　　　　　　　　　答案：B

　　甲要求乙提醒他要做某件事，最合理的對應回答是「我應該什麼時候提醒你呢？」答案為 B。需要打電話給媽媽的人是甲，因此乙用選項 A 回答「你的電話可以借我嗎？」是不合理的。選項 C 前面已經說 Sure 表示同意，後面卻說「你為何不自己來？」也不合乎常理。選項 D 則是利用 call 跟 calling 來干擾作答者，若沒有聽懂整句的意思可能會被誤導。

第 1 回

第 2 回

第 3 回

第 4 回

第 5 回

第 6 回

Q8

All designer bags are now sold at a special discount.
Hurry while stocks last.
所有名牌包現在有特別優惠。還有存貨時，趕快購買。

A. What are we waiting for?
B. How could you do that?
C. Be my guest!
D. What a shame!

A. 我們還在等什麼？
B. 你怎麼能這麼做？
C. 請便！
D. 真可惜，真遺憾！

詳解   **答案：A**

聽到所有的名牌包現在有特別優惠，最為合理的回應是「我們還在等什麼？」，表示現在就去買，因此答案為 A。

|單字片語| **stock** [stɑk] 存貨；股票

Q9

Are you in favor of spending the vacation in London?
你贊同在倫敦渡假嗎？

A. I am not a British.
B. I am not in England now.
C. I am not up to it.
D. I am not against it.

A. 我不是英國人。
B. 我現在不在英格蘭。
C. 我沒辦法做到。
D. 我並不反對。

詳解   **答案：D**

選項中回答「你贊同在倫敦渡假嗎？」的適當回應只有一個，答案為 D。

|單字片語| **for** [fɔr] 贊成 / **against** [ə'gɛnst] 反對

Q10

Janet has been feeling under the weather lately.
Janet 最近身體有些不適。

A. I will do it whether she likes it or not.

B. I hope she gets well before the exams.

C. I am sure she will come up with something.

D. I believe we can expect fair weather.

A. 無論她喜不喜歡，我都會這麼做。

B. 我希望在考試前她能康復。

C. 我很確定她會想出辦法的。

D. 我相信我們可以期待好天氣。

詳解 　　　　　　　　　　　　　　　　　　　　答案：B

　　英文跟中文一樣，也有所謂的成語和俗語之類的表達方式。under the weather 的意思是「身體有些不舒服」，通常是指感冒了。聽到朋友生病了，最合理的回應是希望她能早日康復，答案為 B。

補充說明

　　寫信給生病的外國朋友時，可以寫上 Get well soon.（祝你早日康復。）

Q11

Why can't you do both tasks at the same time?
為什麼你不能一心二用，同時做兩件事呢？

A. I promise I won't do it again.

B. I will get distracted.

C. I think three is even better.

D. I suppose it's cheaper that way.

A. 我答應以後不會再這樣了。

B. 我會被分心。

C. 我認為三個甚至更好。

D. 我猜想這樣比較便宜。

詳解 　　　　　　　　　　　　　　　　　　　　答案：B

　　如果只聽到 Why can't you...，可能會以為答案是 A，不過聽完整句後，會發現對方並沒有指責的意思，只是在問「為什麼你不能一心二用，同時做兩件事？」最合理的回答是「我不能一心二用，我會被分心。」答案為 B。

補充說明

　　現代社會講求辦事效率，一個常聽到的概念是 multi-tasking，意思是同時可

以完成很多項任務。其含意並不是指一心多用，而是利用妥善的安排，能在最短時間內完成很多事情。例如：把衣服放進洗衣機後開始準備晚餐，在等米飯煮熟的時候洗好衣服，利用等待電飯鍋跳起來的時候把衣服拿去晾乾，這都是multi-tasking。

第1回
第2回
第3回
第4回
第5回
第6回

Q12

Wow! These stamps are at least a hundred years old.
哇！這些郵票至少有一百多年了。

A. I told you they can live for a long time.　A. 我告訴過你，他們可以活很久。
B. It's such a pity.　B. 真是可惜。
C. They must be worth a small fortune.　C. 它們肯定值不少錢。
D. We need to get her a birthday present.　D. 我們需要買生日禮物給她。

詳解　　　　　　　　　　　　　　　　　　　　　**答案：C**

　　一百多年的郵票，照理說應該很值錢，因此合理的回答是「它們肯定值不少錢」，答案為 C。

|單字片語| **make a fortune**（靠某件事）發財/ **make a killing**（在短期內輕易地）大賺一筆

Q13

My car was towed away before I even realized it.
在我還來不及察覺之前，我的車子已經被拖吊了。

A. It is never too late to say sorry.　A. 說對不起永遠不會嫌太晚。
B. I suppose you have to pay a fine.　B. 我猜想你必須要付罰金。
C. Someone told me the car is his.　C. 有人告訴我，這台車子是他的。
D. Maybe you should ride a bike.　D. 或許你應該騎腳踏車。

詳解　　　　　　　　　　　　　　　　　　　　　**答案：B**

　　聽到朋友說他的車子被拖吊，可以同情地安慰他，也可以率直地告訴他後果。這道題目中，符合的回應是指出沒有遵守交通規則的代價，答案為 B。

|單字片語| **tow away** 拖吊 / **pull over**（車輛）駛到路邊 / **break down**（車輛）拋錨

Q14

It's hard to tell who will win the match.
很難去判斷誰會贏得這場比賽。

A. Both players are talented.	A. 兩個球員都很有天分。
B. White goes well with any color.	B. 白色配任何顏色都好看。
C. It's no big deal.	C. 沒什麼大不了的。
D. Let's keep this between ourselves.	D. 我們自己知道就好。

詳解　　　　　　　　　　　　　　　　　　　　　　　答案：A

　　從以上句子可判斷，應該有兩個人一起觀看球賽，甲對乙說「很難判斷誰會贏得這場比賽」，乙可以贊同或反對甲的看法。「兩個球員都很有天分」，表示乙贊同甲的看法，答案為 A。

〈補充說明〉

　　若不想表明立場，可說 It's hard to say.（很難說。）、It's too early to say.（現在說言之過早。）

Q15

I can't stand my job anymore.
我再也受不了我的工作了。

A. Have a seat over here.	A. 請坐這裡。
B. That's the only one left.	B. 只有剩下那個。
C. Let's go over it again.	C. 我們再複習一遍。
D. You had better think twice before you quit.	D. 你辭職之前最好要三思。

詳解　　　　　　　　　　　　　　　　　　　　　　　答案：D

　　當朋友說「我再也受不了我的工作了」，身為朋友的我們應該回應「你辭職之前最好要三思」，答案為 D。

|單字片語| can't stand it anymore、can't take it anymore 再也受不了

第 1 回

第 2 回

第 3 回

第 4 回

第 5 回

第 6 回

第三部分 / 簡短對話

Q16

W: This month's electricity bill has gone through the roof. I will limit the use of the air-conditioners to a maximum of two hours every night.

這個月的電費破表了。我將要把冷氣使用時間限制在每晚最多兩小時。

M: What? I can't sleep without air-conditioning.

什麼？沒有冷氣我睡不著。

W: You will have to get used to it. We didn't even have fans back in the old days, remember?

你將會習慣的。以前我們連電風扇也沒有，記得嗎？

Q: What is the woman trying to tell the man?
這位女子想要告訴男子什麼？

A. He should use the air-conditioner the whole night.
A. 他應該一整晚都吹冷氣。

B. He should learn to appreciate what he has.
B. 他該學習感謝他所擁有的。

C. He should try to stay young and healthy.
C. 他應該保持年輕和健康。

D. He shouldn't use the air-conditioner at all.
D. 他根本不應該使用冷氣。

詳解　　　　　　　　　　　　　　　　　　　　　　**答案：B**

　　說話的女子明確規定冷氣只能吹兩個小時，選項 A 和 D 都是錯誤的。從 in the old days（從前）可得知，以前沒有冷氣可以吹，就連電風扇也沒有。這位女子的意思是做人要懂得惜福，並珍惜眼前擁有的，答案為 B。

〈補充說明〉

　　use to 有三種用法，與其死背，不如用句子來理解。

1. used to V 表示「以前經常做，現在沒有做」

　　He **used to** smoke but he quit it last year.　他以前抽菸，但是去年戒掉了。

2. be used to V-ing 表示「習慣」

　　He **is used to** getting up late.　他習慣很晚起床。

3. use...to V 表示「用…來…」

　　He **used** the paper **to** make a boat.　他用那張紙來摺船。

Q17

W: Please do not bring unpaid items beyond this point. The cashier is over there.　請不要把尚未結帳的商品帶出去。收銀員在那裡。

M: But I need to visit the bathroom and I am not done with my shopping yet. 但是我需要去廁所，而且我還有東西要買。

W: In that case, I would be glad to look after the merchandise for you, sir. 先生，這樣的話，我很樂意幫您保管商品。

Q: What does the woman suggest the man do?
這位女子建議男子做什麼？

A. Let her take care of his belongings. A. 讓她保管他的隨身物品。
B. Pay for the items before leaving the store. B. 在離開商店前先付款。
C. Leave the things he wants to buy with her. C. 把他要買的東西放在她那裡。
D. Take the merchandise to the bathroom. D. 把商品帶到廁所。

詳解　　　　　　　　　　　　　　　　　　　　　　　　　　　**答案：C**

　　從對話中可想像出，廁所的位置在商店外，未結帳的商品不能帶去廁所，選項 D 不合常理。說話的女子是店員，男子是顧客，男子的隨身物品並不是商店的物品，不需要交給店員保管，選項 A 是錯誤的。男子已經表示他還想繼續購物，照理說應該等東西買齊了再一次結帳，選項 B 也是錯誤的。因此，最為合理的答案是先把要買的東西放在店員那裡，上完廁所再繼續購物，答案為 C。

I單字片語I belongings [bə'lɔŋɪŋz] 隨身物品；財物 / a sense of belonging 歸屬感

Q18

W: This building is considered the landmark of Rome. Until today, some people are still puzzled by the wisdom of the ancient Romans. 這棟建築被認為是羅馬的地標。直到今天，古代羅馬人的智慧對有些人來說還是個謎。

M: How long ago was it built? 這是多久以前建造的？

W: It can be dated back to 700 B.C. 這可以追溯到西元前 700 年。

Q: What is the woman's profession?
這位女子的職業是什麼？

A. She is a guide. A. 她是一名導遊。
B. She is an accountant. B. 她是一名會計師。
C. She is a diplomat. C. 她是一位外交官。
D. She is an interior designer. D. 她是一位室內設計師。

詳解　　　　　　　　　　　　　　　　　　　　　　　　　　　**答案：A**

　　從四個選項可以得知，這題要問的是說話者的職業。從 building（建築），

landmark（地標）和 ancient（古代），可推斷出這位女子的職業是導遊，答案
為 A。

|單字片語| can be dated back to、can be traced back to 可追溯到

第1回
第2回
第3回
第4回
第5回
第6回

Q19

W: Good morning, Mr. Anderson. I received your email, but I think you forgot to attach the file that you need me to print out.
　　Anderson 先生，早安。我收到了您的電子郵件，但是我想你好像忘了附上您要我列印的檔案。

M: Did I? I guess I still need my morning coffee after all. You'll have it in a minute.
　　是嗎？我猜我早上還是需要一杯咖啡。一分鐘後馬上給你

W: Thank you.　謝謝。

Q: What's the matter with the man?　這位男子怎麼了？
A. He needs more time to finish his work.　A. 他需要更多時間完成他的工作。
B. He received a strange email.　B. 他收到一封奇怪的電子郵件。
C. He's a little absent-minded this morning.　C. 他今天早上有一點健忘。
D. He has a poor sense of humor.　D. 他的幽默感很差。

詳解　　　　　　　　　　　　　　　　　　　　　　　　　**答案：C**

　　從說話者的談話內容，可猜想這位男子可能是女子的雇主或客戶。男子忘了在電子郵件中附上要列印的檔案，是自己的疏失。西方人喜歡用幽默的方式來化解尷尬，當男子說自己早上沒喝咖啡，意思是因為他沒靠咖啡提神，所以才忘東忘西的，答案為 C。從對話中可以知道，男子會用幽默感化解尷尬，選項 D 是錯誤的。

|單字片語| **absent-minded** [ˈæbsntˈmaɪndɪd] 健忘的；心不在焉的
　　　　 open-minded [ˈopənˈmaɪndɪd] 能接受新思想的
　　　　 narrow-minded [ˈnæroˈmaɪndɪd] 心胸狹窄的

Q20

M: Let me explain how to stop a wound from bleeding. Apply a certain amount of pressure on the wound with your palms.
　　讓我解釋如何讓傷口止血。用你的手掌在傷口處用一點力道按壓。

W: Do we need to press down and let go?　我們需要壓下去、然後放手嗎？

M: No. Just apply pressure until the bleeding stops.
　　不。只要保持一定的壓力，直到不再流血為止。

Q: What is the woman doing?　這位女子在做什麼？

A. Doing aerobics.　　　　　　　A. 在做有氧健身操。
B. Having an operation.　　　　　B. 在動手術。
C. Applying makeup.　　　　　　C. 在化妝。
D. Taking a first aid course.　　　D. 在上急救課程。

詳解　　　　　　　　　　　　　　　　　　　　　　答案：D

　　從四個選項可猜測，這題要問的是說話者在做什麼。從關鍵詞 wound（傷口）和 bleeding（流血），可判斷說話者正在上急救課程，答案為 D。

|單字片語| **aid** [ed] 幫助；輔助器材 / **first aid** 急救 / **hearing aid** 助聽器

Q21

W: Career planning should be taken seriously before entering university.
　　在進入大學之前，就應該認真做職涯規畫。

M: What if I am not sure where my interests lie?
　　假設我不確定我的興趣在哪裡呢？

W: You can't major in something just for the sake of getting a degree.
　　你不能只是為了獲得文憑而主修某個科系。

Q: What are the speakers discussing?
說話者在談論什麼？

A. The man's future profession.　　A. 這位男子未來的職業。
B. The man's college life.　　　　B. 這位男子的大學生活。
C. The man's qualifications.　　　C. 這位男子的學歷資格。
D. The man's health condition.　　D. 這位男子的健康狀況。

詳解　　　　　　　　　　　　　　　　　　　　　　答案：A

　　從對話中的關鍵詞 career planning（生涯規畫）可判斷，說話者正在談論未來的職業，答案為 A。對話中雖然提到了與大學有關的單字，但男子還未進大學，所以自然沒有大學生活，因此 B 是錯誤的。而雖然有提到學歷資格，但主要的重點是要男子「先確定未來的職業走向，再來選擇學歷資格」，因此 A 是比 C 更好的選項。

〈補充說明〉

　　sake 是口語中常聽到單字，然而用法有些複雜，有必要解釋一下，直接看例句比較清楚，例句：

I did this for your sake. 我這麼做都是為了你。
For your own sake, quit smoking. 為了你自己好，戒菸吧。
Don't do it for the sake of doing it. 不要只是為了做而做。

Q22

M: Miss. You got to pull over. You got a flat tire.
小姐。你必須靠路邊停。你的輪胎沒氣了。

W: Oh no! What should I do? 糟了！我該怎麼辦？

M: You're in luck. You have a spare tire and I am a mechanic.
你很幸運。你有個備用輪胎，而我是技師。

Q: **What will the man probably do next?**
接下來這位男子應該會做什麼？

A. Send the woman to the hospital.
B. Give the woman a massage.
C. Take the woman home.
D. Help the woman fix her car.

A. 送這位女子到醫院。
B. 給這位女子按摩。
C. 帶這位女子回家。
D. 幫這位女子維修她的車子。

詳解

答案：D

第一句聽到 pull over（把車開到路邊），剛開始或許會以為這位男子是警察，後來男子提到他是技師（mechanic）。既然車子已經停靠在路邊，這位男子接下來應該會幫這位女子換輪胎，答案為 D。

I單字片語I **machine** [məˋʃin] 機器 / **mechanic** [məˋkænɪk] 技師

Q23

M: Mutual respect is very important between couples. Never criticize your husband in public.
夫妻之間互相尊重是非常重要的。千萬別在大庭廣眾下批評你的丈夫。

W: I see. But sometimes I was only offering him some suggestions.
我明白。但是有時候我只是給他一些建議。

M: It's better to let him ask for them instead of telling him what to do all the time.
讓他自己來問會比較好，而不是每次都告訴他要做什麼。

第1回
第2回
第3回
第4回
第5回
第6回

Q: What is the man's occupation?
這位男子的職業是什麼？

A. A marriage counselor.
B. A fitness instructor.
C. A publicity officer.
D. A travel agent.

A. 一名婚姻輔導員。
B. 一名健身教練。
C. 一名負責宣傳的人員。
D. 一名旅行社的職員。

Q24

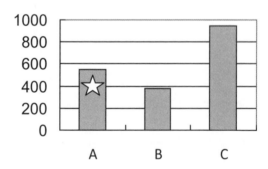

M: I was surprised by some natural disaster statistics over the past 50 years.
我對過去 50 年來的一些自然災害統計資料感到驚訝。

W: Sound interesting. What did you find?　聽起來很有趣，你發現了什麼？

M: Before I read them, I thought there should be plenty of volcanic eruptions. But I found that floods were greater.
在我閱讀之前，我認為應該有很多火山爆發，但是我發現洪災更多。

W: Really? How about tornadoes? It should be quite a number.
真的嗎？那龍捲風如何呢？數量應該相當多。

M: Well, the amount was like volcanic eruptions. In fact, other natural disasters occurred far less frequently than thunderstorms.
嗯，數量和火山爆發相似。事實上，其他自然災害的發生頻率遠低於大雷雨。

第 1 回

第 2 回

第 3 回

第 4 回

第 5 回

第 6 回

Q: **Look at the bar graph. What does the rectangular bar marked with a star refer to?**
請看長條圖，標示著星星的長條指的是甚麼？

A. The floods.

B. The thunderstorms.

C. The volcano eruption.

D. The tornadoes.

A. 洪水。

B. 大雷雨。

C. 火山爆發。

D. 龍捲風。

詳解

答案：A

　　在聽到題目前，從選項中可以猜測題目跟自然災害相關，因此聽敘述時要注意各個自然災害可能對應在長條圖上的位置。整段對話沒有直接表達各種災害的數量，但是從 I thought there should be plenty of volcano eruption. But I found that floods were greater. 可以知道洪水多於火山爆發。接著，從How did tornadoes go? Well, the amount was like volcano eruption. 可以知道龍捲風和火山爆發一樣很少發生。最後，從 other natural disasters occurred far less frequently than thunderstorms. 可以知道雷暴雨的次數多於其他自然災害很多。從以上的資訊可以推論出，長條圖上最多的是雷暴雨，洪水次之，最少的是火山爆發和龍捲風。因此長條圖上有星星標記的是洪水，答案為 A。

Movie Schedule
電影時刻表

Arch (Sci-fi) 拱門（科幻片）	09:05 – 10:55
Competitor (Animated) 競爭對手（動畫片）	11:05 – 13:05
Leopard (Action) 豹（動作片）	13:05 – 15:05
The Horizon (Horror) 地平線（恐怖片）	15:15 – 17:05

W: It's kind of exhausting after a long week. I'm planning on seeing a movie tomorrow. Would you like to come?
在漫長的一週後有點累。我打算明天去看電影。你想要來嗎？

M: Why not? Bruce Johnson's latest Sci-fi movie has been released. Are you interested?
何不呢？Bruce Johnson 最新的科幻電影上映了。你有興趣嗎？

W: Sure. But I don't want to get up before ten. I think we can have brunch first.
當然。但是我不想在 10 點之前起床。我想我們可以先吃早午餐。

M: Good idea. But my part-time job starts at 5 p.m. Also, animated films aren't my style. 好主意。但是我的兼職工作是從下午 5 點開始。而且，動畫電影不是我的風格。

W: Don't worry about it. We can see the movie right after the meal. 不用擔心。飯後我們可以接著去看電影。

M: Great. I will pick you up at your apartment. 太好了。我會到你的公寓接你。

Q: Look at the movie schedule. Which movie will the speakers most likely see?
請看電影時間表，說話者最有可能是看哪一部電影？

A. Arch.   A. 拱門。
B. Competitor.   B. 競爭對手。
C. Leopard.   C. 豹。
D. The Horizon.   D. 地平線。

詳解   答案：C

　　在聽到敘述前，從電影時刻表和選項可以猜測題目跟電影相關，所以聽敘述之前要注意電影時刻表上四部電影的個別資訊，並推論說話者的意思和觀點，才能知道說話者最後選擇的電影。首先，女子提到 But I don't want to get up before te. 就可以先刪除選項 A。女子又提到 I think we can have brunch first. 以及男子說 Also, animated film isn't my style，就可以刪去選項 B。接著男子說 my part-time job starts at 5 p.m.，就可以刪去選項 D。由此推論出，他們最有可能看的電影是 Leopard，答案為 C。

Q26

M: If the life that you used to live is considered abnormal in the new country, it can easily cause certain symptoms. You may suffer from headaches or stomachaches, isolation, sleeping and eating disturbances, or critical reactions to the host culture. The above physical and emotional discomfort can be described as culture shock.

如果你過去的生活方式在新居住的國家被認為是不正常的，這可能容易引起某些症狀。你可能會承受頭痛或胃痛、孤立感、睡眠和進食障礙，或對新文化的批判反應。上述身體和情緒上的不適可以被稱為文化衝擊。

Q: **Who most likely is the audience?**
誰最有可能是聽眾？

A. New doctors.　　　　　　　A. 新來的醫生。
B. New researchers.　　　　　B. 新來的研究人員。
C. New residents.　　　　　　C. 新住民。
D. New hosts.　　　　　　　　D. 新主人。

詳解　　　　　　　　　　　　　　　　　　　　**答案：C**

　　在聽到敘述前，從選項可以猜測可能有四種不同身分的人。所以，聽敘述時要注意說話者所說與這些人相關的內容。從說話者的第一句 If the lifeway that you used to live is considered abnormal in the new country, it can easily cause certain symptoms. 以及第二句 You may suffer from headaches or stomachaches… 可知，聽眾剛移居到另一個國家，而且是在文化上尚未融入當地的新住民，答案為 C。

|單字片語| **symptom** [ˋsɪmptəm] 症狀 / **isolation** [͵aɪsļˋeʃən] 孤立
　　　　　host culture 新文化

Q27

W: Much of Taiwan is expected to receive rain or thunderstorms over the next few days. For those of you planning outdoor activities over the weekend, you might want to change your plans. As the front passes through, rainfall in central and southern Taiwan could increase. The rain should let up by Sunday afternoon.

在未來幾天台灣大部分地區預期會下雨或大雷雨。對於那些計劃在周末進行戶外活動的人，您可能需要更改您的計畫。由於鋒面經過，台灣中部和南部的降雨量可能會增加。應該在星期天下午之前會停止下雨。

Q: Which kind of activities would be least likely to be affected?
哪一種活動較不可能被影響？

A. A mall anniversary sale.
B. A beach birthday party.
C. An outdoor flea market.
D. A soccer match.

A. 購物中心周年慶。
B. 海灘生日派對。
C. 戶外跳蚤市集。
D. 足球比賽。

答案：A

在聽到敘述前，從選項可以看到有四種不同的活動。所以，聽敘述時要注意說話者提到與活動相關的內容。從說話者的 For those of you planning outdoor activities over the weekend, you might want to change your plan. 可以知道，說話者提醒聽眾週末的天氣狀況不佳，會影響戶外活動，選項中不在戶外舉辦的「購物中心週年慶」是最不可能受到影響的活動，答案為 A。

Q28

M: Hi, Ashley. This is Harris. I got accepted at the University of Pennsylvania, but my family wasn't able to afford my full tuition and expenses. So, I'm currently working on the application for a full academic scholarship. I heard that you were awarded one last year. I wonder if you could share your experience with me.

嗨，Ashley。我是 Harris。我錄取賓夕法尼亞大學了，但我的家人無法負擔我全部學費和支出。因此，我目前正在申請全額獎學金。聽說你去年獲得一個獎學金。我想知道你是否可以與我分享你的經驗。

Q: What is the message for?
這則訊息是為了什麼？

A. To share the good news.
B. To accept an offer.
C. To deliver advice.
D. To request assistance.

A. 分享好消息。
B. 接受邀約。
C. 提供建議。
D. 請求協助。

答案：D

在聽到敘述前，從選項可以猜測敘述會與四種不同的事情有關。而說話者可能一開始就說出答案，也有可能在最後才說出。因此，聆聽時要注意從頭到尾，專心聆聽。從說話者的留言訊息中，最後一句 I wonder if you could share your experience with me. 可以理解 Harris 在請求 Ashley 的協助，答案為 D。

第 1 回
第 2 回
第 3 回
第 4 回
第 5 回
第 6 回

Q29

W: If the pressure decreases, you should put on an oxygen mask at once. Pull it tightly toward you, place it over your nose and mouth, place the elastic band around the back of your head, and breathe normally. It is important to secure your mask before helping someone else.

如果壓力降低，你應該立即佩戴氧氣面罩。將其緊緊拉向自己，完全包覆住口、鼻，將鬆緊帶綁在頭後部，並正常呼吸。在幫助他人之前，請務必要戴好氧氣面罩。

Q: **What is the purpose of this announcement?**
這段通知的目的是什麼？

A. To educate people about reducing air pressure.　A. 教育人們關於氣壓減低。
B. To force people put on an oxygen mask.　B. 強迫人們戴上氧氣面罩。
C. To guide people on how to use an oxygen mask.　C. 指導人們如何使用氧氣面罩。
D. To request people to assist others.　D. 要求人們去協助其他人。

詳解　　　　　　　　　　　　　　　　　　　　　　　　**答案：C**

　　在聽到敘述前，從選項可以猜測是和氧氣面罩有關。因此，聽敘述時要注意有關氧氣面罩的重要資訊。從說話者的通知訊息中，第一句 If the pressure decreases, you should wear an oxygen mask at once. 接著介紹使用氧氣面罩的步驟。由此可以知道，這是飛機上使用氧氣面罩的說明，答案為 C。

|單字片語| **elastic** [ɪˈlæstɪk] 有彈性的

Q30

M: Attention all faculty and students. An earthquake disaster drill will take place on National Disaster Prevention Day. The alarm messages will be connected to television sets in each classroom to broadcast emergency information at 9:21 a.m. By receiving the alert, everyone should drop, cover, and hold on. Everyone should learn how to take simple steps to strengthen disaster management capacity.

全體教職員及學生注意。全國防災日將進行一場地震防災演習。警報訊息將會連接到每間教室的電視機上，在上午 9:21 廣播緊急資訊。在收到警報的時候，每個人都應該蹲下、掩護、穩住動作。每個人都應該學會運用簡單的步驟來增強災害應變能力。

Q: What are all students requested to do during the drill?
在演習期間，所有學生被要求做什麼？

A. Watch TV programs.
B. Seek safe cover.
C. Find television sets.
D. Cover the alarm.

A. 觀看電視節目。
B. 尋求安全掩護。
C. 尋找電視機組。
D. 蓋住警報器。

詳解

答案：B

　　這段敘述是校內廣播，而四個選項都是不同的動作指令。廣播中提到 An earthquake disaster drill will take place on the National Disaster Prevention Day. 所以，聽敘述時要注意地震防災演習中的重要資訊。從說話者在廣播中提到 By receiving the alert, everyone should drop, cover, and hold on，清楚說明全體教職員工在收到警報訊息時應該做的事，也就是避難步驟：蹲下、掩護、穩住動作，答案為 B。

|單字片語| **disaster drill** 災難演習 / **drop, cover, hold on** 蹲下，掩護，穩住

Q31

W: After stirring the pasta with water in the bowl of the pressure cooker, you need to place a rack on top of the pasta. Then, mix the tomatoes, garlic, red pepper flakes, and 1/4 teaspoon of salt together in a round cake pan. Put the pan on the rack, seal and lock the lid. Select high pressure and 3 minutes of cook time.

在壓力鍋的碗中將義大利麵加水攪拌後，你需要在義大利麵上放一個架子。接著，在圓形蛋糕盤中將番茄、大蒜、紅辣椒片和 1/4 茶匙的鹽混合在一起。將盤子放在架子上，蓋子蓋緊並鎖住。選擇高壓以及烹飪時間 3 分鐘。

Q: Which is the first step in pasta cooking?
烹煮義大利麵的第一步是什麼？

A. Combine water and the pasta.
B. Mix together the pasta with tomatoes.
C. Place a rack in the pressure cooker.
D. Set the time of cooking.

A. 混合水和義大利麵。
B. 將義大利麵和番茄混合在一起。
C. 放一個架子到壓力鍋中。
D. 設定烹煮時間。

詳解

　　這段敘述是煮義大利麵的教學，四個選項均為烹煮的步驟。聽敘述時要注意煮義大利麵的各個步驟。從說話者的教學中提到 After stirring the pasta with water in the bowl of the pressure cooker, you need to place a rack above the pasta，可以知道應該第一個步驟是義大利麵加水在壓力鍋的碗中攪拌，答案為 A。

|單字片語| **rack** [ræk] 架子 / **flake** [flek] 小薄片

Q32

M:　If you want an activity tracker which looks like a smart watch, this is your best choice. It tracks all of your physical activity and monitors your health fitness features. Moreover, it also goes beyond the basics such as heart rate zone notifications. There is an integrated GPS tracking, so you can monitor your runs and walks.

　　如果你想要一支看起來像智慧手錶的運動追蹤手環，這是你的最佳選擇。它會追蹤你所有的身體活動並監測你的健康健身特點。此外，它超越基本功能，例如：心跳區通知。內建全球衛星定位系統追蹤，因此你可以監測自己跑步和走路的狀況。

Q: What is the speaker presenting?
說話者正在展示什麼？

A. A GPS watch.
B. A fancy watch.
C. A workout class.
D. A fitness tracker.

A. 全球衛星定位系統手錶。
B. 時髦的手錶。
C. 健身課程。
D. 運動追蹤手環。

詳解

　　這則廣告的四個選項都是和手錶及健身相關的商品，因此可推測談話內容和手錶及健身相關。聽敘述時需注意選項內容出現的關鍵句。從說話者的第一句話 If you want an activity tracker which looks like a smart watch, this is your best choice. 可以知道這是追蹤運動的商品，後面的敘述也講述各個追蹤身體資訊的功能，答案為 D。

Q33

W:　It is not hard, but the whole point of a zipper is to keep the teeth in sync. When the teeth are evenly together, try raising the zipper. If you cannot do that, then use a flat head screwdriver to lift the opening wider. Or you may replace a new one. It costs less to do this yourself if you know how to sew things.

這並不難，拉鍊的整個重點是在使拉鍊齒保持同步。當鍊齒均勻地排列在一起時，試著將拉鍊拉起來。如果你無法這樣做，請使用螺絲起子將開口拉開。或者你可以更換一個新的拉鍊。如果你知道如何縫製東西，自己動手做的費用就會較低。

Q: Who will be interested in the short talk?
誰會對這則簡短談話感興趣？

A. A person who is screwing something. A. 一個正在擰東西的人。
B. A person who is raising something. B. 一個正在舉起東西的人。
C. A person who is fixing something. C. 一個正在修理東西的人。
D. A person who is sewing something. D. 一個正在縫東西的人。

詳解　　　　　　　　　　　　　　　　　　　　　　　　　答案：C

在這則談話中，四個選項均和人正在做的一件事有關，因此，聽敘述時需注意所述內容的目的，才能知道答案。從說話者提到 It is not hard, but the whole point of a zipper is to keep the teeth in sync，接著提到 Try raising the zipper. Use a screwdriver to lift the opening wider，可知對這則簡短談話感興趣的人應該是正在修理東西的人，答案為 C。

Q34

March 三月

Sun. 星期日	
Mon. 星期一	1　Online market meeting　線上市場會議
Tue. 星期二	2　Product marketing promotion　產品行銷推廣
Wed. 星期三	3　Market research survey　市場研究調查
Thu. 星期四	4　Visit the North Market　參觀北方市場
Fri. 星期五	5　Visit the Nice Market　參觀美好市場
Sat. 星期六	6

M: Earlier, you texted me to rearrange the online meeting time for two days later. I am afraid my schedule will be full by then. Actually, I will be occupied all week. How about putting it off until the next week? If you would still like to hold the meeting during the first week of March, I can postpone one market visit plan by four days.

稍早你傳訊息給我，要把線上會議時間重新安排在兩天後。恐怕我的時間表到那時候已經滿了。實際上，我整週都排滿了，延後到下週如何呢？如果你仍然想在三月的第一周舉行會議，我可以將一個市場參觀計畫延遲四天。

第1回
第2回
第3回
第4回
第5回
第6回

Q: What plan does the speaker already have for the postponed date?
說話者在延遲的日期已經有什麼計畫？

A. Product marketing promotion.
B. Market research survey.
C. Visit the North Market.
D. Visit the Nice Market.

A. 產品行銷推廣。
B. 市場研究調查。
C. 參觀北方市場。
D. 參觀美好市場。

詳解

答案：B

　　在聽到敘述前，從圖表和選項可以猜測題目跟計畫項目與日程表相關，所以，聽敘述時要注意聽計畫項目的細節，說話者第一句提到 Earlier, you texted me to rearrange the online meeting time to two days later，可以知道說話者原本排的會議時間會被延到原計畫的兩天後。對照日曆，那一天的計畫是 Market research survey。可以推論出，說話者在推遲日期已經排的計畫為是市場研究調查，答案為 B。

Q35

Park Ave. West 公園大道西側 ｜ North street 北街 ｜ Main street 主街 ｜ South street 南街 ｜ Park Ave. East 公園大道東側

W: Road work will be carried out along Park Avenue, from North Street to South Street. The work also includes improvement to sidewalks along this section. The project will begin on February tenth and end before April tenth. The road will be closed while work is in progress, so it will be a temporary zone with no-parking. Thank you for your cooperation and patience throughout the construction period.

道路施工將沿著公園大道，從北街到南街進行。這項工程也包括改善沿著這個區域的人行道。這項計畫將從 2 月 10 日開始，並到 4 月 10 日之前結束。作業進行時，道路將會被封閉，因此它將是一個禁止停車的臨時區域。感謝您在整個施工期間的合作與耐心。

Q: Which road will be shut down during the project?
在工程期間哪一條路將會被關閉？

A. North street.

B. Main street.

C. South street.

D. Park Ave. East.

A. 北街。

B. 主街。

C. 南街。

D. 公園大道東側。

詳解   **答案：D**

　　在聽到題目前，從地圖和選項可以猜測題目跟四條道路相關，因此聽敘述時要注意和道路相關的資訊。說話者在第一句提到 Road work will be carried out along Park Avenue, from North Street to South Street. 表示施工路段為是在公園大道的東側或西側。而第四句 The road will be closed while work in progress... 表示工程進行時，道路將被封閉。選項中只有 D 才有包含公園大道，答案為 D。

初試 閱讀測驗 解析

\第一部分/ 詞彙

Q1

He can't even walk properly when he is drunk, _____ drive.

在他喝醉的時候，他根本連好好走路都不行，更別說開車了。

A. let alone
B. save for
C. apart from
D. inasmuch as

詳解　　　　　　　　　　　　　　　　　　　　　**答案：A**

　　試題中的動作為走路和開車，整個句意是喝醉後連走路都有問題，開車就更不用說了，因此答案為 A. let alone（更別說）。

補充說明

　　「除外」跟「除此之外」，有時候會因為中文的翻譯而造成誤解。要把 save for 理解為「除了…以外」，表示這是例外，把 apart from 理解為「除了…還有」，表示兩者都有，請看以下例句：

Move everything outside **save for** the chairs.
把每樣東西都搬到外面，除了椅子以外。
Move everything outside **except** the chairs.
把每樣東西搬到外面，除了椅子以外。
Apart from some chairs and a table, we need to get a sofa.
除了一些椅子和一張桌子，我們還需要買一套沙發。
Besides some chairs and a table, we need to get a sofa.
除了一些椅子和一張桌子，我們還需要買一套沙發。

|單字片語| **save for** 除了…之外 / **apart from** 除了…還有 / **inasmuch as** 由於

Q2

It was after years of _____ research that the drug was made available to the public.

經過了多年的大規模研究，這種藥物才提供給大眾使用。

A. conducive
B. extensive
C. productive
D. subjective

　　和 research（研究）搭配最合理的單字是 extensive（大規模的），藥物需要經過大規模的研究和臨床測試才能上架供大眾使用。

I單字片語I **conducive** [kən'djusɪv] 有幫助的 / **productive** [prə'dʌktɪv] 生產的
subjective [səb'dʒɛktɪv] 主觀的

Q3

Traffic congestions have become a common scene as a new underground train _____ is being constructed.

由於新的地下火車總站正在建造中，交通阻塞已經成為常見的景象。

A. permission
B. foundation
C. terminal
D. landscape

　　這題的句意是某個建築正在建造，因此選項 A 和 D 都是錯誤的。而選項 C foundation 也不能和 train 搭配，因此選項 C 也是錯誤的。只有選項 B 是正確的，意思是火車總站（train terminal）正在被建造。

補充說明

　　這題句子中也出現被動語態進行式，以下是被動語態各種時態的例句：
A new bridge was constructed. 一座新的橋被建造了。
The workers are constructing a new bridge. 工人正在建造一座新的橋。
A new bridge is being constructed. 一座新的橋正在被建造中。
A new bridge has been constructed so the old one will be demolished.
一座新的橋已經被建造所以舊的將會被拆除。

I單字片語I **congestion** [kən'dʒɛstʃən] 擁塞 / **permission** [pə'mɪʃən] 允許
foundation [faʊn'deʃən] 建立，創辦 / **landscape** ['lænd,skep] 風景

Q4

Someone with a good command of English who is also _____ in another foreign language such as French or German is more suited for this position.

一個精通英文，同時另一種外語也很流利的人，例如法文或德文，更適合這個職位。

A. encouraging
B. competitive
C. reasonable
D. fluent

第 1 回

第 2 回

第 3 回

第 4 回

第 5 回

第 6 回

 詳解　　　　　　　　　　　　　　　　　　　　　　**答案：D**

　　「a good command of 某個語言」是「精通某種語言」的意思，而 fluent 也是指語言流利的意思。精通外語的人具有競爭力（competitive），公司開出來的條件很合理（reasonable），但這些都不是答案。encouraging 則是來形容某些測試的結果（results）「令人感到樂觀」，特別是醫療方面的測試結果，還有某項產品的銷售數字（sales figures）。

|單字片語| **encouraging** [ɪnˈkɝɪdʒɪŋ] 令人鼓舞的 / **competitive** [kəmˈpɛtətɪv] 競爭的
　　　　reasonable [ˈriznəbl] 合理的；講道理的

Q5

Please note that the deadline for the essay competition is this Friday. Late _____ will not be entertained.

請注意作文比賽的截止日期是這個星期五。遲交的參賽作品都不會被考慮

A. fragments
B. entries
C. emergencies
D. drawbacks

詳解　　　　　　　　　　　　　　　　　　　　　　**答案：B**

　　從 essay competition（作文比賽）這個關鍵詞可以推斷，答案跟作品有關，entry 平常當作「參加；入口」的意思，但這裡則是指「參賽作品」，句意是超過截止日期才交上的參賽作品將不被考慮。

|單字片語| **fragment** [ˈfræɡmənt] 碎片 / **emergency** [ɪˈmɝdʒənsɪ] 緊急情況
　　　　drawback [ˈdrɔˌbæk] 缺點

補充說明

entertainment　本來是指「娛樂」，不過 entertain 也有「應酬他人；接受」的意思。
What do you do for entertainment?　你做什麼來當作娛樂？
The host has to keep the guests entertained.　主持人必須款待嘉賓。
Requests for a refund without a receipt will not be entertained.
我們不會接受沒有收據卻要求退費的要求。

Q6

The Statue of Liberty was given to the United States by France and it is a _____ of freedom.

自由女神像是法國給予美國的，它是自由的象徵。

A. bribery
B. refuge
C. fountain
D. symbol

　　freedom 和 liberty 都是「自由」，自由女神像自然是自由的「象徵（symbol）」，答案為 D。

|單字片語| **bribery** [`braɪbərɪ] 賄賂 / **refuge** [`rɛfjʊdʒ] 避風港；避難所 / **refugee** [ˌrɛfjʊ`dʒi] 難民 **fountain** [`faʊntɪn] 泉源；噴泉 / **foundation** [faʊn`deʃən] 基礎

Q7

According to doctors, exercising on a/an _____ basis is the most effective way to lose weight.

根據醫生的說法，固定時間運動是減重最有效的方法。

A. occasional　　　　　　　　B. particular
C. regular　　　　　　　　　　D. nominal

　　運動要定時、固定，不能三天打魚兩天曬網，on a regular basis 是指「定期做某件事」。每天會做的事情可以用 on a daily basis 來表達，先到先服務（誰先來就優先）的英文則是 on a first-come-first-serve basis。

|單字片語| **occasional** [ə`keʒənl] 偶爾的 / **particular** [pə`tɪkjələ] 特定的 **nominal** [`nɑmənl] 名義上的

Q8

Law enforcement officers are required to _____ orders without any sympathy or fear.

執法人員必須在沒有任何同情心或恐懼下執行命令。

A. modify　　　　　　　　　　B. execute
C. withhold　　　　　　　　　　D. abandon

　　從關鍵詞 order（命令），可知道搭配的單字是 execute（執行），公司裡面的 executive 指的是「行政長官」，換句話說也就是公司「決策並執行的人」。另外，force 是「迫使」，enforce 是「執行」。

|單字片語| **modify** [`mɑdəˌfaɪ] 修改 / **withhold** [wɪð`hold] 抑制；留住 **abandon** [ə`bændən] 拋棄；放棄

第 1 回
第 2 回
第 3 回
第 4 回
第 5 回
第 6 回

Q9

The patient's condition _____ within such a short span of time that his family feared for the worst.

病人的情況在如此短的時間內惡化，以至於家屬害怕最壞的情形會發生。

A. worsened
B. exhausted
C. alleviated
D. improved

詳解

答案：A

從 feared for the worst（害怕最壞的情形會發生），可知道病人的病情不樂觀。選項 C 和 D 是正面意思的單字，不可能是答案。雖然選項 B exhausted（筋疲力盡）有負面的意思，卻不能和 condition（病情）搭配，所以答案為 A。worse 是 bad 的比較級，是形容詞。某些形容詞後面可以加 -en，加了 -en 的形容詞 worsen 則變成動詞。其他例子還有 light 變 lighten（減輕）和 dark 變 darken（變暗）。

I單字片語I **exhaust** [ɪɡˋzɔst] 使精疲力盡 / **alleviate** [əˋliviˏet] 減輕；緩和
improve [ɪmˋpruv] 改善

Q10

My mom _____ the luggage to double-check if we have everything we need for the trip.

我母親仔細檢查行李以再次確認，我們是否有旅程所需要的所有東西。

A. went on
B. went into
C. went around
D. went through

詳解

答案：D

動詞片語的用法變化很多，不管是寫作或對話，都經常用到。問題是，動詞片語很難像一般單字那樣背起來，必須用情境來背比較有效。本題的題意顯然是指「把行李檢查一遍」，所以答案應為 D，而 go through sth 的意思是「仔細檢查某物」。

例句

They **went on** singing though it was almost midnight.
雖然快要午夜了，他們還是繼續唱歌。
We have to agree on this deal before I **go into** the details.
在我談論細節之前，我們必須先同意這筆交易。
It is said that money makes the world **go around**.
據說錢能讓這個世界運轉。

第二部分 / 段落填空

Questions 11-15

Could some of the world's ancient civilizations (11) happen to be aliens instead of humans? That would explain the high level of sophisticated technology they possessed thousands of years ago. If such an assumption is plausible, there is more reason to believe that aliens used to (12) exist on earth. A lot of rumors have been circulated online concerning the highly classified government facility known as Area 51. Area 51 might just be a normal military site and it might not. However, so far there is not a single piece of solid evidence to (13) confirm the suspicions. Many believed that there is more than meets the eye since the US government refused to discuss the matter on numerous (14) occasions. The base has long been a very closely-guarded secret, with lots of "trespassers will be shot" signs around the base itself and a large no-fly zone surrounding it. (15) According to conspiracy theorists, the base allegedly features elaborate underground labs and hidden tunnels.

有些世界古代文明有可能剛好是外星人而不是人類嗎？這就能解釋他們在數千年前就擁有高階的精密科技。如果這樣的假設貌似真實，就有更多理由去相信外星人曾經存在於地球上。在網路上已經流傳了許多謠言，有關政府列為高級機密的設施—第 51 區。第 51 區可能只是一個普通的軍事基地，也可能不是。然而，到目前為止沒有任何一個充份的證據能證實這些懷疑。因為美國政府在很多場合都拒絕談論這件事，許多人相信其中必有不為人知的內情。這個基地一直以來是被嚴加看守的祕密，本身周圍有許多「擅闖者格殺勿論」的警示牌，還有基地上空的一大片的禁飛區。根據陰謀論理論家說法，這個基地據說有精密的地下實驗室和隱藏隧道。

  Q11

A. seem to be   B. claim to be
C. happen to be   D. occur to be

詳解   答案：C

happen 原本是「發生」的意思，不過 happen to 則是「剛好…」，用在疑問

句表示是否有可能。世界古代文明有可能剛好是外星人而非人類嗎？這句話強調的是可能性，所以要用 happen to。

例句

Do you **happen to** have a pair of scissors?
你剛好有一把剪刀嗎？
I **happened to** be there when the accident happened.
當意外發生時，我剛好在那裡。

I單字片語I seem [sim] 似乎 / claim [klem] 宣稱 / occur [əˈkɝ] 發生

Q12

A. exhibit   B. explain
C. exist   D. explode

詳解   答案：C

　　assumption 是「假設」，plausible 有點像 possible，差別在於 possible 是「有可能的」，plausible 則是「聽起來似乎是真的」，用 possible 表示不質疑事情的可能性，然而用 plausible 則表示有點懷疑事情的真實性。這句的意思是如果這樣的假設可以相信的話，就有更多理由相信外星人曾經存在（exist）於地球上。

I單字片語I exhibit [ɪgˈzɪbɪt] 展覽；顯示 / explain [ɪkˈsplen] 解釋 / explode [ɪkˈsplod] 爆炸

Q13

A. contrast   B. control
C. condemn   D. confirm

詳解   答案：D

　　從 evidence（證據）這個關鍵詞，可推斷證據是用來 confirm suspicions（證實懷疑的事）。有些美國人認為政府隱瞞事實，there is more than meets the eye 是形容「事情比眼睛所看到的還要多」的意思，也就是說事情沒這麼簡單和單純。

I單字片語I contrast [ˈkɑnˌtræst] 對照，對比 / control [kənˈtrol] 控制 / condemn [kənˈdɛm] 譴責

Q14

A. situations   B. conditions
C. occasions   D. interpretations

詳解

答案：C

occasion 是「場合；節慶」，numerous 來自 numbers，意思是「許多的」，on numerous occasions 則是「在許多場合，許多時候」。

|單字片語| **situation** [ˌsɪtʃuˈeʃən] 情況；形勢 / **condition** [kənˈdɪʃən] 情況；條件
interpretation [ɪnˌtɜprɪˈteʃən] 解釋

A. According to conspiracy theorists
B. In spite of archeologists' denial
C. Due to the architect's reports
D. Through the astrologist's prediction

詳解

答案：A

前面提到關於美國政府是否已發現外星人的存在，卻因為某些因素不肯承認，引發了許多陰謀論。因為沒有充份的證據，這些人被稱為 conspiracy theorists（陰謀理論家），因此符合敘述的答案為 A，其他選項皆不符合。英文的構字原理十分有趣，theory 是「理論」，theorist 是「理論家」，science 是「科學」，scientist 是「科學家」，type 是「打字」，typist 是「打字員」，piano 是「鋼琴」，pianist 是「鋼琴師」。其他例子還有 artist（藝術家），chemist（化學家），physicist（物理學家）和 pharmacist（藥劑師）。

Questions 16-20

E-books may never replace paper books completely, but they make up a significant portion of book sales and appear (16) destined to become the primary way to read. E-books offer a number of advantages for readers that lead us to wonder why people are still buying paper books. First and foremost, e-books do not (17) consume resources to print and distribute. Books in print consume paper, ink and time, while e-books are available for download through publishers directly via Internet. (18) As a result, they cost only a fraction of printed books, sometimes as low as one-tenth of the listed price of paperbacks. Another huge plus of e-books is weight and space. E-books are weightless and they do not take up any physical space. Furthermore, e-books allow readers to bookmark pages and highlight words, sentences and paragraphs the way we are (19) accustomed to when using paper books. Having said all that, old habits die hard and ultimately, the choice between an e-book or paper book (20) may depend on personal preference.

　　電子書或許不層完全取代紙本書籍，但是他們占書本銷售總額顯著的比例，而且似乎註定將成為主要的閱讀方式。電子書為讀者提供幾個優點，這讓我們好奇為什麼還有人在買紙本書。首先要提到的是，電子書不需要耗費資源去印刷及發行。印刷的書本要耗費紙張、墨水和時間，然而電子書可透過出版社在網路上直接下載。因此，他們只需要花費印刷書一小部分的成本，有時候電子書只需要平裝書定價的一成。電子書的另一大優點是重量和空間。電子書是無重量的，而且也不占據任何實體空間。此外，電子書讓讀者能在頁面標記書籤，以及在單字、句子和段落劃重點，就像我們使用紙本書習慣的方式。該說的都提到了，舊的習慣還是很難在短時間內改變，而到最後，選擇電子書或紙本書可能是取決於個人的喜好。

Q16

A. appointed　　　　　　B. refused
C. tolerated　　　　　　　D. destined

詳解　　　　　　　　　　　　　　　　　　　答案：D

　　destiny 是「命運」，destine 是「註定」，destined to become 是「註定成為…」。這句提到從電子書的銷售數字可預見，電子書將註定成為主要的閱讀方式，指出電子書註定要成為主流，答案為 D。

〈補充說明〉

　　destination 的意思是「目的地」和「終點」，或許因為極受歡迎的恐怖電影《絕命終點站》Final Destination，許多人都聽過或看過這個單字。

|單字片語| **appoint** [ə`pɔɪnt] 指定；委任 / **refuse** [rɪ`fjuz] 拒絕 / **tolerate** [`tɑlə,ret] 容忍

Q17

A. exploit　　　　　　　B. consume
C. replenish　　　　　　D. abuse

詳解　　　　　　　　　　　　　　　　　　　答案：B

　　從上下文推斷，這句的句意是電子書的印刷和發行不需要消耗實際資源（consume resources），電子書不需要耗費紙張和做成書本，更不需要運送。

|單字片語| **exploit** [ɪk`splɔɪt] 剝削 / **replenish** [rɪ`plɛnɪʃ] 補充 / **abuse** [ə`bjus] 濫用

Q18

A. As a result   B. To sum up

C. On the contrary   D. In a way

詳解　　　　　　　　　　　　　　　　　　　　　答案：A

　　句中指出電子書不需要實體書在紙張、墨水、印刷和包裝等成本，因此（As a result），他們只需要花費印刷書一小部分的成本。

|單字片語| **To sum up** 總而言之 / **On the contrary** 相反的 / **In a way** 在某種意義上

Q19

A. dependent on   B. frightened of

C. accustomed to   D. satisfied with

詳解　　　　　　　　　　　　　　　　　　　　　答案：C

　　句中指出在實體書上放書籤（bookmark pages）和劃重點（highlight words）是許多人的習慣，換句話說，許多人已習慣（accustomed to）這麼做，答案應為 C。

|單字片語| **dependent on** 依賴，依靠 / **frightened of** 害怕 / **satisfied with** 滿意

Q20

A. may depend on personal preference

B. doesn't have something to do with the marketing target

C. can stand in for publisher's profits

D. should carry out the government's expectation

詳解　　　　　　　　　　　　　　　　　　　　　答案：A

　　這題需要看前句才能作答，前句提到「舊習慣很難改變，紙本書和電子書之間的選擇…」，因此空格可以看出要填入「取決於個人的喜好」才符合邏輯，因此答案為 A，其他選項的敘述皆不符合。而 depend on 是「取決於…」的意思。

例句

This case **has something to do with** the suspect.　這個案件與這名嫌犯有關。

Can you **stand in for** me today?　今天你可以代替我嗎？

She has **carried out** her boss' request.　她實現了老闆的要求。

第
1
回

第
2
回

第
3
回

第
4
回

第
5
回

第
6
回

Time for Talent Time?

Forget about TV reality shows such as the American Idol because not everyone can be an overnight success. Many schools, camps, and organizations hold talent shows every year because they are fun, involve the community, and give students a chance to show off their special skills.

Turn your Talent Show into a Fund-Raiser. Sell T-shirts, food, glow bracelets, etc. Sell advertising for the printed program and sponsor banners to be prominently posted near the stage. Sell tickets for admission. Sell flowers, ribbons, or other gifts supporters are likely to give to the performers. Record the performance and sell DVDs to both participants and audience.

We specialized in designing and manufacturing the products mentioned above. Call our toll-free number at 0800-543-3388. If the event does not make a profit, we charge nothing for our service.

是才藝表演的時候嗎？

忘了像是美國偶像的電視實境秀吧，因為不是每個人都能一夜之間一炮而紅。許多學校、營區和機構每年主辦才藝表演，是因為這些活動很好玩、能讓社區參與，同時給學生機會炫耀他們的特殊才能。

將你的才藝表演變成募款活動。販賣 T 恤、食物、發光手環等等。為印製的節目冊販賣廣告和贊助商橫幅，使其明顯擺放在舞台附近。販售入場門票。販售花、彩帶、或其他支持者可能會送給表演者的禮物。錄製表演並販售 DVD 光碟給參加者和觀眾。

我們專門設計和製造上述提到的產品。打我們的免付費專線 0800-5433388。倘若活動沒有製造利潤，我們的服務就不用收費。

|單字片語| **organization** [͵ɔrgənəˈzeʃən] 組織，機構 / **sponsor** [ˈspɑnsə] 贊助商
prominent [ˈprɑmənənt] 明顯的 / **admission** [ədˈmɪʃən] 入場費
participant [parˈtɪsəpənt] 參與者 / **performer** [pəˈfɔrmə] 表演者
audience [ˈɔdɪəns] 觀眾，聽眾 / **specialize** [ˈspɛʃəl͵aɪz] 專攻
manufacture [͵mænjəˈfæktʃə] 製造 / **profit** [ˈprɑfɪt] 利潤

Q21

Who might be the writer of this passage?
誰有可能是這篇文章的作者？

A. A school principal　學校校長

B. A talent scout　星探

C. A music instructor　音樂指導員

D. A business owner　生意業主

詳解　　　　　　　　　　　　　　　　　　　　**答案：D**

　　從最後一段 We specialized in designing and manufacturing the products mentioned above. Call our toll-free number at 0800-543-3388. If the event does not make a profit, we charge nothing for our service.（我們專門設計和製造以上提到的產品。打我們的免付費專線 0800-543-3388。倘若活動沒有製造利潤，我們的服務就不用收費。）可得知答案為 D。

Q22

The following statements describe the benefits of organizing a Talent Time Contest EXCEPT statement _____.
下列敘述都描述主辦才藝競賽的好處，除了 _____ 以外。

A. teenagers are mostly in favor of such events
　　青少年大多數支持這類活動

B. students have an opportunity to showcase their talent
　　學生有機會展現他們的才能

C. teachers need to sponsor the event　老師需要贊助活動

D. schools can invite residents in the neighborhood
　　學校可以邀請附近社區的居民

詳解　　　　　　　　　　　　　　　　　　　　**答案：C**

　　文章提到主辦才藝表演的三個好處：because they are fun, involve the community, and give students a chance to show off their special skills（因為這些活動很好玩、能讓社區參與，同時給學生機會表演特殊的才能）可知選項 A、B和 D 是主辦才藝競賽的好處，只有選項 C 不是，答案為 C。

Randy's Kitchen
Dinner Specials

Premium Steak ·································· NT $550
Pork Chop ····································· NT $500
Fish Sandwich ······························· NT $480
Sweet & Sour Pork ·························· NT $450
Fresh Salad ·································· NT $380
Super Hamburger ··························· NT $320

Desserts

Apple Pie ····································· NT $120
Cheesecake ·································· NT $110
Ice Cream ···································· NT $100

Drinks

Coffee ·· NT $120
Juice ··· NT $100
Fruit Tea ····································· NT $90

※Set Dinner: Enjoy a main course, dessert and beverage of your choice for only NT $699.
※Get a 5% discount when you like our Facebook fan page.
Note: 10% service charge not included in prices shown above. No reservation in advance, all customers will be seated on a first-come first-served basis.

Randy's 的廚房
晚餐特別餐點

頂級牛排 ······································ NT $550
豬排 ··· NT $500
魚肉三明治 ··································· NT $480
糖醋豬肉 ····································· NT $450
新鮮沙拉 ····································· NT $380
超級漢堡 ····································· NT $320

甜點

蘋果派 ··· NT $120
起司蛋糕 ·· NT $110
冰淇淋 ··· NT $100

飲料

咖啡 ··· NT $120
果汁 ··· NT $100
水果茶 ··· NT $90

※晚餐套餐：享用一份主餐和你選擇的甜點和飲料，只要 NT $699。

※當你在我們的臉書的粉絲專頁按讚，可享有 95 折的優惠。

注意：以上顯示的價格不含百分之十的服務費。不可事先訂位，所有顧客將以先
到先服務的原則入座。

|單字片語| premium [`primɪəm] 優質的 / beverage [`bevərɪdʒ] 飲料 / service charge 服務費
reservation [ˌrɛzə`veʃən] 預約 / in advance 提前

Q23

Sophia would like to order the premium, ice cream and a cup of coffee. Should she opt for the set dinner?

Sophia 想要點頂級牛排、冰淇淋和一杯咖啡。她是否應該選擇套餐？

A. Yes, they cost the same amount of money.

是的，兩者需要花費同樣的錢。

B. Yes, it is less expensive that way. 是的，這樣比較便宜。

C. No, she will pay more either way. 不，不管哪一個方式她都要付更多錢。

D. No, she will pay less if she orders them separately.

不，如果分開單點她將會付比較少的錢。

詳解

答案：B

　　頂級牛排 550 元、冰淇淋 100 元，一杯咖啡 120 元，共 770 元，若選擇套
餐只需要 699 元，這樣選擇套餐會比較便宜，答案為 B。

〈補充說明〉

　　比較便宜（cheaper）也就是比較沒那麼貴（less expensive），最便宜
（cheapest）也就是最不貴（the least expensive）。

Q24

According to the menu, which statement is NOT true?
根據菜單，哪個敘述不是正確的？

A. You can get an extra discount by accessing to the Internet.
   你可以透過上網得到額外的折扣。
B. "Fruit Tea" is the cheapest one in the menu.
   水果茶是菜單上面最便宜的品項。
C. "Apple Pie" costs as much as "Coffee".　蘋果派的價格跟咖啡一樣。
D. You can order lamb here.　你在這裡點得到羊肉。

〔詳解〕　　　　　　　　　　　　　　　　　〔答案：D〕
　　從菜單上可得知臉書粉絲專頁按讚可以得到另外的 95 折優惠，因此選項 A
是對的。水果茶 90 元，是菜單上最便宜的品項，選項 B 也是對的。蘋果派的
價格跟咖啡都一樣是 120 元，選項 C 也是對的。菜單上有牛排、豬排、魚肉、
豬肉，但就是沒有羊肉，而且我們也不能預設沙拉、漢堡裡面會有羊肉，所以
選項 D 不對，答案是 D。

Q25

How can you ensure that you have a seat in the restaurant?
你要如何確保在餐廳有座位？

A. Make a reservation in advance.　事先訂位。
B. Be there as early as possible.　盡可能早到。
C. Call the manager to make arrangements.　打給經理來做安排。
D. Support the restaurant's online fan page.　支持餐廳的線上粉絲專頁。

〔詳解〕　　　　　　　　　　　　　　　　　〔答案：B〕
　　菜單指出餐廳不接受預約，而且是先到先服務（first-come-first-served），
唯一的辦法就是盡可能早到。

Questions 26-28

　　Dutch people are very friendly and tolerant on the whole, yet they
often keep their distance from strangers. Once you are in the
conversation with the Dutch, you will find that they are helpful. In

第 1 回
第 2 回
第 3 回
第 4 回
第 5 回
第 6 回

general, Dutch people are pleasant but at the same time they can be very straightforward and frank, some people would say blunt. Sometimes you might feel that they make you lose face, which is a taboo in Asian societies. Please remember that it is not done on purpose to hurt people but it is rather a form of honesty and truthfulness. When going out to a restaurant with the Dutch, we have to keep in mind that the Dutch are very pragmatic. Even if you happen to be a lady invited to dinner by a Dutch man, do not expect a man to foot the bill. Many female foreigners were confused and offended, when Dutch men asked the waiter to split the bill into two. This habit is known as "going Dutch".

荷蘭人大體上很友善也很包容別人，不過他們對於陌生人還是會保持距離。一旦你開始跟荷蘭人交談，你會發現他們是很樂於助人的。一般說來，荷蘭人很親切，但同時他們也很直接和坦白，有些人會說是耿直。有時候你可能會覺得他們讓你沒面子，而這在亞洲社會是一種禁忌。請記得這並不是故意這麼做去傷害他人的，反而是一種誠實和真實的表現。跟荷蘭人到餐廳用餐的時候必須切記，荷蘭人是很務實的。即使你剛好是位被荷蘭男子邀請共進晚餐的女子，別期望這位男子會付帳。當荷蘭男子要求服務生把帳單分為兩份時，許多外國女子感到困惑和不愉快。這種各付各的習慣叫做「going Dutch」。

Time is not a fluid concept for the Dutch, but rather something fixed. Therefore, being on time is very important for them. When you have an appointment, please remember to be on time. If for any reasons you cannot be on time for the appointment, you have to inform them in advance. Making an appointment before meeting somebody is almost compulsory, otherwise you will waste your time by getting the answer that they cannot see you because they don't have an appointment with you. Instead of getting upset or angry if you cannot make an appointment at short notice, you should realize that the Dutch often make plans months in advance.

時間對荷蘭人來說不是容易改變的概念，而是相當固定的東西。因此，對他們來說守時是非常重要的。當你有約會，請記得要準時。若你有任何理由無法準時赴約，你必須事前通知他們。在跟別人見面之前要先預約幾乎是必須做的，否則他們會說因為沒有跟你約時間所以無法跟你見面，而讓你浪費自己的時間。與其因為不能臨時預約而生氣，你應該了解到荷蘭人通常在幾個月前就事先規劃好要做的事情。

第 1 回
第 2 回
第 3 回
第 4 回
第 5 回
第 6 回

Q26

What do you need to be aware of when speaking to Dutch friends?

當你跟荷蘭朋友交談時需要知道什麼？

A. They might criticize you in public. 他們可能會當眾批評你。

B. They might ask you for a favor. 他們可能會要你幫忙。

C. They might keep something from you. 他們可能會有事情隱瞞你。

D. They might make fun of you. 他們可能會作弄你。

詳解   答案：A

文中提到荷蘭人很友善可是他們也很直接和坦白（straightforward and frank），甚至到率直（blunt）的程度，因此跟荷蘭朋友交談時需要做好心理準備，他們可能會當眾批評你。

Q27

What does it mean to "go Dutch"?

"go Dutch" 的意思是什麼？

A. Women have to fork out the money. 女性必須付錢。

B. Men will settle the bill. 男性會買單。

C. Each person has to pay for his or her meal. 每人必須付自己的餐點。

D. The restaurant will offer a 50 percent discount.
餐廳會提供五折的優惠。

詳解   答案：C

split the bill into two 是指把「帳單分為兩個部分」，按照荷蘭人的習慣，誰點什麼東西自己付錢，真正落實性別平等主義，因此男子邀請女子用餐並不一定要買單，答案為 C。

Q28

Which of the following actions is considered unacceptable to the Dutch people?

以下哪一種行為對荷蘭人來說是不能接受的？

A. Making comments about your Dutch friends' weaknesses
對於荷蘭朋友的缺點給予評語

B. Asking for your Dutch friends' schedules for the months ahead
   向荷蘭朋友詢問幾個月後的行程
C. Refusing to pay for more than your share in a restaurant
   在餐廳時拒絕支付超過自己的那份
D. Knocking on their doors with a cake without warning
   無預警地捧著蛋糕去敲他們的門

　　荷蘭人很率直，針對他們的缺點直接給予評語並不會得罪他們，荷蘭人能接受別人的批評。荷蘭人喜歡提前做好規劃，所以向荷蘭朋友要幾個月後的行程是合理的要求。用餐時誰點什麼東西就要自己付錢，拒絕支付超過自己那份也是可接受的。因此選項 A、B、C 是符合荷蘭人的習慣。在沒有預約，無預警地出現在荷蘭人的家門口，這是他們不能接受的，因此答案為 D。

Questions 29-31

　　Fashion trends come and go and clothes can easily go out of style quickly. Today, the most popular designer stores online and offline showcase Asian fashion in casual wear, formal wear as well as office wear for men and women. Asians as well as Westerners are interested in purchasing these clothes due to lively colors, creative designs and low prices. Garments made in Asia used to be associated with inferior quality but that has changed over the years.

　　時尚潮流來來去去，衣服也很容易很快就退流行。如今，大多數網路上和非網路上最受歡迎的設計師商店都展示亞洲時尚，無論是男性和女性的輕便服裝、正式服裝，還有上班服裝。亞洲人以及西方人對於購買這些服裝都很感興趣，因為其鮮明的色彩、具有創意的設計還有較低的價格。在亞洲製造的服裝曾經都被視為卑劣品質，不過那種情況近年來已經改變。

　　With Korean dramas taking Asian markets by storm, Korean fashion has replaced the Japanese as the most popular choice in the fashion industry. Korean designers design fashionable clothes that appeal to all classes and with Korean idols showing off these trendy and glamorous clothes on Korean dramas, it is no wonder that sales have gone through the roof. There is also no denying that the fabrics used are of good quality and taste.

　　隨著韓劇襲捲亞洲市場，在時尚產業中，韓國時尚服飾已經取代了日本成為

最受歡迎的選擇。韓國設計師設計吸引各個階層人士的新潮服裝，並且有韓國偶像在韓劇中展示這些時髦又亮麗的衣服，難怪銷售額會高漲。無可否認的，這些衣服所用的布料品質和品味都很好。

The best way to source out the latest fashion wear is by browsing the internet and finding out details about styles, fashion and latest trends. Several online stores offer clothing from any part of the world. It helps to spend time going through the photos and finding something that appeals to your sense of taste. Many stores offer huge discounts and free delivery if bulk purchases are made. This makes the entire process even more affordable especially when one has a budget to consider.

要找到最新的時尚服裝的最好方法是，瀏覽網路並了解關於風格、潮流和最新趨勢的細節。某些網路商店提供來自世界任何一個地方的衣服。這幫助人們花時間檢視這些照片，並找出吸引你的品味的事物。如果下訂大量訂購，許多商店提供大量的折扣及免運費。這讓整個過程更加令人得以負擔，尤其當有人有預算考量的時候。

第 1 回
第 2 回
第 3 回
第 4 回
第 5 回
第 6 回

Q29

Westerners prefer Asian fashion for the following reasons EXCEPT _____.
西方人比較喜歡亞洲時尚服裝是因為以下的原因，除了…

A. Asian fashion is more affordable　亞洲時尚服裝更能負擔得起

B. Asian fashion is colorful　亞洲流行服飾色彩鮮明

C. Asian fashion uses cheaper materials
　亞洲時尚服裝用更便宜的材質

D. Asian fashion uses more ideas to design
　亞洲時尚服裝用比較多的想法來設計

詳解　　　　　　　　　　　　　　　　　　　　　　答案：C

從文章中 Asians as well as Westerners are interested in purchasing these clothes due to lively colors, creative designs and low prices. 可以知道西方人之所以對亞洲流行服飾感興趣，原因在於「鮮明的色彩」（即選項 B）、「創意的設計」（即選項 D）與「較低的價格」（即選項 A），可知西方人要價格便宜，卻不想用較便宜的材質，這兩者雖然有點矛盾，卻是一般消費者的心態。東西要便宜，卻不能用太便宜的材質，答案為 C。

Q30

What accounts for the rising popularity of Korean fashion?

是什麼造成韓國時尚越來越受歡迎？

- A. The subsidy provided by the Korean government.
  韓國政府提供的津貼。
- B. The unique winter wear fabric used by Korean fashion designers.
  韓國時尚設計師使用獨特的冬裝布料。
- C. The low-cost marketing strategies adopted by Korean online stores.
  韓國網路商店採取的低成本的行銷策略。
- D. The success of Korean soap operas. 韓國連續劇的成功。

詳解　　　　　　　　　　　　　　　　　　　　　　　答案：D

　　根據文章所提到的，韓國服裝不斷在韓劇中亮相，韓劇的時尚也帶動韓國服裝的銷售量，所以答案為 D。

Q31

You might be able to enjoy the benefits of a free delivery if _____.

如果…，你或許能夠享有免運費的好處。

- A. you spend enough time browsing　你花足夠的時間瀏覽
- B. you place a large order　你下一大筆的訂單
- C. you find what suits your taste　你找到適合你品味的事物
- D. you have a limited budget　你有受到限制的預算

詳解　　　　　　　　　　　　　　　　　　　　　　　答案：B

　　就算沒學過 bulk 這個單字，還是能從文章中判斷出它的意義，買多一點才能獲得免運費的優惠。bulk 是「大規模；大量」的意思，in bulk 是「大量」的意思。

To:	service@hitech.com
From:	chris099@gmail.com
Subject:	About the product problems

To whom it may concern,

I spent NT$16,000 buying one Hitech tablet with built-in wi-fi on your official site two weeks ago. I also purchased a monthly wireless Internet connection plan for NT$1000 per month. Because it was a pre-paid plan which provided a 10 GB data plan via the Hitech Mobile connection, I had paid in advance for 12 months of service.

I am complaining because when I watch movies on Netflix, the quality of video streaming is restricted to the standard definition. As soon as I learned of this issue, I contacted a customer service representative at your company. I was told that I had to pay $1,599 per month to obtain a high-speed plan. I am highly disappointed with your product and service, so I would like a written statement explaining what you will do with respect to my complaint.

Seriously, I look forward to hearing from you as soon as possible to deal with my problem. The copies of my receipt are enclosed.

Yours sincerely,
Chris Chen

第 1 回
第 2 回
第 3 回
第 4 回
第 5 回
第 6 回

收件人：	service@hightech.com
寄件人：	chris099@gmail.com
主旨：	關於產品的問題

敬啟者，

　　兩週前，我花了 16,000 元在貴公司的官方網站上購買了一款內建 wi-fi 的 Hitech 平板電腦。我還購買了無線網路月租方案，每個月 1000 元。因為這是一個透過 Hitech 行動連線提供 10 GB 的預付資費方案，所以我已經預先支付了 12 個月的服務。

　　我之所以要抱怨是因為當我在 Netflix 上觀賞電影時，線上觀看影片的品質僅限於標準解晰度。我一了解到這項問題就與貴公司的客戶服務專員聯繫。我被告知，我必須每個月支付新台幣 1,599 元才能獲得高速方案。對公司的產品和服務，我感到非常失望。因此，我希望獲得一份書面聲明，解釋貴公司將如何處理我的投訴。

　　認真地，我期待您的回信，以盡快解決我的問題。隨信附上我的收據副本。

謹啟，
Chris Chen

To:	chris099@gmail.com
From:	service@hitech.com
Subject:	Re: About the product problems

第
1
回

第
2
回

第
3
回

第
4
回

第
5
回

第
6
回

Dear Mr. Chen,

Thank you for your email. We are serious about customer satisfaction. First, we would like to apologize for your inconvenience and disappointment that you've been suffered.

We provide several data options that would meet the needs of all consumers. Having checked your current data usage, I noticed that you are a heavy Internet user. No wonder the 10 GB data plan is not suitable for you. That is why our service agent suggested that you could purchase the unlimited data plan. It provides no speed restrictions, no usage limits, and no extra costs.

The unlimited data home Internet package is another option that you can use. It streams a great number of videos and keeps your family connected. Starting at NT $5,999 per month for a family of four lines or NT $4,699 for a family of three, you can also get a free upgrade to a Netflix HD subscription.

Finally, we are truly hoping to serve you better in the future. Please contact the customer service department at 5431-9855 with any questions or assistance.

Best regards,
Michael White
Customer Service Director

收件人：	chris099@gmail.com
寄件人：	service@hightech.com
主旨：	回覆：關於產品的問題

親愛的陳先生，

　　謝謝您的來信。我們相當重視客戶滿意度。首先，對於您所遭受的不便和失望，我們深表歉意。

　　我們提供了幾種滿足所有消費者需求的資費方案。在檢查了您目前的數據使用情況之後，我注意到您是高度的網路使用者，難怪 10 GB 的資費方案並不適合您。這也是為什麼我們的服務專員建議您可以購買無限數據方案。它沒有速度限制，沒有用量限制，也沒有額外的費用。

　　無限數據家庭網路套裝方案是您可以使用的另一種選擇。它可以線上收看大量的影片，並讓您的家人保持連線。家庭用四條網路線路起價為每月新台幣 5,999 元，或是家庭用三條網路線路為新台幣 4,699 元，您還可以免費升級 Netflix 上的高畫質訂閱。

　　最後，我們真的希望未來能為您提供更好的服務。如有任何問題或協助，請致電 5431-9855 與客戶服務部門聯繫。

謹啟，
Michael White
客戶服務主管

|單字片語| **stream** [strim] 線上收聽、收看 / **definition** [ˌdɛfəˈnɪʃən] 解析度

Why did Chris Chen write the E-mail?
為什麼 Chris Chen 寫這封電子郵件？

A. He was disappointed with the limitations in the data plan.
他對資費方案中的限制感到失望。

B. He complained about the function of his new tablet.

他抱怨他的新平板電腦的功能。

C. He was furious with the behavior of a service agent.

他對一位服務專員的行為感到憤怒。

D. He wished to return his new tablet.

他希望能退貨他的新平板電腦。

詳解　　　　　　　　　　　　　　　　　　　　　**答案：A**

　　這題是在詢問第一封電子郵件的內容，問的是寫這封郵件的目的，因此要先閱讀選項，針對電子郵件中哪一些內容與目的相關，就能找出關鍵句。第一封電子郵件中第二段提到 I am complaining because when I watch movies on Netflix, the quality of video streaming is restricted to the standard definition. 可以知道他在抱怨用了這個方案後，看電影只有標準解析度，因此答案為 A。

Q33

Which of the following statements is true in relation to the response of Michael White?

關於 Michael White 的回應，下列哪一項敘述是正確的？

A. He admitted that the customer service representative failed to provide adequate service.

他承認客戶服務代表沒有提供適當的服務。

B. He gave Chris a refund because the quality of the video streaming was limited.

他提供 Chris 退費，因為線上觀看影片的品質受到限制。

C. He provided an additional plan for Chris.

他提供一項額外的方案給 Chris。

D. He asked Chris to alter his data plan right away.

他要求 Chris 馬上更改他的資費方案。

詳解　　　　　　　　　　　　　　　　　　　　　**答案：C**

　　這題是在詢問第二封電子郵件的內容，問的是電子郵件的回應內容，因此要先閱讀選項，針對電子郵件中哪一些內容與回應相關，就能快速地找出關鍵句。第二封電子郵件中第二段提到 The unlimited data home Internet package is another option that you can use. 可以知道他提供了 Chris 另一項方案，而選項 A, B, D 並未提及，答案為C。

第 1 回
第 2 回
第 3 回
第 4 回
第 5 回
第 6 回

Q34

What kind of data plan did the customer service representative propose to Chris?

客戶服務代表建議 Chris 使用哪一項方案？

A. An unlimited data home Internet package for three lines.

三條網路線無限數據家庭網路套裝方案。

B. An unlimited data home Internet package for four lines.

四條網路線無限數據家庭網路套裝方案。

C. An unlimited data plan. 無限數據方案。

D. A 10 GB data plan. 10 GB 數據方案。

詳解　　　　　　　　　　　　　　　　　　　　　　　　　　　　**答案：C**

　　本題需要整合二封電子郵件才能找到正確答案。題目問的是客戶服務代表建議什麼樣的資費方案，第一封電子郵件提到 I was told that I had to pay $1,599 per month to obtain a high-speed plan. 可知此方案的速度較快。而從第二封電子郵件的關鍵句提到 That is why our service agent suggested that you could purchase the unlimited data plan，因此客服代表建議了無限數據方案，答案為 C。

Q35

How much money did Chris pay when he bought the tablet along with the data plan?

Chris 在購買平板電腦和資費方案時付了多少錢？

A. NT$ 16,000. 新台幣 16,000 元。

B. NT$ 17,000. 新台幣 17,000 元。

C. NT$ 24,000. 新台幣 24,000 元。

D. NT$ 28,000. 新台幣 28,000 元。

詳解　　　　　　　　　　　　　　　　　　　　　　　　　　　　**答案：D**

　　這題在詢問第一封電子郵件的內容，問的是 Chris 買平板和網路資費付了多少錢，針對電子郵件中與費用相關的內容，快速地找出關鍵句。第一封電子郵件中第一段提到 Chris 花了新台幣 16,000 元購買平板電腦，並已預先支付了 12 個月新台幣1,000元 / 月的資費方案，16,000 + 1,000 x 12 = 28,000，答案為 D。

全民英檢中級

第四回 初試 聽力測驗

本測驗分四部份，全為四選一之選擇題，共 35 題，作答時間約 30 分鐘。

第一部分　看圖辨義

　　共 5 題，試題冊上有數幅圖畫，每一圖畫有 1~3 個描述該圖的題目，每題請聽錄音播出每題以及四個英語敘述之後，選出與所看到的圖畫最相符的一個答案，每題只播出一遍。

例題：（看）

　　　　　　　　　　　　　　（聽）　Look at the picture.
What does the woman want
the boy to do?
A.　Pick up the rubbish.
B.　Tie his shoelaces.
C.　Carry her luggage.
D.　Hail a cab.

正確答案為 A。

聽力測驗第一部分自本頁開始。

A: <u>Question 1</u>

B: <u>Question 2-3</u>

C: Question 4

D: Question 5

第二部分：問答

共 10 題，每題請聽光碟放音機播出一英語問句或直述句之後，從試題冊上 A、B、C、D 四個回答或回應中，選出一個最適合者作答。每題只播出一遍。

例： （聽） What happened to your feet?
　　 （看） A. They were too hungry.
　　　　　 B. I got a new pair.
　　　　　 C. My new shoes are too small.
　　　　　 D. These are not mine.

正確答案為 C。

6. A. Either now or never.
　 B. Either include it or exclude it.
　 C. Either chemistry or biology.
　 D. Either manual or auto.

7. A. May I have the receipt?
　 B. Could you get me another color?
　 C. Isn't it on the shopping list?
　 D. Are you sure it's bright enough?

8. A. That's more like it.
　 B. What a shame!
　 C. Well done!
　 D. Not again!

9. A. It can't be reversed.
　 B. You had better be quick.
　 C. They don't sell that.
　 D. It slipped my mind.

10. A. Make sure you don't get in the way.
　　 B. I'll check if the windows are secured.
　　 C. We can make it change direction.
　　 D. You might want to ask her out for a date.

11. A. He can only leave after six o'clock.
    B. We must help him to move.
    C. Nothing you say will change his mind.
    D. Don't tell me I have to take his place.

12. A. I can't believe this insect is still alive.
    B. We wanted to make it count.
    C. The air-conditioning is out of order.
    D. You should cover yourself with a blanket.

13. A. Friday afternoon would probably be best.
    B. Shall I inform the others?
    C. The line is busy at the moment.
    D. I'll be there on time.

14. A. What about the classified ads?
    B. How could you say that?
    C. Do you think we should go south instead?
    D. Does teenage romance suit your taste?

15. A. No, we can share the table.
    B. No, you have to sit elsewhere.
    C. Yes, please have a seat.
    D. Yes, I will take it to you.

共 10 題，每題請聽光碟放音機播出一段對話及一個相關的問題後，從試題冊上 A、B、C、D 四個選項中選出一個最適合者作答。每段對話及問題只播出一遍。

例：　(聽)　(Man)　　Did you happen to see my earphones?
　　　　　　　　　　I remember leaving them in the drawer.
　　　　　　(Woman)　Did you search your briefcase?
　　　　　　(Man)　　I did but they are not there. Wait a second. Oh.
　　　　　　　　　　They are right here in my pocket.

　　　　　Question:　Where are the man's earphones?

　　(看)　A.　The woman's pocket.
　　　　　B.　Briefcase.
　　　　　C.　The man's pocket.
　　　　　D.　Drawer.

正確答案為 C。

16. A. How many functions the watch has.
    B. How the watch works.
    C. How expensive the watch is.
    D. How accurate the watch is.

17. A. The woman should try to lose some weight.
    B. The woman should visit the hospital as soon as possible.
    C. There is an expert who can retrieve the information.
    D. There is no way he can help the woman.

18. A. A package tour is more affordable.
    B. A package tour is a great experience.
    C. A free-and-easy tour is more enriching.
    D. A free-and-easy tour is more dangerous.

19. A. He doesn't want the woman to be sick.
    B. He doesn't want his son to catch a cold.
    C. He is running a high fever.
    D. He is looking for his keys.

20. A. A student who is ill.
    B. A student who is late.
    C. A student who is sociable.
    D. A student who is polite.

21. A. The price of a certain product.
    B. The rewards of a certain job.
    C. The balance sheet of a company.
    D. The positions of fresh graduates.

22. A. She doesn't want to be charged for something she didn't use.
    B. She doesn't like the way she is being treated by the man.
    C. She doesn't want the bill to be sent to her.
    D. She doesn't want to total up the figures by herself.

23. A. He feels that he is getting old.
    B. He thinks the woman should slow down.
    C. He wants to catch up with the woman.
    D. He believes he can run for a longer distance.

24.

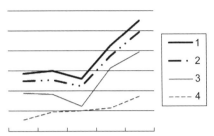

Jan Fed Mar Apr May

    A. Jerry.
    B. Simon.
    C. Ted.
    D. Wesley.

25.

Types of Rooms

Rooms on the Floor 1 – 4	Rooms on the Floor 5 – 6
Standard room Single size bed NT$ 2,300 / per night	Standard room Double size bed NT$ 2,500 / per night
Rooms on the Floor 7 – 8	**Rooms on the Floor 9 – 10**
Luxurious room Single size bed NT$ 2,700 / per night	Luxurious room Double size bed NT$ 3,300 / per night

    A. Rooms on the Floor 9 – 10.
    B. Rooms on the Floor 7 – 8.
    C. Rooms on the Floor 5 – 6.
    D. Rooms on the Floor 1 – 4.

共 10 題，每題請聽光碟放音機播出一段談話及一個相關的問題後，從試題冊上 A、B、C、D 四個選項中選出一個最適合者作答。每段談話及問題只播出一遍。

例：　　　　(聽)　　　Good morning, everyone. Please come over here and take these registration forms. Then, go back to your seats. This is the workshop on APP design. The lecturer of this workshop is an engineer from SBE Software. He has excellent experience in designing smartphone applications. Before you fill in the forms, please look through the forms carefully. If you have any questions, I will answer you later.

　　　　Question:　　What might the listeners do, after they read through the registration forms?

　　　　(看)　　　A. Leave the forms on the desks.
　　　　　　　　B. Pay the registration fee.
　　　　　　　　C. Ask the speaker some questions.
　　　　　　　　D. Go to another location.

正確答案為 C。

26. A. Pork.
　　B. Duck.
　　C. Fish.
　　D. Eggs

27. A. A basketball contest.
　　B. A shooting contest.
　　C. A baseball contest.
　　D. A volleyball contest.

28. A. To book a flight.
　　B. To ask for help.
　　C. To reply to a message.
　　D. To purchase a pillow.

29. A. A skinny person.
　　B. A healthy person.
　　C. An overweight person.
　　D. An overthinker.

30. A. A ballroom dance
       competition
    B. A singing competition.
    C. A composition competition.
    D. A martial arts competition.

31. A. Hailing a taxi.
    B. Looking for a place.
    C. Driving a car.
    D. Giving directions.

32. A. Encourage people to donate
       money.
    B. Make people get rid of the
       drugs.
    C. Inspire people to improve
       their health.
    D. Motivate people to share
       their ideas on prevention.

33. A. Fly a drone.
    B. Push a drone.
    C. Land a drone.
    D. Lift a drone.

34.

Sunny Hotel Saturday Activities

Time	Event	Place
1 pm – 6 pm	Jump Rope Games	Pool Lawn
3 pm – 5 pm	Workout Lesson	Pool Area
3 pm	Water Volleyball	Main Pool
5 pm	Dribble Tag	Pool Area

    A. Dribble Tag.
    B. Workout Lesson.
    C. Jump Rope Games.
    D. Water Volleyball.

35.

**Biggest Worry about Kids
Having Cellphones**

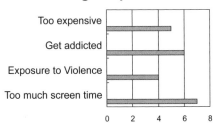

    A. Exposure to violence.
    B. Get addicted.
    C. Too expensive.
    D. Too much screen time.

―結束―

第四回 初試 閱讀測驗

本測驗分三部分,全為四選一的選擇題,共 35 題,作答時間為 45 分鐘。

第一部分:詞彙

共 10 題,每題有一個空格。請由試題冊上的四個選項中選出最適合題意的字或詞作答。

1. These findings are not reliable as they are not _____ established scientific methods.
   - A. resulted in
   - B. based on
   - C. caused by
   - D. due to

2. People who exercise regularly derive a sense of _____ from physical exertion.
   - A. innovation
   - B. recreation
   - C. destruction
   - D. satisfaction

3. The military government was accused of _____ the public by controlling election results as the voting stations were not open to foreign correspondents.
   - A. regulating
   - B. deceiving
   - C. penetrating
   - D. representing

4. The definition of manslaughter is causing another person's death, which is not premeditated or _____ in the first place.
   - A. destructive
   - B. subjective
   - C. intentional
   - D. fundamental

5. Athletes are not allowed to take certain drugs which can _____ their physical performance prior to the Olympic games.
   A. enhance   B. hamper
   C. revive   D. obstruct

6. It is not uncommon to hear complaints of sexual harassment in Japanese firms where men are considered _____ to women.
   A. inferior   B. superior
   C. humorous   D. generous

7. The host forgot to send out the invitation. _____, not a soul turned up for the party.
   A. Nonetheless   B. In general
   C. Hence   D. In particular

8. Only a handful of people made a fortune by _____ on the direction of the stock market, while many have gone broke trying to do so.
   A. forging   B. engraving
   C. gambling   D. assuming

9. Some people consider playing golf a sign of _____ that somewhat sets them apart from those who do not play the sport.
   A. respect   B. deficiency
   C. status   D. ritual

10. How could you _____ me _____? I waited for an hour like an idiot!
    A. stand… off   B. stand… down
    C. stand… out   D. stand… up

第二部分：段落填空

共 10 題，包括二個段落，每個段落各含 5 個空格。請由試題冊上四個選項中選出最適合題意的字或詞作答。

Questions 11-15

While a certain amount of workplace stress is normal ___(11)___ to be expected, excessive stress can interfere with your productivity and impact your physical and emotional health. And your ability to deal with it can mean the difference between success and failure. You can't control everything in your work environment, but that doesn't mean you're powerless—even when you're caught in a difficult ___(12)___. Finding ways to manage workplace stress isn't about making huge changes or rethinking career ambitions, but rather about focusing on the one thing that's always within your control: you. In the current troubled economy, "layoffs" and "budget cuts" have become bywords in the workplace, and the result is increased fear, uncertainty, and higher ___(13)___ of stress. Since job and workplace stress increase in times of economic crisis, it's important to learn new and better ways of ___(14)___. In short, ___(15)___ a positive attitude is the key to stress management.

11. A. as well as
    B. as long as
    C. as soon as
    D. as good as

12. A. arrangement
    B. situation
    C. position
    D. circumstance

13. A. percentage
    B. levels
    C. stages
    D. quantities

14. A. relieving the itching
    B. draining your fortune
    C. coping with pressure
    D. handling the food

15. A. adapting
    B. controlling
    C. selecting
    D. maintaining

244

Music is an integral part of our lives for thousands of years. Before the times of writing and books, music was already prevalent in ancient society. Many studies have been ___(16)___ to find the deeper benefits of listening to and playing music. From the development of babies before birth to everyday emotional healing, the growing field of music ___(17)___ is presenting increasing amounts of evidence supporting the greater powers of music. ___(18)___. The main reason behind this phenomenon is that music has the ability to verbalize and express our feelings better than any other medium. ___(19)___ neurologists, or brain experts as they are commonly known, music enables certain sections of the brain to grow and is also related to academic achievements in math and science. Finally, music can be viewed as a universal language which has no physical ___(20)___. People of different race and tongue are able to enjoy the same music, no matter where they live.

16. A. conducted
    B. researched
    C. directed
    D. liberated

17. A. chemistry
    B. industry
    C. reality
    D. therapy

18. A. The tension of the patient's body can be relieved by food
    B. Music can heighten people's stress when they listen to it
    C. The right song can put listeners in a better mood and comfort soul
    D. Reading can prevent people's brains from aging

19. A. According to
    B. Owing to
    C. Regardless of
    D. On account of

20. A. instruments
    B. borders
    C. limitations
    D. surroundings

第三部分：閱讀理解

　　本部分共 15 題，包括 5 個題組，每個題組含 1 至 2 篇短文，與數個相關的四選一的選擇題。請由試題冊上的選項中選出最適合者作答。

Questions 21-22

Instructions:

Take two pills after meals.

Reduce dosage by half for teenagers.

Children under twelve years old should only take half a pill.

Drink plenty of water.

Do not consume alcohol.

Refrain from driving as the drug may cause drowsiness.

Cease taking the medication should there be any sign of allergy.

21. How many pills should a fifteen-year-old student take?
    A. Two pills
    B. One and a half pills
    C. One pill
    D. Half a pill

22. Which of the following is not advised after taking the medicine?
    A. Eating desserts
    B. Drinking a lot of water
    C. Drinking tea or coffee
    D. Drinking wine or beer

Discover Paris with Tourist Pass

The Paris Tourist Pass is a special travel pass that entitles you to unlimited travel on metro, buses and trains operating within the city area at only 30 euros. In addition, you can visit any two national museums in a day. This pass also offers you the privilege to dine at some restaurants with a complimentary appetizer and up to 100-euro in reduction with participating stores.

- Further 20% discount for youths between 13(inclusive) and 20.
- Half-priced pass for accompanying children from 4 to 12 years old.
- Pass is valid upon purchase for 24 hours.
- Once sold, pass is not refundable.

23. Which of the following statement is a condition for using the tourist pass?
    A. Children are not allowed to board public transportation without parental supervision.
    B. Pass holders are not allowed to travel on trains that go beyond city limits.
    C. Youths are not entitled to any form of discount.
    D. Pass becomes invalid after midnight.

24. Michael just graduated from senior high school this summer. How much does he need to pay for a tourist pass?
    A. 30 euros
    B. 24 euros
    C. 18 euros
    D. 15 euros

25. You have bought the tourist pass, but your friend in Paris offered to give you a city tour in his car. Can you return the pass?
   A. No, but you can use it the next day for another 24 hours.
   B. No, you will not receive any money back.
   C. Yes, you can ask for a refund.
   D. Yes, but you can just get half of your money back.

Questions 26-28

A massive pile up during a whiteout storm in Indiana on Thursday afternoon killed three people and injured more than 20 others. A car lost its power due to engine failure and came to an abrupt stop on the highway. A truck directly behind it was too close to avoid it and led to the first crash. What happened later was described by locals as *a domino effect*. News footage revealed chaotic scenes of jackknifed trailers and the wreckage of cars across three lanes of the highway. More than 40 vehicles were involved in the deadly crash, but weather conditions and the scale of the crash site hindered rescue efforts.

The driver of the first vehicle was still trapped in the car at 6:30 pm, three hours after the crash happened, as rescue crews worked to cut him free. The death toll could rise as some victims were still trapped in the vehicles. Chances of survival are slim as the hours drag on. 'There may be many more fatalities. The clock is working against us,' a rescue worker said.

Some of those who were caught up in the pileup said the snowstorm had severely reduced visibility just before the accident. Even with the blinkers on, they could only see three to five meters ahead. The lucky few who escaped with both body and car unharmed said they kept a distance and were literally crawling along the highway.

26. What can be inferred from the news article?
   A. Three people have been killed, but more deaths are expected.
   B. More than 20 people died in the accident.
   C. A few rescue workers were trapped.
   D. Some victims died from the cold.

27. What is the meaning of a domino effect in line 6?
   A. A gambling urge that involves taking risks
   B. A mental condition that affects judgment
   C. An event that leads to another
   D. An incident that occurs randomly

28. How did some drivers manage to steer clear of the crash site?
   A. They were driving in opposite direction.
   B. They were driving with the blinkers on.
   C. They were driving at a slow speed.
   D. They were driving on the third lane.

There is a school of thought that claims gambling is a vice that does not hurt anyone but the individual doing the gambling. That is not the case. In addition to hurting the gambler's family and loved ones, those who engage in excessive gambling such as spending more money on lottery tickets is also doing great damage to the economy. Money that could be spent on goods and services that would help to stimulate the economy is foolishly wasted. An addicted lottery ticket buyer invariably feels regret and shame but then goes out and does it again. It is a vicious cycle and a horrifying habit that is one of the most difficult addictions to cure.

It is hard to get through to the compulsive gambler. Instead of talking about their actions and feelings, they tend to hide their activity. A friend or a loved one should not ignore any telltale signs that might indicate excessive gambling. While many claim that money lost on such 'lucky draws' are rechanneled to charity, it is nevertheless a form of gambling with hopes of striking it rich. Despite telling themselves that losing is fine, lottery ticket buyers suffered emotionally after each disappointment. Another alarming fact is that gamblers are often drinkers and a high percentage of domestic violence is related to drinking problems.

29. What does gambling have to do with the economy?
    A. Money spent on gambling increases the number of jobs.
    B. Money spent on gambling reduces rural poverty.
    C. Money spent on gambling should be saved in a bank.
    D. Money spent on gambling could be used to improve business.

30. What makes it so difficult for people to quit gambling?
    A. Gambling is like a drug they have to take.
    B. Gambling is a beneficial activity.
    C. Gambling is a form of mental exercise.
    D. Gambling is a way to relieve stress.

31. What is the writer's opinion about gambling?
    A. Gambling must be banned.
    B. Gambling only rewards a small group of people.
    C. Gambling triggers other social ills.
    D. Gambling enhances economic development.

Questions 32-35 are based on the information provided in the following schedule and memorandum.

The Excellent Acting Rehearsal Schedule

In order to set the play perfectly in place, each actor and actress should have a good idea of the individual character as well as of the entire play. Also, each actor and actress must devote their time and energy to memorizing the lines and working on the development of the characters before the rehearsals begin.

Date	Time	Place	Staff
Monday, 3rd March	7pm – 9pm	Studio Theater	Whole cast
Tuesday, 4th March	7pm – 9pm	Dance Theater	Supporting actress, dance company
Tuesday, 4th March	7pm – 9pm	Opera House	Leading actor, Leading actress, Supporting actor
Wednesday, 5th March	7pm – 9pm	Concert Hall	Leading actor, Leading actress, Supporting actor, Supporting actress
Wednesday, 5th March	7pm – 9pm	Studio Theater	dance company
Thursday, 6th March	7pm – 9pm	Concert Hall	Whole cast
Friday, 7th March	7pm – 9pm	Concert Hall	Whole cast

Note: In some cases, the schedule may change at the last minute. Please check the group message daily.

To:	All the cast of the play
From:	Director Gable
Date:	March 1, 2021
Subject:	A reminder of Acting Rehearsal Schedule

Dear all,

The play is just around the corner. I believe all of you have a very thorough preparation to rehearse. Because the studio theater is still under construction, we are going to use the dance theater instead. For a good play, every rehearsal matters. Any lack of discipline leads to a horrible disaster. Before we start the rehearsals, I need to remind you all below.

1. Be ready for your duty. You should have done a lot of preparation. You won't have the script in your hands while rehearsing.
2. Show up on time. There is no excuse for the absences.
3. Respect the stage managers and technicians. They are all part and parcel of the play, and so are you. You have a great interest in working properly together.
4. Stay healthy. You need to take care of your body and your voice from diseases or injuries.

As a good performer, it is important to have good conduct, reliability, and performance. Make sure to step up to the plate. If you have any questions, you should not hesitate to ask a question to clarify right away.

Gable Smith

32. What is the purpose of the memorandum?
    A. To change the rehearsal time.
    B. To inform all actors of some rehearsal rules.
    C. To notify stage managers of some rules.
    D. To call off a rehearsal.

33. Which of the following statements is included in both the schedule and the memo?
    A. Remember all lines.
    B. Come rehearsal on time.
    C. Get along fine with everybody.
    D. Check the group message every day.

34. Where does the dance company have to be on March 5th?
    A. Studio Theater.
    B. Dance Theater.
    C. Opera House.
    D. Concert Hall.

35. Which of the following statements is NOT referred to by Director Gable?
    A. Every cast is expected to attend the rehearsal.
    B. Every cast has the right to ask questions.
    C. Every cast should prevent getting sick.
    D. Every cast needs to respect directors.

—結束—

初試 聽力測驗 解析

第一部分 看圖辨義

Q1

For question one, please look at picture A.

What's the woman's problem?
這位女子的問題是什麼？

A. The kids are getting out of hand.
B. The kids are giving her a hand.
C. The kids are well-behaved.
D. The kids are following orders.

A. 小孩們失控了。
B. 小孩們在幫她的忙。
C. 小孩們都很乖。
D. 小孩們正聽從指示。

詳解　　　　　　　　　　　　　　　　　　　　　　　**答案：A**

　　圖中背景是到處搗蛋的小朋友。有的站在椅子上跳舞，有的在畫牆壁，有的在追逐，而女老師完全控制不住他們，正確答案為 A。

補充說明

　　英文中有許多俚語，不能單從字面上來理解。以下為需要轉個彎聯想的片語，get out of hand（失控），give someone a hand（幫忙），give someone a big hand（熱烈地鼓掌）。

Q2

For questions two and three, please look at picture B.

Which statement best describes the picture?
哪一項敘述最能描述這張圖片？

A. The dog is scared of the woman.
B. The woman has just fainted.
C. The window has shattered.
D. The room is in a mess.

A. 狗很害怕這位女子。
B. 這位女子昏倒了。
C. 窗戶碎裂了。
D. 房子凌亂不堪。

第 1 回
第 2 回
第 3 回
第 4 回
第 5 回
第 6 回

詳解

答案：D

在這個圖片題中，房間裡凌亂不堪，有一隻狗在咬襪子，完全沒把這位主人放在眼裡，正確答案為 D。

Q3

For question three, please refer to picture B again.

Who or what is responsible for what happened?
所發生的事情是因為誰或什麼東西造成的？

A. The dog.
B. The woman.
C. The wind.
D. A burglar.

A. 那隻狗。
B. 那位女子。
C. 風。
D. 一個小偷。

詳解

答案：A

承上題，從圖中可判斷，把房間用得零亂不堪的是那隻狗，正確答案為 A。雖然 responsible 一般會習慣被翻譯成中文「承擔責任的」，進而認為是主人教導無方，或是忽略家中的寵物才會導致小狗亂咬東西，然後被誤導選擇了 B，不過英文的 responsible for 除了做「對⋯負責」解釋外，也有「（不好的情況）起因於⋯」的意思，這裡若只一味的將 responsible 以中文的「承擔責任的」來解釋，就很容易選錯答案。

補充說明

Who is responsible for...? 的意思是「誰造成⋯？」或「誰必須為⋯負責？」，「負責」的其他說法為 accountable 例如：You will be held.（你將需要負起責任。）

Q4

For question four, please look at picture C.

What does the boy want to become in the future? 這個男孩未來想要成為什麼？

A. An author.
B. An engineer.
C. A surgeon.
D. A photographer.

A. 作家
B. 工程師
C. 外科醫師
D. 攝影師

　　圖片中的男孩幻想自己拿著自己的書，可判斷的是他想成為作家，正確答案是 A。

Q5

For question five, please look at picture D.

Which description best fits the picture?
哪一個敘述最適合這個圖片？

A. Both teams are evenly matched.　　　A. 兩隊不相上下。
B. The home team was thoroughly beaten.　B. 主隊被徹底打垮了。
C. The visitors were defeated decisively.　C. 客隊被徹底打垮了。
D. The visiting team won by a small margin. D. 客隊以微小的差距險勝。

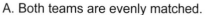

　　圖片是比賽看板，最後的比數（Final Score）為主隊（Home team）：62；客隊（Visiting Team）：99，正確答案為 B。

〈補充說明〉

　　by a small margin（以微小的差距）險勝通常會用來形容選舉，例如： He won the elections by a small margin.（他以微小的差距贏得選舉。）而 no margin for error 則是指「完全沒有出錯的空間」。

第 1 回
第 2 回
第 3 回
第 4 回
第 5 回
第 6 回

Q6

What do you intend to major in?　你打算主修什麼？

A. Either now or never.
B. Either include it or exclude it.
C. Either chemistry or biology.
D. Either manual or auto.

A. 要麼現在不然沒有機會了。
B. 要麼就加入不然就排除它。
C. 要麼是化學不然就是生物。
D. 要麼用手動不然就是自動。

詳解　　　　　　　　　　　　　　　　　　　　　　　　**答案：C**

　　題目問「你打算主修什麼？」最為適當的回應是自己想讀的科目，因此符合回答的答案為 C。

|單字片語| **major** [ˈmedʒə] 主要的；主修 / **mayor** [ˈmeə] 市長

Q7

I would like to exchange this lamp for another item.
我想要把這個桌燈換成另一件商品。

A. May I have the receipt?
B. Could you get me another color?
C. Isn't it on the shopping list?
D. Are you sure it's bright enough?

A. 可以給我收據嗎？
B. 可以幫我拿另外一個顏色嗎？
C. 它不是在購物清單上嗎？
D. 你確定這夠亮嗎？

詳解　　　　　　　　　　　　　　　　　　　　　　　　**答案：A**

　　從句子可推斷，以上對話的場所是在商店，說話者是顧客，回應者是店員。要求對換商品，店員最有可能問的當然是「可以給我收據嗎？」答案為 A。

|單字片語| **receipt** [rɪˈsit] 收據 / **recipe** [ˈrɛsəpɪ] 食譜

Q8

It's time to take your medicine.
吃藥的時間到了。

A. That's more like it.
B. What a shame!
C. Well done!
D. Not again!

A. 這還比較像話。
B. 真是可惜！
C. 做得好！
D. 又來了！不會吧？

詳解

答案：D

　　以上對話或許是媽媽對孩子說「吃藥的時間到了。」沒有人喜歡吃藥，也不會有人覺得吃藥是開心的事情，因此對方的合理反應是「又來了！又要吃藥了，不會吧？」答案為 D。

補充說明

　　以下是選項 A 和 B 的使用情境：
Speaker 1: I have corrected the mistakes in my report.
　　　　　　我已經把報告中的錯誤改正過來了。
Speaker 2: **That's more like it.**　　這還比較像話。
Speaker 1: My son is sick so he can't attend the graduation ceremony.
　　　　　　我兒子感冒了，所以無法參加畢業典禮。
Speaker 2: **What a shame!**　　真是可惜！

Q9

Have you made a reservation?
你已經訂位了嗎？

A. It can't be reversed.
B. You had better be quick.
C. They don't sell that.
D. It slipped my mind.

A. 那是無法還原的。
B. 你最好快一點。
C. 他們不賣那個。
D. 我居然忘了。

詳解

答案：D

　　make a reservation 通常指飯店、餐廳或機票的預訂，當對方問「你已經訂位了嗎？」最為合理的回答是「天啊！我居然忘了。」答案為 D。

|單字片語| **reserve** [rɪˈzɝv] 預留，預訂 / **reverse** [rɪˈvɝs] 還原；回轉

第 1 回

第 2 回

第 3 回

第 4 回

第 5 回

第 6 回

Q10

Looks like a hurricane is heading our way.
看起來颶風正往我們這裡過來。

A. Make sure you don't get in the way.	A. 確保你不要擋路。
B. I'll check if the windows are secured.	B. 我會檢查窗戶是否關緊了。
C. We can make it change direction.	C. 我們可以讓它改變方向。
D. You might want to ask her out for a date.	D. 你或許可以考慮約她出去。

詳解   答案：B

在台灣，typhoon 是「颱風」的音譯，美國人說的 hurricane（颶風）和 cyclone（氣旋），意思都跟 typhoon 差不多。知道颶風要來臨時，最合理的回答是去查看窗戶是否關緊了，答案為 B。若把 hurricane 聽成人名，以為是一位女生，就有可能被誤導而選擇 D。

|單字片語| **hurricane** [`hɜɪˌken] 颶風 / **cyclone** [`saɪklon] 旋風

tornado [tɔr`nedo] 龍捲風 / **twister** [`twɪstə] 捲風

Q11

Michael is on sick leave today.
Michael 今天請病假了。

A. He can only leave after six o'clock.	A. 他要在六點過後才能離開。
B. We must help him to move.	B. 我們一定要幫他搬家。
C. Nothing you say will change his mind.	C. 你說什麼都不能改變他的想法。
D. Don't tell me I have to take his place.	D. 別跟我說我必須代理他。

詳解   答案：D

聽到 sick leave（病假），可推斷說話者在工作場所，兩人是同事。Michael 請了病假表示他不在公司，所以選項 A 是錯誤的。請病假跟搬家毫無關聯，選項 B 也是錯的。選項 C 也不合理，Michael 已經請了病假，不是正在考慮是否要請假。答案為 D，這表示回話者要在 Michael 請假時代理他的職務。

|單字片語| **take one's place** 取代某人的位置，代理某人 / **replace** [rɪ`ples] 取代；把…放回

out of place 格格不入

Don't you think it's getting a little warm in here?
你不覺得這裡面有點熱嗎？

A. I can't believe this insect is still alive.
B. We wanted to make it count.
C. The air-conditioning is out of order.
D. You should cover yourself with a blanket.

A. 我無法相信這隻昆蟲還活著。
B. 我們想要讓它算數。
C. 冷氣故障了。
D. 你應該用毯子把自己蓋住。

詳解　　　　　　　　　　　　　　　　　　　　　　　　答案：C

　　「你不覺得這裡面有點熱嗎？」雖然是一個問句，但日常對話中不一定要用 Yes 或 No 回答，可直接說明看法或原因。這裡面有點熱是因為冷氣故障了，答案為 C。

|單字片語| **out of order** 故障；壞掉 / **everything is in order** 一切都弄好了

We might have to call off the meeting.
我們可能必須要取消會議。

A. Friday afternoon would probably be best.
B. Shall I inform the others?
C. The line is busy at the moment.
D. I'll be there on time.

A. 星期五下午可能是最好的時間。
B. 我應該通知其他人嗎？
C. 目前正在忙線中。
D. 我會準時到那裡。

詳解　　　　　　　　　　　　　　　　　　　　　　　　答案：B

　　當對方說「我們可能必須取消會議」，最為合理的回答是「我應該通知其他人嗎？」答案為 B。

|單字片語| **call off** 取消 / **call on** 拜訪 / **call it quits** 放棄；停止

第 1 回

第 2 回

第 3 回

第 4 回

第 5 回

第 6 回

Q14

Can you recommend a good novel that I can read?
你可以推薦一本好看的小說讓我讀嗎？

A. What about the classified ads?　　　A. 分類廣告如何？
B. How could you say that?　　　　　B. 你怎麼可以這麼說？
C. Do you think we should go south instead?　C. 你認為我們應該改往南走嗎？
D. Does teenage romance suit your taste?　D. 青少年羅曼史合你的胃口嗎？

詳解　　　　　　　　　　　　　　　　　　　　　**答案：D**

　　這應該是朋友之間的對話。當朋友問可否推薦好看的小說，我們應該會先詢問對方的閱讀喜好之後再做推薦，答案為 D。

＜補充說明＞

　　不適合自己口味的東西可以說 It doesn't suit my taste。另外，女生在對話中喜歡把不適合的對象說成 He's not my cup of tea.，意思同樣是這個男生不適合我的品味，另一種說法則是 He's not my type.（他不是我喜歡的類型。）

Q15

Is this seat taken?
這個座位有人坐了嗎？

A. No, we can share the table.　　　A. 沒人坐，我們可共用這張桌子。
B. No, you have to sit elsewhere.　　B. 沒人坐，你必須坐其他地方。
C. Yes, please have a seat.　　　　　C. 有人坐了，請坐下。
D. Yes, I will take it to you.　　　　D. 有人坐了，我會拿給你。

詳解　　　　　　　　　　　　　　　　　　　　　**答案：A**

　　「這個座位有人坐了嗎？」回答「是的」表示位子有人坐了，對方不能坐下。選項 A 說「不，這個位子沒人坐」，說話者願意和對方共用這張桌子，答案為 A。選項 C 說「是的。這個位子有人坐了」，可是卻還要對方坐下，這是矛盾的回答，而選項 B、D 也是不符合敘述的回答。

Q16

W: This smart wristwatch comes with many built-in functions. Besides the usual alarm clock, stopwatch and world time functions, you can also monitor your heartbeat.

這個智慧型腕錶有許多內建功能。除了一般的鬧鐘、碼錶和世界時間功能，你還可以監測你的心跳。

M: How does it manage to do that?　它是怎麼做到的？

W: It takes your pulse. It's wrapped around your wrist, see?

它會測你的脈搏。它戴在你的手腕，看到了嗎？

Q: What is the man interested in?　這位男子對什麼感興趣？

A. How many functions the watch has.　　A. 這支手錶有多少功能。

B. How the watch works.　　　　　　　　B. 這支手錶如何運作。

C. How expensive the watch is.　　　　　C. 這支手錶有多貴。

D. How accurate the watch is.　　　　　 D. 這支手錶有多準確。

詳解　　　　　　　　　　　　　　　　　　　　　**答案：B**

當這位男子問 How does it manage to do that? 這裡的 that 所指的是最後一項檢測心跳的功能。讓這位男子感到好奇的是手錶如何測量心跳，所以他感興趣的是手錶如何運作，答案為 B。

補充說明

function（功能）和 feature（特徵）是不同意義的單字，對許多科技產品而言，其功能就是特徵，但特徵不一定是功能。例如顏色鮮豔是特徵，卻不是功能。

Q17

M: Your computer was hit by a virus. All the information on the hard disk is gone.　你的電腦中毒了。所有硬碟上的資料都不見了。

W: Is there anything you can do about it?　你有什麼辦法嗎？

M: Maybe you can ask an expert for a second opinion, but based on the years of experience I have, I have to say your chances are pretty slim.

或許你可以問專家看看有沒有別的看法，但是根據我多年的經驗，我必須說你的機會很渺茫。

Q: What is the man trying to say? 這位男子想說什麼？

A. The woman should try to lose some weight.
A. 這位女子應該試著去減重。

B. The woman should visit the hospital as soon as possible.
B. 這位女子應該儘快到醫院去。

C. There is an expert who can retrieve the information.
C. 有一個專家能取回資料。

D. There is no way he can help the woman.
D. 他沒辦法幫助這位女子。

詳解　　　　　　　　　　　　　　　　　　　　　　**答案：D**

　　電腦中毒造成硬碟上的資料消失，這是時有所聞的不幸事件。男子以自己多年的經驗（experience），告訴這位女子要取回資料的機會渺茫（chances are pretty slim），表示他也無能為力，答案為 D。

Q18

W: Getting to understand and experience the history, culture and traditions of a place is the main reason I love to go backpacking.
了解並體驗一個地方的歷史、文化和傳統是我愛背包旅行的主要原因。

M: Isn't a group tour more convenient and economical in many ways?
團體旅行在很多方面上不是比較方便也比較省錢嗎？

W: Yes, but then you miss out on a lot of things I just mentioned.
沒錯，但是你會錯過我剛才提到的很多事情。

Q: What is the woman's view?
這位女子的看法是什麼？

A. A package tour is more affordable.
A. 團體旅遊更負擔得起。

B. A package tour is a great experience.
B. 團體旅遊是很棒的體驗。

C. A free-and-easy tour is more enriching.
C. 自助旅遊比較充實。

D. A free-and-easy tour is more dangerous.
D. 自助旅遊比較危險。

詳解　　　　　　　　　　　　　　　　　　　　　　**答案：C**

　　這位女子的看法是背包旅行能夠讓她更深入了解並體驗一個地方的歷史、文化和傳統，也就是說自助旅遊比較充實，答案為 C。男子的看法是團體旅行

的機票、飯店和餐點都是團購,在很多方面比較省錢也比較便宜,若沒有搞清楚題目問的是男子的看法還是女子的看法,就容易誤會而選擇 A。

Q19

M: The temperature is going to drop drastically after the sun goes down.　太陽下山後,溫度會急速下降。

W: There's a sweater in my locker. I'll put it on before I leave the campus.　我的置物櫃裡有一件毛衣。我離開校園前會穿上。

M: I think you should take the gloves with you.
我覺得你也應該把手套帶著。

Q: What is the man worried about?
這位男子在擔心什麼?

A. He doesn't want the woman to be sick.　A. 他不要這位女子生病。
B. He doesn't want his son to catch a cold.　B. 他不要他的兒子感冒。
C. He is running a high fever.　C. 他正在發高燒。
D. He is looking for his keys.　D. 他正在找他的鑰匙。

詳解　　　　　　　　　　　　　　　　　　　　　　　　答案:A

　　對話中男子要女子戴上手套注意保暖,就是擔心女子會因為溫度下降而著涼,答案為 A。

|單字片語| **temperature** [ˈtɛmprətʃə] 溫度 / **temperate** [ˈtɛmprɪt] 溫和的;有節制的

Q20

W: All assignments are to be completed by the deadline. Any late submission will not be accepted.
所有的作業必須在最後期限之前完成。任何遲交的作業都不會被接受。

M: What happens if I have a valid reason?　如果我有正當的理由呢?

W: In that case, I might consider extending the deadline by a few days.
如果是這樣,我可能會考慮延期幾天。

Q: Who can ask for more time to finish his or her work?
誰可以要求更多時間來完成他或她的作業？

A. A student who is ill.
B. A student who is late.
C. A student who is sociable.
D. A student who is polite.

A. 一個生病的學生。
B. 一個遲到的學生。
C. 一個善於社交的學生。
D. 一個有禮貌的學生。

詳解　　　　　　　　　　　　　答案：A

　　這是校園情境的對話，valid reason 是「正當的理由」的意思，選項只有 A 屬於正當的理由，答案是 A。

⟨補充說明⟩

　　因為 date 跟 dead 的發音很接近，有些人會誤以為最後期限（deadline）的英文是 dateline。date 是「日期」，日期跟期限有關聯，所以 dateline 乍看之下挺合理的。但如果聯想成超過這條線（line）你就死定了（dead），這樣最後期限的英文是 deadline 就不會搞混了。

Q21

M: On top of your basic pay, you will receive a commission.
　　除了你的底薪以外，你將會得到一筆佣金。

W: How much will that be?　那會是多少？

M: As new employees, you are entitled to 15% of the net profit.
　　身為新員工，你能享有淨利率的百分之 15。

Q: What are the speakers discussing?
說話者在談論什麼？

A. The price of a certain product.
B. The rewards of a certain job.
C. The balance sheet of a company.
D. The positions of fresh graduates.

A. 某個商品的價格。
B. 某份工作的獎勵。
C. 一家公司的資產負債表。
D. 應屆畢業生的職位。

詳解　　　　　　　　　　　　　答案：B

　　從 basic pay（底薪）和 commission（佣金）這兩個關鍵詞，可判斷說話者在談論工作上的報酬和待遇，報酬和待遇是一種獎勵，答案為 B。

|單字片語| **reward** [rɪˋwɔrd] 獎金；獎賞 / **award** [əˋwɔrd] 獎狀；獎品；授予

Q22

W: There's something wrong with my monthly bill. It doesn't add up.
　　我這個月的帳單有點問題。加總起來不對。

M: Please have a seat while I take a look. Didn't you subscribe for the ringtone service?　請坐，我來看看。您不是有申請來電答鈴的服務嗎？

W: No, I didn't. I want it off my bill.
　　我沒有。我要那筆費用從我的帳單上去除。

Q: What is the woman's request?　這位女子的要求是什麼？

A. She doesn't want to be charged for something she didn't use.

B. She doesn't like the way she is being treated by the man.

C. She doesn't want the bill to be sent to her.

D. She doesn't want to total up the figures by herself.

A. 她不想要為自己沒使用的東西付費。

B. 她不喜歡這位男子對待她的方式。

C. 她不想要帳單寄到她那裡。

D. 她不想要自己把數字加起來。

詳解　　　　　　　　　　　　　　　　　　　　　答案：A

　　學習英文當然是希望可以學以致用，這題的對話情境非常生活化。這位女子看了帳單之後發現有問題，到客服中心詢問，要求把不合理的費用從帳單中刪除，答案為 A。雖然 add up 有「加總」的意思，如果只知道這層意義，可能就會被誤導選擇了 D，然而 not add up 則是有「不合理」的意思。

I單字片語I subscribe [səb'skraɪb] 認捐；訂購 / subscriber [səb'skraɪbə] 訂閱者
　　　　subscription [səb'skrɪpʃən] 訂購；訂閱

Q23

M: I've got to stop. I am having a leg cramp.
　　我必須停下來。我的腳在抽筋。

W: I thought you said a warm-up is not necessary.
　　我以為你說不需要暖身。

M: Age is catching up with me. I used to be able to run for miles straightaway.
　　年紀大了。我以前能夠直接跑好幾英哩。

第 1 回

第 2 回

第 3 回

第 4 回

第 5 回

第 6 回

Q: What is true about the man?
關於這位男子，什麼是正確的？

A. He feels that he is getting old.
B. He thinks the woman should slow down.
C. He wants to catch up with the woman.
D. He believes he can run for a longer distance.

A. 他覺得自己老了。
B. 他認為這位女子應該放慢腳步。
C. 他想要追上這位女子。
D. 他相信他可以跑更長的距離。

詳解

答案：A

　　這位男子原本為了逞強，說自己運動前不需要暖身，結果腳抽筋了。他不得不承認，自己的歲數越來越大了，也就是覺得自己老了，答案為 A。

I單字片語I for people of all ages 老少咸宜

Q24

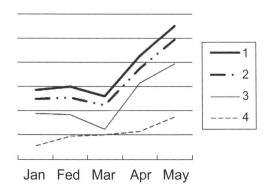

W: Simon told me that the new supervisor had motivated him and helped him get twice the sales amounts in May.

　　Simon 告訴我，新主管激勵了他，並幫助他在五月份獲得了兩倍的銷售額。

M: Jerry and Wesley used to conflict with him. They didn't do well in March, but now both of them have achieved great goals.

　　Jerry 和 Wesley 曾經和他發生衝突。他們在三月份表現不佳，但是現在他們兩個都已經達到很好的目標。

W: Even Ted made some progress. He could barely sell one thousand items in January.

　　甚至 Ted 也有些進步，一月份時他僅僅賣出一千件商品。

M: Yes, although he is not a persuasive person, he is good at following the guidance. The amount of his sales went up all the time. 是的，儘管他不是很有說服力的人，但他遵循了指導。他的銷售額一直在上升。

W: I guess their team will receive the top-selling award this season. 我想他們的團隊將會獲得本季最佳銷售獎。

Q: Look at the line chart. Who does Line 4 refer to?
請看折線圖，4 號線指的是誰？

A. Jerry.
B. Simon.
C. Ted.
D. Wesley.

詳解 　答案：C

　　聽到敘述前，從選項可以猜到與四個人有相關，因此聽的時候要注意聽每個人對應在折線圖上的位置。從 Jerry and Wesley used to conflict with him. They didn't do well in March, but now both of them have achieved great goals，可知 1 號線和 2 號線是 Jerry 和 Wesley。從 Simon told me that the new supervisor had motivated him and helped him get twice the sale amount in May，可知 3 號線是 Simon。從 He could barely sell one thousand items in January 和 The amount of his sale went up all the time，可知 4 號線為 Ted，答案為 C。

I單字片語I **motivate** [`motə͵vet] 激發 / **sale amount** 銷售額
　　　　　 persuasive [pə`swesɪv] 有說服力的 / **guidance** [`gaɪdns] 指導

Types of Rooms

Rooms on the Floor 1 – 4	Rooms on the Floor 5 – 6
Standard room	Standard room
Single size bed	Double size bed
NT$ 2,300 / per night	NT$ 2,500 / per night
Rooms on the Floor 7 – 8	**Rooms on the Floor 9 – 10**
Luxurious room	Luxurious room
Single size bed	Double size bed
NT$ 2,700 / per night	NT$ 3,300 / per night

第 1 回
第 2 回
第 3 回
第 4 回
第 5 回
第 6 回

房間類型

1 – 4 樓客房	5 – 6 樓客房
標準房型 單人床 每晚 / 2,300 元	標準房型 雙人床 每晚 / 2,500 元
7 – 8 樓客房	**9 – 10 樓客房**
豪華房型 單人床 每晚 / 2,700 元	豪華房型 雙人房 每晚 / 3,300 元

W: We are going to Taipei for business next Monday. I want to book accommodations at the National Hotel for a night. What sort of rooms would you like? 下週一我們要去台北做生意。我想在國家飯店住一晚。你喜歡什麼樣的房間？

M: I like that hotel. All the rooms there are pretty nice. Since it's just one night, why not choose a room on the upper level for a view? 我喜歡那間飯店，所有的房間都非常好。既然只待一個晚上，為什麼不要選擇高樓層的房間欣賞美景呢？

W: But I want to sleep alone. I don't want to keep you up because of my snoring. 但我想自己睡，我不想因為我打呼而讓你睡不著。

M: I think if the price for one night is less than $3,000 NT, it should be acceptable. 我認為如果一晚的價格低於 3,000 元應該可以接受。

W: Great. Anything else? 太好了，還要別的嗎？

M: No. You may make the reservations for us now. 沒有，你可以幫我們預訂了。

Q: Look at the types of rooms. Which types of rooms will the speakers most likely book?
查看房間類型。說話者最有可能預訂哪種類型的房間？

A. Rooms on the Floor 9 – 10.
B. Rooms on the Floor 7 – 8.
C. Rooms on the Floor 5 – 6.
D. Rooms on the Floor 1 – 4.

A. 9 – 10 樓的房間。
B. 7 – 8 樓的房間。
C. 5 – 6 樓的房間。
D. 1 – 4 樓的房間。

詳解

答案：B

　　從房間類型的表格和選項可以猜測題目跟飯店房型有關，因此要注意各種房型的個別資訊，才能知道說話者最後選擇的房型。男子提到 why not choose a room on the upper level for a view? 時，可知他們以高樓層為目標。之後男子說 I think if the price for one night is less than $3,000 NT should be acceptable 就可以刪去 9–10 樓的房間。可以推論出，他們最有可能預訂的房型是 7–8 樓的房間，答案為 B。

|單字片語| accommodation [ə,kɑmə'deʃən] 住處 / reservation [,rɛzə'veʃən] 預定

 第四部分 / 簡短談話

Q26

W: It is a required procedure to read the label first before buying meat, poultry, and eggs. You need to find the month as well as the day of the month on the label. In the case of frozen goods, the year should be stated. In addition, there should be a phrase, like "Best if used by", explaining the significance of that date.

在購買肉類、家禽肉和雞蛋之前，先閱讀標籤是一個必要的步驟。你需要在標籤上找到月份以及日期。至於冷凍食品，年份必須被註明。此外，應該有一個片語，像是「最佳賞味期限」，解釋其日期的重要性。

Q: Which product is not mentioned in the speech?
談話中沒有提到哪一項商品？

A. Pork.   A. 豬肉。
B. Duck.   B. 鴨肉。
C. Fish.   C. 魚肉。
D. Eggs.   D. 雞蛋。

詳解   答案：C

從選項中可以預測題目與食物相關，因此聽敘述時要注意與食材相關的內容。第一句提到 It is a required procedure to read the label first before buying meat, poultry, and eggs.，可以知道購買肉類、禽肉和雞蛋前的注意事項，meat 包含羊肉（lamb）、豬肉（pork）和牛肉（beef）等，poultry 包含雞肉（chicken）、鴨肉（duck），可知魚肉沒被提到，答案為 C。

|單字片語| poultry ['poltrɪ] 家禽肉 / best if used by 最佳賞味期限

Q27

M: Number 11 could have shot a layup and scored, but he opted to pass it to Number 5. WOW! Number 5 shoot the ball without a doubt. SWISH! It was an awesome three-pointer. The crowd broke out when Number 5 took the last-second shot and nailed it. Now it extended the lead to double digits.

11 號球員本來可以上籃得分，但他選擇把球傳給 5 號。哇！5 號球員毫不猶豫的投籃。投進！這是一顆很棒的三分球。當 5 號在最後一秒射籃、投進時，觀眾陷入瘋狂。現在，領先分數擴大成兩位數。

Q: **Which kind of activity is the speaker reporting?**
說話者正在報導哪一種活動？

A. A basketball contest.
B. A shooting contest.
C. A baseball contest.
D. A volleyball contest.

A. 一場籃球比賽。
B. 一場射擊比賽。
C. 一場棒球比賽。
D. 一場排球比賽。

詳解　答案：A

從選項可以猜到敘述與運動相關。因此聽敘述時要注意與運動活動相關的內容。從第一句 Number 11 could have shot a layup and scored, but he opted to pass it to Number 5. 和第二、三句 Number 5 shoot the ball without a doubt. SWISH! It was an awesome three-pointer. 都有用到籃球的術語。可判斷出，說話者正在報導籃球比賽，答案為 A。

|單字片語| **layup** [ˈleɪˌʌp] 上籃 / **swish** [swɪʃ]（籃球）直接入網
nail it 搞定；成功 / **break out**（情緒）爆發 / **double digit** 兩位數

Q28

W: Hi, I got a voicemail from your staff saying I'd left a travel pillow on my seat on flight CA0492. The phone number she gave me just keeps ringing, so I'm wondering if you could give me a hand? My seat number was 23C, and the pillow was green. This is Olivia White. My phone number is 942-942-942. Many thanks.

您好，我收到貴公司工作人員的語音訊息，提到我將一個旅行枕頭留在 CA0492 班機的座位上。她給我的電話號碼只有響但沒人接聽，所以我想知道您是否可以幫我？我的座位號碼是 23C，枕頭是綠色的。我是 Olivia White。我的電話號碼是 942-942-942，非常感謝。

273

Q: **What is the purpose of the call?**
這通來電的目的是什麼？

A. To book a flight.	A. 預定航班。
B. To ask for help.	B. 尋求幫助。
C. To reply to a message.	C. 回覆一則訊息。
D. To purchase a pillow.	D. 購買一顆枕頭。

詳解　　　　　　　　　　　　　　　　　　　　　　　　答案：B

　　從選項可以猜測有四種情況，可能與航班相關，因此要注意專心聽敘述。從說話者的留言訊息談話內容中，第二句 The phone number she gave me just rings out, so I'm wondering if you could give me a hand? 可以知道說話者的目的是在尋求協助，答案為 B。

Q29

M:　Do you want to get on the road to weight loss and better health? Try our fitness package. Our program will help you lose weight slowly and steadily, not muscle. Follow along with our personal professional coach. You will get complete individual attention to bring you success. Ask a gym representative to provide details.

你是否想通往減重以及更健康的路上嗎？試試我們的健身套餐。我們的計畫將會幫助你緩慢並穩定地減重，而不是減少肌肉。跟著我們的私人專業教練。你將獲得完全的個人關注，從而使你走向成功。向健身房代表詢問以提供詳細資訊。

Q: **Who will be interested in this announcement?**
誰會對這則公告有興趣？

A. A skinny person.	A. 瘦得皮包骨的人
B. A healthy person.	B. 健康的人
C. An overweight person.	C. 體重過重的人
D. An overthinker.	D. 想太多的人

詳解　　　　　　　　　　　　　　　　　　　　　　　　答案：C

　　從四個選項可以猜測談話與身材及健康有關。所以，聆聽時要注意四種身材及健康在談話內容中的重要資訊。從第三句 Our program will help you lose weight slowly and steadily, not muscle 可以清楚知道談話的內容主要是在減重。由此可以判斷，這則公告是針對超重的人，答案為 C。

第 1 回
第 2 回
第 3 回
第 4 回
第 5 回
第 6 回

Q30

W: The competition is really harsh. The voting line will not open until all candidates have performed. With your votes, your favorite singer can be crowned champion. The SMS fee is according to your mobile carrier. Keep in mind that each phone number is only allowed to vote for one candidate. This Friday is the deadline!

比賽真的非常殘酷。直到所有人選表演過後，才會開放投票。有了您的投票，您最喜歡的歌手就能成為冠軍。簡訊費用取決於您的電信供應商。請記住，每個電話號碼只能投票給一個人選。這個星期五是最後期限！

Q: What kind of event is this?
這是什麼類型的活動？

A. A ballroom dance competition.	A. 國標舞比賽。
B. A singing competition.	B. 唱歌比賽。
C. A composition competition.	C. 寫作比賽。
D. A martial arts competition.	D. 武術比賽。

詳解

答案：B

　　這是一段比賽節目的談話，四個選項指出不同類型的比賽，因此聽敘述時要注意與比賽相關的關鍵詞。談話中提到 With your votes, your favorite singer can be crowned champion，清楚說明參賽者為歌手，可知這是歌唱比賽，答案為 B。

Q31

M: There are several ways to access the museum from here. The best way is to walk down BaDe Road and then turn right at the fourth traffic light. The quickest way is to walk along GuangFu North Road, when you pass a filling station, turn left on BaDe Road. The easiest way is to catch a cab.

從這裡可以有幾種方式到達博物館。最好的方法是沿著八德路走，接著在第四個紅綠燈處右轉。最快的方法是沿著光復北路走，在你經過一間加油站的時候，在八德路左轉。而最簡單的方法是搭乘計程車。

Q: What is the speaker doing?
說話者正在做什麼？

A. Hailing a taxi.	A. 叫計程車。
B. Looking for a place.	B. 尋找一個地方。
C. Driving a car.	C. 開車。
D. Giving directions.	D. 指示方向。

　　這題的四個選項均與交通方式或地點相關，因此聽敘述時要注意與選項相關的內容。雖然談到中提到各種地點和路名，從內容可以知道這是在指示去博物館的路線說明，答案為 D。

Q32

W: National Prevention Week is right around the corner. This is your chance to help yourself and others move toward a healthy lifestyle. You can promote prevention by providing insights, skills, tools, and resources. Or you may be a sponsor to assist communities in preventing substance abuse. You are welcome to visit National Prevention Week's website at www.NPW.com to learn more.

全國預防週就快到了，這是你幫助自己和其他人邁向健康生活方式的機會。你能夠藉由提供洞察力、技能、工具和資源來促進預防。或者你可能成為贊助者，以協助社區預防藥物濫用。歡迎你上國家預防週的網站 www.NPW.com，以了解更多資訊。

Q: What is not mentioned in the announcement?
這則公告沒有提到什麼？

A. Encourage people to donate money.
B. Make people get rid of the drugs.
C. Inspire people to improve their health.
D. Motivate people to share their ideas on prevention.

A. 鼓勵人們捐款。
B. 使人們擺脫毒品。
C. 激勵人們改善健康狀況。
D. 激勵人們分享他們對預防的想法。

詳解

　　在這則公告中，四個選項均與活動行為有關，由於活動內容不完全相似，聽敘述時應注意選項出現的關鍵句。從第二句 This is your chance to help yourself and others move toward a healthy lifestyle. 可知與選項 C 相符，第三句 You can promote prevention by providing insights... 可知與選項 D 相符，第四句 Or you may be a sponsor to assist communities... 可知與選項 A 相符。而選項 B 並未在敘述中被提到，答案為 B。

Q33

M: To get your drone to take off into the air, the only thing you need to do is to press the start button. Slowly push the stick further forward until the drone lifts off the ground. Then get the stick back to zero and let the drone land. Now that you know how to do it, you're good to go.

要將無人機在空中起飛，你唯一需要做的就是按下開始按鈕。慢慢地將桿子更往前推，直到無人機離開地面。接著將桿子調回零，讓無人機降落。既然你知道該怎麼做了，你可以開始使用了。

第 1 回
第 2 回
第 3 回
第 4 回
第 5 回
第 6 回

Q: What would the listener probably do next?
聽者接下來可能會做什麼？

A. Fly a drone.	A. 飛一架無人機。
B. Push a drone.	B. 推一架無人機。
C. Land a drone.	C. 降落一架無人機。
D. Lift a drone.	D. 舉起一架無人機。

詳解　　　　　　　　　　　　　　　　　　　　　　　　　**答案：A**

　　題目的四個選項皆和無人機的操作有關，因此聽敘述時需要注意所述的各種動作，就能知道答案。從第一句 To take off your drone in the air, the only thing you need to do is to press the start button，可知聽者接下來可能會操作無人機起飛到空中，答案為 A。

|單字片語| **drone** [dron] 無人機 / **lift off** （航天器）起飛 / **rod** [rɑd] 桿

 Q34

Sunny Hotel Saturday Activities
Sunny 飯店週六活動

Time 時間	Event 活動	Place 地點
1 pm – 6 pm 下午 1 點到 6 點	Jump Rope Games 跳繩遊戲	Pool Lawn 游泳池草坪
3 pm – 5 pm 下午 3 點到 5 點	Workout Lesson 健身課程	Pool Area 游泳池區
3 pm 下午 3 點	Water Volleyball 水上排球	Main Pool 主游泳池
5 pm 下午 5 點	Dribble Tag 運球競賽	Pool Area 游泳池區

W: Dear guests, today's most inspiring event is about to begin. It's safe and suitable for everyone. When doing simple tasks, you can enhance your posture with ease. By participating in this event, not only can you improve your health and fitness, but you also learn how to exercise without burdening your body. Sufficient exercise is good for you. Come to the Pool Area and experience the passion of exercise.

敬愛的嘉賓，今天最鼓舞人心的活動即將開始。這個活動很安全且適合所有人。在進行簡單的任務時，你可以輕鬆地改善姿勢。透過參加這項活動，你不僅可以提升健康狀況和健身，也可以在不增加身體負擔的情況下，學習如何運動。足夠的運動對你有益。快來游泳池區，並體驗運動的熱情。

Q: Look at the schedule. What event is the speaker introducing? 請看行程表，說話者正在介紹什麼活動？

A. Dribble Tag.

B. Workout Lesson.

C. Jump Rope Games.

D. Water Volleyball.

A. 運球競賽。

B. 健身課程。

C. 跳繩遊戲。

D. 水上排球。

詳解

答案：B

在聽到敘述前，先讀表格和選項有助於在聽敘述時很快找出關鍵詞。這題的表格跟選項主要為四種活動，所以，聽敘述時要注意活動的細部資訊，從第二、三句 By participating in this event, not only can you improve your health and fitness, but you also learn how to exercise without burdening your body，可知活動內容主要在改善姿勢、提升健康狀況和健身以及鍛煉身體。而最後一句提到 Come to the Pool Area...，再去看表格可以推論，說話者在介紹 Workout Lesson，答案為 B。

Q35

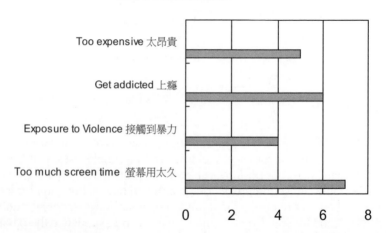

Biggest Worry about Kids Having Cellphones
孩童有手機的最大擔憂

第 1 回
第 2 回
第 3 回
第 4 回
第 5 回
第 6 回

M: Though you all have different parenting styles, your fear about the way your kids use cellphones is similar. The chart shows that most parents share this concern. It certainly has an impact on the development of children's brains. It results in many negative effects, including sleep problems and educational problems. As a teacher, I believe that teaching children how to use cellphones is essential.

儘管你們所有人都有不同的育兒方式,然而你們對孩子使用手機的方式的擔憂是相似的。這張圖表顯示出大多數的父母都有這項擔憂。這肯定是對孩童的大腦發育有影響,導致許多負面影響,包括:睡眠問題和教育問題。身為老師,我認為教導孩子們如何使用手機是必要的。

Q: **Look at the Chart. Which concern is the speaker talking about?** 請看圖表,說話者在說的是哪一項擔憂?

A. Exposure to violence.
B. Get addicted.
C. Too expensive.
D. Too much screen time.

A. 接觸到暴力。
B. 上癮。
C. 太昂貴。
D. 觀看螢幕的時間太久。

詳解   答案:D

　　從圖表和選項猜測題目與孩子擁有手機最大的擔憂相關,因此聽敘述時要注意四種擔憂的資訊。第二句提到 The chart shows that most of parents share this concern. 表示大多數的家長有相同的擔憂。接著提到 It certainly has an impact on the development of children's brains. It results in many negative effects... 表示對大腦發育有影響,導致負面的效應。而從圖表中可以知道,父母最擔憂的是「觀看螢幕的時間太久」,答案為 D。

初試 閱讀測驗 **解析**

第一部分 詞彙和結構

Q1

These findings are not reliable as they are not _____ established scientific methods.

這些研究結果不可靠，因為它們不是根據已制訂的科學方法得來的。

A. resulted in
B. based on
C. caused by
D. due to

詳解

答案：B

這題是指研究結果之所以不可靠，是因為其過程沒有根據已制訂的科學方法，並非指研究結果造成已制訂的科學方法，答案應該是 B 而不是 C。

例句

The heavy rain **resulted in** a flash flood.　大雨造成暴洪。
The flash flood is **caused by** the heavy rain.　暴洪是由大雨造成的。
Due to the heavy rain, the house was flooded.　由於大雨，房子淹水了。

Q2

People who exercise regularly derive a sense of _____ from physical exertion.

規律運動的人們從體能鍛鍊中得到一種滿足感。

A. innovation
B. recreation
C. destruction
D. satisfaction

詳解

答案：D

運動是一種消遣，可是做運動並不會得到一種「消遣感」，運動流汗之後得到是滿足感，答案為 D。

I單字片語I innovation [ˌɪnə'veʃən] 創新，革新 / recreation [ˌrɛkrɪ'eʃən] 消遣，休閒
destruction [dɪ'strʌkʃən] 破壞；毀滅

Q3

The military government was accused of _____ the public by controlling election results as the voting stations were not open to foreign correspondents.

由於投票站不開放給外國記者，軍權政府被指控透過控制選舉結果來欺騙大眾。

A. regulating
B. deceiving
C. penetrating
D. representing

詳解　　　　　　　　　　　　　　　　　　　　　　　　**答案：B**

　　從 accused（指控）這個關鍵詞，可判斷被指控的事情一定是負面的。從上下文判斷，軍權政府被指控透過控制選舉結果來欺騙大眾，答案為 B。

|單字片語| **regulate** [ˈrɛgjəˌlet] 調節；管理 / **penetrate** [ˈpɛnəˌtret] 滲入
　represent [ˌrɛprɪˈzɛnt] 代表

Q4

The definition of manslaughter is causing another person's death, which is not premeditated or _____ in the first place.

過失殺人的定義是造成其他人死亡，當初是沒有預謀或犯意的。

A. destructive
B. subjective
C. intentional
D. fundamental

詳解　　　　　　　　　　　　　　　　　　　　　　　　**答案：C**

　　英文字根、字首就像中文的部首，學會的話將受用無窮。premeditated 的 pre- 是之前的意思，例如 prepare（準備）、prevent（預防）、predict（預測）。meditate 是「沉思」，premeditated 是「事先仔細想過」，也就是「早有預謀」。過失殺人的定義是沒有預謀，也就是不是有意圖的（intentional），答案為 C。

|單字片語| **destructive** [dɪˈstrʌktɪv] 有毀滅性的 / **subjective** [səbˈdʒɛktɪv] 主觀的
　fundamental [ˌfʌndəˈmɛntl] 基本的

第 1 回
第 2 回
第 3 回
第 4 回
第 5 回
第 6 回

Q5

Athletes are not allowed to take certain drugs which can _____ their physical performance prior to the Olympic games.

運動員在奧林匹克比賽前不允許服用某些可以加強體能表現的藥物。

A. enhance   B. hamper
C. revive   D. obstruct

詳解   答案：A

　　運動員在比賽前服用禁藥的事件時有所聞，服用禁藥的目的是在比賽期間提升自己的表現，不可能是為了妨礙自己，因此選項 B 和 D 是錯誤的。試題中沒有提到運動員士氣低落或體力不支，選項 C 也是錯誤的，符合的答案為 A。

|單字片語| hamper [ˋhæmpə] 妨礙 / revive [rɪˋvaɪv] 甦醒；復元
　　　　obstruct [əbˋstrʌkt] 妨礙；阻塞

Q6

It is not uncommon to hear complaints of sexual harassment in Japanese firms where men are considered _____ to women.

在男性被視為優越於女性的日本公司裡，聽到性騷擾的投訴並非不常見的事情。

A. inferior   B. superior
C. humorous   D. generous

詳解   答案：B

　　日本社會一向存在大男人主義的觀念，在日本公司裡男性被視為優越於女性，答案為 B。

|單字片語| inferior [ɪnˋfɪrɪə] 劣等的；下級的 / humorous [ˋhjumərəs] 幽默的
　　　　generous [ˋdʒɛnərəs] 大方的

Q7

The host forgot to send out the invitation. _____, not a soul turned up for the party.

主辦人忘了寄出邀請函。因此，這場派對連一個人影也沒有。

A. Nonetheless
B. In general
C. Hence
D. In particular

詳解　　　　　　　　　　　　　　　　　　　答案：C

　　因為忘了做某件事，造成了某種後果，句首的副詞必須用 Hence（因此），答案為 C。

例句

The host forgot to send out the invitation. **Nonetheless**, a few friends turned up for the party.
主辦人忘了寄出邀請函。雖然如此，還是有幾個朋友出席派對。
In general, we should go to a party only if we received an invitation.
一般而言，我們應該只有收到邀請才去派對。
In particular, the Dutch people will never go to a party without an invitation.
尤其，荷蘭人在沒有收到邀請的情況下是不會去派對的。

Q8

Only a handful of people made a fortune by _____ on the direction of the stock market, while many have gone broke trying to do so.

只有少數的人藉由在股市方向下賭注而致富，然而很多嘗試這麼做的人都破產了。

A. forging
B. engraving
C. gambling
D. assuming

詳解　　　　　　　　　　　　　　　　　　　答案：C

　　股市的方向（the direction of the stock market）誰也不能保證，再精細的分析也只是對於未來的猜測。賭博（gambling）是投機的行為，賭的是股市未來的方向，答案為 C。

|單字片語| **forge** [fɔrdʒ] 鍛鍊；偽造 / **engrave** [ɪnˈgrev] 雕刻 / **assume** [əˈsjum] 假設

第 1 回
第 2 回
第 3 回
第 4 回
第 5 回
第 6 回

Q9

Some people consider playing golf a sign of _____ that somewhat sets them apart from those who do not play the sport.

有些人認為打高爾夫球是一種身分地位的象徵，而這在某種程度上將他們和那些不打高爾夫球的人區別開來。

A. respect
B. deficiency
C. status
D. ritual

詳解 　　　　　　　　　　　　　　　　　　　　　答案：C

　　這題是指打高爾夫球被視為一種榮耀，一種地位象徵。對有些人來說，高爾夫球不僅僅是一種運動，而是提升社會地位（status）的活動，高爾夫球的贊助商通常是高檔的品牌，答案為 C。

I單字片語I respect [rɪ'spɛkt] 尊重 / deficiency [dɪ'fɪʃənsɪ] 缺乏 / ritual ['rɪtʃʊəl] 儀式

Q10

How could you _____ me _____? I waited for an hour like an idiot!

你怎麼可以放我鴿子？我像個傻瓜一樣，等了一個小時！

A. stand… off
B. stand… down
C. stand… out
D. stand… up

詳解 　　　　　　　　　　　　　　　　　　　　　答案：D

　　stand someone up 是「爽約；放某人鴿子」的意思，因此選項 A、B 和 C 都是錯誤的，英文沒有 stand someone off，stand someone down 或 stand someone out 的用法，答案為 D。

〈補充說明〉

　　動詞片語的使用非常靈活，stand up against someone 的用法不同於 stand someone up，stand up against someone 是「對抗、反對某人」的意思。例如：The little boy stood up against the man who kicked the puppy.（那個小男孩和那個踢了小狗一腳的男人對抗。）

第 1 回
第 2 回
第 3 回
第 4 回
第 5 回
第 6 回

第二部分 / 段落填空

Questions 11-15

While a certain amount of workplace stress is normal (11) as well as to be expected, excessive stress can interfere with your productivity and impact your physical and emotional health. And your ability to deal with it can mean the difference between success and failure. You can't control everything in your work environment, but that doesn't mean you're powerless—even when you're caught in a difficult (12) situation. Finding ways to manage workplace stress isn't about making huge changes or rethinking career ambitions, but rather about focusing on the one thing that's always within your control: you. In the current troubled economy, "layoffs" and "budget cuts" have become bywords in the workplace, and the result is increased fear, uncertainty, and higher (13) levels of stress. Since job and workplace stress increase in times of economic crisis, it's important to learn new and better ways of (14) coping with the pressure. In short, (15) maintaining a positive attitude is the key to stress management.

儘管工作環境中一定程度的壓力是正常也是預料中的,過度的壓力可能會妨礙你的做事效率並且影響你的生理和心理健康。你對於應付壓力的能力可能代表著成功或失敗的差異。你無法控制工作環境中的每一件事物,但這不表示你無能為力——即便當你被困在一個窘境。找到方法控制工作上的壓力不是關於做出巨大的改變或重新思考職涯的抱負,而是關於專注於一件永遠在你控制之內的東西:就是你自己。在目前陷入困境的經濟中,「裁員」和「刪減預算」已經成為工作場所常聽到的代名詞,這樣的結果是增加恐懼、不確定性,還有更高程度的壓力。由於工作和工作場所的壓力在經濟危機的時期會增加,學習新的和更好的方法來應對壓力是很重要的。簡言而之,保持正面的態度是壓力管理的關鍵。

Q11

A. as well as
B. as long as
C. as soon as
D. as good as

詳解　　　　　　　　　　　　　　　　　　　　　**答案:A**

這題是指工作壓力是正常「也」是預料中的,as well as 在這裡的用法跟

and 相似，就是「還有、也」的意思。若不把 as well as 看成一個主體，把 well 解讀成 good 的副詞，套進 as ... as 的句型，那麼 as well as 也有「做得跟…一樣好」的意思。

例句

He can play baseball **as well as** a professional player.
他打棒球打得跟職業球員一樣好。
A man, **as well as** a woman, was involved in the accident.
一名男子，還有一名女子，被牽連到這起意外中。

補充說明

在以上例句中，as well as a woman 是兩個逗點中的同位語，是額外的補充資料，主詞只有 A man，所以動詞用 was 才能符合主詞、動詞一致的原則。反之，若用 and 把男子和女子連在一起，主詞就有兩個人，動詞必須用 were。例如：
A man, as well as a woman, **was** involved in the accident.
一名男子，還有一名女子，被牽連到這起意外中。
A man and a woman **were** involved in the accident.
一名男子和一名女子被牽連到這起意外中。

Q12

A. arrangement
B. situation
C. position
D. circumstance

詳解

答案：B

這題是指被困在艱難的情況下，答案為 B，另一種說法是 caught in a dilemma（左右為難，進退兩難）。雖然 circumstance 也是「情況；環境」的意思，但用法是 under such difficult circumstances（在這種艱難的情況下），介系詞要使用 under。

|單字片語| **arrangement** [əˋrendʒmənt] 安排 / **position** [pəˋzɪʃən] 職位；姿勢
　　　　　　circumstance [ˋsɝkəm‚stæns] 情況，環境

Q13

A. percentage
B. levels
C. stages
D. quantities

詳解

答案：B

stress（壓力）是不可數名詞，但壓力的等級則可數，答案為 B。有高壓力層級（high stress levels）的工作，而我們也能把壓力控制在低的層級（keep stress level low）。

|單字片語| **percentage** [pə'sɛntɪdʒ] 百分比 / **stages** [stedʒ] 階段；時期
quantity ['kwɑntətɪ] 數量

Q14

A. relieving the itching
B. draining your fortune
C. coping with pressure
D. handling the food

詳解　　　　　　　　　　　　　　　　　　　　　　　　　**答案：C**

　　這題要根據前後句，才能判斷要選哪個選項，空格處前一句提到「工作和工作環境的壓力在…增加，因此學習新的…方法很重要」，可以看出只有選項 C 符合敘述，其他選項皆不合適。「應付壓力」也以說 cope with stress，也可以說 handle stress，handle 不需要加介系詞，而「紓解壓力」是 relieve stress，也不需要加介系詞。

|單字片語| **relieve** [rɪ'liv] 減緩 / **drain** [dren] 排出；使流出 / **handle** ['hændl] 處理

Q15

A. adapting　　　　　　　　　　B. controlling
C. selecting　　　　　　　　　　D. maintaining

詳解　　　　　　　　　　　　　　　　　　　　　　　　　**答案：D**

　　空格的後面是態度（attitude），雖然態度可以控制，不過外國人比較習慣說改變或保持態度，因此答案為 D。每個人都會有樂觀跟悲觀的時候，維持樂觀和積極的態度是壓力管理的關鍵。maintain 的近義詞是 sustain，但 sustain 用在維持生命方面比較合適，不能說 sustain a positive attitude.。

|單字片語| **adapt** [ə'dæpt] 適應；改編 / **control** [kən'trol] 控制 / **select** [sə'lɛkt] 挑選

Questions 16-20

Music is an integral part of our lives for thousands of years. Before the times of writing and books, music was already prevalent in ancient society. Many studies have been (16) conducted to find the deeper benefits of listening to and playing music. From the development of babies before birth to everyday emotional healing, the growing field of music (17) therapy is presenting increasing amounts of evidence

第 1 回
第 2 回
第 3 回
第 4 回
第 5 回
第 6 回

supporting the greater powers of music. (18) The right song can put listeners in a better mood and comfort the soul. The main reason behind this phenomenon is that music has the ability to verbalize and express our feelings better than any other medium. (19) According to neurologists, or brain experts as they are commonly known, music enables certain sections of the brain to grow and is also related to academic achievements in math and science. Finally, music can be viewed as a universal language which has no physical (20) borders. People of different race and tongue are able to enjoy the same music, no matter where they live.

音樂在幾千年以來已經成為我們生活中不可或缺的部分。在文字和書籍的時代之前，音樂在古代社會已經非常普遍。為了找出聆聽音樂和彈奏音樂更深層的好處，而進行了許多研究。從胎兒在出生前的發展到每天情感上的治療，音樂治療不斷成長的領域持續提出了越來越多的證據來支持音樂具有更大的力量。一首對的歌曲可以讓聆聽者的心情變得更好，並安慰其心靈。這個現象背後的主要原因是音樂有能力用言語描述和表達我們的感受，優於任何其他媒介。根據神經科醫師，或是普遍所知的大腦專家，音樂能夠使大腦的某些區塊成長，音樂也和數學和科學的學術成就有所關聯。最後，音樂可被視為一種沒有實體邊界的通用語言。不同種族和語言的人們都能享受相同的音樂，不管他們住在什麼地方。

Q16

A. conducted   B. researched
C. directed   D. liberated

詳解   答案：A

當 studies 和 research 作為名詞使用，意思都是「研究調查」，research 當作動詞則是「做研究」，不可能對音樂的研究調查再去做研究，因此選項 B 是錯誤的。conduct 是「進行」，「進行研究」是 conduct a research 或 conduct a study，答案為 A。

|單字片語| research [rɪˈsɝtʃ] 探討；研究 / direct [dəˈrɛkt] 指揮 / liberate [ˈlɪbə,ret] 解放

Q17

A. chemistry   B. industry
C. reality   D. therapy

第 1 回

第 2 回

第 3 回

第 4 回

第 5 回

第 6 回

詳解

答案：D

　　從上下文提供的線索 emotional healing（情感上的治療），可判斷這篇文章提到的是 music therapy（音樂療法），答案為 D。

|單字片語| **chemistry** [ˈkɛmɪstrɪ] 化學 / **industry** [ˈɪndəstrɪ] 工業 / **reality** [rɪˈælətɪ] 事實

Q18

A. The tension of the patient's body can be relieved by food

B. Music can heighten people's stress when they listen to it

C. The right song can put listeners in a better mood and comfort the soul

D. Reading can prevent people's brains from aging

詳解

答案：C

　　這個段落都在描述音樂有安慰人們心靈的作用，因此空格處也要填入與音樂有關的選項，符合敘述的答案為 C。選項 B 提到音樂會提高人們的壓力，選項 B 是錯誤的，而選項 A 和 D 都和音樂無關，因此也是錯誤的答案。

|單字片語| **tension** [ˈtɛnʃən] （精神上的）緊張 / **heighten** [ˈhaɪtn]提高，增加

　　　　comfort [ˈkʌmfət] 安慰 / **prevent** [prɪˈvɛnt] 預防；避免

Q19

A. According to　　　　　　B. Owing to

C. Regardless of　　　　　　D. On account of

詳解

答案：A

　　從空格處後面這整段話判斷 neurologists, or brain experts as they are commonly known, music enables...（神經科醫師的說法，音樂能夠…），可知空格處要填入 According to，答案為 A。

例句

Owing to his support, we managed to raise enough funds.
由於他的支持，我們成功籌到了足夠的款項。
Regardless of his support, we will raise enough funds.
不管他是否支持，我們會籌得足夠的款項。
On account of his support, we will make him the chairman.
因為他的支持，我們將讓他成為主席。

A. instruments B. borders

C. limitations D. surroundings

詳解 答案：B

空格處的句子指出 music is universal language（音樂是通用的語言），沒有實體的邊界，答案為 B。

|單字片語| **instrument** [ˈɪnstrəmənt] 儀器 / **limitation** [ˌlɪməˈteʃən] 限制

surroundings [səˈraʊndɪŋz] 周遭

第三部分 / 閱讀理解

第1回
第2回
第3回
第4回
第5回
第6回

Questions 21-22

Instructions:
Take two pills after meals.
Reduce dosage by half for teenagers.
Children under twelve years old should only take half a pill.
Drink plenty of water.
Do not consume alcohol.
Refrain from driving as the drug may cause drowsiness.
Cease taking the medication should there be any sign of allergy.

指示：
餐後服用兩錠藥丸。
青少年須把劑量減半。
十二歲以下的兒童應該只服用半錠。
多喝水補充水分。
請勿飲酒。
請不要開車，因為藥物可能會造成昏睡。
若有任何過敏跡象，請停止服用。

|單字片語| **drowsy** [ˈdrɑʊzɪ] 昏昏欲睡的 / **dizzy** [ˈdɪzɪ] 頭暈目眩的 / **giddy** [ˈgɪdɪ] 暈眩的
instruction [ɪnˈstrʌkʃən] 指示 / **dosage** [ˈdosɪdʒ] （藥的）劑量
alcohol [ˈælkəˌhɔl] 酒精；含酒精飲料 / **allergy** [ˈælədʒɪ] 過敏

Q21

How many pills should a fifteen-year-old student take?
一個十五歲的學生應該服用多少錠的藥丸？

A. Two pills　兩錠
B. One and a half pills　一錠半
C. One pill　一錠
D. Half a pill　半錠

　　　　　　　　　　　　　　　　　　　　　　　　答案：C

　　根據指示的說明，提到青少年須把劑量減半。（Reduce dosage by half for teenagers.）成人服用兩錠，兩錠的一半則是一錠，十五歲的學生應該服用一錠藥丸，十二歲以下的孩子服用半錠，答案為 C。

Which of the following is not advised after taking the medicine?

服用藥物後，以下哪一個選項是不被建議的？

A. Eating desserts　吃甜點
B. Drinking a lot of water　喝許多水
C. Drinking tea or coffee　喝茶或咖啡
D. Drinking wine or beer　喝紅酒或啤酒

　　　　　　　　　　　　　　　　　　　　　　　　答案：D

　　指示中提到請勿飲酒（Do not consume alcohol.），答案為 D。選項 A、C 在指示中看不到，所以無法得知是否被建議還是不被建議，因此不能夠作為答案。指示中建議服用藥物要多喝水（Drink plenty of water.）因此選項 B 是「被建議」而不是「不被建議」的，所以也不能當成答案。

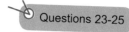

Questions 23-25

Discover Paris with Tourist Pass

　　The Paris Tourist Pass is a special travel pass that entitles you to unlimited travel on metro, buses and trains operating within the city area at only 30 euros. In addition, you can visit any two national museums in a day. This pass also offers you the privilege to dine at some restaurants with a complimentary appetizer and up to 100-euro in reduction with participating stores.

· Further 20% discount for youths between 13 (inclusive) and 20.
· Half-priced pass for accompanying children from 4 to 12 years old.
· Pass is valid upon purchase for 24 hours.
· Once sold, pass is not refundable.

使用遊客周遊證探索巴黎

巴黎遊客周遊證是一個特別的通行證，只要花 30 歐元，它讓你能夠在城市區域內無限次數搭乘地鐵、公車和火車。此外，你能夠在一天中可以拜訪任兩間國立博物館。這個通行證提供優待讓你在某些餐廳享有免費招待的開胃菜，以及在參與的商店中享有最高達 100 歐元的折扣。

- 13 至 20 歲的青少年可額外獲得八折的優惠。
- 隨同的 4 至 12 歲孩童可享半價的周遊證。
- 周遊證有效時間為購買後算起 24 小時。
- 一旦售出，恕不退費。

|單字片語| **entitle to** 讓…享有 / **privilege** [ˈprɪvlɪdʒ] 特權
complimentary [ˌkɑmpləˈmɛntərɪ] 免費贈送的 / **reduction** [rɪˈdʌkʃən] 減少；減免
participate [pɑrˈtɪsəˌpet] 參與 / **accompany** [əˈkʌmpənɪ] 陪同
valid [ˈvælɪd] 有效的 / **benefit** [ˈbɛnəfɪt] 好處 / **refundable** [rɪˈfʌndəbl] 可退費的

Q23

Which of the following statement is a condition for using the tourist pass?
以下哪一項敘述為使用遊客周遊證的條件？

A. Children are not allowed to board public transportation without parental supervision.
孩童在沒有父母監督下，不允許搭乘大眾運輸工具。

B. Pass holders are not allowed to travel on trains that go beyond city limits. 周遊證使用者不得搭乘超越城市界線的火車。

C. Youths are not entitled to any form of discount.
青少年不能享有任何形式的折扣。

D. Pass becomes invalid after midnight. 周遊證過了午夜將變無效。

詳解

答案：B

accompanying children 是指「隨同的兒童」，兒童並非一定要父母陪同才能搭乘大眾運輸工具，選項 A 不對。說明中很清楚的提到青少年有八折優惠，選項 C 不對。周遊證的有效期限是購買後的 24 小時，跟過不過午夜無關，選項 D 不對。周遊證限用於都市範圍之內（within the city area），答案為 B。

主題遊樂園中一些具有危險性的娛樂設施，通常會出現 children below ~ years of age must be accompanied by adults（…歲以下兒童必須由成人陪伴）的警示標語。

Q24

Michael just graduated from senior high school this summer. How much does he need to pay for a tourist pass?

Michael 今年夏天剛從高中畢業。他需要付多少錢購買一張遊客周遊證？

A. 30 euros　30 歐元
B. 24 euros　24 歐元
C. 18 euros　18 歐元
D. 15 euros　15 歐元

詳解　　　　　　　　　　　　　　　　　　　　　　　　　答案：B

文中提到全票 30 歐元，而 Michael 的年紀票價可扣除 20% discount，等於打八折，30 × 0.8 = 24 歐元，答案為 B。

Q25

You have bought the tourist pass, but your friend in Paris offered to give you a city tour in his car. Can you return the pass?

你已經買了遊客周遊證，但是你在巴黎的朋友提議用他的車子載你遊覽城市。你可以退還通行證嗎？

A. No, but you can use it the next day for another 24 hours.
　　不，但是你可在隔天多使用 24 小時。
B. No, you will not receive any money back.　不，你將不會拿回任何錢。
C. Yes, you can ask for a refund.　是的，你可以要求退費。
D. Yes, but you can just get half of your money back.
　　是的，但你只能拿回一半的錢。

詳解　　　　　　　　　　　　　　　　　　　　　　　　　答案：B

文中的最後一個條約規定：Once sold, pass is not refundable.（一旦售出，恕不退費。）答案為 B。

Questions 26-28

A massive pile up during a whiteout storm in Indiana on Thursday afternoon killed three people and injured more than 20 others. A car lost its power due to engine failure and came to an abrupt stop on the highway. A truck directly behind it was too close to avoid it and led to the first crash. What happened later was described by locals as *a domino effect*. News footage revealed chaotic scenes of jackknifed trailers and the wreckage of cars across three lanes of the highway. More than 40 vehicles were involved in the deadly crash, but weather conditions and the scale of the crash site hindered rescue efforts.

星期四下午於印第安那州在白茫茫的暴風雪中發生了連環車禍，有三人喪命、超過二十人受傷。一輛汽車由於引擎熄火失去動力，而在高速公路上突然停止。跟隨在正後方的大卡車因距離太近而無法避開它，導致第一起相撞意外。當地人用「骨牌效應」來形容之後發生的事。新聞畫面顯示混亂的現場情景：折疊起來的聯結車和幾輛車子的殘骸橫越高速公路的三條車道上。這起致命的意外超過四十輛車子受到牽連，但天氣的條件和車禍現場的規模阻礙了救援行動。

The driver of the first vehicle was still trapped in the car at 6:30 pm, three hours after the crash happened, as rescue crews worked to cut him free. The death toll could rise as some victims were still trapped in the vehicles. Chances of survival are slim as the hours drag on. 'There may be many more fatalities. The clock is working against us,' a rescue worker said.

在傍晚六點三十分，車禍發生後的三個小時，第一輛車的駕駛還被困在車子內，雖然救難人員嘗試著破壞車體把他救出來。由於還有一些受害者被困在車內，死亡人數可能還會攀升。隨著時間流失，生存的機會越來越渺茫。一名救難人員說：「可能會有更多死者。時間對我們非常不利。」

Some of those who were caught up in the pileup said the snowstorm had severely reduced visibility just before the accident. Even with the blinkers on, they could only see three to five meters ahead. The lucky few who escaped with both body and car unharmed said they kept a distance and were literally crawling along the highway.

有一些被捲入這場連環車禍意外的人表示，就在車禍發生前，暴風雪嚴重降低能見度。即使打開了閃光警示燈，他們只能看到前方三至五公尺遠的地方。那

些幸運躲過這場意外，身體和車子都沒有受傷的少數人說，他們保持安全距離，而且可說是在高速公路上慢速行進。

Q26

What can be inferred from the news article?
從這則新聞中可以推斷出什麼？

A. Three people have been killed, but more deaths are expected.
三個人已經喪命，但預期會有更多死亡人數。

B. More than 20 people died in the accident.
超過二十個人在這場意外中死亡。

C. A few rescue workers were trapped.　有幾個救難人員受困。

D. Some victims died from the cold.　有些受害者死於寒冷的天氣。

詳解　　　　　　　　　　　　　　　　　　　　　　　　**答案：A**

　　從報導的第一句可得知目前的死亡人數為三人，第二段提到 death toll could rise（死亡人數可能會增加），答案為 A。

Q27

What is the meaning of a domino effect in line 6?
第 6 行中 a domino effect 的意思是什麼？

A. A gambling urge that involves taking risks　一種包含冒險的賭博慾望

B. A mental condition that affects judgment　一種影響判斷能力的精神狀況

C. An event that leads to another　一起事件導致另一起事件

D. An incident that occurs randomly　一場隨機發生的事件

詳解　　　　　　　　　　　　　　　　　　　　　　　　**答案：C**

　　domino 是「骨牌」，domino effect 指的是「骨牌效應」。從文章中可以知道，從第一起的車禍衍生出後面的連環追撞事故，就算不知道 domino 是「骨牌」，也可以猜到它的意思是一起事件導致另一起事件，如此接連發生的連環效應，因此答案為 C。

〈補充說明〉

　　ripple effect 是指「漣漪效應」，意思是事情的影響範圍逐漸擴大。

How did some drivers manage to steer clear of the crash site?
有些駕駛如何成功避開車禍現場？

A. They were driving in opposite direction.　他們逆向。
B. They were driving with the blinkers on.　他們打開閃光警示燈。
C. They were driving at a slow speed.　他們以慢速行駛。
D. They were driving on the third lane.　他們行駛在第三車道。

詳解　　　　　　　　　　　　　　　　　　　　答案：C

　　steer 是「掌舵」，steering wheel 是「方向盤」，steer clear of 是「繞過；避開」的意思。選項 A 文章沒提到，所以是錯誤的。目擊者提到，即便打開閃光警示燈，能見度還是很低，可見光靠打開閃光警示燈無法避免車禍。幸運避開這場意外的車主說他們保持安全距離，而且可說是在高速公路上慢速爬行（they kept a distance and were literally crawling along the highway）所以避開意外的關鍵是放慢速度，答案為 C。

Questions 29-31

　　There is a school of thought that claims gambling is a vice that does not hurt anyone but the individual doing the gambling. That is not the case. In addition to hurting the gambler's family and loved ones, those who engage in excessive gambling such as spending more money on lottery tickets is also doing great damage to the economy. Money that could be spent on goods and services that would help to stimulate the economy is foolishly wasted. An addicted lottery ticket buyer invariably feels regret and shame but then goes out and does it again. It is a vicious cycle and a horrifying habit that is one of the most difficult addictions to cure.

　　有一門思想學派宣稱賭博是一種惡習，並不會傷害其他人，卻只會傷害在賭博的人，而不是其他人。真實情況並非如此。除了傷害賭徒的家人和其所愛的人，那些從事過度賭博行為的人，例如花很多錢買彩券，他們也對經濟造成極大的傷害。原本可以花在用來幫助刺激經濟的商品和服務的錢，都被愚蠢地浪費掉了。一個上癮的樂透彩券買家常常會感到後悔和羞恥，可是卻一而再、再而三地重覆這些行為。這是一種惡性循環，也是其中一個最難治療上癮的可怕習慣。

第1回
第2回
第3回
第4回
第5回
第6回

It is hard to get through to the compulsive gambler. Instead of talking about their actions and feelings, they tend to hide their activity. A friend or a loved one should not ignore any telltale signs that might indicate excessive gambling. While many claim that money lost on such 'lucky draws' are rechanneled to charity, it is nevertheless a form of gambling with hopes of striking it rich. Despite telling themselves that losing is fine, lottery ticket buyers suffered emotionally after each disappointment. Another alarming fact is that gamblers are often drinkers and a high percentage of domestic violence is related to drinking problems.

要跟無法抗拒賭博的人溝通是很困難的。與其談論自己的行為和感受，他們反而傾向隱藏自己的活動。朋友或愛人不應該忽略任何可能暗示出過度賭博的藏不住的徵兆。雖然許多人宣稱輸在「抽獎遊戲」的錢會再轉到慈善團體，這始終還是一種希望一夕發達的賭博行為。儘管告訴自己輸錢沒關係，樂透彩券的買家卻在每一次失望之後在情緒上受到折磨。另一個令人擔憂的事實是，賭徒往往也是酒鬼，而很高比例的家庭暴力跟酗酒問題有關。

What does gambling have to do with the economy?
賭博跟經濟有什麼關係？

A. Money spent on gambling increases the number of jobs.
花在賭博的錢增加工作數量。

B. Money spent on gambling reduces rural poverty.
花在賭博的錢減少農村的貧窮。

C. Money spent on gambling should be saved in a bank.
花在賭博的錢應該存在銀行。

D. Money spent on gambling could be used to improve business.
花在賭博的錢可用於改善生意。

詳解　　　　　　　　　　　　　　　　　　　　　　　　　　　答案：D

依作者的看法，原本用來賭博的錢可以藉由購買商品和服務來刺激經濟（stimulate the economy），也就是改善生意（improve business），商家的生意好會對經濟有幫助，答案為 D。

Q30

What makes it so difficult for people to quit gambling?
人們要戒賭會這麼困難是因為什麼？

    A. Gambling is like a drug they have to take.
       賭博就像是他們必須服用的毒品。
    B. Gambling is a beneficial activity.　賭博是一種有益的活動。
    C. Gambling is a form of mental exercise.　賭博是一種心理運動的形式。
    D. Gambling is a way to relieve stress.　賭博是一種紓解壓力的方法。

　詳解　　　　　　　　　　　　　　　　　　　　　　　答案：A

　　compulsive behavior 是指「無法克制的強迫行為」，文中也提到賭博是一種癮（addiction），因此讓很多人難以戒賭的原因是，賭博就像是他們必須服用的毒品，因此答案為 A。作者提到賭博對經濟的發展不利，賭博並不是一種有益的活動，選項 B 是錯誤的。雖然有些人說小賭怡情，偶爾打打牌對頭腦有幫助，有助於紓壓，不過文章中提及的是已經泥足深陷的賭徒，選項 C、D 也是錯誤的。

Q31

What is the writer's opinion about gambling?
作者對於賭博的看法是什麼？

    A. Gambling must be banned.　賭博必須被禁止。
    B. Gambling only rewards a small group of people.
       賭博只獎勵一小部分的人。
    C. Gambling triggers other social ills.　賭博引起其它社會弊端。
    D. Gambling enhances economic development.　賭博提升經濟發展。

　詳解　　　　　　　　　　　　　　　　　　　　　　　答案：C

　　作者在最後一段提到 gamblers are often drinkers and a high percentage of domestic violence is related to drinking problems.（賭徒往往也是酒鬼，而很高比例的家庭暴力跟酗酒問題有關）。作者的看法是好賭的人通常會酗酒，會酗酒的人會造成家庭暴力，可推論出賭博會間接造成其他社會問題，答案為 C。

 Questions 32-35

The Excellent Acting Rehearsal Schedule

In order to set the play perfectly in place, each actor and actress should have a good idea of the individual character as well as of the entire play. Also, each actor and actress must devote their time and energy to memorizing the lines and working on the development of the characters before the rehearsals begin.

Date	Time	Place	Staff
Monday, 3rd March	7pm – 9pm	Studio Theater	Whole cast
Tuesday, 4th March	7pm – 9pm	Dance Theater	Supporting actress, dance company
Tuesday, 4th March	7pm – 9pm	Opera House	Leading actor, Leading actress, Supporting actor
Wednesday, 5th March	7pm – 9pm	Concert Hall	Leading actor, Leading actress, Supporting actor, Supporting actress
Wednesday, 5th March	7pm – 9pm	Studio Theater	dance company
Thursday, 6th March	7pm – 9 pm	Concert Hall	Whole cast
Friday, 7th March	7pm – 9pm	Concert Hall	Whole cast

Note: In some cases, the schedule may change at the last minute. Please check the group message daily.

優秀演技排練的時間表

　　為了使戲劇演出完美到位，每位男演員和女演員都應該對個人角色以及整場戲劇有一個很好的構想。再者，在排練開始之前，每位男演員和女演員必須花費他們的時間和精力來記住台詞，並著重在角色的發展。

日期	時間	地點	工作人員
3／3 星期一	下午 7－9點	攝影棚劇場	全體演員
3／4 星期二	下午 7－9點	舞蹈劇場	女配角、舞團
3／4 星期二	下午 7－9點	歌劇院	男主角、女主角、男配角
3／5 星期三	下午 7－9點	音樂廳	男主角、女主角、男配角、女配角
3／5 星期三	下午 7－9點	攝影棚劇場	舞團
3／6 星期四	下午 7－9點	音樂廳	全體演員
3／7 星期五	下午 7－9點	音樂廳	全體演員

注意：在某些情況下，時間表可能會在最後一刻更改，請每天查看群組訊息。

MEMO

To:	All the cast of the play
From:	Director Gable
Date:	March 1, 2021
Subject:	A reminder of Acting Rehearsal Schedule

Dear all,

The play is just around the corner. I believe all of you have a very thorough preparation to rehearse. Because the studio theater is still under construction, we are going to use the dance theater instead. For a good play, every rehearsal matters. Any lack of discipline leads to a horrible disaster. Before we start the rehearsals, I need to remind you all below.

1. Be ready for your duty. You should have done a lot of preparation. You won't have the script in your hands while rehearsing.
2. Show up on time. There is no excuse for the absences.
3. Respect the stage managers and technicians. They are all part and parcel of the play, and so are you. You have a great interest in working properly together.
4. Stay healthy. You need to take care of your body and your voice from diseases or injuries.

As a good performer, it is important to have good conduct, reliability, and performance. Make sure to step up to the plate. If you have any questions, you should not hesitate to ask a question to clarify right away.

Gable Smith

備忘錄

收件人：	戲劇全體演員
寄件人：	Gable 導演
日期：	2021 年 3 月 1 日
主旨：	演技排練時間表提醒

大家好，

　　這齣戲劇即將演出。我相信你們所有人都有充分的準備進行排練。由於攝影棚劇場仍在施工中，我們將會改用舞蹈劇場。對於一齣好的戲劇而言，每次排練都很重要。缺乏紀律會導致可怕的災難。在我們開始排練前，我需要提醒大家以下事項。

1. 準備好你的職責。你應該已經做了很多準備。在排練時，你的手中不能拿著劇本。
2. 準時出席。沒有藉口缺席。
3. 尊重舞台經理和技術人員。他們都是戲劇很重要的一部分，你也是。你們適當地一起共事會擁有很大的利益。
4. 保持健康。你需要照顧好自己的身體和聲音，免於疾病或傷害。

　　身為一位出色的表演者，重要的是要有良好的行為、可靠性和表演，對遇到的事情做出行動。如有任何問題，請立即提出以澄清疑問。

Gable Smith

|單字片語| under construction 在建造中 / part and parcel 主要部分
step up to the plate 對機會或危機做出行動

What is the purpose of the memorandum?
這封備忘錄的目的是什麼？

A. To change the rehearsal time. 更改排練時間。

B. To inform all actors of some rehearsal rules.
告知所有演員一些排練規則。

C. To notify stage managers of some rules. 通知舞台經理一些規則。

D. To call off a rehearsal. 取消一場排練。

詳解　　　　　　　　　　　　　　　　　　　　　　　答案：B

　　這題是針對第二篇的備忘錄，問的是備忘錄的目的，因此先閱讀選項，針對備忘錄與目的相關的內容，就能快速地找出關鍵句。備忘錄的收件人為 All the cast of the play，而第二段也提到 Before we start rehearsals, I need to remind you all below，可知導演在排演前要告訴演員一些規則，答案為 B。

Q33

Which of the following statements is included in both the schedule and the memo?
下列哪一項敘述皆包含在時間表和備忘錄之中？

A. Remember all lines. 記住所有台詞。

B. Come rehearsal on time. 準時來排練。

C. Get along fine with everybody. 與每個人相處融洽。

D. Check the group message every day. 每天檢查群組訊息。

詳解　　　　　　　　　　　　　　　　　　　　　　　答案：A

　　這題需要整合排練時間表和備忘錄才能找到答案。因此要先看選項，進而分辨出哪一些選項在排練時間表和備忘錄中都有提到，就能快速地找出關鍵答案。在排練時間表第二句 Each actor and actress must devote their time and energy to memorizing the lines... 及備忘錄第二段第一點 You won't have the script in your hands while rehearsing. 說明應記住劇本台詞再去排練。而選項 B、C 只有在備忘錄提到，選項 D 只在排練時間表提到，答案為 A。

Q34

Where does the dance company have to be on March 5th?
舞團在 3 月 5 日必須在哪裡？

A. Studio Theater. 攝影棚劇場。

B. Dance Theater. 舞蹈劇場。

C. Opera House. 歌劇院

D. Concert Hall. 音樂廳。

　　　　　　　　　　　　　　　　　　　　　　　答案：B

　　這題需要整合排練時間表和備忘錄才能找到答案。先看到排練時間表，舞團當天是在實驗劇場排演。接著，在備忘錄第一段最後一句提到 Because the studio theater is still under construction, we are going to use the dance theater instead，可知攝影棚劇場無法使用，地點會改到舞蹈劇場，答案為 B。

Q35

Which of the following statements is NOT referred to by Director Gable?

導演 Gable 沒有提到哪一項敘述？

A. Every cast is expected to attend the rehearsal.
   每位演員被預期參加排演。

B. Every cast has the right to ask questions.　每位演員有權利問問題。

C. Every cast should prevent getting sick.　每位演員應該要預防生病。

D. Every cast needs to respect directors.　每位演員需要尊重導演。

　　　　　　　　　　　　　　　　　　　　　　　答案：D

　　本題內容是針對備忘錄，題目問的是導演未提及的內容，因此先閱讀選項後，針對備忘錄找哪一項描述沒被提到，就能快速地找出關鍵句。選項 A 為導演 Gable 所提到的第二點，選項 B 在備忘錄的最後一句，選項 C 為第四點，而第三點是要求演員要尊重舞台經理和技術人員，但沒有提到尊重導演，答案為 D。

全民英檢中級

第五回 初試 聽力測驗

本測驗分四部份,全為四選一之選擇題,共 35 題,作答時間約 30 分鐘。

第一部分　看圖辨義
　　共 5 題,試題冊上有數幅圖畫,每一圖畫有 1~3 個描述該圖的題目,每題請聽錄音播出每題以及四個英語敘述之後,選出與所看到的圖畫最相符的一個答案,每題只播出一遍。

例題:(看)

　　　　　　　　　　　　　　(聽) Look at the picture.
　　　　　　　　　　　　　　　　 What does the woman want
　　　　　　　　　　　　　　　　 the boy to do?
　　　　　　　　　　　　　　　　 A. Pick up the rubbish.
　　　　　　　　　　　　　　　　 B. Tie his shoelaces.
　　　　　　　　　　　　　　　　 C. Carry her luggage.
　　　　　　　　　　　　　　　　 D. Hail a cab.

正確答案為 A。

聽力測驗第一部分自本頁開始。

A:　Question 1

B:　Question 2

C: Question 3

D: Question 4-5

第二部分：問答

　　共 10 題，每題請聽光碟放音機播出一英語問句或直述句之後，從試題冊上 A、B、C、D 四個回答或回應中，選出一個最適合者作答。每題只播出一遍。

例： （聽）　What happened to your feet?
　　　（看）　A. They were too hungry.
　　　　　　　B. I got a new pair.
　　　　　　　C. My new shoes are too small.
　　　　　　　D. These are not mine.

正確答案為 C。

6. A. I can't wait for the new
　　　　semester.
　　B. I am not sure if it will be
　　　　here.
　　C. I have a suggestion.
　　D. I'd rather not talk about it.

7. A. You can always play it
　　　　again.
　　B. I promise I won't take long.
　　C. Let's go there by train.
　　D. This doesn't belong to you.

8. A. No, the company is sending
　　　　him to Paris.
　　B. No, he is definitely going.
　　C. Yes, he's working on his
　　　　French.
　　D. Yes, he will be in Germany
　　　　next month.

9. A. That's cheating.
　　B. They might get wet.
　　C. Maybe yellow will be a
　　　　better choice.
　　D. I'll go get it.

10. A. Perhaps it is a different
　　　　brand.
　　B. Your watch has slowed
　　　　down.
　　C. We ran out of gasoline.
　　D. An accident most likely.

11. A. I usually carry a shopping bag.
    B. I have had enough.
    C. I can adjust the volume.
    D. I believe it is round.

12. A. I can give you some advice.
    B. I can think of no more questions.
    C. There is no way it is going to happen.
    D. There are many ways to do it.

13. A. They are kind and friendly.
    B. I haven't returned her call.
    C. Something inexpensive but practical.
    D. It's made of wood and plastic.

14. A. My IQ is above average.
    B. You have to be creative sometimes.
    C. They can communicate using sounds.
    D. This is the latest technology.

15. A. She didn't see the poster.
    B. She has always been considerate.
    C. She hasn't gotten over the death of her pet
    D. She promised she will be early.

第三部分：簡短對話

　　共 10 題，每題請聽光碟放音機播出一段對話及一個相關的問題後，從試題冊上 A、B、C、D 四個選項中選出一個最適合者作答。每段對話及問題只播出一遍。

例：　(聽)　(Man)　　　Did you happen to see my earphones?
　　　　　　　　　　　I remember leaving them in the drawer.
　　　　　　(Woman)　Did you search your briefcase?
　　　　　　(Man)　　I did but they are not there. Wait a second. Oh. They are right here in my pocket.

　　　　　　Question:　Where are the man's earphones?

　　(看)　A.　The woman's pocket.
　　　　　B.　Briefcase.
　　　　　C.　The man's pocket.
　　　　　D.　Drawer.

正確答案為 C。

16. A.　Her son's grades.
　　B.　Her son's health.
　　C.　Her son's classmate.
　　D.　Her son's illness.

17. A.　In a garment store.
　　B.　In a post office.
　　C.　In a stationery shop.
　　D.　In a bakery.

18. A.　A landslide is taking place.
　　B.　A flood is happening.
　　C.　An earthquake is occurring.
　　D.　A typhoon is approaching.

19. A.　In a library.
　　B.　In a gallery.
　　C.　In a clinic.
　　D.　In a terminal.

20. A.　Get a software program from the Internet.
　　B.　Print out the train schedule.
　　C.　Write down an address.
　　D.　Tell the driver her destination.

21. A. An unfair hike in fare.
    B. A surcharge for late hours.
    C. A way to get home safely.
    D. A sacrifice people have to make.

22. A. He is an expert.
    B. He is not interested in chess.
    C. He wants to join the club.
    D. He is the chairman of a chess club.

23. A. He couldn't get the first place in the competition.
    B. He couldn't pass his exams.
    C. He couldn't see two women at the same time.
    D. He couldn't understand what went wrong.

24.

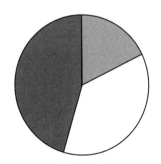

    A. Facebook.
    B. Snapchat.
    C. YouTube.
    D. Instagram.

25.

Receipt
Saturday, March 12, 2021

ITEM	QUANTITY	PRICE	AMOUNT
Plastic bag	1	$ 2	$ 2
Book bag	1	$ 1,300	$ 1,300
Pen bag	2	$ 100	$ 200
Pad	2	$ 200	$ 400
		TOTAL	$ 1,902

    A. $ 2.
    B. $ 100.
    C. $ 200.
    D. $ 300.

共 10 題，每題請聽光碟放音機播出一段談話及一個相關的問題後，從試題冊上 A、B、C、D 四個選項中選出一個最適合者作答。每段談話及問題只播出一遍。

例：　　　　（聽）　　Good morning, everyone. Please come over here and take these registration forms. Then, go back to your seats. These is the workshop on APP design. The lecturer of this workshop is an engineer from SBE Software. He has excellent experience in designing smartphone applications. Before you fill in the forms, please look through the forms carefully. If you have any questions, I will answer you later.

　　　　Question:　　What might the listeners do, after they read through the registration forms?

　　　　（看）　　A. Leave the forms on the desks.
　　　　　　　　　B. Pay the registration fee.
　　　　　　　　　C. Ask the speaker some questions.
　　　　　　　　　D. Go to another location.

正確答案為 C。

26. A. Attitude.
　　B. Relationship.
　　C. Appearance.
　　D. Rumors.

27. A. A construction.
　　B. A traffic jam.
　　C. A protest march.
　　D. A road run.

28. A. Buy an enormous quantity of goods.
　　B. Having some technical problems.
　　C. File your complaint.
　　D. Request payment of an invoice.

29. A. Watch a performance.
    B. Enjoy the rhythm.
    C. Applaud loudly.
    D. Dress up.

30. A. Heat-related illness.
    B. Foreign exchange risk.
    C. Stronger hurricanes.
    D. More melting ice.

31. A. Hollywood movies.
    B. Korean dramas.
    C. Taiwan documentary films.
    D. British commercials.

32. A. Force parents to make a dentist appointment for their children.
    B. Warn parents to make a dentist appointment for their children.
    C. Assist parents to make a dentist appointment for their children.
    D. Encourage parents to make a dentist appointment for their children.

33. A. Changing a bulb.
    B. Threading a screw.
    C. Placing a fan.
    D. Rotating a clock.

34.

Compare prices on Electric Toothbrushes

Brand	Price
Brand A	$ 1,200
Brand B	$ 1,900
Brand C	$ 1,500
Brand D	$ 1,700

    A. Brand A.
    B. Brand B.
    C. Brand C.
    D. Brand D.

35.

Metro Route Map

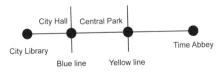

    A. City Library.
    B. City Hall.
    C. Central Park.
    D. Time Abbey.

—結束—

第五回 初試 閱讀測驗

本測驗分三部分，全為四選一的選擇題，共 35 題，作答時間為 45 分鐘。

第一部分：詞彙

共 10 題，每題有一個空格。請由試題冊上的四個選項中選出最適合題意的字或詞作答。

1. After the third attempt, the little boy realized that riding a bike was not so difficult _____.
   A. in general
   B. instead
   C. after all
   D. ultimately

2. Postgraduate students are advised not to take things _____, as it is the professors' duties to point out their mistakes and shortcomings.
   A. immediately
   B. awkwardly
   C. personally
   D. formally

3. Nuclear power is now seen as a threat to public safety. The government is exploring other _____ such as solar and hydro energy.
   A. alternatives
   B. animations
   C. appliances
   D. achievements

4. Some scientists put forth the hypothesis that black holes are expanding at a _____ rate.
   A. static
   B. secured
   C. constant
   D. necessary

5. With the _____ of credit cards, it has become much more difficult to suppress the urge to make purchases on impulse.
   A. invitation
   B. investigation
   C. invasion
   D. invention

6. The recruit had the enemy soldier at his _____ yet he could not muster the courage to pull the trigger.
   A. begging
   B. mercy
   C. disposal
   D. request

7. The exact sales figures are yet to be _____. Sales from the next few days will also have to be factored in before we can make a comparison with the previous year.
   A. fabricated
   B. determined
   C. negotiated
   D. confiscated

8. Arthur skipped dinner again as he was so _____ his work that he lost track of time.
   A. wary of
   B. absorbed in
   C. persuaded by
   D. bestowed on

9. Once in office, politicians who raise funds to run for elections are expected to return the favor of _____ who supported them. Whether this is seen as corruption remains a controversial issue.
   A. challengers
   B. sponsors
   C. lecturers
   D. translators

10. I love you with all my heart and I will not let anything _____ us.
    A. come up with
    B. come between
    C. come apart
    D. come down with

第二部分：段落填空

共 10 題，包括二個段落，每個段落各含 5 個空格。請由試題冊上四個選項中選出最適合題意的字或詞作答。

Questions 11-15

A tsunami is a natural ___(11)___ caused by an earthquake. During a tsunami, huge masses of ocean water rushed inland in tidal waves and the costs to human life can be ___(12)___. The deadliest tsunami in recorded history was the Christmas tsunamis of 2004 in the Indian Ocean. On December 26, 2004, an earthquake registering 9.2 magnitude occurred on one of the islands around Sumatra. It created a deadly series of tsunamis that swept Indonesia, India, Madagascar, and Ethiopia. The death toll was ___(13)___ to be in the neighborhood of 300,000 to 350,000. The immediate destruction of lives and property is only the beginning of the damage. After the waters retreated there was the increased of diseases ___(14)___. Many who survived the initial flood perished due to starvation or dehydration. Many more were lost to diseases that were ___(15)___ as dead bodies exposed to the scorching sun began to decompose out in the open.

11. A. accident
    B. event
    C. tragedy
    D. phenomenon

12. A. exclusive
    B. horrifying
    C. indifferent
    D. emphatic

13. A. estimated
    B. imagined
    C. proposed
    D. organized

14. A. affecting people's cognition
    B. causing animal's weird behavior
    C. created by stagnant and polluted water
    D. spread by people's saliva and body fluid

15. A. thorough
    B. intensive
    C. primitive
    D. widespread

Questions 16-20

Baseball has been woven into the very fabric of American society for many years now. Children of all ages take up baseballs and gloves in order to have fun, and mothers and fathers find themselves ___(16)___ their nurseries for their baby boy with baseballs and other equipment ___(17)___. No matter where you roam in the United States, you'll never be too far away from a great baseball game, or just a small corner shop which specializes in baseball cards. To some, there is a season for baseball, but to ___(18)___, baseball is always in season. Older generations of Americans are more familiar with baseball card collecting than younger generations, and because of this, many people believe that baseball card collecting is a ___(19)___ art. This is simply not the case, as many cards which have been saved over the years only increase in ___(20)___, and many collectors take advantage of this knowledge to make a killing. You'll find card collectors at many types of sales in which people get rid of their old belongings.

16. A. decorate
    B. to decorate
    C. decorating
    D. decoration

17. A. which has nothing to do with sports
    B. that is disliked by their child
    C. which goes along with the sport
    D. that is related with movies

18. A. another
    B. the other
    C. others
    D. some other

19. A. lost
    B. dying
    C. growing
    D. contemporary

20. A. length
    B. status
    C. value
    D. weight

第三部分：閱讀理解

本部分共 15 題，包括 5 個題組，每個題組含 1 至 2 篇短文，與數個相關的四選一的選擇題。請由試題冊上的選項中選出最適合者作答。

Questions 21-22

To: Customer Service Officer

I am a loyal customer of your company for five years. Your company has always provided the best telecom service in terms of price and quality. Nevertheless, I regret to inform you that I had a rather unpleasant experience in one of your local stores on Ziyou Rd, Kaohsiung yesterday. I went there during lunch hours and I was surprised to see only one clerk at the counter. There was a long queue and I waited for half an hour before I was served. I intend to purchase a phone for my son so I tried to clarify the various subscription plans offered. The clerk sounded annoyed and told me to refer to a piece of paper she printed. I am in my late forties and I have trouble reading fine print. I requested that she explained the details to me and she raised her voice at me and told me she is not a teacher, causing me much embarrassment. In the end, I left the store in anger. I demand a written apology from this employee, failure of which might lead me to legal actions against her for insulting me in public.

Your customer,
Angela Wang

21. Why did the problem happen?
    A. The clerk was impatient.
    B. The customer was kept waiting for half an hour.
    C. The piece of paper was well printed.
    D. The customer is nearly 50 years old.

22. What actions might the customer take if the clerk failed to apologize?
    A. She might cancel her account.
    B. She might raise her voice.
    C. She might take her to court.
    D. She might purchase another phone.

True Nature Photography Prize 2022

Each quarterly issue of True Nature magazine contains two images selected from entries for the annual Nature Photography Prize. This is a chance for your photographs to be published. You will also be awarded US$ 500 plus a whole year's subscription of True Nature magazine.

Who may enter: Anyone except individuals related to True Nature employees or board members. By submitting an entry, each contestant agrees to the rules of the contest.

Photograph eligibility: Photographs must be taken outdoors and bring out the beauty of mother nature. Photos that violate or infringe upon another person's rights, including but not limited to copyright, are not eligible.

Entry deadline: Photographs must be received by 1 July 2022 to be considered for the 2022 prize. Images received after this date will automatically be entered into the competition for 2023.

How to enter: Entry is free and each entrant may submit up to five images. Entries should be sent to editor@truenature.com.us with the entrant's name and a brief description of what the image shows. Entries should be sent as digital image files, in either TIF or JPEG format, and each file may not be larger than 10MB.

23. Who is not allowed to take part in the contest?
    A. Anyone below 18 years of age
    B. Someone who sent five images
    C. Readers of True Nature magazine
    D. Relatives of the magazine's editor

24. Can you send in photographs for the competition after July the first?
    A. No, your entry will automatically be canceled.
    B. No, entries after the deadline will not be entertained.
    C. Yes, you can ask for an extension to be considered for the 2022 prize.
    D. Yes, but you will take part in next year's contest.

25. What is a basic requirement for all entries?
    A. All imitations are welcome.
    B. Photographs have to be original.
    C. Pictures need to be developed.
    D. Only plant owners are eligible.

Since PLAY & PAY opened its doors in July 2007, we have cemented our position in the market as a leader of this industry. With a total of four offices in Australia (Sydney, Melbourne, Brisbane and Perth), one in New Zealand (Auckland) and two in Canada (Toronto and Vancouver), we have become the largest and most significant service provider for young people who wish to work to get paid and find time to play at the same time. In 2012, we serviced over 5500 members from 17 different countries.

What makes our service unique is that it is completely tailored towards the individual needs and objectives of our members. Our packages, however, are designed to suit everyone and all budgets. We work very closely with our partners to develop new packages that match the requirements of their individual markets. Our ambitious product development strategy has enabled us to remain competitive with regards to the quality of our service and the individual package prices.

Our essential start-up kits include Orientation, Sim Cards and On-the-Job Support. Once members are in their destination country, they are able to contact us by our toll-free number anytime. Our service also covers personal travel advice, accommodation and transport reservation services and a wide range of tours and travel packages. Our dedicated and multilingual consultants have been thoroughly trained to provide our members with accurate information and advice.

26. What can be said about PLAY & PAY?
    A. It is a leader that specializes in cement.
    B. Its members are from Australia, New Zealand and Canada.
    C. It is the biggest player in the packaged-tour industry.
    D. Its services allow members to secure a job and travel.

27. What can you expect if you enroll in the program provided by PLAY & PAY?
    A. You can get in touch with PLAY & PAY staff by phone.
    B. You have to stay with a friend or a relative.
    C. You will learn how to lead a guided tour.
    D. You are required to report your whereabouts.

28. Which of the following is included in the service?
    A. Student loan packaged tours
    B. Immigration advice and application
    C. Assistance in overcoming language barriers
    D. Driving classes to obtain international passport

Questions 29-31

The United States currently relies heavily on coal, oil, and natural gas for its energy. Fossil fuels are non-renewable, that is, they draw on finite resources that will eventually dwindle, becoming too expensive or too environmentally damaging to retrieve. In contrast, the many types of renewable energy resources, such as wind and solar energy, are constantly replenished and will never run out. Sunlight, or solar energy, can be used directly for heating and lighting homes and other buildings, for generating electricity, and for hot water heating. There's a catch though; there is no solar electricity when the Sun does not shine, and no wind energy when there is no wind. Neither wind nor solar energy can ever replace coal or natural gas for power generation until these basic limitations are dealt with.

Another alternative to fossil fuels is hydro energy. In countries with abundant water supply all year round, water flowing downhill from mountains into rivers or streams can be converted to hydroelectric power. Nuclear power used to be thought of as a cheap and efficient way to produce power but has now been frowned on after a series of disasters brought about by radiation. Renewable energy is a viable option but it needs to be steady, reliable and available round the clock if it will ever power the world. The race has begun. Car makers have poured millions of dollars into the research and development of highly efficient electric vehicles that depend solely on green energy. Some other questions they have to answer include, "Where can drivers charge their cars the way they can charge a phone? Will the cost of recharging batteries be higher than filling up tanks in a gas station?"

29. What can be said about fossil fuels a few decades from now?
    A. They will be entirely replaced by solar energy.
    B. They will be used up.
    C. They will be recycled and reused.
    D. They will be cheaper to produce.

30. According to the passage, what advantage might hydro energy have over wind energy?
    A. Hydro energy is more reliable.
    B. Hydro energy is more economical.
    C. Hydro energy is friendlier to the environment.
    D. Hydro energy is cleaner and better.

31. What challenge do car makers face?
    A. To create a car that requires little electricity to run
    B. To develop a gasoline-free car before rival companies do
    C. To set up kiosks where motorists can plug in to charge their vehicles
    D. All of the above

Questions 32-35 are based on the information in the following letter and confirmation.

To all the graduates,

Congratulations! You set your goal, and you reached it. You have worked hard to complete your degree at the International University. And that's something you and your loved ones want to celebrate together.

Taking part in this wonderful ceremony and seeing you receive your diploma should be an unforgettable experience for them. If you want to invite your family and relatives to come to the United States, you need to request verification letters. First, you must visit the International University website to fill out the form in order to provide certain necessary information about your guests.

The deadline for this form is January 20, 2020. All letters will be issued in Portable Document Format (PDF) and emailed to you. You should remind your guests to visit the U.S. Embassy website for procedures to fill the forms, pay the appropriate fees, and book a visa interview appointment. Once they receive the confirmation of the visa application, they can bring their passports along with the letters for a visa interview.

Best Regards,
Michelle Miller
Executive director of International Student Affairs

Confirmation

This confirms the submission of the Non-immigrant visa application form:

Name Provided:	Allen Chen	Location Selected
Date of Birth:	05/11/1970	American Institute in
Place of Birth:	Keelung, Taiwan	Taiwan – Kaohsiung
Gender:	Male	Branch Office
Nationality:	Republic of China	5F, No.88, Chenggong
Passport number:	9842357	2nd Road, Qianzhen
Purpose of Travel:	pleasure visitor	Dist., Kaohsiung 80661,
Completed on:	31 JAN 2020	Taiwan
Confirmed No:	AA144P4IMW	
This is not a VISA		

YOU MUST BRING the confirmation page and the following document(s) with you at all steps during the application process: Passport, the verification letter from the university
You may also provide any additional documents you feel will support your case.

32. What is the purpose of the letter?
    A. To congratulate everyone who graduated.
    B. To advise all the guests of graduated to apply for a visa.
    C. To inform all the graduates to apply for verification letters.
    D. To make all guests of graduates aware of the graduation ceremony.

33. What is the family name of the visa applicant?
    A. Michelle.
    B. Miller.
    C. Allen.
    D. Chen.

34. What is the next step when people get the confirmation page?
    A. Applying for verification letters.
    B. Attending the graduation ceremony.
    C. Waiting for an international mail.
    D. Participating in a visa interview appointment.

35. According to the letter and the confirmation page, which of the following is true?
    A. Those who get the letters are the students of the International University.
    B. Allen Chen was born in Kaohsiung in 1970.
    C. The graduation ceremony will be held on January 20, 2020.
    D. The International University is located in Taiwan.

—結束—

第五回

初試 聽力測驗 解析

第一部分 看圖辨義

Q1

For question one, please look at picture A.

What can you tell from the picture?
你從圖片中可看出什麼？

A. The woman is doing two things at a time.

B. The woman is typing in some information.

C. The woman is suspended from work.

D. The woman is overwhelmed by her duties.

A. 這位女子同一時間在做兩件事。

B. 這位女子正在輸入一些資料。

C. 這位女子被停職了。

D. 這位女子因為工作而不知所措。

答案：D

詳解

　　圖中可見辦公桌上放滿了文件還有便利貼，女子狂抓頭髮，窮於應付，答案為 D。

補充說明

　　overwhelm 原來的意思是指「淹沒」，英文單字有所謂的字面上（literal）的用法，也就是原來的意思，但很多時候也有修辭上（figurative）的用法。overwhelmed by 通常被用來做比喻令人不知所措的情況，而非真正的被洪水淹沒。

Q2

For question two, please look at picture B.

Who does the man need to call for help?
這位男子需要向誰求助？

A. A plumber.
B. A barber.
C. An electrician.
D. A veterinarian.

A. 水管工人。
B. 男理髮師。
C. 電工。
D. 獸醫。

〔詳解〕　　　　　　　　　　　　　　　　　　　　　　　　答案：A

　　在圖片題中，男子在廚房，水龍頭不斷噴出水，使男子十分慌張，他需要找會維修水管的技工幫忙，答案為 A。

〈補充說明〉

　　在台灣，水電工可從事電路與水管的業務。然而在外國，負責電路和水管是兩個不同的專業領域，plumber 負責維修水管、水龍頭和馬桶等，並不負責和電相關的工作。

Q3

For question three, please look at picture C.

Why are the players so excited?
為何這些球員如此興奮？

A. They won the lottery.
B. They are the champions.
C. They are the first runners-up.
D. They came in second.

A. 他們中了樂透。
B. 他們是冠軍。
C. 他們是亞軍。
D. 他們得到第二名。

〔詳解〕　　　　　　　　　　　　　　　　　　　　　　　　答案：B

　　圖片中的足球隊員捧著上面寫著「1」的冠軍獎盃，可以知道他們是冠軍（champion），答案為 B。runner-up 是指第二名或之後的名次，所以 first runner-up 就是「第二名」，「第三名」則是 second runner-up，請注意複數型字尾 s 所在的位置。

〈補充說明〉

　　英國人習慣把一樓叫 ground floor（地面樓層），二樓才是第一層 first floor，跟台灣一般熟悉的美式英文狀況不同。

第 1 回
第 2 回
第 3 回
第 4 回
第 5 回
第 6 回

Q4

For questions four and five, please look at picture D.

What information is true based on this brochure?　在這本手冊上，什麼資訊是正確的？

Summer Travel Fair:
Adults: NT$200.
Students: NT$100
Student tickets are required for children.

taller than 110 cm.
Admission is free for senior citizens aged 65 and above.

A. All adults have to pay an entrance fee.

B. All children are required to purchase tickets.

C. Students can get tickets at half-price.

D. Admission is free for kids who are eleven years old.

A. 所有成人必須付入場費。

B. 所有兒童必須購票。

C. 學生可享有半價優惠。

D. 十一歲的兒童入場免費。

詳解　　　　　　　　　　　　　　　　　　　　　　　答案：C

　　從圖中旅展手冊可得知，並非所有成人必須付入場費，65 歲以上的年長者無需購票，選項 A 是錯誤的。身高 110 公分以上的兒童才需購票，選項 B 也是錯的。成人票價為 $200，學生價為 $100，學生可享有半價優惠是正確的，答案為 C。兒童需不需要購票取決於身高而不是年齡，圖片中並沒有說明十一歲兒童的身高，選項 D 不能算是正確的訊息。

|單字片語| **Summer Travel Fair** 夏季旅展 / **adult** [əˋdʌlt] 成年人
　　　　 admission [ədˋmɪʃən] 入場費；門票 / **citizen** [ˋsɪtəzn̩] 市民；居民

Q5

For question five, please refer to picture D again.

Mr. Clifford is seventy years old and his wife is sixty years old. How much do they have to pay?
Clifford 先生今年 70 歲，而他的太太 60 歲，他們必須付多少錢？

Summer Travel Fair:
Adults: NT$200.
Students: NT$100
Student tickets are required for children.

taller than 110 cm.
Admission is free for senior citizens aged 65 and above.

A. NT$400.
B. NT$200.
C. NT$100.
D. NT$0.

A. 台幣 400 元。
B. 台幣 200 元。
C. 台幣 100 元。
D. 台幣 0 元。

詳解　　　　　　　　　　　　　　　　　　　　　　　答案：B

　　承上題，70 歲的 Mr. Clifford 入場免費，但他的太太不符合免費入場的條件，需要購買成人票，他們必須付 NT$200，答案為 B。

第二部分 問答

Q6

Let's discuss about what to do for the summer vacation.
讓我們討論一下暑假要做什麼。

A. I can't wait for the new semester.
B. I am not sure if it will be here.
C. I have a suggestion.
D. I'd rather not talk about it.

A. 我好期待新的學期。
B. 我不確定它是否會在這裡。
C. 我有一個提議。
D. 我寧可不談這件事。

詳解　　　　　　　　　　　　　　**答案：C**

　　既然要討論暑假要做什麼，選項中最合理的回應是「我有一個提議」，答案為C。選項 A 直接跳過暑假，完全沒有針對說話者的問題做出回應，因此選項 A 是錯誤的。選項 D 在以上情境中聽起來會十分無禮，而且討論暑假活動時，心情會低迷到不想談也不合常理，反而是當對方問了一些會讓人感到不開心的事時，可以用選項 D 回答。

〈補充說明〉

I rather not talk about it 的使用情境：
Speaker 1: I heard that your car broke down again.　我聽說你的車子又拋錨了。
Speaker 2: I rather not talk about it.　我寧可不談這件事。

Q7

Visiting hours are over.
探病時間過了。

A. You can always play it again.
B. I promise I won't take long.
C. Let's go there by train.
D. This doesn't belong to you.

A. 你可以一直再玩一次。
B. 我保證我不會太久。
C. 我們坐火車去吧。
D. 這不是屬於你的。

詳解　　　　　　　　　　　　　　**答案：B**

　　從試題可判斷，說話者在醫院，說話對象應該是病患的朋友或家屬。除非是加護病房，否則探病時間一般都能通融，即使探病時間過了也可以跟病患見上一面。在這樣的情境中，選項 B 是最為合理的答案。

|單字片語| visiting hours 探病時間 / business hours 營業時間 / rush hours 尖峰時段

Q8

Aaron is going to Paris on business, isn't he?
Aaron 要去巴黎出差，不是嗎？

A. No, the company is sending him to Paris.　A. 不，公司派他去巴黎。
B. No, he is definitely going.　B. 不，他肯定會去的。
C. Yes, he's working on his French.　C. 是的，他正在苦練法文。
D. Yes, he will be in Germany next month.　D. 是的，他下個月將會在德國。

詳解　　　　　　　　　　　　　　　　　　　**答案：C**

　　這是附加問句，後半句的 isn't he?（不是嗎？）的目的是強調前半句。「Aaron 要去巴黎出差，不是嗎？」表示說話者很肯定 Aaron 將要到巴黎出差。選項 A 和 B 既然表示認同，應該用 Yes 回答，所以 A 和 B 都是錯誤的。最合理的答案為 C，因為 Aaron 要到巴黎出差，所以正在苦練法文。選項 D 則是陷阱題，若不知道法國的首都是巴黎，就有可能被誤導。

〈補充說明〉

　　以下是歐洲主要國家的首都：
英國首都 London（倫敦），德國首都 Berlin（柏林），義大利首都 Rome（羅馬），荷蘭首都 Amsterdam（阿姆斯特丹）。

Q9

The copier is out of paper again.
這台影印機又沒紙了。

A. That's cheating.　A. 那是作弊。
B. It might get wet.　B. 它可能會弄濕。
C. Maybe yellow will be a better choice.　C. 或許黃色是更好的選擇。
D. I'll go get it.　D. 我去拿紙。

詳解　　　　　　　　　　　　　　　　　　　**答案：D**

　　當對方說「影印機又沒紙了」，最合適的對應句是「我去拿紙」，答案為 D。

|單字片語| copier [ˈkɑpɪə] 影印機 / Xerox machine 影印機
　　　　fax [fæks] 傳真 / telegram [ˈtɛləˌgræm] 電報

Why is there such a big jam? We are stuck for almost an hour. 為什麼會大塞車？我們已經被卡住快一個小時了。

A. Perhaps it is a different brand.
B. Your watch has slowed down.
C. We ran out of gasoline.
D. An accident most likely.

A. 或許是一個不同的品牌。
B. 你的手錶已經慢下來了。
C. 我們的汽油用完了。
D. 最有可能的是發生意外吧。

詳解　　　　　　　　　　　　　　　　　　　　　**答案：D**

　　從說話者的說話內容可推斷，他們遇到了交通阻塞，解釋造成交通阻塞最合理的原因是發生交通意外，答案為 D。

We should do our part to help save the earth.
我們應該出一份力來拯救地球。

A. I usually carry a shopping bag.
B. I have had enough.
C. I can adjust the volume.
D. I believe it is round.

A. 我通常會拿一個購物袋。
B. 我已經受夠了。
C. 我可以調整音量。
D. 我相信它是圓的。

詳解　　　　　　　　　　　　　　　　　　　　　**答案：A**

　　這題要轉個彎才可以選出答案，題目談到每個人都要出一份力來拯救地球，而其中一個方法是自己攜帶購物袋，以減少塑膠袋的使用，並減少垃圾，答案為 A。另外，如果只聽到 earth 卻沒有理解整句話，就可能會被選項 D 誤導，因此一定要聽完整個敘述，並看過所有的選項才能作答。

|單字片語| **do one's part** 盡一分力 / **have a part to play** 有責任和義務

第 1 回
第 2 回
第 3 回
第 4 回
第 5 回
第 6 回

Q12

Have you prepared yourself for the interview?
你已經為這場面試做好準備了嗎？

A. I can give you some advice.
B. I can think of no more questions.
C. There is no way it is going to happen.
D. There are many ways to do it.

A. 我可以給你一些建議。
B. 我想不到更多的問題了。
C. 這是不可能會發生的。
D. 有很多方法做這件事。

詳解　　　　　　　　　　　　　　　　　　　**答案：B**

　　甲問乙是否已經為面試做好準備，表示要參加面試的人是乙，至於甲是否也要去參加面試不得而知，所以選項 A 是錯的，這句話應該是甲說的，不是乙。最合理的回應是「我想不到更多的問題了」，表示已經做好充分的準備，答案為 B。

＜補充說明＞

　　語言是活學活用的工具，「我想不到更多的問題」可以說 I can't think of any more questions，也可以說 I can think of no more questions。還有其他例句：I can't think of anyone else.（我想不到還有誰。）/ I can think of no one.（我想不到任何一個人。）

Q13

What kind of present would you like to receive?
你想要得到什麼樣的禮物呢？

A. They are kind and friendly.
B. I haven't returned her call.
C. Something inexpensive but practical.
D. It's made of wood and plastic.

A. 他們很親切也很友善。
B. 我還沒回她的來電。
C. 某一個不貴但實用的東西。
D. 它是由木頭和塑膠做的。

詳解　　　　　　　　　　　　　　　　　　　**答案：C**

　　「你想要得到什麼樣的禮物？」最合理的回應是「某一個不貴但實用的東西」，答案為 C。

|單字片語| **practical** [ˋpræktɪkl] 實際的；實用的 / **practically** [ˋpræktɪklɪ] 實際上

Dolphins are really intelligent creatures.
海豚是很聰明的生物。

A. My IQ is above average.
B. You have to be creative sometimes.
C. They can communicate using sounds.
D. This is the latest technology.

A. 我的智商在平均之上。
B. 有時候你必須有創意。
C. 牠們能夠用聲音來溝通。
D. 這是最新的科技。

詳解　　　　　　　　　　　　　　　　　　　　**答案：C**

　　要和外國人對答如流，必須依照場合和情境對答，不一定要等對方疑問才開口回答。假設兩個人看一部紀錄片，當對方做出評語，我們可以把自己知道的說出來與對方做互動，因此回應「海豚是很聰明的生物」最為合理的回應為 C。

|單字片語| intelligent [ɪnˈtɛlədʒənt] 有智慧的 / Intelligence Quotient 智商指數

Did you notice that Elaine looks kind of depressed lately?
你有沒有注意到 Elaine 最近看起來有點沮喪？

A. She didn't see the poster.
B. She has always been considerate.
C. She hasn't gotten over the death of her pet.
D. She promised she will be early.

A. 她沒有看到海報。
B. 她一直以來都很體貼。
C. 她對於寵物的過世還沒釋懷。
D. 她答應我她會早點到的。

詳解　　　　　　　　　　　　　　　　　　　　**答案：C**

　　題目提到朋友最近看起來有點沮喪，最合理的回應是說出她感到沮喪的原因，答案為 C。

|單字片語| get over 釋懷 / get rid of 除掉
　　　　　 get away from 暫時離開 / get away with 逍遙法外

第1回
第2回
第3回
第4回
第5回
第6回

Q16

W: Did you wash your hands with soap? Go do it before you get a disease.
你有用肥皂洗手嗎？在你感染疾病之前趕快去做。

M: Mom, you are always making such a big fuss.
媽，你總是小題大作。

W: One of your classmates spent two days in a hospital because his mom didn't make a big fuss about personal hygiene.
你其中一位同學就是因為他的媽媽沒有在個人衛生上小題大作，在醫院住院兩天。

Q: What is the woman concerned about?
這位女子擔心的是什麼？

A. Her son's grades.
B. Her son's health.
C. Her son's classmate.
D. Her son's illness.

A. 她兒子的成績。
B. 她兒子的健康。
C. 她兒子的同學。
D. 她兒子的病情。

詳解　　　　　　　　　　　　　　　　　　　　　　　　答案：B

　　全民英檢的對話題大多是一男一女，所以從四個選項中判斷，我們可預期將會聽到的有可能是母子的對話，或是男女間討論女子的小孩的對話，而這裡的對話就是母子間的對話，說話者是媽媽和兒子。這位媽媽要求兒子勤洗手注意個人衛生（personal hygiene），非常關心孩子的健康問題，答案為 B。

|單字片語| **hygiene** [ˈhaɪdʒin] 衛生 / **hygienic** [ˌhaɪdʒɪˈɛnɪk] 衛生（學）的

Q17

W: I am more used to wearing pants with a zip.
我比較習慣穿有拉鍊的褲子。

M: Buttons are just as convenient. In fact, they look more fashionable.
鈕扣也一樣方便。事實上，他們看起來比較時尚。

W: Maybe you're right. I don't have to worry about the zip getting stuck.
也許你是對的。我也不需要擔心拉鍊被卡住。

Q: Where are the speakers most likely?
說話者最有可能在什麼地方？

A. In a garment store.　　A. 在服裝店。
B. In a post office.　　　B. 在郵局。
C. In a stationery shop.　C. 在文具店。
D. In a bakery.　　　　　D. 在麵包店。

詳解　　　　　　　　　　　　　　　　　　答案：A

　　從選項即可知道這題問的是說話者在什麼地方，從拉鍊（zip）和鈕扣（button）等關鍵詞，可判斷他們在談論服裝，答案為 A。

I單字片語I **garment** [ˈgɑrmənt] 衣服 / **apparel** [əˈpærəl] 服裝
　　　　clothing [ˈkloðɪŋ] 衣服 / **attire** [əˈtaɪr] 服裝

Q18

M: You had better get inside. Wind speed is picking up.
　　你最好進來裡面。風速在增強了。

W: It's not even raining. Maybe the weather forecast is a little
　　exaggerated.　甚至連雨也沒下。或許氣象預報有點誇張。

M: Get in here. I don't want you to be hit by a falling object.
　　進來這裡。我不想要你被掉落的東西砸到。

Q: What can we tell from the conversation?
從這段對話中可以知道什麼？

A. A landslide is taking place.　A. 正在發生塌方。
B. A flood is happening.　　　　B. 正在發生淹水。
C. An earthquake is occurring.　C. 有地震發生。
D. A typhoon is approaching.　　D. 颱風正要靠近。

詳解　　　　　　　　　　　　　　　　　　答案：D

　　選項中提到四種天然災難，而對話中的關鍵詞為風速（wind speed），氣象預報（weather forecast）和掉落物（falling object），可見說話者在談論的是颱風，答案為 D。

I單字片語I **hurricane** [ˈhɜɪˌken] 颶風 / **cyclone** [ˈsaɪklon] 氣旋
　　　　tornado [tɔrˈnedo] 龍捲風 / **twister** [ˈtwɪstə] 旋風

第 1 回

第 2 回

第 3 回

第 4 回

第 5 回

第 6 回

Q19

W: Please lower your volume. You are disturbing the rest.
請降低音量。你打擾到其他人。

M: I'm terribly sorry. I'm looking for some research material.
我很抱歉。我正在找一些研究資料。

W: You may make use of the computer to narrow your search.
你可以用電腦來縮小要尋找的範圍。

Q: **Where is the conversation taking place?**
這段對話在什麼地方發生的？

A. In a library.
B. In a gallery.
C. In a clinic.
D. In a terminal.

A. 在圖書館。
B. 在畫廊。
C. 在診所。
D. 在車站。

詳解

答案：A

光看選項可知道題目要問的是對話發生的地點，在畫廊、和圖書館或診所都不應該大聲喧嘩，從降低聲量（lower your volume）無法判斷合理答案。要找研究資料（research material），最有可能去的地方是圖書館，答案為 A。

〈補充說明〉

要求別人說話小聲一點可以說 lower your volume，若是要求別人把收音機的音量調低，可以說 turn down the volume a little。

Q20

W: May I have a copy of the train schedule, please? Oh my! This is complicated.　請問可以給我一份火車時刻表嗎？天啊！這個好複雜喔。

M: Why don't you download the smart phone version? We have a free user-friendly application and all you need to do is enter your current location plus the destination.

你為何不去下載智慧型手機的版本呢？我們有一個非常對使用者友善的免費應用程式。你全部需要做的，就是輸入你目前的所在地還有想要去的目的地。

W: That would be great!　那太棒了！

Q: What was the man's suggestion?
這位男子的建議是什麼？

A. Get a software program from the Internet.　A. 從網路上取得軟體程式。
B. Print out the train schedule.　B. 把火車行程表列印出來。
C. Write down an address.　C. 寫下一個地址。
D. Tell the driver her destination.　D. 告訴司機她的目的地。

詳解　　　　　　　　　　　　　　　　　　　　　　**答案：A**

　　手機和平板應用程式的 APP，是 application 的縮寫，從下載（download）和版本（version）這兩個關鍵詞，可判斷男子建議女子從網路上取得一個軟體程式，答案為 A。

|單字片語| **download** [ˈdaʊnˌlod] 下載 / **upload** [ʌpˈlod] 上傳 / **update** [ʌpˈdet] 更新

Q21

W: We have to pay an extra 20% on the fare after midnight.
　　午夜過後，我們必須多付百分之 20 的車資。

M: That's pretty reasonable to me. Some people are sacrificing their sleep to make sure we get home safe and sound.
　　對我來說那很合理。有些人犧牲他們的睡眠，以確保我們平安到家。

W: All right. If you say so.　好吧。如果你這麼說的話。

Q: What are the speakers discussing?
說話者在談論什麼？

A. An unfair hike in fare.　A. 不合理的車資調漲。
B. A surcharge for late hours.　B. 凌晨時分的額外收費。
C. A way to get home safely.　C. 安全回家的方法。
D. A sacrifice people have to make.　D. 人們必須做出的犧牲。

詳解　　　　　　　　　　　　　　　　　　　　　　**答案：B**

　　在對話中，男子表示午夜過後的附加收費是合理的，而且後來女子也認同他的看法，因此選項 A 是錯誤的。如果沒有聽完對話的內容，光靠關鍵詞 safe（安全）和 sacrifice（犧牲），還是無法判斷正確答案，因此要注意聽完整個對話。而說話者在討論的是凌晨時分額外收費的合理性，答案為 B。

第 1 回
第 2 回
第 3 回
第 4 回
第 5 回
第 6 回

Q22

M: I didn't know there are so many strategies when it comes to playing chess.

我不知道説到下西洋棋會有這麼多的策略。

W: You have to learn them if you want to be a top player.

你若想成為頂級的選手，就必須把它們學起來。

M: Does your chess club welcome amateurs?

你的棋社歡迎業餘人士嗎？

Q: What is true about the man?
關於這位男子，什麼是正確的？

A. He is an expert.
B. He is not interested in chess.
C. He wants to join the club.
D. He is the chairman of a chess club.

A. 他是一位專家。
B. 他對下西洋棋不感興趣。
C. 他想參加這個社團。
D. 他是棋社的社長。

詳解

答案：C

　　這位男子承認自己不知道原來下棋有許多策略，這表示他不是專家，選項 A 是錯誤的。雖然他不是專家，卻想要加入棋社，這表示他對下棋有興趣，選項 B 也是錯誤的。對話的最後一句，既然他是業餘愛好者（amateur），也表示他想要參加棋社，因此他就不可能是棋社社長，選項 D 也是錯誤的。男子問是否歡迎業餘人員，表示他有參加意願，答案為 C。

|單字片語| **amateur** [ˈæməˌtʃʊr] 業餘愛好者 / **novice** [ˈnɑvɪs] 新手 / **layman** [ˈlemən] 外行人

Q23

M: It's been a year and I still can't get over her. I wonder why she broke up with me in the first place. She left without a word.

已經一年了，我還是忘不了她。我想知道她當初為何跟我分手。她一句話都沒説就離開了。

W: It's time you should start seeing someone else.

是時候你應該開始另外找對象了。

M: I don't think anyone can replace her.　我不認為有任何人可以取代她。

341

Q: Why is the man so upset? 為何這位男子如此煩惱？

A. He couldn't get the first place in the competition.
A. 他無法在比賽中取得第一名。

B. He couldn't pass his exams.
B. 他無法通過考試。

C. He couldn't see two women at the same time.
C. 他無法同時跟兩個女人交往。

D. He couldn't understand what went wrong.
D. 他不明白哪裡出了問題。

詳解

答案：D

　　四個選項都是 He couldn't，可預想到聽取對話的焦點應該放在對話中男子遇到的問題。從 broke up（分手），left without a word（不告而別）和 replace（取代）等關鍵詞，可得知這名男子忘不了他的前女友。男子也提到他想知道前任離開的原因，因此符合敘述的答案為 D。

〈補充說明〉

　　in the first place 可理解為「一開始」，在口說和寫作中都很常會用到。
We shouldn't have come here **in the first place**.　我們一開始就不應該來這裡。
You could have told me you don't like it **in the first place**.
你一開始就可以告訴我，你不喜歡這個。

Q24

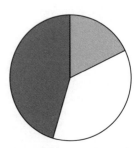

M: Yesterday, my professor showed us this poll regarding the three most favorite social media platform among teenagers.
昨天，我的教授給我們看了這項針對青少年最喜歡的三種社群媒體的民調。

W: Let me have a look. YouTube is on the top.
讓我看看，YouTube 是第一名。

M: Yes, even though I have heard that teens spend more time on

Instagram, the result shows that it only came in second.

沒錯，即使我聽說了青少年花更多時間在 Instagram 上，結果卻顯示它只在第二名。

W: Interestingly, Snapchat, which I have never used, ranked third.

有趣的是，我從來沒用過的 Snapchat 排名第三名。

M: Me neither. I guess we are kind of old school.

我也沒用過，我想我們有點老派。

W: Yeah. Didn't you notice that Facebook was not on the chart? From what I know, Facebook has the most users around the globe.

對啊，你沒發現 Facebook 沒有在這張圖表裡面嗎？就我所知道的，Facebook 在全球擁有最多用戶。

Q: **Look at the pie chart. What does the largest section refer to?** 請看這張圓餅圖，最大的部分指的是什麼？

A. Facebook.
B. Snapchat.
C. YouTube.
D. Instagram.

詳解　　　　　　　　　　　　　　　　　　　　　　　　　答案：C

　　從圓餅圖和選項可知題目可能跟前三大社群媒體有關，因此聽敘述時要注意各社群媒體對應到圖表上的位置。從 YouTube is on the top，可以知道 YouTube 是第一、佔最大部份。而 teens spend more time on Instagram, the result shows that it only came in the second 指出第二是 Instagram。Snapchat ranked third，可知 Snapchat 排名第三。Facebook was out of the chart. 因此臉書不在圖表中。整合以上的資訊，可以推論出，圓餅圖中佔最大的部份是 YouTube，答案為 C。

Q25

Receipt 收據

Saturday, March 12, 2021

2021 年 3 月 12 日 星期六

ITEM 品項	QUANTITY 數量	PRICE 金額	AMOUNT 合計
Plastic bag 塑膠袋	1	$ 2	$ 2
Book bag 書包	1	$ 1,300	$ 1,300
Pen bag 筆袋	2	$ 100	$ 200
Pad 便條紙	2	$ 200	$ 400
		TOTAL 總計	$ 1,902

第 1 回
第 2 回
第 3 回
第 4 回
第 5 回
第 6 回

W: Excuse me. I bought some stuff at your store last Saturday. There seems to be something wrong with the receipt.

不好意思。我上週六在你的商店買了一些東西。這張收據上有些項目似乎有錯。

M: May I see your receipt first? 我可以先看你的收據嗎？

W: Here you are. There was a sign on the bookshelf. It said, "Buy one book bag and get one pen bag for free." 在這裡。書架上有個牌子，上面寫道：「買一個書包，免費獲得一個筆袋。」

M: Yes. The promotion was from March 1st to 15th, and your purchase was on March 12th.

是的，這個促銷是從 3 月 1 日到 15 日，而你是在 3 月 12 日購買的。

W: Which means I should get one pen bag for free.

這代表我應該免費得到一個筆袋。

M: I apologize for making the mistake. Let me give you your money back for this.

很抱歉犯了這個錯誤，讓我歸還你這筆錢。

Q: Look at the receipt. How much money will the woman get from the store?

請看這張收據，這位女子將從這間店拿到多少錢？

A. $ 2.
B. $ 100.
C. $ 200.
D. $ 300.

詳解

答案：B

　　從收據和選項可以猜測題目跟費用有關，因此聽敘述時要注意收據上四個物品的資訊，才能知道女子能從商店裡拿到多少錢。女子提到 Buy one book bag and get one pen bag for free，可以知道買了書包，就可免費獲得一個筆袋。男子提到 The promotion was from March 1st to 15th, and your purchase was on March 12th，可以知道女子的消費符合促銷資格，再看到收據上筆袋的價錢為 100 元，因此答案為 B。

第四部分 / 簡短談話

Q26

M: With social media widely used in high schools, many teenagers suffer from cyberbullying. The most common reason is generally looks. Anything put on the Internet is spreading rapidly. The worst part is that even if you eliminate the post, someone else could repost it. The minds of the victims are severely affected so that they may blame themselves and even hurt themselves.

隨著社群媒體在中學廣泛被使用，許多青少年遭受到網路霸凌。最常見的原因通常是外表。任何放在網路上的事情會迅速傳播。最糟糕的部分是，即使你刪除了貼文，其他人也可能會將它重新發佈。受害人的心靈嚴重受到影響，以致於他們可能會自責，甚至傷害自己。

> **Q: What type of bullying is mentioned in this speech?**
> 這篇演講中提到了哪一種霸凌行為？
>
> | | |
> |---|---|
> | A. Attitude. | A. 態度。 |
> | B. Relationship. | B. 關係。 |
> | C. Appearance. | C. 外表。 |
> | D. Rumors. | D. 謠言。 |

答案：C

詳解

　　從選項中可以猜測題目與人相關。所以，聽敘述時要注意與人相關的內容。從第二句 The most common reason is generally looks，可知網路霸凌最常見的原因通常是外表，答案為 C。

|單字片語| **cyberbully** [ˈsaɪbəˈbʊlɪ] 網路霸凌 / **eliminate** [ɪˈlɪməˌnet] 消除

Q27

W: The shoulder and single lane between the 210 km and 250 km makers on Highway 68 will be closed every night from March 10th to 20th. This will start from 9 p.m. and go to 6 a.m. Flags, arrow boards, and cones will be displayed. Drivers are advised to be cautious while traveling through the work area and be aware of personnel and traffic control devices.

68 號高速公路在 210 公里至 250 公里之間的路肩和單行道，將於 3 月 10 日至 20 日每天晚上關閉。從晚上 9 點開始、直到凌晨 6 點結束。旗子、指示板和圓錐會被擺放出來。建議駕駛在通過施工區時要小心，並且要注意人員和交通控制設備。

第 1 回
第 2 回
第 3 回
第 4 回
第 5 回
第 6 回

Q: **What will happen on the shoulder and single lane of Highway 68?** 68 號高速公路的路肩和單行道會發生什麼事？

A. A construction.　　　　　　　　A. 施工。
B. A traffic jam.　　　　　　　　B. 交通擁塞。
C. A protest march.　　　　　　　C. 抗議遊行。
D. A road run.　　　　　　　　　D. 公路路跑。

詳解　　　　　　　　　　　　　　　　　　　　　　**答案：A**

　　從選項可以猜測是四種與道路相關的事件，這些事件都會進行道路管制或封閉，因此聽敘述時要注意相關的內容。從第一句 The shoulder and single lane between 210 km and 250 km on Highway 68 will be closed every night from March 10th to 20th，可知道路被封閉數個晚上，最後一句 Drivers are advised to be cautious while traveling through the work area and be aware of personnel and traffic control devices 提醒駕駛在通過施工區時要小心，可知這是針對道路施工的報導，答案為 A。

Q28

M: Hello and thank you for calling Sharper Company. If you know the extension number you are trying to reach, you may dial it at any time. For sales inquiries, press 1. For customer support agents, press 2. For accounting, press 3. For all other inquiries, press 9, or press 0 to repeat the available options.

您好，感謝您致電 Sharper 公司。如果您知道要聯繫的分機號碼，您可以隨時撥號。關於銷售詢問，請按 1。關於客戶支援專員，請按 2。關於會計，請按 3。對於所有其他的詢問，請按 9，或按 0 重聽可用的選項。

Q: **For what service would you press three?**
你會為了什麼服務而按 3？

A. Buy an enormous quantity of goods.　　　A. 購買大量的商品。
B. Having some technical problem.　　　　B. 有一些技術上的問題。
C. File your complaint.　　　　　　　　　C. 提出你的投訴。
D. Request payment of an invoice.　　　　D. 要求一張發票的付款。

詳解　　　　　　　　　　　　　　　　　　　　　　**答案：D**

　　從選項可以猜測可能會提到四種不同的商業行為，分別為：購買、技術、投訴、會計，並從這段電話語音中，對應相關的按鍵。選項 A 與銷售詢問有關，要按 1。選項 B 與技術問題有關，要按 2。選項 C 與其他查詢有關，要按 9。選項 D 與付款帳務的會計相關，因此要按 3，答案為 A。

Q29

W: Our dancers have shown their confidence and dedication. All the hard work and practice of the dancers paid off. Their rhythms, outfits, and movements were so precise and perfect. That wrapped up our annual ballet performance. All of us appreciate you for taking the time out of your busy schedules to be with us this beautiful evening. We wish you all a pleasant night.

我們的舞者表現出了自己的信心和專心致力的精神。舞者們的所有努力和練習都得到了回報。他們的節奏、服裝和動作是如此嚴謹和完美。我們的年度芭蕾舞表演在此結束。我們全體人員感謝您抽出寶貴的時間與我們一起度過這個美好的晚上。我們祝大家有個愉快的夜晚。

Q: What might the audience do next?
聽眾接下來可能會做什麼？

A. Watch a performance.
B. Enjoy the rhythm.
C. Applaud loudly.
D. Dress up.

A. 觀看表演。
B. 享受節奏。
C. 大聲鼓掌。
D. 盛裝打扮。

詳解 答案：C

從選項可以推測這段談話和表演有關，因此聽敘述時要注意許其相關的關鍵詞。從第三句 That wrapped up our annual ballet performance 可以知道年度芭蕾舞表演結束。選項 A（Watch a performance）、B（Enjoy the rhythm）、D（Dress up）都不是在表演節結束時會做的行為，因此刪去這些選項後可以知道，聽眾接下來會大聲鼓掌，答案為 C。

Q30

M: As a result of climate change, hot days become hotter and more common. The temperatures in summer never stopped rising every year. The heatwaves will increase intensely due to reduced soil moisture. Furthermore, heatwaves do not only occur on the ground. Consequently, extreme heat increases both the risk of disasters and the threat to human health, and ecosystems.

由於氣候變遷，炎熱的日子變得越來越熱，也越來越普遍。每年，夏天的溫度都不曾停止上升。由於土壤的水分減少，熱浪急劇增加。此外，熱浪不僅發生在地面上。因此，極度高溫既增加了災害的風險，也增加了對人類健康和生態系統的威脅。

Q: **What is not caused by climate change?**
什麼不是氣候變遷造成的？

A. Heat-related illness.
B. Foreign exchange risk.
C. Stronger hurricanes.
D. More melting ice.

A. 與熱相關的疾病。
B. 外匯風險。
C. 更強的颶風。
D. 更多冰融化。

詳解

答案：B

　　這是一段與氣候變遷有關的談話，四個選項都是不好的狀況，因此聽敘述時要注意與四個選項相關的內容。最後一句提到 Consequently, extreme heat increases both the risk of disasters and the threat to human health, and ecosystems.，清楚說明極端高溫產生的風險和威脅。選項 C（Stronger hurricanes）為災害的風險，選項 A（Heat-related illness）為對人的威脅，選項 D（More melting ice）為生態威脅。選項 B（Foreign Exchange Risk）是經濟問題，與氣候變遷並無直接關連，答案為 B。

|單字片語| **heatwave** [`hitwev] 熱浪 / **ecosystem** [`ɛko,sɪstəm] 生態系統

Q31

W: Netflix offers award-winning television series, films, and documentaries in limitless numbers. It is very easy to create an account on Netflix. There are multiple plans that you can select, and you can downgrade or upgrade anytime. If you choose not to use it, you are free to cancel it online anytime. Why don't you give it a shot?

Netflix 提供無數的得獎電視連續劇、電影和紀錄片。在 Netflix 上建立帳戶非常容易。有多種方案供您選擇，並且能隨時降級或升級。如果您選擇不使用它，可以隨時在網路上取消。您為什麼不試用看看呢？

Q: **What can't you watch on Netflix?**
你在 Netflix 上無法看到什麼？

A. Hollywood movies.
B. Korean dramas.
C. Taiwan documentary films.
D. British commercials.

A. 好萊塢電影。
B. 韓國戲劇。
C. 台灣紀錄片。
D. 英國商業廣告。

詳解

　　從選項可以猜測是對話和不同類型的影片相關，因此聽敘述時要注意這些類型的影片在談話中出現的情況。從第一句 Netflix offers award-winning television series, films and documentaries in limitless numbers 可以知道在 Netflix 可以看到電視連續劇、電影和紀錄片。選項 B（Korean dramas）是為電視連續劇，選項 A（Hollywood movies）是為電影，選項 C（Taiwan documentary films）是為紀錄片。選項 D（British commercials）並沒有被提及，答案為 D。

Q32

M:　Are you aware that it is necessary for your kids to consult a dentist on a regular basis? Children's teeth can easily decay, so they should go to the dentist at least once a year. You are lucky now. Dr. Cruise, a dentist with more than 15 years of experience, specializes in dental care for kids. She joined the Shining Dental Clinic a month ago. Appointments can be made by phone.

　　您是否意識到定期看牙醫對您的孩子是必要的呢？兒童的牙齒很容易蛀牙，所以他們每年至少應該看一次牙醫。現在，您很幸運。Cruise 醫生是一位擁有 15 年以上經驗的牙醫，專精於兒童牙齒保健。一個月前，她加入了 Shining 牙科診所。可以透過電話進行預約。

Q: What is the purpose of this announcement?
這則通知的目的是什麼？

A. Force parents to make a dentist appointment for their children.

B. Warn parents to make a dentist appointment for their children.

C. Assist parents to make a dentist appointment for their children.

D. Encourage parents to make a dentist appointment for their children.

A. 強迫父母為孩子預約牙醫。

B. 警告父母為孩子預約牙醫。

C. 協助父母為孩子預約牙醫。

D. 鼓勵父母為孩子預約牙醫。

詳解

　　選項雖然都是長句，但仔細看會發現只有第一個字不同。而四個選項都和父母為孩子預約牙醫有關，可以推測內容和兒童的牙齒保健相關。聽敘述時需注意與選項的第一個字相關的關鍵句。從第二句 Children's teeth can easily decay, so they should go at least once a year，可知通知的目的是告訴家長每年應該至少去看牙醫一次，最後一句 Appointments can be made by phone 說明預約的方式，答案為 D。

|單字片語| **on a regular basis** 定期地

Q33

W: You just have to find a step stool and place it under a ceiling fan for easy access to the light. The light's screws are round-headed without any slots, so you can rotate them left with your fingers. After removing the broken light bulb, you can thread a new one into the socket until it is tightened. The final step is to replace the screws. Look! It's not difficult.

你只需要找到一個踏凳,並將它放置在吊扇下,來輕鬆地觸及到燈具。燈具的螺釘是圓頭的、沒有任何插槽,所以你用手指就可以將其向左旋轉。卸下損壞的燈泡後,你就能將一個新的燈泡插入插槽,直到它被轉緊為止。最後一步是放回螺釘。你看!沒有很難。

Q: What is the speaker demonstrating?
說話者在示範什麼?

A. Changing a bulb.
B. Threading a screw.
C. Placing a fan.
D. Rotating a clock.

A. 更換一顆燈泡。
B. 鎖上一顆螺絲。
C. 裝上一個風扇。
D. 旋轉一個時鐘。

詳解

答案:A

談話中,說話者在示範一段動作流程,而四個選項和使用家中用品有關,因此聽敘述時要注意所述的動作,才知道答案。從第三句話 After removing the broken light bulb, you thread a new one into the socket until it is tightened ,可知說話者示範的是更換燈泡,答案為 A。

|單字片語| **slot** [slɑt] 狹縫 / **socket** [ˈsɑkɪt] 插座

Q34

Compare prices on Electric Toothbrushes
電動牙刷品牌的價格比較

Brand 品牌	Price 價格
Brand A 品牌 A	$ 1,200
Brand B 品牌 B	$ 1,900
Brand C 品牌 C	$ 1,500
Brand D 品牌 D	$ 1,700

M: I've been considering buying an electric toothbrush for a while. A dental expert recommends several brands to me as they are good at lowering the risk of gum recession. At first, I wanted to buy the least expensive one. Then I found its brush heads cost five hundred dollars, which is way more expensive than the others. Therefore, I chose another one. Although this toothbrush costs three hundred more than the cheapest one, I guess this one is suitable for me.

我已經考慮購買一支電動牙刷一段時間了。一位牙科專家向我推薦了幾個品牌，因為它們善於降低牙齦萎縮的風險。起初，我想購買最不昂貴的品牌。後來，我發現它的刷頭費用是 500 元，比其他的貴很多。因此我選了另一支，儘管這一支牙刷比最便宜的要多花 300 元，我猜這款很適合我。

Q: Which brand does the speaker decide to buy?
說話者決定購買哪一個品牌？

A. Brand A.	A. 品牌 A。
B. Brand B.	B. 品牌 B。
C. Brand C.	C. 品牌 C。
D. Brand D.	D. 品牌 D。

詳解 　　　　　　　　　　　　　　　　　　　　　　　答案：C

　　這題的表格跟選項主要為四種不同品牌的電動牙刷和價格，因此聽敘述時要注意聽針對品牌與價格關係的細節，從第三句 At first, I want to buy the least expensive one，可知一開始說話者想購買最便宜的牙刷，對照表格可以知道最便宜的是品牌 A、1200 元。但最後又提到 I choose another one. Although this toothbrush costs three hundred more than the cheapest one... ，可以推論出，說話者在最後的決定比最低價多 300 元的那一隻電動牙刷，對照表格可知是品牌 C、1500 元，答案為 C。

|單字片語| gum recession 牙齦萎縮

Metro Route Map 捷運路線圖

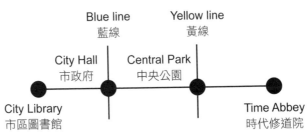

W: Ladies and Gentlemen, this is the Red Line bound for Time Abbey. Please move down inside the cabins and do not block the doors.

第 1 回
第 2 回
第 3 回
第 4 回
第 5 回
第 6 回

The next stop is City Hall. The doors will open on the right side.
Passengers going to City Park can change here to the Blue Line.
Passengers getting off this stop, please don't forget your personal
belongings and watch the gap between the train and the platform.

先生女士您好，這是前往時代修道院的紅線。請往車廂內移動，不要堵住
車門。下一站是市政府，車門將在右側開啟。要前往城市公園的乘客可以
在此處轉乘藍線。在這一站下車的乘客，請不要忘記您的個人物品，並留
意電車和月台之間的空隙。

Q: At which stop should a passenger get off to get to City Park? 要去城市公園的乘客應該在哪一站下車？

A. City Library.　　　　　　　　　A. 市區圖書館。
B. City Hall.　　　　　　　　　　B. 市政府。
C. Central Park.　　　　　　　　C. 中央公園。
D. Time Abbey.　　　　　　　　　D. 時代修道院。

詳解　　　　　　　　　　　　　　　　　　　　　　　　　　**答案：B**

　　在聽敘述前，從路線圖和選項可以猜測題目跟捷運車站有關，因此聽敘述
時要注意四種車站的內容。第三句提到 The next stop is City Hall，表示下一站為
市政府。在第五句提到 Passengers are going to City Park can change here to the
Blue Line，表示前往城市公園的乘客需在那一站轉乘藍線。再對照圖表，前往
城市公園的乘客應該在市政府站下車，答案為 B。

初試 閱讀測驗 解析

第一部分 / 詞彙

Q1

After the third attempt, the little boy realized that riding a bike was not so difficult _____.

在第三次嘗試之後，那個小男孩發現騎單車畢竟沒有那麼困難。

A. in general
B. instead
C. after all
D. ultimately

詳解　　　　　　　　　　　　　　　　　　　　　　　**答案：C**

　　after all（畢竟；終究）的用法比較困難，意思是原本的事情並沒有想像中那樣。句意是小男孩第三次嘗試之後終於成功了，發現騎單車畢竟沒有原本想像中那麼困難，答案為 C。

例句

You don't have to mad. He's just a kid **after all**.
你不必生氣。他畢竟只是一個小朋友。
After all, someone will have to finish the job.
終究，還是需要有人把這件事情完成。

|單字片語| in general 一般而言 / instead [ɪn`stɛd] 反而 / ultimately [`ʌltəmɪtlɪ] 最終

Q2

Postgraduate students are advised not to take things _____, as it is the professors' duties to point out their mistakes and shortcomings.

研究生被建議不要把事情認為是針對個人，因為指出他們的錯誤和缺點是教授的職責。

A. immediately
B. awkwardly
C. personally
D. formally

personal 是「私人的，個人的」，personally 則是它的副詞。take things personally 是指「把事情認為是針對個人」，中文的「對事不對人」用英文表達是 Don't take things personally. ，而 Do it personally. 則是「親自去做」的意思。

|單字片語| **immediately** [ɪ'midɪɪtlɪ] 立即 / **awkwardly** ['ɔkwɜdlɪ] 尷尬地
formally ['fɔrm|ɪ] 正式地

Q3

Nuclear power is now seen as a threat to public safety. The government is exploring other _____ such as solar and hydro energy.

核電現在被視為是公共安全的威脅。政府正在探討其他替代方案，例如：太陽能和水力發電。

A. alternatives   B. animations
C. appliances   D. achievements

詳解 答案：A

太陽能和水力發電是核能發電的替代選擇，alternative 並不只是選擇（choice），而是可以取代另一個方法的替代選擇。There are no alternatives. 意思是「別無選擇」。

|單字片語| **animation** [͵ænə'meʃən] 動畫片 / **appliance** [ə'plaɪəns] 器具
achievement [ə'tʃivmənt] 成就

Q4

Some scientists put forth the hypothesis that black holes are expanding at a _____ rate.

有些科學家提出這個假說，黑洞正以固定的速度擴大。

A. static   B. secured
C. constant   D. necessary

詳解 答案：C

若是靜止的（static），就不會擴大（expand），選項 A 是錯誤的。而選項 B（以安全的速度擴大）跟選項 D（以必要的速度擴大）語意看起來也很奇怪，因此也是錯誤的。可知最合理的搭配是選項 C（以固定的速度擴大）。

第 1 回
第 2 回
第 3 回
第 4 回
第 5 回
第 6 回

Q5

With the _____ of credit cards, it has become much more difficult to suppress the urge to make purchases on impulse.

有了信用卡的發明，壓抑一時衝動購物的慾望變得更加困難。

A. invitation

B. investigation

C. invasion

D. invention

詳解   答案：D

　　這題顯然是想利用拼字相似的單字去混淆考生的題目，不仔細看拼字的話很容易會被誤導而選錯。從關鍵詞 on impulse（在一時衝動下）和 urge（慾望），可推斷是在信用卡發明後買東西很方便，因此變得更難壓抑想買東西的慾望，答案為 D。

|單字片語| invitation [ˌɪnvəˈteʃən] 邀請 / investigation [ɪnˌvɛstəˈgeʃən] 調查；偵查
　　　　 invasion [ɪnˈveʒən] 入侵；侵略

Q6

The recruit had the enemy soldier at his _____ yet he could not muster the courage to pull the trigger.

那位新兵已掌控敵對士兵的生死，可以他卻沒辦法鼓起勇氣扣下板機開槍。

A. begging

B. mercy

C. disposal

D. request

詳解   答案：B

　　這題要考的是片語，題目中 at someone's mercy 的意思是「完全任人宰割」。而 have something at someone's disposal 是指「有某個資源供某人利用」。

|單字片語| beg [bɛg] 請求；乞討 / beggar [ˈbɛgə] 乞丐
　　　　 disposal [dɪˈspozl] 處置 / request [rɪˈkwɛst] 要求

Q7

The exact sales figures are yet to be _____. Sales from the next few days will also have to be factored in before we can make a comparison with the previous year.

精確的銷售數字尚未被確定。在我們可以和前年做比較之前，接下來幾天的銷售額也將需要被納入考量。

A. fabricated
B. determined
C. negotiated
D. confiscated

詳解
答案：B

精確的銷售數字不可以捏造（fabricate），因此選項 A 是錯誤的。談判（negotiate）的事情應該是價格，而不是銷售數字，數字也不可能被沒收（confiscated），因此選項 C 和 D 都是錯誤的。由此可知，題目要表達的是銷售數字尚未確定（determined），答案為 B。

Q8

Arthur skipped dinner again as he was so _____ his work that he lost track of time.

Arthur 又忘了吃晚餐了，因為他如此全神貫注於他的工作上，以至於他沒注意時間過了多久。

A. wary of
B. absorbed in
C. persuaded by
D. bestowed on

詳解
答案：B

從 lost track of time（沒注意時間過了多久）和 skipped dinner（忘了吃晚餐）這些關鍵詞，可以推斷 Arthur 正全神貫注於（absorbed in）某件事情上。

|單字片語| wary of 謹慎於… / persuaded by 被…說服 / bestowed on 把…贈與

Q9

Once in office, politicians who raise funds to run for elections are expected to return the favor of _____ who supported them. Whether this is seen as corruption remains a controversial issue.

一旦上任後，募款來參加選舉的政治人物就會被支持他們的贊助者期待償還人情。這是否被視為貪汙依然是一項具有爭議性的議題。

A. challengers   B. sponsors
C. lecturers   D. translators

詳解   答案：B

　　do someone a favor 是「幫某人一個忙」，被幫忙表示你欠幫助你的人一個
人情，return the favor 是「償還所欠的人情債」。接受幫忙的人有義務要幫忙曾
經幫助他的人，即贊助者（sponsors），因此答案為 B。

〈補充說明〉

　　favor 是「小忙；小恩惠」，I owe you a favor. 表示「我欠你一份人情。」
Do me a favor. 則是「幫我一個忙。」favor 也可以表示「比較喜歡；比較看好某
一方」，例如：in favor of（贊成），fall out of favor（失寵）。

|單字片語| **challenger** [ˈtʃælɪndʒə] 挑戰人 / **lecturer** [ˈlɛktʃərə] 講師
　　　　translator [trænsˈletə] 譯者

Q10

I love you with all my heart and I will not let anything _____ us.

我全心全意地愛你，而我不會讓任何事情介入到我們之間。

A. come up with   B. come between
C. come apart   D. come down with

詳解   答案：B

　　這題考的是動詞片語，動詞片語必須用情境來記，才能明白其用法，come
between sb 就是「介入…之間」的意思，答案為 B。

例句

Who can **come up with** a solution?　誰能想出一個解決方法？
The bumper **came apart** after he kicked it.
他踢了保險桿一腳後，整個保險桿掉落。
He **came down with** the flu two days ago.　他在兩天前得了流感。

第 1 回
第 2 回
第 3 回
第 4 回
第 5 回
第 6 回

Questions 11-15

A tsunami is a natural (11) phenomenon caused by an earthquake. During a tsunami, huge masses of ocean water rushed inland in tidal waves and the costs to human life can be (12) horrifying. The deadliest tsunami in recorded history was the Christmas tsunamis of 2004 in the Indian Ocean. On December 26, 2004, an earthquake registering 9.2 magnitude occurred on one of the islands around Sumatra. It created a deadly series of tsunamis that swept Indonesia, India, Madagascar, and Ethiopia. The death toll was (13) estimated to be in the neighborhood of 300,000 to 350,000. The immediate destruction of lives and property is only the beginning of the damage. After the waters retreated, there was the increased risk of diseases (14) created by stagnant and polluted water. Many who survived the initial flood perished due to starvation or dehydration. Many more were lost to diseases that were (15) widespread as dead bodies exposed to the scorching sun began to decompose out in the open.

海嘯是一種由地震引發的自然現象。海嘯發生時，大量的海水以巨浪灌入內陸，這對人命傷亡的代價是極為恐怖的。歷史紀錄中最致命的海嘯為 2004 年在印度洋發生的聖誕節海嘯。在 2004 年 12 月 26 日，規模為 9.2 的地震發生在蘇門達臘周圍的其中一座島嶼。地震引發一連串致命的海嘯，橫掃了印尼、印度、馬達加斯加和衣索比亞。死亡人數估計大約為三十萬至三十五萬人。生命和財產的立即毀滅只是破壞的開始。當海水退去後，增加了因無法流動且受汙染的水所造成的傳染病風險。許多在第一次洪水中倖存的人因為飢餓和脫水而死亡。由於曝曬在烈日下的屍體開始腐爛，還有許多人死於廣泛擴散的疾病。

Q11

A. accident   B. event

C. tragedy   D. phenomenon

詳解   答案：D

海嘯是一種由地震造成的自然現象，這種自然現象（natural phenomenon）不同於意外（accident），是無法避免的。而事件（event）都是人為的，並不是

自然發生的，而英文也沒有所謂的自然悲劇（natural tragedy）和自然喜劇（natural comedy）的說法，答案為 D。

<補充說明>

　　phenomenon 的複數為 phenomena，跟 criterion（條件）複數為 criteria 一樣，兩者都是源自拉丁文的單字。

第 1 回
第 2 回
第 3 回
第 4 回
第 5 回
第 6 回

Q12

A. exclusive
C. indifferent

B. horrifying
D. emphatic

詳解　　　　　　　　　　　　　　　　　　　　　答案：B

　　空格處的句子指的是海嘯所帶來的恐怖代價，因此要填入 horrifying，考生也可以聯想到發生在日本福島的 311 事件，也同樣是海嘯所帶來的災難，新聞報道提醒人們海嘯可帶來嚴重的破壞，對人命的代價是極為恐怖的，答案為 B。

|單字片語| exclusive [ɪkˈsklusɪv] 獨有的 / indifferent [ɪnˈdɪfərənt] 不感興趣的；冷淡的
　　　　　 emphatic [ɪmˈfætɪk] 強調的

Q13

A. estimated
C. proposed

B. imagined
D. organized

詳解　　　　　　　　　　　　　　　　　　　　　答案：A

　　從段落中 300,000 to 350,000 範圍的數字，可得知這些數字是估計（estimate）出來的，答案為 A。

|單字片語| imagine [ɪˈmædʒɪn] 想像 / propose [prəˈpoz] 提議 / organize [ˈɔrgəˌnaɪz] 組織

Q14

A. affecting people's cognition
B. causing animals' weird behavior
C. created by stagnant and polluted water
D. spread by people's saliva and body fluid

　　這題要根據空格處的前後文來判斷應填入的子句選項，前一句提到：「生命和財產的立即毀滅只是破壞的開始。當海水退去後增加了…的傳染病風險」因此要從選項找出造成傳染病風險增加的原因，可以推測海水退去後，陸地會滯留許多骯髒的積水，這些受汙染的水會使人生病，答案為 C。

|單字片語| **cognition** [kɑɡˋnɪʃən] 認知 / **stagnant** [ˋstæɡnənt] 不流動的；（水）汙濁的
　　saliva [səˋlɑɪvə] 唾液

Q15

A. thorough
C. primitive

B. intensive
D. widespread

　　要確認應該使用什麼形容詞，必須先了解所形容的對象。這題要形容的對象是 disease（疾病），spread 是「蔓延，散播」，wide 是「廣泛的」，因此最合理的答案為 D。widespread 除了形容傳染病的「擴散」，也可以用來形容消息、語言或某種情緒的散播。

|單字片語| **thorough** [ˋθɝo] 徹底的 / **intensive** [ɪnˋtɛnsɪv] 密集的
　　primitive [ˋprɪmətɪv] 原始的

Questions 16-20

　　Baseball has been woven into the very fabric of American society for many years now. Children of all ages take up baseballs and gloves in order to have fun, and mothers and fathers find themselves (16) decorating their nurseries for their baby boy with baseballs and other equipment (17) which goes along with the sport. No matter where you roam in the United States, you'll never be too far away from a great baseball game, or just a small corner shop which specializes in baseball cards. To some, there is a season for baseball, but to (18) others, baseball is always in season. Older generations of Americans are more familiar with baseball card collecting than younger generations, and because of this, many people believe that baseball card collecting is a (19) dying art. This is simply not the case, as many cards which have been saved over the years only increase in (20) value, and many collectors take advantage of this knowledge to make a killing. You'll find card collectors at many types of sales in which people get rid of their old belongings.

　　如今棒球已經融入美國社會的每一個環節很多年了，所有年齡的兒童會拿起棒球和手套來玩耍，而爸爸、媽媽則會發現自己在佈置男寶寶的育嬰室時，都會用棒球和這項運動有關的其他設備。無論你漫步在美國任何地方，在不遠處都會有精彩的棒球比賽，或者是某個小角落就有一家專賣棒球卡片的商店。對有些人來說，棒球只有一個賽季的，但對其他人來說，一年四季都是棒球季。老一輩的美國人比年輕一代更熟悉蒐集棒球卡片，也因為如此，許多人認為蒐集棒球卡片是一門逐漸消失的藝術。然而事情並不這樣的，由於許多保存多年的棒球卡片只會增值，也有很多收藏家會利用這個知識來大賺一筆。你會在人們想要處理舊物的眾多種類的特賣會中發現這些卡片收藏家。

Q16

A. decorate
C. decorating

B. to decorate
D. decoration

詳解　　　　　　　　　　　　　　　　　　　　　　　**答案：C**

　　這題考的是文法概念，find oneself V-ing 意思是「發現自己忙於做某件事」，所以跟 busy V-ing 一樣，必須加動名詞，答案為 C。

Q17

A. which has nothing to do with sports
B. that is disliked by their child
C. which goes along with the sport
D. that is related with movies

詳解　　　　　　　　　　　　　　　　　　　　　　　**答案：C**

　　此題要配合空格處前後文來判斷適合填入的子句選項，前一句提到「爸爸、媽媽則會發現自己在佈置男寶寶的育嬰室時，都會用棒球和…的其他設備」後一句提到「無論到美國任何地方，在不遠處都會有精彩的棒球比賽」，可以推測空格處應該要填入和棒球這項運動有關的子句，因此答案為 C。

第 1 回
第 2 回
第 3 回
第 4 回
第 5 回
第 6 回

Q18

A. another   B. the other
C. others   D. some other

詳解   答案：C

　　理解這一題的關鍵在於前半句的 To some（對某些人來說），後半句則必須要填入的是 but to others（但是對其他的人來說），答案為 C。

例句

I dropped my fork. May I have **another** one?
我把叉子用掉了。可以再給我一把嗎？
He is holding a knife in one hand and a fork in **the other**.
他一手握著刀子，另一手握著叉子。

Q19

A. lost   B. dying
C. growing   D. contemporary

詳解   答案：B

　　文章提到年輕一代不像老一輩那麼喜歡蒐集棒球卡片，表示這門珍藏棒球卡片的藝術可能會逐漸消失，die out 的意思是「絕種」，也就是完全消失。a dying art 通常用來形容沒有年輕人願意傳承的藝術或手藝，答案為 B。

|單字片語| **contemporary** [kən'tɛmpə,rɛrɪ] 當代的

Q20

A. length   B. status
C. value   D. weight

詳解   答案：C

　　段落中提到 make a killing（大賺一筆），可見作為一種珍藏品，某些棒球卡片會隨著時間增值（increase in value）。

|單字片語| **length** [lɛŋθ] 長度 / **status** ['stetəs] 地位 / **weight** [wet] 重量

第三部分 / 閱讀理解

第 1 回
第 2 回
第 3 回
第 4 回
第 5 回
第 6 回

Questions 21-22

To: Customer Service Officer

I am a loyal customer of your company for five years. Your company has always provided the best telecom service in terms of price and quality. Nevertheless, I regret to inform you that I had a rather unpleasant experience in one of your local stores on Ziyou Rd, Kaohsiung yesterday. I went there during lunch hours and I was surprised to see only one clerk at the counter. There was a long queue and I waited for half an hour before I was served. I intend to purchase a phone for my son so I tried to clarify the various subscription plans offered. The clerk sounded annoyed and told me to refer to a piece of paper she printed. I am in my late forties and I have trouble reading fine print. I requested that she explained the details to me and she raised her voice at me and told me she is not a teacher, causing me much embarrassment. In the end, I left the store in anger. I demand a written apology from this employee, failure of which might lead me to legal actions against her for insulting me in public.

Your customer,
Angela Wang

至：客服人員

我是貴公司長達五年的忠誠顧客。貴公司一直以來在價格和品質方面都提供最好的電信服務。儘管如此，我很遺憾要告知您，我昨天在高雄自由路的當地門市有一個相當不愉快的經驗。我是在午餐時段過去的，我很驚訝看到店裡只有一名店員。排了很長的隊伍，而在輪到我被服務前，我等了半個小時。我打算給我兒子買一隻手機，所以我試著要把提出的不同月租費方案搞清楚。店員的口氣聽起來很煩躁，並告訴我去參考她所列印的一張紙。我已經四十幾快五十歲了，所以閱讀這麼小的字對我有點困難。我要求店員把細節解釋給我聽，她居然對我大聲，還跟我說她不是老師，這使我非常難堪。最後，我憤怒地離開門市。我要求這位員工以書信的方式向我道歉，若沒有的話可能使我對她採取法律行動，因為她公然侮辱我。

您的客戶，
Angela Wang

|單字片語| **quality** [ˈkwɑlətɪ] 品質 / **regret** [rɪˈɡrɛt] 後悔；遺憾
unpleasant [ʌnˈplɛzn̩t] 使人不愉快的 / **refer to** 參考
request [rɪˈkwɛst] 請求 / **fine print** 字體小的印刷品
embarrassment [ɪmˈbærəsmənt] 難堪；尷尬 / **demand** [dɪˈmænd] 要求
insult [ɪnˈsʌlt] 侮辱

Why did the problem happen?
為什麼這個問題會發生？

A. The clerk was impatient.　這位店員沒有耐心。

B. The customer was kept waiting for half an hour.
這位顧客持續等了半個小時。

C. The piece of paper was well printed.　那張紙被印得很好。

D. The customer is nearly 50 years old.　這位顧客快要五十歲了。

詳解　　　　　　　　　　　　　　　　　　　　　　　　答案：A

　　文章提到當事人等了半個小時，當事人的年紀快 50 歲，這也是事實，但這些並非是整件事情發生的主要原因。從 The clerk sounded annoyed（店員的口氣聽起來有點煩躁）、I requested that she explained the details to me and she raised her voice at me and told me she is not a teacher（我要求店員把細節解釋給我聽，她居然對我大聲，還跟我說她不是老師）可知道一切的主因是因為店員對顧客沒有耐心，答案為 A。文章裡的 fine print，主要是指印刷品的字體很小，並不是指印刷品印得很好，因此選項 C 根本與文章的情況不符。

What actions might the customer take if the clerk failed to apologize?
如果店員沒有道歉，這位顧客可能會採取甚麼行動？

A. She might cancel her account.　她可能會取消她的帳號。

B. She might raise her voice.　她可能會提高音量。

C. She might take her to court.　她可能會起訴她。

D. She might purchase another phone.　她可能會購買另一隻手機。

詳解　　　　　　　　　　　　　　　　　　　　　　　　答案：C

　　信中提到 legal actions（法律行為），表示如果店員沒有道歉，當事人可能會對她採取法律行動，答案為 C。

第 1 回
第 2 回
第 3 回
第 4 回
第 5 回
第 6 回

<補充說明>

court 有「球場」和「法庭」的意思，不過也可以當動詞使用，意思為「追求」。例如：He spent a great deal of time courting girls when he was in university.（他在大學時期花很多的時間追求女生。）You are courting your own death.（你在自找死路。）

Questions 23-25

True Nature Photography Prize 2022

Each quarterly issue of True Nature magazine contains two images selected from entries for the annual Nature Photography Prize. This is a chance for your photographs to be published. You will also be awarded US$ 500 plus a whole year's subscription of True Nature magazine.

Who may enter: Anyone except individuals related to True Nature employees or board members. By submitting an entry, each contestant agrees to the rules of the contest.

Photograph eligibility: Photographs must be taken outdoors and bring out the beauty of mother nature. Photos that violate or infringe upon another person's rights, including but not limited to copyright, are not eligible.

Entry deadline: Photographs must be received by 1 July 2022 to be considered for the 2022 prize. Images received after this date will automatically be entered into the competition for 2023.

How to enter: Entry is free and each entrant may submit up to five images. Entries should be sent to editor@truenature.com.us with the entrant's name and a brief description of what the image shows. Entries should be sent as digital image files, in either TIF or JPEG format, and each file may not be larger than 10MB.

真自然攝影獎 2022

每一季的真自然雜誌期號會從一年一度真自然攝影獎的參賽作品中挑選兩張照片刊登。這是讓你的照片出版的機會。你也將獲得 500 美元加上訂閱一整年的真自然雜誌的獎勵。

誰可參加：任何人，除了與真自然雜誌員工或董事會成員有關的人。透過提交參賽作品，參賽者即同意比賽的規則。

照片資格：照片必須在戶外拍攝，並且強調大自然的美。照片違反或侵犯他人權利，包含版權但不限於版權，將不具參賽資格。

參賽截止期限：若要參與 2022 年的獎項，照片必須在 2022 年 7 月 1 日之前收到。在這個日期後收到的照片將自動進入 2023 年的比賽。

如何參賽：參賽是免費的，而且每個參賽者最多可以投稿五張照片。參賽作品請寄至 editor@truenature.com.us，並附上參賽者的姓名還有照片所要表達的簡短說明。參賽作品必須是數位影像檔案，以 TIF 或 JPEG 的格式，每個檔案不得超過 10MB。

|單字片語| issue [ˈɪʃʊ] 期號；發行量 / annual [ˈænjʊəl] 一年一度的 / publish [ˈpʌblɪʃ] 出版
award [əˈwɔrd] 獎項 / subscription [səbˈskrɪpʃən] 訂閱
individual [ˌɪndəˈvɪdʒʊəl] 個人 / submit [səbˈmɪt] 提交
eligible [ˈɛlɪdʒəbl] 有資格的 / violate [ˈvaɪəˌlet] 違反 / infringe [ɪnˈfrɪndʒ] 侵犯
copyright [ˈkɑpɪˌraɪt] 版權 / imitation [ˌɪməˈteʃən] 模仿
deadline [ˈdɛdˌlaɪn] 期限 / digital [ˈdɪdʒɪtl] 數位的 / image [ˈɪmɪdʒ] 影像；形象
file [faɪl] 檔案

Q23

Who is not allowed to take part in the contest?
誰不被允許參加比賽？

A. Anyone below 18 years of age　任何未年滿 18 歲的人
B. Someone who sent five images　一個寄了五張照片的人
C. Readers of True Nature magazine　真自然雜誌的讀者
D. Relatives of the magazine's editor　雜誌編輯的親戚

詳解　　　　　　　　　　　　　　　　　　　　　　　　　答案：D

關於參賽者的資格，文中提到 Anyone except individuals related to True Nature employees or board members（任何人，除了與真自然雜誌員工或董事會成員有關的人），答案為 D。

Q24

Can you send in photographs for the competition after July the first?
七月一日之後你還可以把相片寄進去來參加比賽嗎？

A. No, your entry will automatically be canceled.
不行，你的稿件將自動被取消。

B. No, entries after the deadline will not be entertained.

不行，截止日期後的投稿將不被接受。

C. Yes, you can ask for an extension to be considered for the 2022 prize. 可以，你可以要求延期來參與 2022 年的獎項。

D. Yes, but you will take part in next year's contest.

可以，但是你將參與明年的比賽。

詳解

2022 年度的參賽截止日期為七月一日，不過 Images received after this date will automatically be entered into the competition for 2023（這個日期後收到的影像將自動進入 2023 年的比賽），答案為 D。

Q25

What is a basic requirement for all entries?
所有參賽作品的基本要求是什麼？

A. All imitations are welcome. 歡迎所有仿冒品。

B. Photographs have to be original. 照片必須是原創的。

C. Pictures need to be developed. 照片必須被沖洗出來。

D. Only plant owners are eligible. 只有植物的擁有者才有資格參賽。

詳解

參賽條件註明：Photos that violate or infringe upon another person's rights, including but not limited to copyright, are not eligible（照片違反或侵犯他人權利，包含版權但不僅限於版權，將不具參賽資格），也就是說照片必須是原創的，答案為 B。

Questions 26-28

Since PLAY & PAY opened its doors in July 2007, we have cemented our position in the market as a leader of this industry. With a total of four offices in Australia (Sydney, Melbourne, Brisbane and Perth), one in New Zealand (Auckland) and two in Canada (Toronto and Vancouver), we have become the largest and most significant service provider for young people who wish to work to get paid and find time to play at the same time. In 2012, we serviced over 5500 members from 17 different countries.

自從 PLAY & PAY 在 2007 年開市營業以來，我們已經牢牢鞏固我們在這個產業市場龍頭的地位。總共有四間辦公室在澳洲（雪梨、墨爾本、布里斯本和伯斯），一間在紐西蘭（奧克蘭），以及兩間在加拿大（多倫多和溫哥華），我們已經成為最大以及最重要的服務提供者，為希望同時在工作賺錢和找時間遊玩的年輕人提供服務。在 2012 年，我們服務了來自 17 個不同國家、超過 5500 名會員。

What makes our service unique is that it is completely tailored towards the individual needs and objectives of our members. Our packages, however, are designed to suit everyone and all budgets. We work very closely with our partners to develop new packages that match the requirements of their individual markets. Our ambitious product development strategy has enabled us to remain competitive with regards to the quality of our service and the individual package prices.

讓我們的服務獨一無二的是，它是完全針對我們會員的個人需求和目標量身打造的。然而我們的套裝方案，也為了符合每個人、所有預算所設計。我們和合夥人緊密合作，以發展符合其個別市場需求的全新套裝方案。我們有抱負的產品發展策略已經使我們能夠在服務品質和個別套裝方案的價格上維持競爭力。

Our essential start-up kits include Orientation, Sim Cards and On-the-Job Support. Once members are in their destination country, they are able to contact us by our toll-free number anytime. Our service also covers personal travel advice, accommodation and transport reservation services and a wide range of tours and travel packages. Our dedicated and multilingual consultants have been thoroughly trained to provide our members with accurate information and advice.

我們主要的基本配套包含定位、手機晶片還有在工作上的支援。一旦會員在目的地國家後，他們可以透過我們的免付費專線隨時與我們聯絡。我們的服務也包含個人旅遊建議、住宿和交通運輸預訂服務，以及各式各樣的旅遊套裝行程。我們全心投入而且會使用多種語言的顧問都受過了徹底的訓練，為的是提供我們的會員正確的資訊和建議。

 Q26

What can be said about PLAY & PAY?
關於 PLAY & PAY 可以說什麼？

A. It is a leader that specializes in cement.　它是專門製造水泥的龍頭。

B. Its members are from Australia, New Zealand and Canada.
他的會員來自澳洲、紐西蘭和加拿大。

C. It is the biggest player in the packaged-tour industry.
它在團體旅遊業是最大的參與者。

D. Its services allow members to secure a job and travel.
它的服務讓會員可以找到工作並旅遊。

詳解　　　　　　　　　　　　　　　　　　　　　　　　**答案：D**

　　cement 當名詞使用是「水泥」的意思，當動詞使用則是「用水泥黏合」的意思，但這裡則是像是用水泥黏合一般「鞏固某事」的意思，PLAY & PAY 並非製造水泥的公司，選項 A 是錯誤的。PLAY & PAY 的辦公室在澳洲、紐西蘭和加拿大，不過成員來自 17 個不同國家，選項 B 也不對。PLAY & PAY 提供年輕人出國工作兼旅遊的機會，也提供團體旅遊，但沒提到它是團體旅遊業最大的參與者，因此選項 C 也是錯誤的。PLAY & PAY 的服務是讓會員可以找到工作並旅遊，答案為 D。

Q27

What can you expect if you enroll in the program provided by PLAY & PAY?
如果你報名 PLAY & PAY 所提供的計畫，可以期待什麼？

A. You can get in touch with PLAY & PAY staff by phone.
你可以透過電話和 PLAY & PAY 的員工聯繫。

B. You have to stay with a friend or a relative.
你必須跟一位朋友或親戚住。

C. You will learn how to lead a guided tour.　你將會學習如何帶旅行團。

D. You are required to report your whereabouts.　你需要報備你的行蹤。

詳解　　　　　　　　　　　　　　　　　　　　　　　　**答案：A**

　　PLAY & PAY 提供的服務之一是會員可以透過免付費專線隨時與他們聯絡，答案為 A。文中並沒提到會員需要報備個人行蹤，因此選項 D 是不對的。PLAY & PAY 會安排住宿（accommodation），會員不需要跟朋友或親戚住，選項 B 是錯的。有需要的話，會員可以參加 PLAY & PAY 提供的團體旅遊，但文中沒有提到要學習如何帶旅行團，選項 C 是錯的。

第 1 回
第 2 回
第 3 回
第 4 回
第 5 回
第 6 回

Which of the following is included in the service?
以下哪一項包含在服務內？

A. Student loan packaged tours　學生套裝旅遊貸款
B. Immigration advice and application　移民建議和申請
C. Assistance in overcoming language barriers　克服語言障礙的協助
D. Driving classes to obtain international passport
　　獲得國際駕照的駕訓班

| 詳解 |

　　文章說 PLAY & PAY 有會使用多種語言的顧問（multilingual consultants），合理推斷是幫助會員克服語言障礙，其他選項的服務都沒有在文中提到，答案為 C。

Questions 29-31

　　The United States currently relies heavily on coal, oil, and natural gas for its energy. Fossil fuels are non-renewable, that is, they draw on finite resources that will eventually dwindle, becoming too expensive or too environmentally damaging to retrieve. In contrast, the many types of renewable energy resources, such as wind and solar energy, are constantly replenished and will never run out. Sunlight, or solar energy, can be used directly for heating and lighting homes and other buildings, for generating electricity, and for hot water heating. There's a catch though; there is no solar electricity when the Sun does not shine, and no wind energy when there is no wind. Neither wind nor solar energy can ever replace coal or natural gas for power generation until these basic limitations are dealt with.

　　美國目前非常依賴煤炭、石油和天然氣來當作它的能源。化石燃料是不能再生的，也就是說，他們抽用最後將會變少的有限資源，取得這些資源將變得太過昂貴，或對環境造成太大的破壞。相對地，許多種類的再生能源，例如：風力和太陽能，都能不斷地補充而且也不會耗盡。陽光，或太陽能，可以直接用來溫暖、照亮住家和其他建築，並能拿來產生電力及加熱熱水。不過有個條件；當太陽不照射的時候就沒有太陽能，當沒有風的時候就沒有風力。不管是風力或太陽能都不能取代煤炭或天然氣來發電，直到這些基本的限制能被解決為止。

第 1 回
第 2 回
第 3 回
第 4 回
第 5 回
第 6 回

Another alternative to fossil fuels is hydro energy. In countries with abundant water supply all year round, water flowing downhill from mountains into rivers or streams can be converted to hydroelectric power. Nuclear power used to be thought of as a cheap and efficient way to produce power but has now been frowned on after a series of disasters brought about by radiation. Renewable energy is a viable option but it needs to be steady, reliable and available round the clock if it will ever power the world. The race has begun. Car makers have poured millions of dollars into the research and development of highly efficient electric vehicles that depend solely on green energy. Some other questions they have to answer include, "Where can drivers charge their cars the way they can charge a phone? Will the cost of recharging batteries be higher than filling up tanks in a gas station?"

化石燃料的另一個替代選擇是水力。在整年水源充沛的國家，從山上流入河川和小溪的水可以轉換為水力發電。核能之前被視為一種便宜和有效率的發電方法，不過現在輻射引發的一連串災難後，使這項科技遭到反對。再生能源是一個可行的選擇，但如果它要為全世界供電的話，它需要是穩定、可靠而且二十四小時皆可使用的。而這場競賽已經開始。汽車製造商已經投入數百萬元在研究並發展只靠綠色能源供電的高效能電動車。有些廠商必須回答的問題包括：「駕駛者要到哪裡，才能像手機充電那樣為車子充電？電池充電的花費會比在加油站加油來得更高嗎？」

What can be said about fossil fuels a few decades from now?

再過數十年，關於化石燃料可以得知什麼？

A. They will be entirely replaced by solar energy.
它們會完全被太陽能取代。

B. They will be used up. 它們會被用完。

C. They will be recycled and reused. 它們會被回收再利用。

D. They will be cheaper to produce. 它們的生產會比較便宜。

詳解 答案：B

從 dwindle（逐漸變少）這個關鍵字可得知，再過數十年化石燃料將會被用完。文中提到太陽能的限制，但沒有明確說明太陽能會完全取代化石燃料，因

此選項 A 是不對的。化石燃料是不能再生的，無法回收再利用，因此選項 C 是錯誤的。容易挖掘的化石燃料已經快耗盡，若繼續挖掘埋藏在深層的化石燃料，成本和費用將會提高，不可能會更便宜，文章也說變得太過昂貴（becoming too expensive），因此選項 D 是錯的。從敘述中可知化石燃料終究會被用盡，答案為 B。

Q30

According to the passage, what advantage might hydro energy have over wind energy?

根據這篇文章，水力發電相較於風力發電可能有什麼好處？

A. Hydro energy is more reliable.　水力發電比較可靠。

B. Hydro energy is more economical.　水力發電比較經濟實惠。

C. Hydro energy is friendlier to the environment.
水力發電對環境比較友善。

D. Hydro energy is cleaner and better.　水力發電比較好，也比較乾淨。

詳解　　　　　　　　　　　　　　　　　　　　　　　　　　答案：A

　　水力發電和風力發電都是對環境友善的綠色能源，而文章沒有說明水力發電比風力發電乾淨或便宜，因此選項 B、C、D 是錯的。但比起供應較不穩定的風力（no wind energy when there is no wind），水力的供應似乎較為可靠，因為有些河流一年四季都川流不息（In countries with abundant water supply all year round, water flowing downhill from mountains into rivers or streams can be converted to hydroelectric power.），可推測出答案為 A。

Q31

What challenge do car makers face?

汽車製造業者面對什麼樣的挑戰？

A. To create a car that requires little electricity to run
創造一種需要很少電力來運作的車子

B. To develop a gasoline-free car before rival companies do
趕在敵對公司之前發展無需汽油的車子

C. To set up kiosks where motorists can plug in to charge their vehicles
設立駕駛者可以讓車子充電的充電站

D. All of the above　以上皆是

第 1 回

第 2 回

第 3 回

第 4 回

第 5 回

第 6 回

詳解

　　從 development of highly efficient electric vehicles 可推論出選項 A。vehicles that depend solely on green energy 則可推論出選項 B。Where can drivers charge their cars the way they can charge a phone? 跟選項 C 有關，所以答案為 D。All of the above（以上皆是）和 None of the above（以上皆非）這樣的選擇，是歐美國家閱讀測驗常出的，主要是測試考生是否理解每一個選項的內容。

Questions 32-35

To all the graduates,

　　Congratulations! You set your goal, and you reached it. You have worked hard to complete your degree at the International University. And that's something you and your loved ones want to celebrate together.

　　Taking part in this wonderful ceremony and seeing you receive your diploma should be an unforgettable experience for them. If you want to invite your family and relatives to come to the United States, you need to request verification letters. First, you must visit the International University website to fill out the form in order to provide certain necessary information about your guests.

　　The deadline for this form is January 20, 2020. All letters will be issued in Portable Document Format (PDF) and emailed to you. You should remind your guests to visit the U.S. Embassy website for procedures to fill the forms, pay the appropriate fees, and book a visa interview appointment. Once they receive the confirmation of the visa application, they can bring their passports along with the letters for a visa interview.

Best Regards,
Michelle Miller
Executive director of International Student Affairs

致所有的畢業生：

　　恭喜！你設立了你的目標，也達成了。你已經努力去完成國際大學的學位。而那也是你和你所愛的人想要一起慶祝的事情。

　　參加這個美好的典禮，並看到你獲得文憑，對他們來說應該是一次難忘的體驗。如果你想邀請家人和親戚來到美國，你需要索取驗證信件。首先，你必須到國際大學網站上填寫表格，以提供關於你所邀請客人的一些必要資訊。

　　這份表格的截止日期是 2020 年 1 月 20 日。所有信件將以可攜式文件格式（PDF）發行並以電子郵件發送給你。你應該提醒你的客人到美國大使館網站，以完成填寫表格、支付適當的費用，與預約簽證面談的程序。一旦他們收到簽證申請的確認書，便可以攜帶護照以及信件進行簽證面試。

謹啟
Michelle Miller
國際學生事務執行主任

Confirmation

This confirms the submission of the Non-immigrant visa application form:

Name Provided:	Allen Chen	Location Selected
Date of Birth:	05/11/1970	American Institute in
Place of Birth:	Keelung, Taiwan	Taiwan – Kaohsiung
Gender:	Male	Branch Office
Nationality:	Republic of China	5F, No.88, Chenggong
Passport number:	9842357	2nd Road, Qianzhen Dist.,
Purpose of Travel:	pleasure visitor	Kaohsiung 80661, Taiwan
Completed on:	31 JAN 2020	
Confirmed No:	AA144P4IMW	
This is not a VISA		

YOU MUST BRING the confirmation page and the following document(s) with you at all steps during the application process:
Passport, the verification letter from the university
You may also provide any additional documents you feel will support your case.

第 1 回
第 2 回
第 3 回
第 4 回
第 5 回
第 6 回

確認書

這份文件確認提交非移民簽證申請表：

提供的姓名：	Allen Chen	選擇地點
出生日期：	05/11/1970	美國在臺協會
出生地點：	臺灣基隆市	高雄分處
性別：	男性	80661 高雄市前鎮區成功二路
國籍：	中華民國	88 號 5 樓
護照號碼：	9842357	
旅行目的：	愉悅的旅客	
完成填表時間：	2020 年 1 月 31日	
確認編號：	AA144P4IMW	
這不是簽證		

申請過程的所有過程中，您都必須隨身攜帶確認頁面和以下文件：
護照、大學的證明信
您也可以提供任何您認為會支持您的案件的其他文件。

|單字片語| **diploma** [dɪˈplomə] 學位證書 / **verification** [ˌvɛrɪfɪˈkeʃən] 證明
nationality [ˌnæʃəˈnælətɪ] 國籍 / **visa** [ˈvizə] （護照等上的）證據

Q32

What is the purpose of the letter?
這封信的目的是什麼？

A. To congratulate everyone who graduated. 恭喜每位畢業生。

B. To advise all the guests of graduated to apply for a visa.
建議所有畢業生的賓客申請簽證。

C. To inform all the graduates to apply for verification letters.
通知所有畢業生應申請證明信件。

D. To make all guests of graduates aware of the graduation ceremony.
使所有畢業生的賓客知道這場畢業典禮。

詳解　　　　　　　　　　　　　　　　　　　　答案：C

這題是針對信件的內容，題目問的是信件的目的，因此先閱讀信件各段的
第一句和最後一句，再對應選項後，就能快速地找出關鍵句。第二段很明確地

提到出信件的目的（If you want to invite your family and relatives to come to the United States, you need to request verification letters.），答案為 C。

Q33

What is the family name of the visa applicant?
簽證申請人的姓氏是什麼？

A. Michelle.
B. Miller.
C. Allen.
D. Chen.

詳解　　　　　　　　　　　　　　　　　　　　　　　答案：D

　　這題是針對確認書的內容，題目問的是申請人的姓氏，找出 Name Provided: 即可知道他的名字是 Allen Chen。英文姓名一般都是先寫名（given / first name），再寫姓（surname / last name），答案為 D。

Q34

What is the next step when people get the confirmation page?
當人們取得確認書時，下一個步驟是什麼？

A. Applying for verification letters.　申請驗證信。
B. Attending the graduation ceremony.　參加畢業典禮。
C. Waiting for an international mail.　等一封國際郵件。
D. Participating in a visa interview appointment.　參加簽證面試預約。

詳解　　　　　　　　　　　　　　　　　　　　　　　答案：D

　　這題是針對信件的內容，題目問的是取得確認書後的下一個步驟。第三段最後一句明確提到 Once they receive the confirmation of the visa application, they can bring their passports along with the letters for a visa interview（一旦他們收到簽證申請的確認書，便可以攜帶護照以及信件進行簽證面試），答案為 D。

Q35

According to the letter and the confirmation page, which of the following statement is true?

根據信件和確認信，下列哪一項敘述是正確的？

A. Those who get the letters are the students of the International University. 收到信件的人是國際大學的學生。

B. Allen Chen was born in Kaohsiung in 1970.
Allen Chen 於 1970 年在高雄出生。

C. The graduation ceremony will be held on January 20, 2020.
畢業典禮將舉辦於 2020 年 1 月 20 日。

D. The International University is located in Taiwan.
國際大學位於臺灣。

詳解　　　　　　　　　　　　　　　　　　　　　　**答案：A**

　　這題是針對信件和確認書的內容，由於題目問的是哪個選項的內容是正確的，因此要一一確認。對應表格 Date of Birth: 05/11/1970 和 Place of Birth: Keelung, Taiwan，Allen Chen 於 1970 年出生在基隆，因此選項 B 錯誤。對應信件第三段 The deadline for this form is January 20, 2020，可知 2020 年 1 月 20 日是截止日期，選項 C 錯誤。對應信件第二段 If you want to invite your family and relatives to come to the United States...，可知國際大學位於美國，選項 D 錯誤。對應信件第一段 To all the graduates，可知收件者是國際大學的畢業生，當然是該校學生，答案為 A。

全民英檢中級

第六回 初試 聽力測驗

本測驗分四部份，全為四選一之選擇題，共 35 題，作答時間約 30 分鐘。

第一部分　看圖辨義

　　共 5 題，試題冊上有數幅圖畫，每一圖畫有 1~3 個描述該圖的題目，每題請聽錄音播出每題以及四個英語敘述之後，選出與所看到的圖畫最相符的一個答案，每題只播出一遍。

例題：（看）

（聽）　Look at the picture.
　　　　What does the woman want
　　　　the boy to do?
　　　　A.　Pick up the rubbish.
　　　　B.　Tie his shoelaces.
　　　　C.　Carry her luggage.
　　　　D.　Hail a cab.

正確答案為 A。

聽力測驗第一部分自本頁開始。

A: Question 1

B: Question 2

C: <u>Question 3</u>

D: <u>Question 4-5</u>

Notice: Ferry services terminated due to severe weather conditions. Shuttle bus service will be provided to take passengers back to the main island.

共 10 題，每題請聽光碟放音機播出一英語問句或直述句之後，從試題冊上 A、B、C、D 四個回答或回應中，選出一個最適合者作答。每題只播出一遍。

例：　（聽）　What happened to your feet?
　　　（看）　A.　They were too hungry.
　　　　　　　B.　I got a new pair.
　　　　　　　C.　My new shoes are too small.
　　　　　　　D.　These are not mine.

正確答案為 C。

6. A. I need a broom.
   B. I can't do both things at the same time.
   C. I think that is fair.
   D. I will turn the volume down.

7. A. Where do I need to sign?
   B. How can you purchase it without telling me?
   C. Will I have to be there tomorrow?
   D. Do you mean it's weird in some way?

8. A. Yes, we accept both credit card and cash.
   B. Yes, it will be valid for three days.
   C. No, unless you wish to extend your stay.
   D. No, you need it in the first place.

9. A. We have to work harder than before.
   B. You need to check the engine.
   C. It is not going to work.
   D. I have already called for an ambulance.

10. A. Why don't you go there yourself?
    B. Do I have access to the Internet?
    C. Where can I find the answers?
    D. Will my postal address be required?

11. A. The line is still busy.
    B. She is spending her money unwisely.
    C. We will visit her at the hospital later.
    D. So she finally realized it is time to settle down.

12. A. Let me take the patient's temperature.
    B. There is still room for improvement.
    C. Where are the eggs and flour?
    D. Why didn't you greet me at the door?

13. A. We can't rule out the possibility.
    B. There is a parking lot here.
    C. You have to be careful.
    D. I want to remain where I am.

14. A. I usually have it with some sugar.
    B. I guess listening to music helps.
    C. I wonder who can do it.
    D. I can't just ignore it.

15. A. I have already made up my mind.
    B. There are two things required.
    C. Hurry up or you will regret it.
    D. It's just a form of recreation.

第三部分：簡短對話

共 10 題，每題請聽光碟放音機播出一段對話及一個相關的問題後，從試題冊上 A、B、C、D 四個選項中選出一個最適合者作答。每段對話及問題只播出一遍。

例：（聽）　(Man)　　　Did you happen to see my earphones?
I remember leaving them in the drawer.

　　　　　(Woman)　Did you search your briefcase?

　　　　　(Man)　　　I did but they are not there. Wait a second. Oh.
They are right here in my pocket.

　　　　　Question:　Where are the man's earphones?

　　（看）　A. The woman's pocket.
　　　　　　B. Briefcase.
　　　　　　C. The man's pocket.
　　　　　　D. Drawer.

正確答案為 C。

16. A. In an aquarium.
    B. In an art gallery.
    C. In a theater.
    D. In a hospital.

17. A. She is taking a blood test.
    B. She is purchasing an item.
    C. She is enrolling in a university.
    D. She is designing a webpage.

18. A. She's a housewife.
    B. She is a school teacher.
    C. She's a sales representative.
    D. She is a toy designer.

19. A. He needs to spend more time with his dog.
    B. He needs to be more serious at work.
    C. He needs to learn how to relieve stress.
    D. He needs to exercise more regularly.

20. A. 5500 bucks.
　　B. 5000 bucks.
　　C. 4500 bucks.
　　D. 4000 bucks.

21. A. They just made a lot of
　　　 money.
　　B. They just got married.
　　C. They are going on a tour.
　　D. They feel more energetic.

22. A. Go dining.
　　B. Go diving.
　　C. Go surfing.
　　D. Go skiing.

23. A. Learning English doesn't
　　　 take a lot of time.
　　B. Learning English is free but
　　　 troublesome.
　　C. Learning English can be
　　　 costly.
　　D. Learning English requires
　　　 determination.

24.

The Amount of Customers

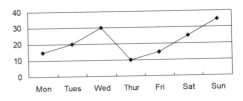

　　A. It was warming up.
　　B. It was warm and dry.
　　C. It was getting drier.
　　D. It was chilly and rainy.

25.

Noah's Profit Income

Investment	2018	2019	2020
Gold	$1,000	$1,000	$1,100
Stocks	-$2,500	$2,000	-$3,000
Funds	$2,000	-$4,000	$2,000
Bonds	-$3,000	$2,000	$3,000

　　A. Gold.
　　B. Stocks.
　　C. Funds.
　　D. Bonds.

請 翻 頁 ▷ 385

共 10 題，每題請聽光碟放音機播出一段談話及一個相關的問題後，從試題冊上 A、B、C、D 四個選項中選出一個最適合者作答。每段談話及問題只播出一遍。

例：　　　(聽)　　　Good morning, everyone. Please come over here and take these registration forms. Then, go back to your seats. This is the workshop on APP design. The lecturer of this workshop is an engineer from SBE Software. He has excellent experience in designing smartphone applications. Before you fill in the forms, please look through the forms carefully. If you have any questions, I will answer you later.

Question:　　　What might the listeners do, after they read through the registration forms?

(看)　　　A. Leave the forms on the desks.
B. Pay the registration fee.
C. Ask the speaker some questions.
D. Go to another location.

正確答案為 C。

26. A. Mountain bike racing.
    B. Road bicycle racing.
    C. Leisure cycling.
    D. Track cycling.

27. A. Wearing protective glasses.
    B. Reducing time on smartphones.
    C. Putting more research into it.
    D. Turning off electronic devices.

28. A. Whale watching.
    B. Tasting of seafood.
    C. Beach visit.
    D. Modern tour.

29. A. A creative agency.
    B. An online agency.
    C. A real estate agency.
    D. A marketing agency.

30. A. Outer space.
    B. World War I.
    C. Artificial Intelligence.
    D. Time traveler.

31. A. At 2:30 p.m.
    B. At 3:00 p.m.
    C. At 3:30 p.m.
    D. At 4:00 p.m.

32. A. On an aircraft.
    B. At a parking apron.
    C. At a check-in counter.
    D. At an airport.

33. A. Send a voice mail.
    B. Turn an app on.
    C. Press a number.
    D. Find a conference.

34.

General Scholastic Ability Test (GSAT) Result

Subject	Top percentile	Average percentile
Chinese	13th grade	11th grade
English	13th grade	8th grade
Mathematics	12th grade	11th grade
Sciences	13th grade	12th grade
Social studies	13th grade	10th grade

    A. Chinese.
    B. English.
    C. Mathematics.
    D. Social Studies.

35.

    A. Living room.
    B. Bedroom 1.
    C. Bedroom 2.
    D. Bedroom 3.

― 結束 ―

第六回 初試 閱讀測驗

本測驗分三部分，全為四選一的選擇題，共 35 題，作答時間為 45 分鐘。

第一部分：詞彙

共 10 題，每題有一個空格。請由試題冊上的四個選項中選出最適合題意的字或詞作答。

1. All group leaders are to return to your _____ groups and inform your group members of the change.
   - A. absolute
   - B. exceptional
   - C. considerable
   - D. respective

2. We do not foresee any danger, but nonetheless your parent or guardian's _____ is required before you sign up for the excursion.
   - A. approval
   - B. concern
   - C. hesitation
   - D. recipe

3. In view of the increased terrorist activities, the local police have been advised to beef up _____ for the upcoming international conference.
   - A. confession
   - B. dominance
   - C. security
   - D. invasion

4. Windows play a crucial role in a house since air _____ through the rooms helps to prevent the walls from getting damp.
   - A. flattery
   - B. compensation
   - C. alternative
   - D. circulation

5. The teenage girl wore oversized clothes in an attempt to _____ the fact that she was pregnant.
   - A. deceive
   - B. verify
   - C. conceal
   - D. alter

6. The three-hour battle of wits between the two chess masters ended in
   a _____. It will take another match to decide the winner.
   A. draw   B. crescendo
   C. triumph   D. venture

7. According to a study done by a group of university students, police
   records revealed the fact that men who consume excessive alcohol have
   a _____ to hit their wives and children.
   A. preference   B. motivation
   C. tendency   D. withdrawal

8. All efforts to revive the little boy were _____ and the doctor had no
   choice but to pronounce him dead.
   A. in pursuit   B. in vain
   C. on target   D. on air

9. Rather than wasting money to organize a/an _____ wedding
   banquet, the couple opted to have a simple dinner with an inner circle
   of family and friends.
   A. luxurious   B. rational
   C. substantial   D. inferior

10. The week before Chinese New Year is a good time to _____ things
    you no longer need in the house.
    A. get away with   B. get down to
    C. get used to   D. get rid of

第二部分：段落填空

　　本部分共 10 題，包括二個段落，每個段落各含 5 個空格。請就試題冊上 A、B、C、D 四個選項中選出<u>最適合</u>題意的字詞或片語作答。

Questions 11-15

　　The richest man on planet earth, Bill Gates, was born on Oct. 28, 1955, in Seattle, Washington.　　(11)　　the son of a lawyer and a schoolteacher, he was expected to practice law but he exceeded his parents' expectations　　(12)　　their wildest dream. Since young, Bill Gates was argumentative and refused to accept the world as it was. As a teenager, his　　(13)　　for knowledge was so great that he read the entire "World Book Encyclopedia" series from start to finish. After graduating from a private high school in 1973, Gates went on to Harvard. Two years later, Gates made a decision that would change the world.　　(14)　　Microsoft released Windows in 1985 and the software company went public in 1986. By 1987 at the age of thirty-one, Gates was already a billionaire. With such a vast amount of　　(15)　　at his disposal, Gates devoted his time and money to charity and donated billions of dollars to third world countries.

11. A. To be
    B. Being
    C. Been
    D. Having been

12. A. beneath
    B. despite
    C. beyond
    D. upon

13. A. appetite
    B. obsession
    C. improvement
    D. progress

14. A. He dropped out of school to set up Microsoft with Paul Allen
    B. He finished his college degree and became an attorney
    C. He decided to work in a finance company to gain experience
    D. He and his friends started a restaurant to serve all kinds of customers

15. A. carbon
    B. force
    C. wealth
    D. literature

Questions 16-20

In ___(16)___ to the rising cases of bullying and abuse in schools, the ministry of education of England introduced a new measure aimed at preventing and dealing with such cases. Bullying is ___(17)___ as undesirable and negative behavior, whether in verbal, psychological or physical form, conducted by an individual or group against another person (or persons) and which is repeated over time. School ___(18)___ and school personnel are required to adhere to the procedures in the new measure in dealing with allegations and incidents of bullying. The purpose of these procedures is to prevent school-based bullying behavior amongst its pupils and deal with any negative ___(19)___ within school of bullying behavior that occurs elsewhere. Nevertheless, parents have raised concerns ___(20)___. Some pointed out that teaching children to respect one another should be a top priority.

16. A. advice
    B. view
    C. response
    D. contrast

17. A. ratified
    B. simplified
    C. confined
    D. defined

18. A. authorities
    B. pirates
    C. manufacturers
    D. souvenirs

19. A. attack
    B. impact
    C. result
    D. attitude

20. A. of their children's body health
    B. about the nutrition of their children's lunch
    C. regarding the effectiveness of such measures
    D. of the schools' facility safety

第三部分：閱讀理解

本部分共 15 題，包括 5 個題組，每個題組含 1 至 2 篇短文，與數個相關的四選一的選擇題。請由試題冊上的選項中選出最適合者作答。

Questions 21-22

Tranquil Two-Story Villa

Come and feel the serenity of country life and enjoy the waves, the breeze, the sunshine, and....

The Tranquil Two-Story Villa is located thirty kilometers outside the downtown by the seashore, and it takes you only fifteen to twenty minutes through the super highway from the city center. Surrounded by waters, hills and woods, the villa offers you and your family the country life at its best.

Laundry facilities, central heating, air conditioning, and a fireplace are provided. Three unfurnished bedrooms are available. Children are welcome here, but not pets.

What is more, there are one swimming pool, a ten-hectare garden, and basketball and tennis courts. Parking spaces of two for each villa are free of charge.

For more rental details, please contact Mr. Huang: 02-4333-8886.

21. What do you think the main purpose of the description is?
    A. To find a roommate
    B. To build the villa
    C. To rent out the house
    D. To introduce the hotel

22. What can you do within the villa with the supplied equipment?
    A. Playing baseball
    B. Playing table tennis
    C. Skiing
    D. Washing clothes

- Enjoy Unlimited Internet Access.
- Rent a Wi-Fi device from the airport today and get connected anywhere, anytime in Singapore.

Do It Now! Our offices are open 24/7.

1. Visit the SG Wi-Fi booths located at Terminal 1, Basement 1, #2308. (Next to a fountain)
2. Provide us with your passport, return air ticket and credit card.
3. Fill in and sign the agreement form.
4. Pick up the Wi-Fi device and enjoy instant Internet connection.

Please Read:

Plan A: SGD $20/day for unlimited access.

Recommended if you play online games.

Plan B: SGD $10/day for usage below 5G.

Recommended if you watch a movie or two a day.

Plan C: SGD $5/day for usage below 1G.

Recommended if you only use the Internet to read your emails.

Plan C will be automatically upgraded to Plan B should usage exceed 1G and Plan B to Plan A should usage exceed 5G.

Billing starts on the first day and ends on the day of return. Rental charges will be based on full days, regardless of number of hours used per day.

For damages / lost / stolen / unreturned items, the following charges will apply:

- Wi-Fi device $200
- SIM card $50
- USB cable and plug $30
- Bag holder $20

23. What is NOT required if you wish to rent the Wi-Fi device?
    A. Passport
    B. USB cable
    C. Credit Card
    D. Air Ticket

24. What happens if you use more than 5G a day?
    A. You need to pay SGD $5 a day.
    B. You need to pay SGD $10 a day.
    C. You need to pay SGD $20 a day.
    D. You need to pay more than SGD $20 a day.

25. What can be inferred about the information above?
    A. Rental fee is based on number of hours used.
    B. You can only return the device during normal business hours.
    C. Billing starts on the day the device is activated.
    D. The device can be used at once.

Deprived of natural resources, Switzerland places emphasis on the education of its people. It claims to have one of the world's best education systems and the fact that it generates one of the highest GDP in Europe goes to show that the education system is indeed successful. For many Europeans, Switzerland is the Promised Land with higher income, better welfare, charming landscape and a much lower crime rate.

Switzerland is divided into districts and each district is responsible for educational services from kindergarten all the way to universities. Education policies may vary significantly between districts. For example, some districts start to teach the first foreign language at fourth grade, while others start at seventh grade. This can make people with children moving between districts a nightmare. In Switzerland, most children go to public schools. Private schools usually are expensive and people tend to think that students of private schools probably didn't make it at the public school. There are eleven universities in Switzerland; nine are run by districts, while two are run by the central government.

After elementary school, kids may either choose to go to secondary school or to start an apprenticeship. In the latter case, after finishing the apprenticeship, it is still possible to start an academic career at either a secondary school or a so called technical college. The Swiss are pragmatic people who value technical skills as well as academic achievement.

26. Why did Switzerland pay so much attention to education?
    A. Proper education eliminates criminal activities.
    B. Switzerland has always been top in every area.
    C. Human resource is viewed as the only asset.
    D. Immigrants have to adopt the Swiss culture.

27. Switzerland is considered the first choice for work by foreigners
    because _____.
    A. they can enjoy more freedom
    B. they can transfer their children to different schools with ease
    C. they can contribute to the Swiss economy
    D. they can afford a higher standard of living

28. What can be observed about the Swiss people?
    A. Technical skills and academic knowledge are equally important.
    B. Vocation schools are more useful than university degrees.
    C. Students are encouraged to leave school at an early age.
    D. Universities are only for private school students.

Just a century ago, raising children is something newly-weds do without much thought. Nowadays, couples go through serious financial considerations and planning before they decide to have babies. With women receiving higher levels of education, many have become career-minded and the burden of being a full-time housewife is not as appealing as it used to be. Developed countries all over the world face a common challenge: a low birthrate and a high percentage of aging citizens.

The aging of populations does raise concerns at many levels for governments around the world. There is concern over the possibility that a shrinking proportion of working-age people (ages 15 to 64) in the population may lead to an economic slowdown. The smaller working-age populations must also support growing numbers of older dependents, possibly creating financial stress for social insurance systems and dimming the economic outlook for the elderly.

Graying populations will also fuel demands for changes in public investments, such as the reallocation of resources from the needs of children to the needs of seniors. At the more personal level, longer life spans may strain household finances, cause people to extend their working lives or rearrange family structures. Perhaps not surprisingly, an aging China announced a relaxation of its one-child policy in November 2013.

29. Why are women less willing to have children based on reasons given in the passage?
    A. They are indifferent.
    B. They are fearful.
    C. They are infertile.
    D. They are ambitious.

30. In what way does an aging population affect the economy?
    A. Senior citizens refuse to give up their positions.
    B. The workforce decreases significantly.
    C. Young people have difficulty advancing their career.
    D. Retirement age is extended to 70.

31. Why did China reverse its population control policy?
    A. The burden of the younger generation is too much to bear.
    B. The older generation demands to have more grandchildren.
    C. Young couples are now willing to have more children.
    D. Modern science has enabled more new-borns to survive.

Questions 32-35 are based on the information provided in the following Internship program and resume.

Oversea Internship Program

This program is currently open to juniors and seniors in college who are interested in real jobs related to their major in the world. Please refer to the following available opportunities.

Company / Country	Responsibilities	Preferred students' field	Requirements	Opening
Sound Strategy Company, Korea	Support systems engineering and passenger technology	engineering, technology	1. Proficiency in Microsoft Office (Word, PowerPoint, Excel) 2. Fluency in English and Korean	2
Alright Technologies, India	Assist the finance team in developing new applications	finance, economics	1. Strong Microsoft Excel skills 2. Fluency in spoken and written English	1
Coast Development, Canada	Contribute to climate risk evaluation and conduct systematic research	economics, statistics, technology	1. Experience in the climate change research 2. Fluency in English and French	4
First Property, Singapore	General support to a content management program	management, finance	1. Microsoft Excel skills are absolutely essential	2

Internship Resume

Mason Thomas
Business Student
Date of birth: 10/01/1998
Phone number: 0919-111-222
Email address: mason.thomas@gmail.com

Education

Global Business
University of Taiwan
09/2018 – present
Main courses
Strategy, organization, and
market creation
Data analysis and systematic
reviews

Volunteer Experience

Foxcoon Education Foundation
October 2018 – May 2020
Offered school work guidance
and care for juniors
Greenpeace, Taiwan
July 2019 – Present
Help improve environment
protection projects

Technical Skills

Proficient user in Microsoft
Office
Digital marketing strategy
Big data analysis

Soft Skills

Time management
Leadership
Critical thinking

Languages

English (Advanced)
French (Advanced)
Mandarin Chinese (Native)

Hobbies

Travel
Play basketball
Reading

---

32. Which of the following statements is NOT Mr. Thomas' strength?
    A. Motivate people to work together.
    B. Analyze information and make a reasoned decision.
    C. Write some coding languages, like C++.
    D. Make effective decisions by using large amounts of raw data.

33 Which of the following statements about the four companies is true?
   A. Sound Strategy Company's interns need to develop new applications.
   B. Alright Technologies is open for one intern.
   C. Coast Development expects the interns with Microsoft Excel skills.
   D. First Property is looking for interns who major in technology.

34. Which firm is the least likely to have Mr. Thomas as an intern?
   A. Sound Strategy Company.
   B. Alright Technologies.
   C. Coast Development.
   D. First Property.

35. Which company is outside of Asia?
   A. Sound Strategy Company.
   B. Alright Technologies.
   C. Coast Development.
   D. First Property.

—結束—

初試 聽力測驗 解析

第一部分 / 看圖辨義

第 1 回
第 2 回
第 3 回
第 4 回
第 5 回
第 6 回

Q1

For question one, please look at picture A.

What time will the train arrive?
列車什麼時候會抵達？

A. A quarter past four.   A. 4:15
B. A quarter past five.   B. 5:15
C. A quarter to four.   C. 3:45
D. A quarter to five.   D. 4:45

詳解   **答案：D**

　　圖片中的時鐘顯示當時的時間是 4:40，而上方的電視螢幕指出下一班列車將在 5 分鐘後抵達，也就是 4:45，答案為 D。

補充說明

　　英文說明時間的方式有幾種，除了一般按照小時、分鐘順序的說法，如 4:15 唸作 four fifteen 之外，也有像題目那樣，先聽到的數字是分鐘，後面的數字是小時的講法。另外聽到 past 或 after 用加法，ten past two = 2 點加 10 分等於 2:10。聽到 to 則是用減法，ten to two = 2 點減掉 10 分等於 1:50。

Q2

For question two, please look at picture B.

What might the woman be telling the man?
這位女子可能在跟老先生說什麼？

A. Please call the number on this paper.

B. Please cut the line and go to counter number one.

C. Please read out your identification card number.

D. Please take a number and wait for your turn.

A. 請把紙上的號碼叫出來。

B. 請插隊，接著到一號櫃檯。

C. 請念出你的身分證號碼。

D. 請拿一個號碼，然後等你的叫號。

詳解　　　　　　　　　　　　　　　　　　　　　　**答案：D**

　　圖片背景可能在銀行或郵局，行員對著老先生微笑，並指著抽號碼牌的機器，可合理推斷行員要老先生抽取號碼牌，答案為 D。

Q3

For question three, please look at picture C.

What did the player in jersey number 10 do?
身穿 10 號球衣的籃球員做了什麼？

A. He made a perfect shot.

B. He violated the rules of the game.

C. He snatched the ball from another player.

D. He did not hear the whistle.

A. 他投進了完美的一球。

B. 他違反了比賽的規則。

C. 他從另一名球員手中把球搶走。

D. 他沒有聽到哨聲。

詳解　　　　　　　　　　　　　　　　　　　　　　**答案：B**

　　圖片中身穿 10 號球衣的籃球員用手肘推了另一名在防守他的球員，可知他已經犯規了，答案為 B。

|單字片語| **foul** [faul] 犯規 / **foul out** 犯規出局

Q4

For questions four and five, please look at picture D.

What can we learn from the notice?
從這張通知可得知什麼？

A. Ship rides are temporarily cancelled.　　A. 輪船服務暫時取消。
B. Boating is reserved for certain passengers.　B. 划船只保留給某些乘客。
C. The weather is pleasant.　　C. 天氣宜人。
D. Bus services will be terminated.　　D. 公車服務將會被終止。

詳解　　答案：A

　　圖片為一張通知單，通告上寫著：Ferry services terminated due to severe weather conditions.（由於天氣狀況惡劣所有渡輪服務將停止。）Shuttle bus service will be provided to take passengers back to the main island.（將提供接駁公車載送乘客回本島。）根據以上的訊息，答案為 A。

Q5

For question five, please refer to picture D again.

Why can't the passengers get back to the main island by ship?
為什麼乘客不能坐船回到本島？

A. It could be dangerous.　　A. 可能會有危險。
B. The view by bus is better.　　B. 坐公車的景觀比較好。
C. There is something wrong with the ferry.　C. 這艘渡輪有問題。
D. They can exercise if they travel on foot.　D. 用走的他們可以運動。

詳解　　答案：A

　　承上題，從通知上的關鍵詞 severe weather conditions（天氣狀況惡劣）可推斷風浪可能很大，乘坐這艘渡輪可能會發生危險，答案為 A。

第1回
第2回
第3回
第4回
第5回
第6回

Q6

Could you vacuum the floor while I do the laundry?
當我在洗衣服的同時，你可以用吸塵器吸地板嗎？

A. I need a broom.
B. I can't do both things at the same time.
C. I think that is fair.
D. I will turn the volume down.

A. 我需要掃把。
B. 我不能同時做兩件事。
C. 我認為那很公平。
D. 我會把音量調低。

詳解　　　　　　　　　　　　　　　　　　　　　　**答案：C**

　　對方用 Could you... 來表示禮貌，提出一個合理的要求。一個人負責洗衣服，另一個負責用吸塵器，這是公平的工作分配，答案為 C。

補充說明

　　Can 跟 Could 翻譯成中文都是「可以；能夠」的意思，在用法上卻不同。
Could you turn down the volume a little?　你是否可以把音量調小聲一點？
Can you turn down the volume?　你把音量調小聲可以嗎？
Could you do me a favor?　你是否能幫我一個忙？
Can you come to my party?　你可以來我的派對嗎？

Q7

The assignment I got today is really unusual.
我今天拿到的作業跟平時的很不一樣。

A. Where do I need to sign?
B. How can you purchase it without telling me?
C. Will I have to be there tomorrow?
D. Do you mean it's weird in some way?

A. 我需要在哪裡簽名？
B. 你怎麼可以沒告訴我就買下來？
C. 我明天需要去那裡嗎？
D. 你的意思是在某方面怪怪的嗎？

詳解　　　　　　　　　　　　　　　　　　　　　　**答案：D**

　　聽到 assignment（作業），可猜想這是校園對話，說話者應是學生。今天的作業不尋常（unusual），不尋常的近義詞是奇怪的（weird），答案為 D。請注意，不要聽到 assignment 有 sign 的發音就選 A。

|單字片語| **odd** [ad] 奇特的 / **peculiar** [pɪˈkjʊljə] 奇怪的；獨特的

第 1 回
第 2 回
第 3 回
第 4 回
第 5 回
第 6 回

Q8

Will a visa be necessary for a thirty-day trip?
三十天的行程將會需要簽證嗎？

A. Yes, we accept both credit card and cash.
B. Yes, it will be valid for three days.
C. No, unless you wish to extend your stay.
D. No, you need it in the first place.

A. 是的，信用卡和現金我們都接受。
B. 是的，有效期為三天。
C. 不，除非你想延長停留時間。
D. 不，你本來就需要簽證。

詳解

答案：C

多數人都知道 visa 是「信用卡」，因為很多信用卡上都有這個字樣，不過 visa 也是「簽證」的意思。而試題中 visa 的意思是指「簽證」，選項 A 是錯的。說話者問的是三十天的行程，因此簽證的有效期為三天不符合邏輯，選項 B 也是錯誤的。三十天內不需要簽證，想延長停留時間的話才需要申請，這是最合理的說明，答案為 C。選項 D 前後矛盾，前面說不用簽證，後面又說本來就需要簽證。

|單字片語| **extend** [ɪkˈstɛnd] 擴展；延伸 / **extent** [ɪkˈstɛnt] 程度；範圍
extension [ɪkˈstɛnʃən] 延伸；增長部分 / **extension number** 分機號碼

Q9

This is an emergency. A child is badly injured.
這是個緊急事故。有個孩童受了重傷。

A. We have to work harder than before.
B. You need to check the engine.
C. It is not going to work.
D. I have already called for an ambulance.

A. 我們必須比之前更加努力。
B. 你需要檢查引擎。
C. 這是行不通的。
D. 我已經打電話叫救護車了。

詳解

答案：D

從以上情境中，可以得知有個孩童的傷勢很嚴重，最為合理的回答是「我已經打電話叫救護車了」，答案為 D。

〈補充說明〉

急診室的英文是 emergency room，簡稱 ER。一些緊急逃生設備也常會註明：In case of emergency, break glass.（若有緊急狀況，打破玻璃。）

Q10

Please provide us with your personal information.
請提供我們您的個人資料。

A. Why don't you go there yourself?
B. Do I have access to the Internet?
C. Where can I find the answers?
D. Will my postal address be required?

A. 你為何不自己去？
B. 我能連接網路嗎？
C. 我能在哪裡找到答案？
D. 需要我的郵政地址嗎？

【詳解】 　　　　　　　　　　　　　　　　　　　　　　　【答案：D】

　　從以上題目可猜想，應該是在申請某個東西或詢問某件事時，對方才會要求我們提供個人資料，而個人資料包括郵政地址，答案為 D。

Q11

Have you heard that Adeline is getting engaged?
你聽說 Adeline 要訂婚了嗎？

A. The line is still busy.
B. She is spending her money unwisely.
C. We will visit her at the hospital later.
D. So she finally realized it is time to settle down.

A. 電話還在忙線中。
B. 她都在亂花錢。
C. 我們晚點到醫院探訪她。
D. 所以她終於發現是時候要安定下來了。

【詳解】 　　　　　　　　　　　　　　　　　　　　　　　【答案：D】

　　聽說另一個朋友要訂婚了，最為合理的回應是「所以她終於發現是時候要安定下來了」，答案為 D。

|單字片語| fiance [ˌfiənˈse] 未婚夫 / fiancee [ˌfiənˈse] 未婚妻

Q12

Make sure we have all the ingredients ready.
確保我們都有準備好所有食材。

A. Let me take the patient's temperature.
B. There is still room for improvement.
C. Where are the eggs and flour?
D. Why didn't you greet me at the door?

A. 讓我測量這位病人的體溫。
B. 還是有進步的空間。
C. 雞蛋跟麵粉在哪裡？
D. 為何你沒在門口跟我打招呼？

詳解

答案：C

　　從關鍵詞 ingredients（食材），可知道答案是 C，因為雞蛋（eggs）和麵粉（flour）都是食材。唯一可能造成疑惑的是，flower（花朵）和 flour（麵粉）的發音相同，可能會選錯。

Q13

Are there aliens out there in space?
外太空那裡會有外星人嗎？

A. We can't rule out the possibility.
B. There is a parking lot here.
C. You have to be careful.
D. I want to remain where I am.

A. 我們不能排除這個可能性。
B. 這裡有一個停車位。
C. 你必須小心一點。
D. 我想要留在原來的地方。

詳解

答案：A

　　關於外星人是否存在的爭議已然沒有答案，因此最好的回應是不排除任何可能性，答案為 A。

|單字片語| **rule out** 排除 / **overrule** [ˌovəˋrul] 否決；駁回

Q14

How do you cope with stress?
你如何應付壓力？

A. I usually have it with some sugar.
B. I guess listening to music helps.
C. I wonder who can do it.
D. I can't just ignore it.

A. 我通常會加一點糖。
B. 我猜聽音樂會有幫助。
C. 我不曉得誰能做得到。
D. 我不能就這樣忽略它。

詳解

答案：B

　　應付壓力的方法很多，而聽音樂是不錯的選擇，答案為 B。

|單字片語| **deal with** 處理；對待 / **handle** [ˋhændl] 對待，處理 / **relieve** [rɪˋliv] 緩和

It's always better to think twice before making a decision.
在做決定之前，三思而後行總是比較好的。

A. I have already made up my mind.
B. There are two things required.
C. Hurry up or you will regret it.
D. It's just a form of recreation.

A. 我已經下定決心了。
B. 需要兩樣東西。
C. 快點，不然你會後悔。
D. 這只是一種消遣。

〔詳解〕　　　　　　　　　　　　　　　　　　　　　　　　　〔答案：A〕

　　這題說話者在勸對方要三思而行，然而對方回答他已經下定決心了，答案為 A。

〈補充說明〉

　　以下是一些英文的慣用語：

　　think twice 三思而行，have second thoughts 反悔，once bitten twice shy 一朝被蛇咬、十年怕井繩。

第 1 回
第 2 回
第 3 回
第 4 回
第 5 回
第 6 回

Q16

W: Excuse me, sir. No flash photography allowed. Marine life is extremely sensitive to strong lights.
先生，抱歉。不准使用閃光燈。海洋生物對強光非常敏感。

M: I'm sorry. Is it all right for me to take some pictures?
對不起。我可以拍一些照片嗎？

W: As long as no flash is used. 只要不要開閃光燈就可以了。

Q: Where are the man and woman?
這位男子和女子在什麼地方？

A. In an aquarium.　　　　　　A. 在水族館。
B. In an art gallery.　　　　　B. 在藝術畫廊。
C. In a theater.　　　　　　　C. 在戲院。
D. In a hospital.　　　　　　　D. 在醫院。

詳解　　　　　　　　　　　　　　　　　　　　　答案：A

　　只從選項可推敲，這題要問的是說話者目前所在的地方。從 marine life（海洋生物）可猜測，說話者應該是在水族館，答案為 A。水族館或海生館內可以拍照，但生物對強光很敏感，所以禁止使用閃光燈（flash）。

|單字片語| aquarium [əˋkwɛrɪəm] 魚缸；水族館 / aqua [ˋækwə] 水；水綠色

Q17

M: Prior to admission, you will have to take an entrance test. The results of the test will determine the courses available to you in the first semester.
在入學之前，你將必須參加入學考試。考試的成績將會決定你第一學期可以選修的課程。

W: Are there any materials that I can use for preparation?
有任何我可以用來做準備的資料嗎？

M: Sure. Past years' questions can be found on our website.
當然。歷屆考題都可以在我們的網站上找到。

Q: What is the woman doing? 這位女子在做什麼？
A. She is taking a blood test. A. 她正在做血液檢驗。
B. She is purchasing an item. B. 她正在購買一件物品。
C. She is enrolling in a university. C. 她正在登記入學大學。
D. She is designing a webpage. D. 她正在設計網頁。

詳解　　　　　　　　　　　　　　　　　　　　　　　　**答案：C**

　　聽到 entrance test（入學考試）、course（課程）和 semester（學期），可推測這是在校園的情境對話，答案為 C。最後提到的網站（website）上有可以下載歷屆考題的地方，並不是要這位女子設計網頁。

I單字片語I **admission** [əd`mɪʃən] 入學；入場 / **enrolment** [ɪn`rolmənt] 登記；入學
　　　　　 application [ˌæplə`keʃən] 申請；應用

Q18

M: I'm looking for a Christmas present for my daughter. She's in fifth grade and I'm not sure if she is still into Barbie Dolls and all that.
我在找一份聖誕節禮物給我女兒。她五年級了，我不確定她是否還喜歡芭比娃娃之類的禮物。

W: Let's take some time to find out what she needs. As a mother, I hate to buy things that my kids never use.
我們來花點時間看看她到底需要什麼。身為母親，我不喜歡買一些孩子不會用到的東西。

M: That's very kind of you. OK. Let me see.
你人真好。好的。讓我想想。

Q: What is the woman's job? 這位女子的工作是什麼？
A. She's a housewife. A. 她是一位家庭主婦。
B. She is a school teacher. B. 她是一名學校老師。
C. She's a sales representative. C. 她是一位銷售代表。
D. She is a toy designer. D. 她是一名玩具設計師。

詳解　　　　　　　　　　　　　　　　　　　　　　　　**答案：C**

　　從選項可預測，這題要問的是這位女子的職業。男子想購買聖誕節禮物給女兒，而女子說她可以提供意見，這位女子的職業應該是銷售員，答案為 C。這位女子說她也是一位媽媽，但這不表示媽媽就是家庭主婦。

I單字片語I **represent** [ˌrɛprɪ`zɛnt] **(v.)** 代表 / **representative** [ˌrɛprɪ`zɛntətɪv] **(n.)** 代表；代理人

Q19

W: Physically he is fine. I think he is just upset because there is no one to play with him when you are at work.

身體方面，他很好。我認為他只是因為你在工作時，沒有人跟他玩在難過而已。

M: Do you mean he is biting and chewing on the sofa because he wants my attention? 你的意思是，他咬沙發是為了要引起我的注意嗎？

W: That's right. Most pets need some kind of companionship. For his size, you will need to walk him at least twice a day.

沒錯。多數的寵物都需要有個伴。以他的體型，你需要一天帶他出去散步最少兩次。

Q: What is the man's problem? 這位男子的問題是什麼？

A. He needs to spend more time with his dog. A. 他需要多花時間陪他的狗。
B. He needs to be more serious at work. B. 他需要在工作時更加嚴謹。
C. He needs to learn how to relieve stress. C. 他需要學習如何紓解壓力。
D. He needs to exercise more regularly. D. 他需要更定期去運動。

【詳解】　　　　　　　　　　　　　　　　　　　　　答案：A

　　從四個選項看來，可預判大概是對話中的男子需要做哪方面的改善，來解決目前的問題，聽對話前可以朝這方面預作準備。嚴格來說寵物是動物，代名詞應該用 it，不過許多人把寵物當成家中的一分子，所以也可以用 he 或 she。選項中的 he 則是指男主人，說話的女子應該是獸醫或動物專家，她給這位男主人的建議是多花時間陪伴寵物，答案為 A。

|單字片語| get sb's attention 引起注意 / center of attention 專注的焦點

Q20

M: Come on. Stop bargaining. I have quoted you the best price possible. 拜託，不要再討價還價了。我已經報給你最優惠的價格了。

W: 5000 bucks is still unacceptable. I guess I don't need a new handbag after all.

五千元還是不能接受。那我想我也不需要新的手提包了。

M: Just a second. I will buy it using my name, so you are entitled to the extra 10% discount for staff. Take it or leave it.

慢著。我用我的名義來買，這樣你就能得到員工額外的九折優惠。只能這樣，不要就拉倒。

Q: How much does the woman have to pay?
這位女子需要付多少錢？

A. 5500 bucks.	A. 五千五百元。
B. 5000 bucks.	B. 五千元。
C. 4500 bucks.	C. 四千五百元。
D. 4000 bucks.	D. 四千元。

詳解　　　　　　　　　　　　　　　　　　　　　　　　答案：C

　　從對話內容可得知，說話者是店員和顧客，既然顧客嫌五千元太貴，選項 A 和 B 都不可能。最後男子給女子打九折，因此這題要考一點點的數學概念，5000 的 10% 是 500，5000 - 500 = 4500，答案為 C。

〈補充說明〉

　　英文表達折扣的方式是能省下多少錢，相反的是，中文則關注在最後要付多少錢。看到 15% OFF 等優惠，最簡單的方式是用 100 扣掉 15，等於打 85 折。25% OFF 則可理解為 100 扣掉 25，等於打 75 折。值得注意的是，考生作答時，要聽清楚題目問是最後要付的總額，還是可以省下多少錢。

Q21

W: I told you a vacation would be a good investment. I am beginning to look at things from different perspectives.
　我告訴過你度假是個很好的投資。我開始從不同的觀點來看待事物。

M: I can't argue with that. I feel refreshed and I can't wait to get back to work.　這一點我不能否認。我覺得煥然一新，而且等不及想回去工作。

W: Same here. Let's enjoy the last day of the trip tomorrow to the fullest.　我也是。讓我們盡情享受明天最後一天的行程。

Q: Why are the speakers so excited?
說話者為何如此興奮？

A. They just made a lot of money.	A. 他們剛賺了很多錢。
B. They just got married.	B. 他們剛結婚。
C. They are going on a tour.	C. 他們將要去旅行。
D. They feel more energetic.	D. 他們覺得更精力充沛。

詳解　　　　　　　　　　　　　　　　　　　　　　　　答案：D

　　光從關鍵詞 investment（投資），或許會以為答案會跟錢有關，不過對話

中所謂的投資並非指錢方面的回報，而是指看不見的收穫。對話中並沒有提到說話者是否在渡蜜月，因此選項 B 無法確認。而選項 C 也是錯誤的，因為說話者已經在旅行，並不是將要去旅行。他們花錢去渡假，感覺自己煥然一新，表示很期待回到工作崗位，答案為 D。

|單字片語| **fresh** [frɛʃ] 新鮮的；有精神的 / **refresh** [rɪˈfrɛʃ] 恢復精神
refreshment [rɪˈfrɛʃmənt] 精力恢復；茶點

第 1 回
第 2 回
第 3 回
第 4 回
第 5 回
第 6 回

Q22

M: Please check your gear one last time. The oxygen tank will last you an hour but for safety's sake, we will return to the surface in 40 minutes.

請最後一次檢查你的裝備。氧氣筒可以提供一小時的氧氣，但為了安全起見，我們在 40 分鐘後會回到水面。

W: This is the first time I will be seeing coral reefs with my own eyes.

這將會是我第一次親眼看到珊瑚礁。

M: I understand that you guys are first-timers. I do have to remind you not to take anything as a souvenir.

我明白你們都是第一次。我必須提醒你們不要把任何東西帶回去當紀念品。

Q: What will the speakers probably do next?
接下來說話者應該會做什麼？

A. Go dining.   A. 去用餐。
B. Go diving.   B. 去潛水。
C. Go surfing.   C. 去衝浪。
D. Go skiing.   D. 去滑雪。

詳解   **答案：B**

選項列出四種運動，可以知道對話跟運動有關，而從對話中的 oxygen tank（氧氣筒）和 coral reef（珊瑚礁）等關鍵詞可判斷，說話者接下來會去潛水，答案為 B。

|單字片語| **snorkeling** [ˈsnɔrklɪŋ] 浮潛 / **scuba diving** 配戴氧氣筒潛水

Q23

W: You can improve your English without spending a lot of money. As a matter of fact, sometimes you can learn English totally free.

你可以不用花很多錢就能加強你的英文。實際上，有時候你可以完全免費來學英文。

M: Really? I thought I have to go to a cram school or something.

真的嗎？我以為必須去補習班什麼的。

W: There are free English lessons on YouTube, tons of information on the Internet, a dozen programs you can view on TV, you name it. The question is, are you disciplined enough to do it on a regular basis?

YouTube 上有免費的英文課程，在網路上有非常多的資訊，而電視上也有十幾個可以觀看的節目，要什麼都有。問題是，你有足夠的自律來定期學習英文嗎？

Q: **What is the woman's advice to the man?**
這位女子給男子的建議是什麼？

A. Learning English doesn't take a lot of time.   A. 學英文不會花很多時間。
B. Learning English is free but troublesome.   B. 學英文是免費的，但是很麻煩。
C. Learning English can be costly.   C. 學英文可能會花很多錢。
D. Learning English requires determination.   D. 學英文需要決心。

詳解   **答案：D**

從對話中可得知，學習英文可以是方便而且免費的，不過需要花很多時間。而最後這位女子所提到的自律，指的是學習的決心，答案為 D。

|單字片語| **determination** [dɪˌtɝməˈneʃən] 決心 / **perseverance** [ˌpɝsəˈvɪrəns] 堅持不懈

The Amount of Customers
顧客的人數

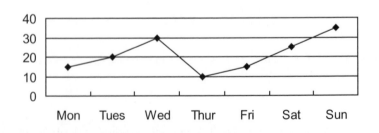

M: I heard that you run an outdoor dining café. How's your business going?

416

第 1 回

第 2 回

第 3 回

第 4 回

第 5 回

第 6 回

我聽說你經營一間露天餐飲咖啡館，你的生意如何？

W: It could be better as it's warming up lately. I believe the weather is the most significant factor influencing customers.

因為最近變暖了，可能會更好。我相信天氣是影響顧客最重要的因素。

M: Are you saying that chilly weather means fewer customers?

你是說冷颼颼的天氣代表更少的顧客嗎？

W: I mean it. Not only the temperature, but people also don't want to eat out on a rainy day.

沒錯，不僅是氣溫，人們也不想在下雨天外出吃飯。

M: Were the tables less during the rainy season?

在雨季時的桌數比較沒那麼多嗎？

W: That's correct. In my experience, as the weather is getting drier, we will have more guests.

沒錯。就我的經驗，因為天氣越來越乾燥，我們將會有更多的客人。

Q: **Look at the graph. What will the weather be like on Thursday?** 請看這張圖表，週四的天氣會如何呢？

A. It was warming up.   A. 天氣會變暖。
B. It was warm and dry.   B. 天氣很溫暖、乾燥。
C. It was getting drier.   C. 天氣越來越乾燥。
D. It was chilly and rainy.   D. 天氣陰冷且有雨。

詳解   **答案：D**

　　從圖表和選項可知題目跟顧客人數及天氣狀況有關，因此聽敘述時要注意聽這兩項因素之間的關係。從 It could be better as it's warming up lately，可知氣溫漸漸變暖。而 Not only the temperature, but people also don't want to eat out on a rainy day，因此推斷出雨季的用餐桌數較少。再加上 as the weather is getting drier, we will have more guests，可知天氣越乾燥，用餐客人就較多。整合以上的資訊、在對照圖表，可知週四用餐人數最少，以及女子所述的天氣狀況，週四的天氣狀況應該是陰冷且有雨，答案為 D。

Noah's Profit Income
Noah 的利潤收入

Investment 投資	2018	2019	2020
Gold 黃金	$1,000	$1,000	$1,100
Stocks 股票	-$2,500	$2,000	-$3,000
Funds 基金	$2,000	-$4,000	$2,000
Bonds 債券	-$3,000	$2,000	$3,000

W: Hi, Noah. I want to start investing. Would you share your experience with me?

嗨，Noah。我想要開始投資，你可以和我分享你的經驗嗎？

M: No problem. Wise investors know not to blindly place all their eggs in one basket. There are many different types of investments. You need to know what your investment options are.

沒問題。明智的投資者知道不要盲目地將所有雞蛋放在一個籃子裡。投資有許多不同的類型。你需要知道你的投資選擇是什麼。

W: As a new investor, I'd like to begin with a low-risk investment.

身為新的投資者，我想從一項低風險的投資開始。

M: Well, it is a good place to start, but the return will be low.

嗯，這是一個很好開始的起點，但回報會很低。

W: That's fine with me. A small reward is better than losing money.

對我來說還可以，小的報酬比賠錢還好。

M: That is for sure.　那是肯定的。

Q: **Look at Noah's Profit Income. What type of investment would Noah most likely suggest the woman begin with?**
請看 Noah的利潤收入表，Noah 最有可能會建議女子開始哪種類型的投資？

A. Gold.
B. Stocks.
C. Funds.
D. Bonds.

A. 黃金。
B. 股票。
C. 基金。
D. 債券。

詳解

　　從 Noah 的利潤收入表和選項可以猜出題目跟投資相關，因此聽敘述時要注意四種投資的利潤。從女子提到 I'd like to begin with a low-risk investment 和 A small reward is better than losing money，可知她選擇低風險的投資。而 Noah 的利潤收入表可以看到他三年來的投資情況，只有黃金的利潤少，但也沒有賠錢。由此可知，Noah 最有可能建議女子從黃金開始投資，答案為 A。

|單字片語| **put all your eggs in one basket** 孤注一擲 / **return** [rɪˋtɜn] 回報

Q26

M: A top-down approach doesn't work for young people. Teenagers are not resistant to do more physical activity. If we work with them, rather than acting on their behalf, they will be more active in school and in the community. Boys want the freedom to socialize out of the classroom. Girls want the opportunity for casual and fun activities, instead of traditional competitive sports.

用由上而下的方法對年輕人是不適用的。青少年並不抗拒進行更多的體能活動。如果我們與他們合作，而不是代替他們做事，他們會在學校和社區中更加活躍。男孩們希望自由自在地在教室外社交。女孩們希望有進行休閒、有趣活動的機會，而不是傳統的競技運動。

Q: What type of physical activity would girls like to take part in? 女孩們會喜歡參加哪一種體能活動？

A. Mountain bike racing.	A. 登山自行車賽。
B. Road bicycle racing.	B. 公路自行車賽。
C. Leisure cycling.	C. 休閒自行車。
D. Track cycling.	D. 場地自由車

詳解

答案：C

從選項可以知道敘述會提到四種不同的自行車活動，因此聽的時候要注意與自行車活動相關的內容。從最後一句 Girls want the opportunity for casual and fun activities, instead of the traditional competitive sports，可知女孩們不想要參加競技運動，而是想要休閒娛樂活動。選項 A（Mountain bike racing）、選項 B（Road bicycle racing）、選項 D（Track cycling）都是屬於競技運動，選項 C（Leisure cycling）則是休閒娛樂活動，答案為 C。

|單字片語| **act on behalf of sb.** 代理某人的職務 / **socialize** ['soʃə,laɪz] 參與社交
track cycling 場地自由車

Q27

W: Increasingly, people spend more time on devices with screens. As a result, they often experience sleep disturbances. It is believed that blue light confuses the internal clock of the body. Researchers found that wearing special glasses can block out blue light emissions by digital devices. They may help tech-addicted people sleep better at night.

越來越多地，人們花更多時間在有螢幕的裝置上。因此，他們經常遭受睡眠障礙之苦。人們相信，藍光會使人體的內部時鐘混亂。研究人員發現，戴上特殊眼鏡可以阻擋數位裝置散發的藍光。他們可能會幫助科技成癮的人晚上睡得更好。

Q: What is the speaker's suggestion?
說話者的建議是什麼？

A. Wearing protective glasses.
B. Reducing time on smartphones.
C. Putting more research into it.
D. Turning off electronic devices.

A. 戴上防護眼鏡。
B. 減少用智慧型手機的時間。
C. 對此進行更多研究。
D. 關閉電子裝置。

詳解

答案：A

從選項可以猜出這題與數位裝置的主題相關，因此聽敘述時要注意與數位裝置有關的內容。從第三句 The researchers found that wearing special glasses can block out the emission of blue light by digital devices 和最後一句 They may help tech-addicted people sleep better at night，可以知道說話者建議配科技成隱者戴特殊眼鏡來阻擋會傷害身體的藍光，答案為 A。

|單字片語| **block out** 擋住 / **emission** [ɪˈmɪʃən] 放射；散發

Q28

M: Hi, Annie! Thanks for such an unforgettable four-day vacation. A soothing walk along the beach was truly relaxing. Nothing could be fresher and more delightful than the flavor of the seafood. The richest and most memorable part was whale watching on the vessel. Please pay a visit to us next summer. Let me and my wife organize a magnificent visit to our modern city for your family.

嗨，Annie！感謝你提供如此難忘的四天假期。沿著海灘平靜地散步真是令人放鬆。沒有什麼比海鮮的味道更新鮮、更令人愉悅了。而最豐富和最難忘的部分是在船上賞鯨。明年夏天請來拜訪我們。讓我和我太太為你的家人安排一段現代化城市的壯麗之旅。

Q: What will the speaker offer?
說話者將會提供什麼？

A. Whale watching.
B. Tasting of seafood.
C. Beach visit.
D. Modern tour.

A. 賞鯨。
B. 品嚐海鮮。
C. 去海灘。
D. 現代之旅。

從選項猜測敘述可能會出現四種旅遊活動，因此聽敘述時要注意與旅遊活動相關的訊息。選項 A（Whale watching）、選項 B（Tasting of seafood）、選項 C（Beach visit）都是說話者感謝對方所提供的旅遊活動。而從最後一句 Let me and my husband organize a magnificent visit to our modern city for your family，可知說話者希望能安排一段自己住在現代城市的參觀旅遊，答案為 D。

Q29

W: Sweet Seller is the best company that you should choose. We are willing to help sell your home efficiently and professionally. Your home will be in front of the most qualified buyers through means of magazines, online listing sites, and advertising in local papers. Give us a call now to get your home in the marketplace and to get it presented on our website.

Sweet Seller 是您應該選擇的最佳公司。我們願意有效、專業地幫助您出售您的房屋。您的房屋將會透過雜誌、線上登錄網站和地區報紙廣告的方式，呈現在最符合資格的買家面前。立即打電話給我們，讓您的房屋進入市場，並展示在我們的網站上。

Q: What sort of business is Sweet Seller?
Sweet Seller 是什麼樣的產業呢？

A. A creative agency.　　　　　A. 創意代理商。
B. An online agency.　　　　　B. 線上代理商。
C. A real estate agency.　　　　C. 房地產仲介。
D. A marketing agency.　　　　D. 銷售代理商。

四個選項都與代理商機構有關，可以猜測是題目要問某個營運機構，因此聽敘述時要注意在廣播內容中出現的商業活動。從第二句 We are willing to help sell your home efficiently and professionally，可知 Sweet Seller 主要在銷售房屋，因此是房地產仲介商，答案為 C。

Q30

M: Science fiction is a literature of great ideas and problem resolutions. This imagination of more advanced species offers a possibility for humanity. From sci-fi novels and films, we can explore how mankind would react to them. Even though it is tough, I still have 10 good movies for you. There's no shame in never having seen them, but with today's introduction, there is no excuse not to check them out. Okay. Here we go!

科幻小說是一種關於偉大構想和解決問題的文學。更先進物種的想像力提供了人類的可能性。從科幻小說和電影中，我們可以探索人類會如何對它們反應。即使這很困難，我仍然有十部好電影要推薦給你。不曾看過這些電影並不會很丟臉，但是有了今天的介紹，就沒有任何理由不去觀賞它們了。好的，開始吧！

第 1 回
第 2 回
第 3 回
第 4 回
第 5 回
第 6 回

Q: Which movie might not be introduced?
哪一部電影可能不會被介紹？

A. Outer space.
B. World War I.
C. Artificial Intelligence.
D. Time traveler.

A. 外太空。
B. 第一次世界大戰。
C. 人工智慧。
D. 時空旅行者。

詳解

答案：B

這題的四個選項都是電影名稱，因此需要注意有關電影的細節。獨白的第二句 From sci-fi novels and films, we can explore how mankind would react to them，提到了科幻小說及電影。第三句 Even though it is tough, I still have 10 good movies for you，代表要介紹的十部電影。選項 A（Outer space）、選項 C（Artificial Intelligence）、選項 D（Time traveler）可推測這些都是科幻片。而選項 B（World War I）則是已經發生的第一次世界大戰的歷史電影，最不可能被介紹，答案為 B。

Q31

W: An old Japanese proverb says that if a man has no tea in him, he is unable to comprehend truth and beauty. At Osaka Tea House, our tea experts will serve various flavors of strong tea for you at three o'clock this afternoon. If you are interested in sipping the finest teas and enjoying the atmosphere of the traditional tea ceremony, register at the reception before half past two. This unique event is only half an hour long.

一句日本古老的諺語提到，如果一個人沒有喝茶，他就無法理解真理和美麗。在大阪茶館，我們的茶專家將在今天下午三點為您提供各種口味的濃茶。如果您有興趣品嚐最上乘的茶水，並享受傳統茶道的氣氛，請在下午 2:30 前在接待處登記。這項獨特的活動只有半小時的時間。

Q: When will the event come to an end?
活動什麼時候會結束？

A. At 2:30 p.m.	A. 下午 2:30。
B. At 3:00 p.m.	B. 下午 3:00。
C. At 3:30 p.m.	C. 下午 3:30。
D. At 4:00 p.m.	D. 下午 4:00。

詳解　　　　　　　　　　　　　　　　　　　　　　　　　　答案：C

　　從四個選項可知題目可能會提到這些時間，因此聽敘述時要特別注意各個時間所對應的內容，並掌握關鍵詞。從第二句 In Osaka Tea House, all tea experts will serve you with various flavors of strong tea at three o'clock this afternoon，可知活動開始的時間是在下午三點。最後一句提到 This unique event is only half an hour long，說明活動只會進行 30 分鐘，因此活動結束的時間在下午 3:30，答案為 C。

|單字片語| comprehend [ˌkɑmprɪˈhɛnd] 理解 / reception [rɪˈsɛpʃən] 接待處

Q32

M: May I have your attention, please? Passengers, Liam Huang and Alan Chen, please proceed to Gate 11 immediately. This is the final boarding call for passengers, Liam Huang and Alan Chen, booked on Flight 7712 bound for Taipei City. The final checks have been completed and the captain will order to close the aircraft door in approximately five minutes.

請大家注意這裡好嗎？旅客 Liam Huang 和 Alan Chen，請立即前往 11 號登機門。這是針對預定 7712 航班飛往台北的旅客 Liam Huang 和 Alan Chen 的最後登機廣播。最後檢查已完成，機長將會命令在大約五分鐘內關閉飛機的機門。

Q: Where would you hear this announcement?
你會在哪裡聽到這則廣播？

A. On an aircraft.	A. 在飛機上。
B. At a parking apron.	B. 在停機坪。
C. At a check-in counter.	C. 在報到櫃台。
D. At an airport.	D. 在機場。

詳解　　　　　　　　　　　　　　　　　　　　　　　　　　答案：D

　　從四個選項可以判斷題目會詢問地點，因此聽敘述時需注意相關的關鍵語

句，就可以知道答案。從第二句 Passengers, Liam Huang and Alan Chen, please proceed to Gate 11 immediately，可知廣播的目的是請兩位旅客到登機門。最後一句 The final checks have been completed and the captain will order to close the aircraft door in approximately five minutes，表示飛機的機門即將關閉，因此廣播地點應該是機場，答案為 D。

第 1 回
第 2 回
第 3 回
第 4 回
第 5 回
第 6 回

Q33

W: It's easy to invite your colleagues or classmates to participate in your online conference. Our application allows you to send invitations by email, contacts, or phone numbers. The process is slightly different whether you choose to do it on a mobile device application or on your desktop. You can click the icon and follow the instructions to learn what to do.

發送會議邀請給您的同事或同學來參加您的線上會議是很容易的。我們的應用程式讓您能夠透過電子郵件、聯絡人或電話號碼來發送邀請。無論您選擇在行動裝置的應用程式上，或是在桌機上進行，其程序都有些微的不同。您可以點擊圖示，並按照說明來學習怎麼做。

Q: **What does the speaker expect the listener to do next?**
說話者期待聽眾接下來會做什麼？

A. Send a voice call.
B. Turn an app on.
C. Press a number.
D. Find a conference.

A. 發送語音訊息。
B. 打開一個應用程式。
C. 按一個數字。
D. 找出一個會議。

詳解

答案：B

從四個選項可知題目和動作有關，雖然動作不同，但是都和操作應用程式有關，因此聽敘述時需注意其目的才能知道答案。在最後一句 You can click the icon and follow the instructions to learn what to do，可知聽眾正在學習如何邀請他人參加線上會議，所以說話者希望聽眾接下來要點擊一個圖示，以學習後續操作，答案為 B。

General Scholastic Ability Test (GSAT) Result

Subject	Top percentile	Average percentile
Chinese	13th grade	11th grade
English	13th grade	8th grade
Mathematics	12th grade	11th grade
Sciences	13th grade	12th grade
Social studies	13th grade	10th grade

學科能力測驗結果

科目	頂標	均標
國文	13 級分	11 級分
英文	13 級分	8 級分
數學	12 級分	11 級分
自然	13 級分	12 級分
社會	13 級分	10 級分

M: As expected, the average percentile dipped below the 10th grade this year. Since the original purpose of the GSAT was to evaluate students' general scholastic ability, it can be seen that the root of the problem lies in the students' basic capacities. Although its top percentile is the same as other subjects, we still need to come up with some solutions to help the teachers enhance the learning outcomes of students.

就如預期的，今年的均標下降到 10 級分以下。由於學測的最初目的是評估學生的總體學業能力，可以看出，問題的根源是在於學生的基本能力。儘管它的頂標與其他學科相同，但我們仍然需要提出一些解決方案，來幫助教師提升學生的學習成效。

Q: **Which subject does the speaker talk about?**
說話者在談論哪一個科目？

A. Chinese.
B. English.
C. Mathematics.
D. Social Studies.

A. 國文。
B. 英文。
C. 數學。
D. 社會。

詳解 答案：B

　　這題的表格與選項內容主要有五種學測科目及其頂標和均標的級分，因此聽敘述時要注意聽針對科目與其頂標和均標級分的關係，從第一句 As expected, the average percentile dipped below the 10th grade this year，可知這個科目今年的均標下降到 10 級分以下。再加上，說話者又提到 Although its top percentile is the same as other subjects…，可以推論出說話者在討論的是英文科成績，答案為 B。

|單字片語| **percentile** [pə'sɛntaɪl] 百分位數 / **scholastic** [skə'læstɪk] 學校的

Q35

W: My family is going to move into a new flat. My room only has one single bed, but my sister's room has a double bed. My parents have a contemporary bathroom in their room. My room is a little bit far away from the kitchen, but it is next to the bathroom. So, I can take a shower faster and more easily.

　　我家將要搬到一間新公寓了。我的房間只有一張單人床，但我姊姊的房間有一張雙人床。我的父母的房間裡有一間現代的浴室。我的房間離廚房有點遠，但它在浴室旁邊。所以，我可以更快、更輕鬆地去洗澡。

Q: Which room is the speaker going to have?
說話者將擁有哪一間房間？

A. Living room.　　　　　　　A. 客廳。
B. Bedroom 1.　　　　　　　B. 臥室 1。
C. Bedroom 2.　　　　　　　C. 臥室 2。
D. Bedroom 3.　　　　　　　D. 臥室 3。

詳解 答案：D

　　從圖表和選項猜測出題目與四種房間相關，因此聽敘述時要留意四種房間的資訊。第二句提到 My room only has one single bed，可知他的房間有一張單人床。最後提到 it is next to the bathroom，表示房間在浴室旁邊。由此推論出，說話者的是房間是 Bedroom 3，答案為 D。

初試 閱讀測驗 **解析**

\第一部分/ 詞彙和結構

Q1

All group leaders are to return to your _____ groups and inform your group members of the change.

所有的小組組長必須回到你們各自的小組，並通知組員關於這項改變。

A. absolute
B. exceptional
C. considerable
D. respective

詳解　　　　　　　　　　　　　　　　　　　　　　**答案：D**

　　respect 是「尊敬」，然而 respective 跟尊敬的意思完全沒關係，是指「各自的」。

|單字片語| **absolute** [ˋæbsəˏlut] 絕對的 / **exceptional** [ɪkˋsɛpʃən!] 例外的；優秀的
　　　　 considerable [kənˋsɪdərəb!] 相當多的

Q2

We do not foresee any danger, but nonetheless your parent or guardian's _____ is required before you sign up for the excursion.

我們沒預見會有任何危險，但儘管如此，在你報名這次戶外教學前，請取得你的父母或監護人同意。

A. approval
B. concern
C. hesitation
D. recipe

詳解　　　　　　　　　　　　　　　　　　　　　　**答案：A**

　　去戶外教學必須得到家長或監護人的「同意」，答案為 A。除了 approval，也可以用 consent 或 permission。

例句

Do not enter people's houses without their **consent**.
沒有別人的同意，不要進入他們的家中。
Students should not enter the teachers' office without **permission**.
沒有得到許可，學生不應該進入老師的辦公室。

|單字片語| **concern** [kənˋsɝn] 擔心；關心的事 / **hesitation** [ˌhɛzəˋteʃən] 猶豫
　　　　 recipe [ˋrɛsəpɪ] 食譜；處方

Q3

In view of the increased terrorist activities, the local police
have been advised to beef up _____ for the upcoming
international conference.

鑑於恐怖分子的活動增加，當地警察已經被建議要在即將來臨的國際會議
加強戒備。

A. confession
B. dominance
C. security
D. invasion

詳解　　　　　　　　　　　　　　　　　　　　　　　　　　**答案：C**

　　從 terrorist（恐怖分子）和 police（警察）等關鍵詞，可推斷試題和安全問
題有關。beef up security 是固定的用法，意思是「加強戒備」，答案為 C。

|單字片語| **confession** [kənˋfɛʃən] 承認；懺悔 / **dominance** [ˋdɑmənəns] 優勢
　　　　 invasion [ɪnˋveʒən] 入侵

Q4

Windows play a crucial role in a house since air _____
through the rooms helps to prevent the walls from getting
damp.

房子裡窗戶扮演一個關鍵的角色，因為空氣流通到房間有助於防止牆壁變
潮濕。

A. flattery
B. compensation
C. alternative
D. circulation

詳解　　　　　　　　　　　　　　　　　　　　　　　　　　**答案：D**

　　從 windows（窗戶）和 damp（潮濕）這些關鍵詞，可得知試題在說的是空
氣流通（air circulation）的問題，答案為 D。

|單字片語| **flattery** [ˋflætərɪ] 諂媚 / **compensation** [ˌkɑmpənˋseʃən] 補償；賠償
　　　　 alternative [ɔlˋtɝnətɪv] 替代方案；選擇

Q5

The teenage girl wore oversized clothes in an attempt to
_____ the fact that she was pregnant.

這位少女穿著大尺碼的衣服，試圖隱藏她懷有身孕的事實。

A. deceive

B. verify

C. conceal

D. alter

詳解

答案：C

我們可以欺騙某人，卻不能欺騙事實（fact），選項 A 是錯誤的。試圖「證實」自己懷孕的事實而穿大尺碼的衣服也不合理，選項 B 是錯誤的。事實是不容「修改」的，選項 D 也是錯的。少女穿著大尺碼的衣服，是試圖隱藏（conceal）她懷有身孕的事實。

|單字片語| **deceive** [dɪˋsiv] 欺騙 / **verify** [ˋvɛrəˏfaɪ] 證實 / **alter** [ˋɔltə] 改變；修改

Q6

The three-hour battle of wits between the two chess
masters ended in a _____. It will take another match to
decide the winner.

兩位棋藝大師之間長達三個小時的機智對決最後不分勝負。將需要另一場比賽來決定誰是贏家。

A. draw

B. crescendo

C. triumph

D. venture

詳解

答案：A

要決定誰是贏家將需要另一場比賽，這表示尚未分出勝負，draw 當名詞使用時有「平手」的意思，答案為 A。 draw 當動詞除了「畫畫」還有「抽取；吸引」的意思，所抽的東西也是 draw，幸運抽獎的英文為 lucky draw，到銀行提款為 withdrawal。

＜補充說明＞

西洋棋有一些專有名詞，stalemate 是「和棋；僵局」，check 是「將…一軍」，checkmate 是「將軍，死棋」。當對方的將帥還有地方可逃，只能說 check，而當對方的將帥無路可逃時，就是 checkmate。

|單字片語| **crescendo** [krɪˋʃɛnˏdo] 聲音漸強 / **triumph** [ˋtraɪəmf] 勝利

venture [ˋvɛntʃə] 冒險；投機活動

Q7

According to a study done by a group of university students, police records revealed the fact that men who consume excessive alcohol have a _____ to hit their wives and children.

根據由一群大學生所做的研究，警方的紀錄顯示了飲酒過度的男性有毆打妻子和孩子的傾向。

A. preference

B. motivation

C. tendency

D. withdrawal

詳解 答案：C

　　這題考的不只是單字，還有一些文法概念。have a tendency to V 和 have a preference for V-ing 的意思相似，兩者都是「有…傾向」的意思，have a tendency 必須加不定詞，have a preference for 必須加動名詞。

|單字片語| **preference** [ˈprɛfərəns] 喜好，偏愛 / **motivation** [ˌmotəˈveʃən] 動機
　　　withdrawal [wɪðˈdrɔəl] 撤回；收回

Q8

All efforts to revive the little boy were _____ and the doctor had no choice but to pronounce him dead.

所有想讓這位小男孩甦醒的努力都徒勞無功，而醫生別無選擇，只能宣佈他已經死亡。

A. in pursuit

B. in vain

C. on target

D. on air

詳解 答案：B

　　題目指出因為到最後男孩還是宣告不治，表示所有的努力都白費了，所以答案為 B。

例句

Some people sacrifice their family **in pursuit** of wealth.
有些人為了追求財富而犧牲家庭。
He fired several shots and each shot was right **on target**.
他開了幾槍，而每一槍都命中目標。
He swore at his colleagues without realizing he was **on air**.
他咒罵同事的時候，沒發現正在實況轉播。

第1回
第2回
第3回
第4回
第5回
第6回

Q9

Rather than wasting money to organize a/an _____ wedding banquet, the couple opted to have a simple dinner with an inner circle of family and friends.

與其浪費錢籌劃奢華的婚宴，這對夫妻選擇跟比較親密的家人和朋友吃簡單的晚餐。

A. luxurious
B. rational
C. substantial
D. inferior

詳解

答案：A

　　從 Rather than 這個關鍵詞可得知，前半句和後半句的意思會是相反的，後半句是簡單的晚餐，那麼前半句應該是指奢華的（luxurious）婚宴，答案為 A。

|單字片語| rational [ˈræʃənl] 理性的 / substantial [səbˈstænʃəl] 真實的
　　　　inferior [ɪnˈfɪrɪə] 劣等的

Q10

The week before Chinese New Year is a good time to _____ things you no longer need in the house.

農曆新年的前一週是丟棄你不再需要的物品的好時機。

A. get away with
B. get down to
C. get used to
D. get rid of

詳解

答案：D

　　這題考的是動詞片語的意思，答案是有「丟棄」意思的 get rid of，動詞片語必須用情境來背，才能記得比較久。

例句

The killer will not **get away with** it.　殺人犯不會逍遙法外的。
Let's **get down to** business.　我們開始談生意，講正經的事。
You will **get used to** the weather here.　你將會習慣這裡的天氣的。

第 1 回
第 2 回
第 3 回
第 4 回
第 5 回
第 6 回

第二部分 / 段落填空

Questions 11-15

The richest man on planet earth, Bill Gates, was born on Oct. 28, 1955, in Seattle, Washington. (11) Being the son of a lawyer and a schoolteacher, he was expected to practice law but he exceeded his parents' expectations (12) beyond their wildest dream. Since young, Bill Gates was argumentative and refused to accept the world as it was. As a teenager, his (13) appetite for knowledge was so great that he read the entire "World Book Encyclopedia" series from start to finish. After graduating from a private high school in 1973, Gates went on to Harvard. Two years later, Gates made a decision that would change the world. (14) He dropped out of school to set up Microsoft with Paul Allen. Microsoft released Windows in 1985 and the software company went public in 1986. By 1987 at the age of thirty-one, Gates was already a billionaire. With such a vast amount of (15) wealth at his disposal, Gates devoted his time and money to charity and donated billions of dollars to third world countries.

地球上最有錢的人，比爾・蓋茲，出生於 1955 年 10 月 28 日華盛頓州的西雅圖。身為律師和學校老師的兒子，他被期待從事法律領域，但他超乎雙親的期望，超過他們想都沒想過的事情。自從年輕時，比爾・蓋茲就好辯論，並且拒絕接受這個世界原來的樣子。當他是青少年的時候，他對知識的渴望如此之大，以至於他把整套世界百科全書從頭到尾都讀完了。1973 年畢業於一所私立高中後，蓋茲進入了哈佛大學。兩年後，蓋茲做了一個將會改變世界的決定。他為了跟保羅・艾倫一起建立的微軟公司而從哈佛輟學。微軟在 1985 年推出 Windows，這個軟體公司在 1986 年上市。到了 1987 年，比爾・蓋茲在 31 歲的時候，他已經是個億萬富翁了。有了如此龐大的財富供他使用，蓋茲把他的時間和金錢投入在慈善，並捐贈數十億元給第三世界國家。

Q11

A. To be

B. Being

C. Been

D. Having been

詳解

　　這題考的是分詞構句的概念，分詞分為現在分詞和過去分詞，現在分詞構句強調「在…」，過去分詞強調「被…」。比爾・蓋茲身為律師和學校老師的兒子，為人子的身分是進行的狀態，必須用現在分詞，答案為 B。

例句

現在分詞構句：**Taking** her dog to the vet, she met her friend.
帶著她的狗去獸醫那裡時，她遇到了她的朋友。
過去分詞構句：**Taken** to the vet, her dog started wailing.
被帶到獸醫那裡時，她的狗開始哀嚎。

Q12

A. beneath   B. despite
C. beyond   D. upon

詳解

答案：C

　　從文中可得知，比爾・蓋茲超出父母的期待（exceeded... expectations），所以答案為具有「超出，超越」意思的 beyond。達到期待可以說 live up to expectations，意思是「不負眾望」。沒達到期待則可以說 fall short of expectations，意思是「令人大失所望」。

I單字片語I **beneath** [bɪˋniθ] 在…的下方 / **despite** [dɪˋspaɪt] 儘管，不管
　　　　 upon [əˋpɑn] 在…上面

Q13

A. appetite   B. obsession
C. improvement   D. progress

詳解

答案：A

　　英文單字分為字面上（literal）還有修辭上（figurative）的用法，對食物的胃口可以延伸為對其他東西的渴望，這裡是對知識（knowledge）的渴望，所以是修辭的用法。另外我們也要特別注意與單字所搭配的介系詞，例如：appetite for、obsession with、improvement in、progress of，從空格後的 for 我們也可以推測空格是 appetite，答案為 A。

補充說明

　　既然 appetite 有修辭上的用法，stomach（胃）也可以延伸為勇氣的意思。例如：I do not have the stomach for sashimi.（我沒有吃生魚片的勇氣。）

|單字片語| obsession [əb`sɛʃən] 著迷 / improvement [ɪm`pruvmənt] 改善
progress [prɑ`grɛs] 進步；進展

第 1 回
第 2 回
第 3 回
第 4 回
第 5 回
第 6 回

Q14

A. He dropped out of school to set up Microsoft with Paul Allen

B. He finished his college degree and became an attorney

C. He decided to work in a finance company to gain experience

D. He and his friends started a restaurant to serve all kinds of customers

詳解　　　　　　　　　　　　　　　　　　　　　　　**答案：A**

　　這題要根據空格的前後文才能作答，前句提到「兩年後，蓋茲做了一個將會改變世界的決定」，而後句提到「微軟在 1985 年推出 Windows…」因此可以推測空格的句子應該要和微軟有關，因此符合敘述的答案為 A。

例句

　　以下是與 set 有關的動詞片語：
We are going to **set up** camp here.　我們要在這裡紮營。
I didn't steal anything. Someone **set** me **up**.　我沒有偷任何東西。有人陷害我。
We will **set out** at sunrise.　我們在日出的時候出發。
Let's set out before the rain **sets in**.　我們在開始下雨前出發吧。
The burglar **set off** the alarm.　這個竊賊觸動了警鈴。

Q15

A. carbon

B. force

C. wealth

D. literature

詳解　　　　　　　　　　　　　　　　　　　　　　　**答案：C**

　　have something at someone's disposal 是英語常見的用法，意思是「有某個東西供某人使用，任憑處置」。文中提到比爾・蓋茲在 31 歲就已經是億萬富翁（billionaire），因此指出他有龐大數量的「財富」供他使用，答案為 C。

|單字片語| carbon [`kɑrbən] 碳；複寫紙 / force [fors] 力量；勢力
literature [`lɪtərətʃə] 文學；文學作品

Questions 16-20

In (16) response to the rising cases of bullying and abuse in schools, the ministry of education of England introduced a new measure aimed at preventing and dealing with such cases. Bullying is (17) defined as undesirable and negative behavior, whether in verbal, psychological or physical form, conducted by an individual or group against another person (or persons) and which is repeated over time. School (18) authorities and school personnel are required to adhere to the procedures in the new measure in dealing with allegations and incidents of bullying. The purpose of these procedures is to prevent school-based bullying behavior amongst its pupils and deal with any negative (19) impact within school of bullying behavior that occurs elsewhere. Nevertheless, parents have raised concerns (20) regarding the effectiveness of such measures. Some pointed out that teaching children to respect one another should be a top priority.

為了因應校園霸凌和虐待案件不斷攀升的問題，英國教育部推出了一項新的措施，其目的在於預防並處理這類型的案件。霸凌的定義是由一個人或一群人對他人，無論是以言語、精神或身體的形式，不斷重複令人討厭和負面的行為。學校當局和學校職員必須遵守新措施中的流程來處理霸凌的指控和事件。這些流程的目的是預防學生之間以學校為主的霸凌行為，並處理其他地方發生的校外霸凌行為任何對校內的負面影響。儘管如此，家長對於這些措施的有效性提出了一些擔憂。有些家長指出，教導孩子互相尊重才是首要的任務。

Q16

A. advice   B. view

C. response   D. contrast

【詳解】   答案：C

     response 原本是「回應」的意思，in response to 是「對…的反應」，因此這句是指為了因應校園霸凌和虐待案件不斷攀升的問題，英國教育部推出了一項新的措施，其目的是預防和處理這類事件，答案為 C。

|單字片語| in view of 鑑於；考慮到 / in contrast to 與…形成對比

Q17

A. ratified
C. confined

B. simplified
D. defined

[詳解]

答案：D

文中提到霸凌（bullying）是一種令人討厭和負面的行為（undesirable and negative behavior），這句話解釋霸凌的定義，所以答案為 D。

|單字片語| ratify [ˈrætəˌfaɪ]（正式）批准 / simplify [ˈsɪmpləˌfaɪ] 簡化
confine [kənˈfaɪn] 限制

Q18

A. authorities
C. manufacturers

B. pirates
D. souvenirs

[詳解]

答案：A

這題的關鍵詞是 adhere to（遵守）跟 procedures（程序），而從文中推測遵守反霸凌程序的對象顯然是校方。authority 是「權力」，用為複數 authorities 則是指「擁有管轄權的單位」，通常指政府機構或官方，答案為 A。

|單字片語| pirates [ˈpaɪrət] 海盜 / manufacturers [ˌmænjəˈfæktʃərəs] 製造業者
souvenir [ˈsuvəˌnɪr] 紀念品

Q19

A. attack
C. result

B. impact
D. attitude

[詳解]

答案：B

impact（影響）可分為正面和負面的情況，霸凌事件顯然是產生負面的影響，答案為 B。除了 impact 還可以用 effect 和 influence。

|單字片語| attack [əˈtæk] 攻擊 / result [rɪˈzʌlt] 結果 / attitude [ˈætətjud] 態度

Q20

A. of their children's body health
B. about the nutrition of their children's lunch
C. regarding the effectiveness of such measures
D. of the schools' facility safety

437

　　這題要從前後句來判斷空格處要填入的子句，前句提到「學校要遵守預防霸凌的程序和措施，有些家長提出了一些擔憂…」，而後句提到「有些家長認為教導孩子互相尊重才是重要的」，因此空格處要填入與反霸凌措施有關的敘述，因此答案為 C。

I單字片語I **nutrition** [njuˋtrɪʃən] 營養 / **effectiveness** [əˋfɛktɪvnɪs] 有效性

　　　　　　facility [fəˋsɪlətɪ] 設備

第1回
第2回
第3回
第4回
第5回
第6回

Questions 21-22

Tranquil Two-Story Villa

Come and feel the serenity of country life and enjoy the waves, the breeze, the sunshine, and...

The Tranquil Two-Story Villa is located thirty kilometers outside the downtown by the seashore, and it takes you only fifteen to twenty minutes through the super highway from the city center. Surrounded by waters, hills and woods, the villa offers you and your family the country life at its best.

Laundry facilities, central heating, air conditioning, and a fireplace are provided. Three unfurnished bedrooms are available. Children are welcome here, but not pets.

What is more, there are one swimming pool, a ten-hectare garden, and basketball and tennis courts. Parking spaces of two for each villa are free of charge.

For more rental details, please contact Mr. Huang: 02-4333-8886.

寧靜雙層別墅

來感受鄉間生活的寧靜,並享受海浪、微風、陽光,和其他事物。

寧靜雙層別墅座落於離市區外三十公里的海岸邊,而從市中心走高速公路只要花您十五至二十分鐘便可到達。環繞在海水、山丘和森林,這間別墅給您和家人最棒的鄉村生活。

這裡提供洗衣設備、中央暖氣系統、空調及壁爐,另有三間未裝潢過的臥房可供使用,我們歡迎孩童來到這裡,但恕不接受寵物。

此外,這裡還有一座游泳池,一座十公頃的花園、籃球場及網球場。每棟別墅配有兩個免費的停車位。

欲知更多租用細節,請聯繫 02-4333-8886,黃先生。

單字片語 **tranquil** [ˈtræŋkwɪl] 平靜的 / **story** [ˈstorɪ] 樓層;故事
breeze [briz] 微風 / **villa** [ˈvɪlə] 別墅 / **facility** [fəˈsɪlətɪ] 設備
hectare [ˈhɛktɛr] 公頃 / **detail** [ˈditel] 細節

Q21

What do you think the main purpose of the description is?

你認為這段描述主要的目的是什麼？

A. To find a roommate　找一位室友

B. To build the villa　蓋別墅

C. To rent out the house　出租房子

D. To introduce the hotel　介紹飯店

詳解　

　　從 rental details（出租細節）可得知這棟別墅是要出租，答案為 C。

Q22

What can you do within the villa with the supplied equipment?

藉由別墅提供的設備，你可以做什麼？

A. Playing baseball　打棒球

B. Playing table tennis　打桌球

C. Skiing　滑雪

D. Washing clothes　洗衣服

詳解　

　　文中有提到籃球場和網球場，但選項 A 是棒球，而選項 B 是桌球，這兩個選項是藉由拼字的相似度所設的陷阱。雖然別墅有提供壁爐和暖氣，但沒提到別墅內有適合滑雪的場地，選項 C 是錯的。別墅有洗衣設備（Laundry facilities），因此顯然洗衣服沒什麼問題，答案是 D。

Questions 23-25

· Enjoy Unlimited Internet Access

· Rent a Wi-Fi device from the airport today and get connected anywhere, anytime in Singapore.

Do It Now! Our offices are open 24/7.

　　1.Visit the SG Wi-Fi booths located at Terminal 1, Basement 1,

#2308. (Next to a fountain)

2.Provide us with your passport, return air ticket and credit card.

3.Fill in and sign the agreement form.

4.Pick up the Wi-Fi device and enjoy instant Internet connection.

Please Read:

Plan A: SGD $20/day for unlimited access.

Recommended if you play online games.

Plan B: SGD $10/day for usage below 5G.

Recommended if you watch a movie or two a day.

Plan C: SGD $5/day for usage below 1G.

Recommended if you only use the Internet to read your emails.

Plan C will be automatically upgraded to Plan B should usage exceed 1G and Plan B to Plan A should usage exceed 5G.

Billing starts on the first day and ends on the day of return. Rental charges will be based on full days, regardless of number of hours used per day.

For damages / lost / stolen / unreturned items, the following charges will apply:

- Wi-Fi device $200

- SIM card $50

- USB cable and plug $30

- Bag holder $20

・享受無限網路連線。

・今天就從機場租一台 Wi-Fi 分享器,在新加坡隨時隨地都能連線。

現在就行動吧!我們的辦公室二十四小時全年無休。

一、請至第一航廈,地下一樓 2308 號的 SG Wi-Fi 攤位。(在噴泉旁邊)

二、提供我們您的護照、回程機票和信用卡。

三、填寫並簽署同意書。

四、領取 Wi-Fi 分享器,享受立即的網路連線。

請閱讀以下資訊:

方案 A:二十元新加坡幣/日,無限上網吃到飽。

如果您有玩線上遊戲,建議您選擇這個方案。

第 1 回
第 2 回
第 3 回
第 4 回
第 5 回
第 6 回

方案 B：十元新加坡幣／日，用量在 5G 以下。

如果您一天看一、兩部電影，建議您選擇這個方案。

方案 C：五元新加坡幣／日，用量在 1G 以下。

如果您只用網路來查看電子郵件，建議您選擇這個方案。

萬一用量超過 1G，方案 C 將會自動升級成方案 B，萬一用量超過 5G，方案 B 則會自動升級成方案 A。

計費日期從第一天開始，至退還分享器當天截止。出租費用將以全天計算，無論每天使用多少的時數。

若有毀損、遺失、遭偷竊、未歸還物品，將另外收取以下費用：

- Wi-Fi 分享器 $200
- SIM 卡 $50
- USB 傳輸線和插座 $30
- 分享器袋子 $20

|單字片語| **device** [dɪˋvaɪs] 裝置；器具 / **connect** [kəˋnɛkt] 連結 / **instant** [ˋɪnstənt] 立即的 **unlimited** [ʌnˋlɪmɪtɪd] 無限的 / **usage** [ˋjusɪdʒ] 使用量 **automatic** [ˌɔtəˋmætɪk] 自動的 / **upgrade** [ˋʌpˋgred] 升級 / **exceed** [ɪkˋsid] 超出 **regardless** [rɪˋgɑrdlɪs] 無論如何 / **charge** [tʃɑrdʒ] 費用，計費

Q23

What is NOT required if you wish to rent the Wi-Fi device?
若你想要租 Wi-Fi 分享器，不需要什麼？

A. Passport　　護照
B. USB cable　　USB 傳輸線
C. Credit Card　　信用卡
D. Air Ticket　　機票

詳解　　　　　　　　　　　　　　　　　　　　　　　　　　答案：B

　　文中提到，欲租用 Wi-Fi 分享器，須提供護照、回程機票和信用卡（Provide us with your passport, return air ticket and credit card），USB 傳輸線會隨分享器出租，答案為 B。

Q24

What happens if you use more than 5G a day?
如果你一天的用量超過 5G，會發生什麼事？

A. You need to pay SGD $5 a day.　　你需要付一天五元新加坡幣。

B. You need to pay SGD $10 a day.　你需要付一天十元新加坡幣。

C. You need to pay SGD $20 a day.　你需要付一天二十元新加坡幣。

D. You need to pay more than SGD $20 a day.

你需要付一天超過二十元新加坡幣。

詳解　　　　　　　　　　　　　　　　　　　　　　　　**答案：C**

　　從出租條文可以得知，方案 B 的使用量若超出 5G，方案 B 自動升級成方案 A（Plan B to Plan A should usage exceed 5G），而方案 A 是吃到飽方案，因此最多只需要付方案 A 的費用，也就是一天 20 元新加坡幣，答案為 C。

Q25

What can be inferred about the information above?

從以上資訊可推知什麼？

A. Rental fee is based on number of hours used.

出租費用根據時數來計算。

B. You can only return the device during normal business hours.

你只能在一般的上班時間歸還分享器。

C. Billing starts on the day the device is activated.

在分享器在啟動當天開始收費。

D. The device can be used at once.　分享器可以立刻使用。

詳解　　　　　　　　　　　　　　　　　　　　　　　　**答案：D**

　　選項 A 是錯誤的，因為出租費用是以全天計算而非小時計算。選項 B 是錯誤的，因為出租攤位的營業時間為 24/7，24 指一天 24 小時，7 指每週 7 天，也就是全年無休，隨時都開放的意思。選項 C 說在分享器啟動當天開始收費，但是條約寫的是計費日期從第一天開始（billing starts on the first day）跟有沒有啟動無關。從這句話：領取 Wi-Fi 分享器，享受立即的網路連線（Pick up the Wi-Fi device and enjoy instant Internet connection），可得知領取 Wi-Fi 分享器後無須等待，可以立刻使用，答案為 D。

Questions 26-28

　　Deprived of natural resources, Switzerland places emphasis on the education of its people. It claims to have one of the world's best education systems and the fact that it generates one of the highest GDP in Europe goes to show that the education system is indeed successful. For many Europeans, Switzerland is the Promised Land with higher income, better welfare, charming landscape and a much lower crime rate.

　缺乏天然資源的情況下，瑞士把重點放在國民的教育上。它宣稱擁有世界上最好的教育體系，它能製造歐洲其中一個最高的國民平均所得這項事實，顯示這個教育體系的確很成功。對許多歐洲人來說，瑞士是擁有更高的收入、更好的福利、迷人景色，還有相對較低犯罪率的應許之地。

Switzerland is divided into districts and each district is responsible for educational services from kindergarten all the way to universities. Education policies may vary significantly between districts. For example, some districts start to teach the first foreign language at fourth grade, while others start at seventh grade. This can make people with children moving between districts a nightmare. In Switzerland, most children go to public schools. Private schools usually are expensive and people tend to think that students of private schools probably didn't make it at the public school. There are eleven universities in Switzerland; nine are run by districts, while two are run by the central government.

　瑞士分為不同的區域，每個區域負責從幼兒園一直到大學的教育服務。各區域之間的教育政策可能會有明顯變化。例如，有些區域在四年級就開始教第一個外語，而其他區域則在七年級才開始。對有孩子的人來說，搬到其他區域可能是一場惡夢。在瑞士，大多數的兒童是上公立學校。私立學校通常很昂貴，而人們傾向於認為私立學校的學生可能是考不上公立學校。瑞士有十一所大學；其中九所是由區域管理的，而另外兩所是中央政府管理的。

After elementary school, kids may either choose to go to secondary school or to start an apprenticeship. In the latter case, after finishing the apprenticeship, it is still possible to start an academic career at either a secondary school or a so called technical college. The Swiss are pragmatic people who value technical skills as well as academic achievement.

　小學畢業後，孩子可以選擇上中學或開始學徒培訓。而後者的案例中，完成學徒培訓之後，還是可以在中等學校或技術大學開始學業生涯。瑞士人是非常務實的人民，他們重視技術技能也重視學術成就。

第 1 回

第 2 回

第 3 回

第 4 回

第 5 回

第 6 回

Q26

Why did Switzerland pay so much attention to education?

為什麼瑞士如此注重在教育上？

A. Proper education eliminates criminal activities.

適當的教育排除犯罪行為。

B. Switzerland has always been top in every area.

瑞士在每個領域一直是第一名。

C. Human resource is viewed as the only asset.

人力資源被視為唯一的資產。

D. Immigrants have to adopt the Swiss culture.

移民必須採納瑞士的文化。

詳解　　　　　　　　　　　　　　　　　　　　　　　　　　答案：C

　　文中提到，瑞士缺乏天然資源（deprived of natural resources），所以把重點放在國民的教育（emphasis on the education of its people），也就是把人力資源被視為唯一的資產，因此瑞士非常注重教育，答案為 C。

Q27

Switzerland is considered the first choice for work by foreigners because _____.

瑞士被視為外國人工作的首要選擇，因為…

A. they can enjoy more freedom　他們可以享有更多自由

B. they can transfer their children to different schools with ease

他們可以輕鬆地把孩子轉到不同學校

C. they can contribute to the Swiss economy

他們可以為瑞士的經濟做出貢獻

D. they can afford a higher standard of living

他們可以負擔更高的生活水準

詳解　　　　　　　　　　　　　　　　　　　　　　　　　　答案：D

　　瑞士是歐洲其中一個擁有最高的國民平均所得（one of the highest GDP in Europe）的國家，有了更高的所得，就能負擔得起更高的生活水準。文章也提到 For many Europeans, Switzerland is the Promised Land with higher income, better welfare, charming landscape and a much lower crime rate. 這些都能證明瑞士的生活水準，答案為 D。

What can be observed about the Swiss people?
關於瑞士人，可以觀察到什麼？

A. Technical skills and academic knowledge are equally important.
技術能力和學術知識同樣重要。

B. Vocation schools are more useful than university degrees.
職業學校比大學學位更有用。

C. Students are encouraged to leave school at an early age.
學生在很小的年紀被鼓勵離開學校。

D. Universities are only for private school students.
只有私立學校的學生才能進大學。

詳解　　　　　　　　　　　　　　　　　　　　　　答案：A

　　文中提到瑞士人重視技術能力也重視學術成就（value technical skills as well as academic achievement），職業學校和大學學歷一樣有用，因此選項 B 是錯的，答案為 A。

Questions 29-31

Just a century ago, raising children is something newly-weds do without much thought. Nowadays, couples go through serious financial considerations and planning before they decide to have babies. With women receiving higher levels of education, many have become career-minded and the burden of being a full-time housewife is not as appealing as it used to be. Developed countries all over the world face a common challenge: a low birthrate and a high percentage of aging citizens.

在一個世紀以前，扶養孩子對新婚夫婦來說是一件不用想太多就會做的事。如今，夫妻在決定生小孩之前，會經過嚴謹的財務考量和計畫。隨著女性接受更高等的教育，許多女生已經變得有事業心，而當一個全職家庭主婦的重擔似乎沒有像以前一樣那麼吸引人。全世界的已開發國家都面對一項共同的挑戰：低生育率和高比例的老化人口。

The aging of populations does raise concerns at many levels for governments around the world. There is concern over the possibility that a shrinking proportion of working-age people (ages 15 to 64) in the population may lead to an economic slowdown. The smaller working age populations must also support growing numbers of older dependents, possibly creating financial stress for social insurance systems and dimming the economic outlook for the elderly.

人口的老化確實在許多層面上引起世界各地的政府擔憂。一個顧慮是工作年齡人數（15 至 64 歲）在人口上的比例減少的可能性或許會導致經濟衰退。比較小的工作年齡人口也必須支撐逐漸增加的較年長的需供養者，可能會對社會保險制度製造財務上的壓力，對於老年人的經濟前景也相當不樂觀。

Graying populations will also fuel demands for changes in public investments, such as the reallocation of resources from the needs of children to the needs of seniors. At the more personal level, longer life spans may strain household finances, cause people to extend their working lives or rearrange family structures. Perhaps not surprisingly, an aging China announced a relaxation of its one-child policy in November 2013.

銀髮族人口也將會刺激大眾投資改變的需求，例如：資源的重新分配，從兒童的需求轉移到年長者的需求。在更個人的層面上，較長的壽命可能會讓家庭經濟有壓力，造成人們必須延長他們的工作生涯或重新安排家庭結構。或許不會感到驚訝的是，人口老化的中國在 2013 年 11 月宣佈放鬆一胎制的政策。

Q29

Why are women less willing to have children based on reasons given in the passage?
根據文章中所給的原因，為什麼女性比較不願意生小孩？

A. They are indifferent.　她們漠不關心。
B. They are fearful.　她們充滿恐懼。
C. They are infertile.　她們無法生育。
D. They are ambitious.　她們很有野心。

[詳解]

答案：D

根據文章中所給的原因，女性比較不願意生小孩是因為她們受過更高等的教育後變得有事業心（career-minded），也就是在工作方面比較有野心，不想因為生小孩而耽誤自己的事業，因此答案為 D。

第 1 回
第 2 回
第 3 回
第 4 回
第 5 回
第 6 回

Q30

In what way does an aging population affect the economy?

人口老化在什麼方面影響經濟？

A. Senior citizens refuse to give up their positions.
老年人拒絕放棄他們的職位。

B. The workforce decreases significantly. 勞動力明顯減少。

C. Young people have difficulty advancing their career.
年輕人在增進職業方面有困難。

D. Retirement age is extended to 70. 退休年齡延長到 70 歲。

詳解　　　　　　　　　　　　　　　　　　　　　　答案：B

　　人口老化等於工作年齡的人口開始縮小（shrink），加上少子化的影響，勞動力將會大幅減少，因此答案為 B。

Q31

Why did China reverse its population control policy?

為什麼中國要逆轉控管人口的政策？

A. The burden of the younger generation is too much to bear.
年輕一代的負擔太過沉重。

B. The older generation demands to have more grandchildren.
老一輩的人要求更多孫子。

C. Young couples are now willing to have more children.
年輕夫妻現在願意生更多孩子。

D. Modern science has enabled more new-borns to survive.
現代科學已經讓更多新生嬰兒能夠活下來。

詳解　　　　　　　　　　　　　　　　　　　　　　答案：A

　　一胎化的政策下，導致一個小孩必須照顧兩個老人，壽命較長可能會造成家庭經濟壓力（longer life spans may strain household finances），也就是說年輕一代的負擔太過沉重，答案為 A。

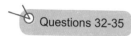

Questions 32-35

第 1 回
第 2 回
第 3 回
第 4 回
第 5 回
第 6 回

Oversea Internship Program

This program is currently open to juniors and seniors in college who are interested in real jobs related to their major in the world. Please refer to the following available opportunities.

Company / Country	Responsibilities	Preferred students' field	Requirements	Opening
Sound Strategy Company, Korea	Support systems engineering and passenger technology	engineering, technology	1. Proficiency in Microsoft Office (Word, PowerPoint, Excel) 2. Fluency in English and Korean	2
Alright Technologies, India	Assist the finance team in developing new applications	finance, economics	1. Strong Microsoft Excel skills 2. Fluency in spoken and written English	1
Coast Development, Canada	Contribute to climate risk evaluation and conduct systematic research	economics, statistics, technology	1. Experience in the climate change research 2. Fluency in English and French	4
First Property, Singapore	General support to a content management program	management, finance	1. Microsoft Excel skills are absolutely essential	2

海外實習計畫

這項計畫目前開放給對世界各地與主修相關的實際工作有興趣的大三、大四生。請參考以下可利用的機會。

公司／國家	職責	優先的學生領域	必要條件	空缺
韓國，Sound Strategy 公司	支援系統工程與乘客技術	工程、科技	1. 熟悉 Microsoft Office 軟體（Word、Power Point、Excel） 2. 具備流利的英語和韓語能力	2
印度，Alright 科技	協助財務團隊發展出新的應用程式	財務、經濟	1. 具備 Microsoft Office Excel 的超強技能 2. 具備流利的英語口說、寫作能力	1
加拿大，Coast 開發	投入氣候風險評估，並進行系統性研究	經濟、統計、科技	1. 具備氣候變遷研究經驗 2. 具備流利的英語和法語能力	4
新加坡，First 房地產	一般支援內容管理計畫	管理、財務	1. 具備 Microsoft Office Excel 的能力是絕對必要的	2

Internship Resume

Mason Thomas
Business Student
Date of birth: 10/01/1998
Phone number: 0919-111-222
Email address: mason.thomas@gmail.com

Education
Global Business
University of Taiwan
09/2018 – present
Main courses
Strategy, organization, and market creation
Data analysis and systematic reviews

Volunteer Experience
Foxcoon Education Foundation
October 2018 – May 2020
Offered school work guidance and care for juniors
Greenpeace, Taiwan
July 2019 – Present
Help improve environment protection projects

Technical Skills
Proficient user in Microsoft Office
Digital marketing strategy
Big data analysis

Soft Skills
Time management
Leadership
Critical thinking

Languages
English (Advanced)
French (Advanced)
Mandarin Chinese (Native)

Hobbies
Travel
Play basketball
Reading

第1回
第2回
第3回
第4回
第5回
第6回

實習生履歷表

Mason Thomas
商科學生
出生日期：1998 年 10 月 1 日
電話號碼：0919-111-222
電子郵件地址：mason.thomas@gmail.com

教育
全球商業
臺灣大學
2018 年 9 月－至今
主要課程
策略、組織和市場創立
數據分析和系統性審查

志工經歷
鴻海教育基金會
2018 年 10 月－2020 年 5 月
提供國中生課業輔導與關懷
綠色和平，臺灣
2019 年 7 月－至今
幫助改善環境保護專案

專業技能
精通使用 Microsoft Office 軟體
數位行銷策略
大數據分析

軟實力
時間管理
領導能力
批判性思考

語言
英語（精通）
法語（精通）
中文（母語）

嗜好
旅行
打籃球
閱讀

I單字片語I internship [ˈɪntɝnˌʃɪp] 實習職位 / proficiency [prəˈfɪʃənsɪ] 精通
fluency [ˈfluənsɪ] 流利 / essential [ɪˈsɛnʃəl] 必要的 / digital [ˈdɪdʒɪtl] 數位的

Which of the following statement is NOT Mr. Thomas' strength?
下列哪一項敘述不是 Thomas 先生的長處？

A. Motivate people to work together. 激勵人們一起工作。
B. Analyze information and make a reasoned decision.
   分析資訊並做出一項合理的決定。

C. Write some coding languages, like C++.

編寫一些程式語言，例如：C++。

D. Make effective decisions by using large amounts of raw data.

透過使用大量的原始數據來做出有效的決定。

詳解　　　　　　　　　　　　　　　　　　　　　　　　　答案：C

　　這題內容是針對實習履歷表，題目問的是 Thomas 先生擅長什麼？因此要先閱讀履歷表上的兩種能力（Technical Skills 和 Soft Skills），再對應選項，就能快速找出關鍵句。選項 A 和 B 分別是他的軟實力（Leadership 和 critical thinking），選項 D 則是他的專門技能（Big data analysis）。而履歷中沒有提及他能編寫一些程式語言，因此程式語言不是他的長處，答案為 C。

Q33

Which of the following statements about the four companies is true?

關於四間公司的下列敘述哪一個是正確的？

A. Sound Strategy Company's interns need to develop new applications.

Sound Strategy 公司的實習生需要開發新的應用程式。

B. Alright Technologies is open for one intern.

Alright 科技有一位實習生的空缺。

C. Coast Development expects the interns with Microsoft Excel skills.

Coast 開發期望實習生具備 Microsoft Excel 的技能。

D. First Property is looking for interns who major in technology.

First 房地產正在尋找主修在科技領域的實習生。

詳解　　　　　　　　　　　　　　　　　　　　　　　　　答案：B

　　這題的內容是針對實習計畫，題目與各家公司有關，因此要先閱讀實習計畫，再對應選項就能快速找出關鍵句。選項 A 需要開發新的應用程式的公司不是 Sound Strategy 公司，而是 Alright 科技；選項 C 的 Coast 開發並未列出實習生需具備 Microsoft Excel 的技能；選項 D 希望實習生的專業領域不是在 technology，而是在 management, finance。選項 B Alright 科技的實習生空缺為 1 名，答案為 B。

Q34

Which firm is the least likely to have Mr. Thomas as an intern?

哪一間公司最不可能錄取 Thomas 先生當實習生？

A. Sound Strategy Company.　Sound Strategy 公司。

B. Alright Technologies.　Alright 科技。

C. Coast Development.　Coast 開發。

D. First Property.　First 房地產。

詳解

答案：A

　　這題的內容需整合實習計畫和 Thomas 先生的履歷表才能作答。從履歷表可知 Thomas 先生是商科學生，而從各家公司希望實習生的專業領域可以看出，除了 Sound Strategy 公司，其他三家公司的實習生專業都與商業相關，答案為 A。

Q35

Which company is outside of Asia?

哪一間公司在亞洲之外？

A. Sound Strategy Company.　Sound Strategy 公司。

B. Alright Technologies.　Alright 科技。

C. Coast Development.　Coast 開發。

D. First Property.　First 房地產。

詳解

答案：C

　　這題的內容是針對實習計畫，題目與各家公司的所在位置相關，因此要先閱讀實習計畫，再對應選項就能快速地找出關鍵句。選項 A 在韓國、選項 B 在印度、選項 D 在新加坡，都是位於亞洲的國家。而選項 C 在加拿大，是位於美洲的國家，答案為 C。

國際學村

全民英語能力分級檢定測驗 初級初試試題答案紙（第一回）

聽力測驗答對題數與分數對照表

答對題數	分數	答對題數	分數	答對題數	分級
35	120	23	80.5	11	38.5
34	115.5	22	77	10	35
33	112	21	73.5	9	31.5
32	108.5	20	70	8	28
31	105	19	66.5	7	24.5
30	101.5	18	63	6	21
29	98	17	59.5	5	17.5
28	94.5	16	56	4	14
27	91	15	52.5	3	10.5
26	87.5	14	49	2	7
25	85	13	45.5	1	3.5
24	84	12	42	0	0

閱讀測驗答對題數分數對照表

答對題數	分數	答對題數	分數	答對題數	分級
35	120	23	80.5	11	38.5
34	115.5	22	77	10	35
33	112	21	73.5	9	31.5
32	108.5	20	70	8	28
31	105	19	66.5	7	24.5
30	101.5	18	63	6	21
29	98	17	59.5	5	17.5
28	94.5	16	56	4	14
27	91	15	52.5	3	10.5
26	87.5	14	49	2	7
25	85	13	45.5	1	3.5
24	84	12	42	0	0

考生姓名：＿＿＿＿＿＿＿

注意事項：

1. 限用 2B 鉛筆作答，否則不予計分。
2. 劃記要粗黑、清晰，不可出格、擦拭要清潔，若劃記過
   輕或汙損不清，不為機器所接受，考生自行負責。
3. 作答樣例：

正確方式 ■ 錯誤方式 ☑ ⊠ ▢ ●

聽力能力測驗

1	A B C D		26	A B C D
2	A B C D		27	A B C D
3	A B C D		28	A B C D
4	A B C D		29	A B C D
5	A B C D		30	A B C D
6	A B C D		31	A B C D
7	A B C D		32	A B C D
8	A B C D		33	A B C D
9	A B C D		34	A B C D
10	A B C D		35	A B C D
11	A B C D			
12	A B C D			
13	A B C D			
14	A B C D			
15	A B C D			
16	A B C D			
17	A B C D			
18	A B C D			
19	A B C D			
20	A B C D			
21	A B C D			
22	A B C D			
23	A B C D			
24	A B C D			
25	A B C D			

閱讀能力測驗

1	A B C D		26	A B C D
2	A B C D		27	A B C D
3	A B C D		28	A B C D
4	A B C D		29	A B C D
5	A B C D		30	A B C D
6	A B C D		31	A B C D
7	A B C D		32	A B C D
8	A B C D		33	A B C D
9	A B C D		34	A B C D
10	A B C D		35	A B C D
11	A B C D			
12	A B C D			
13	A B C D			
14	A B C D			
15	A B C D			
16	A B C D			
17	A B C D			
18	A B C D			
19	A B C D			
20	A B C D			
21	A B C D			
22	A B C D			
23	A B C D			
24	A B C D			
25	A B C D			

國際學村 全民英語能力分級檢定測驗 初級初試試答案紙（第二回）

聽 力 能 力 測 驗

1	A B C D	26	A B C D
2	A B C D	27	A B C D
3	A B C D	28	A B C D
4	A B C D	29	A B C D
5	A B C D	30	A B C D
6	A B C D	31	A B C D
7	A B C D	32	A B C D
8	A B C D	33	A B C D
9	A B C D	34	A B C D
10	A B C D	35	A B C D
11	A B C D		
12	A B C D		
13	A B C D		
14	A B C D		
15	A B C D		
16	A B C D		
17	A B C D		
18	A B C D		
19	A B C D		
20	A B C D		
21	A B C D		
22	A B C D		
23	A B C D		
24	A B C D		
25	A B C D		

閱 讀 能 力 測 驗

1	A B C D	26	A B C D
2	A B C D	27	A B C D
3	A B C D	28	A B C D
4	A B C D	29	A B C D
5	A B C D	30	A B C D
6	A B C D	31	A B C D
7	A B C D	32	A B C D
8	A B C D	33	A B C D
9	A B C D	34	A B C D
10	A B C D	35	A B C D
11	A B C D		
12	A B C D		
13	A B C D		
14	A B C D		
15	A B C D		
16	A B C D		
17	A B C D		
18	A B C D		
19	A B C D		
20	A B C D		
21	A B C D		
22	A B C D		
23	A B C D		
24	A B C D		
25	A B C D		

聽力測驗答對題數與分級對照表

答對題數	分數	答對題數	分數	答對題數	分級
35	120	23	80.5	11	38.5
34	115.5	22	77	10	35
33	112	21	73.5	9	31.5
32	108.5	20	70	8	28
31	105	19	66.5	7	24.5
30	101.5	18	63	6	21
29	98	17	59.5	5	17.5
28	94.5	16	56	4	14
27	91	15	52.5	3	10.5
26	87.5	14	49	2	7
25	85	13	45.5	1	3.5
24	84	12	42	0	0

閱讀測驗答對題數與分級對照表

答對題數	分數	答對題數	分數	答對題數	分級
35	120	23	80.5	11	38.5
34	115.5	22	77	10	35
33	112	21	73.5	9	31.5
32	108.5	20	70	8	28
31	105	19	66.5	7	24.5
30	101.5	18	63	6	21
29	98	17	59.5	5	17.5
28	94.5	16	56	4	14
27	91	15	52.5	3	10.5
26	87.5	14	49	2	7
25	85	13	45.5	1	3.5
24	84	12	42	0	0

考生姓名：＿＿＿＿＿＿

注意事項：

1. 限用 2B 鉛筆作答，否則不予計分。
2. 劃記要粗黑、清晰、不可出格，擦拭要清潔，若劃記過輕或污損不清，不烏機器所接受，考生自行負責。
3. 作答樣例：

正確方式 ▬

錯誤方式 ☑ ☒ □ ●

國際學村

全民英語能力分級檢定測驗
初級初試試答案紙（第三回）

聽力測驗答對題數與分數對照表

答對題數	分數	答對題數	分數	答對題數	分級
35	120	23	80.5	11	38.5
34	115.5	22	77	10	35
33	112	21	73.5	9	31.5
32	108.5	20	70	8	28
31	105	19	66.5	7	24.5
30	101.5	18	63	6	21
29	98	17	59.5	5	17.5
28	94.5	16	56	4	14
27	91	15	52.5	3	10.5
26	87.5	14	49	2	7
25	85	13	45.5	1	3.5
24	84	12	42	0	0

閱讀測驗答對題數與分數對照表

答對題數	分數	答對題數	分數	答對題數	分級
35	120	23	80.5	11	38.5
34	115.5	22	77	10	35
33	112	21	73.5	9	31.5
32	108.5	20	70	8	28
31	105	19	66.5	7	24.5
30	101.5	18	63	6	21
29	98	17	59.5	5	17.5
28	94.5	16	56	4	14
27	91	15	52.5	3	10.5
26	87.5	14	49	2	7
25	85	13	45.5	1	3.5
24	84	12	42	0	0

考生姓名：_____

注意事項：

1. 限用 2B 鉛筆作答，否則不予計分。
2. 劃記要粗黑、清晰，不可出格、擦拭要清潔，若劃記過輕或污損不清，不為機器所接受，考生自行負責。
3. 作答樣例：

正確方式　■

錯誤方式

☑　☒　▢　◖●

聽力測驗

1	A B C D	26	A B C D
2	A B C D	27	A B C D
3	A B C D	28	A B C D
4	A B C D	29	A B C D
5	A B C D	30	A B C D
6	A B C D	31	A B C D
7	A B C D	32	A B C D
8	A B C D	33	A B C D
9	A B C D	34	A B C D
10	A B C D	35	A B C D
11	A B C D		
12	A B C D		
13	A B C D		
14	A B C D		
15	A B C D		
16	A B C D		
17	A B C D		
18	A B C D		
19	A B C D		
20	A B C D		
21	A B C D		
22	A B C D		
23	A B C D		
24	A B C D		
25	A B C D		

閱讀測驗

1	A B C D	26	A B C D
2	A B C D	27	A B C D
3	A B C D	28	A B C D
4	A B C D	29	A B C D
5	A B C D	30	A B C D
6	A B C D	31	A B C D
7	A B C D	32	A B C D
8	A B C D	33	A B C D
9	A B C D	34	A B C D
10	A B C D	35	A B C D
11	A B C D		
12	A B C D		
13	A B C D		
14	A B C D		
15	A B C D		
16	A B C D		
17	A B C D		
18	A B C D		
19	A B C D		
20	A B C D		
21	A B C D		
22	A B C D		
23	A B C D		
24	A B C D		
25	A B C D		

國際學村　全民英語能力分級檢定測驗
初級初試答案紙（第四回）

聽 力 能 力 測 驗

#	A	B	C	D
1	A	B	C	D
2	A	B	C	D
3	A	B	C	D
4	A	B	C	D
5	A	B	C	D
6	A	B	C	D
7	A	B	C	D
8	A	B	C	D
9	A	B	C	D
10	A	B	C	D
11	A	B	C	D
12	A	B	C	D
13	A	B	C	D
14	A	B	C	D
15	A	B	C	D
16	A	B	C	D
17	A	B	C	D
18	A	B	C	D
19	A	B	C	D
20	A	B	C	D
21	A	B	C	D
22	A	B	C	D
23	A	B	C	D
24	A	B	C	D
25	A	B	C	D
26	A	B	C	D
27	A	B	C	D
28	A	B	C	D
29	A	B	C	D
30	A	B	C	D
31	A	B	C	D
32	A	B	C	D
33	A	B	C	D
34	A	B	C	D
35	A	B	C	D

閱 讀 能 力 測 驗

#	A	B	C	D
1	A	B	C	D
2	A	B	C	D
3	A	B	C	D
4	A	B	C	D
5	A	B	C	D
6	A	B	C	D
7	A	B	C	D
8	A	B	C	D
9	A	B	C	D
10	A	B	C	D
11	A	B	C	D
12	A	B	C	D
13	A	B	C	D
14	A	B	C	D
15	A	B	C	D
16	A	B	C	D
17	A	B	C	D
18	A	B	C	D
19	A	B	C	D
20	A	B	C	D
21	A	B	C	D
22	A	B	C	D
23	A	B	C	D
24	A	B	C	D
25	A	B	C	D
26	A	B	C	D
27	A	B	C	D
28	A	B	C	D
29	A	B	C	D
30	A	B	C	D
31	A	B	C	D
32	A	B	C	D
33	A	B	C	D
34	A	B	C	D
35	A	B	C	D

聽力測驗答對題數與分數對照表

答對題數	分數	答對題數	分數	答對題數	分級
35	120	23	80.5	11	38.5
34	115.5	22	77	10	35
33	112	21	73.5	9	31.5
32	108.5	20	70	8	28
31	105	19	66.5	7	24.5
30	101.5	18	63	6	21
29	98	17	59.5	5	17.5
28	94.5	16	56	4	14
27	91	15	52.5	3	10.5
26	87.5	14	49	2	7
25	85	13	45.5	1	3.5
24	84	12	42	0	0

閱讀測驗答對題數與分數對照表

答對題數	分數	答對題數	分數	答對題數	分級
35	120	23	80.5	11	38.5
34	115.5	22	77	10	35
33	112	21	73.5	9	31.5
32	108.5	20	70	8	28
31	105	19	66.5	7	24.5
30	101.5	18	63	6	21
29	98	17	59.5	5	17.5
28	94.5	16	56	4	14
27	91	15	52.5	3	10.5
26	87.5	14	49	2	7
25	85	13	45.5	1	3.5
24	84	12	42	0	0

考生姓名：＿＿＿＿＿＿

注意事項：

1. 限用 2B 鉛筆作答，否則不予計分。
2. 劃記要粗黑、清晰，不可出格，擦拭要清潔，若劃記過輕或汙損不清，不為機器所接受，考生自行負責。
3. 作答樣例：

正確方式 ■　　錯誤方式 ☑ ☒ ▨ ◖ ●

國際學村　全民英語能力分級檢定測驗
初級初試試答案紙（第六回）

聽力測驗答對題數與分數對照表

答對題數	分數	答對題數	分數	答對題數	分級
35	120	23	80.5	11	38.5
34	115.5	22	77	10	35
33	112	21	73.5	9	31.5
32	108.5	20	70	8	28
31	105	19	66.5	7	24.5
30	101.5	18	63	6	21
29	98	17	59.5	5	17.5
28	94.5	16	56	4	14
27	91	15	52.5	3	10.5
26	87.5	14	49	2	7
25	85	13	45.5	1	3.5
24	84	12	42	0	0

閱讀測驗答對題數與分數對照表

答對題數	分數	答對題數	分數	答對題數	分級
35	120	23	80.5	11	38.5
34	115.5	22	77	10	35
33	112	21	73.5	9	31.5
32	108.5	20	70	8	28
31	105	19	66.5	7	24.5
30	101.5	18	63	6	21
29	98	17	59.5	5	17.5
28	94.5	16	56	4	14
27	91	15	52.5	3	10.5
26	87.5	14	49	2	7
25	85	13	45.5	1	3.5
24	84	12	42	0	0

考生姓名：＿＿＿＿＿

注意事項：

1. 限用 2B 鉛筆作答，否則不予計分。
2. 劃記要粗黑、清晰、不可出格、擦拭要清潔，不爲機器所接受，考生自行負責。輕擦或汙損不清，不爲機器所接受，考生自行負責。
3. 作答樣例：

   正確方式 ■　　錯誤方式 ☑ ☒ ●

聽力能力測驗

1	A	B	C	D
2	A	B	C	D
3	A	B	C	D
4	A	B	C	D
5	A	B	C	D
6	A	B	C	D
7	A	B	C	D
8	A	B	C	D
9	A	B	C	D
10	A	B	C	D
11	A	B	C	D
12	A	B	C	D
13	A	B	C	D
14	A	B	C	D
15	A	B	C	D
16	A	B	C	D
17	A	B	C	D
18	A	B	C	D
19	A	B	C	D
20	A	B	C	D
21	A	B	C	D
22	A	B	C	D
23	A	B	C	D
24	A	B	C	D
25	A	B	C	D
26	A	B	C	D
27	A	B	C	D
28	A	B	C	D
29	A	B	C	D
30	A	B	C	D
31	A	B	C	D
32	A	B	C	D
33	A	B	C	D
34	A	B	C	D
35	A	B	C	D

閱讀能力測驗

1	A	B	C	D
2	A	B	C	D
3	A	B	C	D
4	A	B	C	D
5	A	B	C	D
6	A	B	C	D
7	A	B	C	D
8	A	B	C	D
9	A	B	C	D
10	A	B	C	D
11	A	B	C	D
12	A	B	C	D
13	A	B	C	D
14	A	B	C	D
15	A	B	C	D
16	A	B	C	D
17	A	B	C	D
18	A	B	C	D
19	A	B	C	D
20	A	B	C	D
21	A	B	C	D
22	A	B	C	D
23	A	B	C	D
24	A	B	C	D
25	A	B	C	D
26	A	B	C	D
27	A	B	C	D
28	A	B	C	D
29	A	B	C	D
30	A	B	C	D
31	A	B	C	D
32	A	B	C	D
33	A	B	C	D
34	A	B	C	D
35	A	B	C	D

測驗成績記錄表

（自己的姓名）＿＿＿＿＿＿＿＿＿ 這次英檢中級初試一定會過！

填表日期：＿＿＿年＿＿＿月＿＿＿日

達成日期：＿＿＿年＿＿＿月＿＿＿日

完成每次測驗後，請將所得到的成績用黑點●標示在表格上，就能感受到自己分數的進步。

台灣廣廈 國際出版集團
Taiwan Mansion International Group

國家圖書館出版品預行編目（CIP）資料

NEW GEPT全新全民英檢中級聽力＆閱讀題庫解析【新制修訂版】／國際
語言中心委員會, 郭文興, 許秀芬著. -- 初版. -- 新北市：國際學村, 2021.06
　　面；　公分
ISBN 978-986-454-158-4（平裝）
1.英語 2.讀本

805.1892　　　　　　　　　　　　　　　　　　　　110007015

國際學村

NEW GEPT 全新全民英檢中級聽力＆閱讀題庫解析【新制修訂版】
110年起最新改版英檢中級題型！6回試題完全掌握最新內容與趨勢！

作　　　者／國際語言中心委員會、　編輯中心編輯長／伍峻宏・編輯／陳怡樺
　　　　　　郭文興、許秀芬　　　　　封面設計／何偉凱・內頁排版／菩薩蠻數位文化有限公司
　　　　　　　　　　　　　　　　　　製版・印刷・裝訂／東豪・紘億・秉成

行企研發中心總監／陳冠蒨　　　　　媒體公關組／陳柔彣
　　　　　　　　　　　　　　　　　　綜合業務組／何欣穎

發　行　人／江媛珍
法 律 顧 問／第一國際法律事務所 余淑杏律師・北辰著作權事務所 蕭雄淋律師
出　　　版／國際學村
發　　　行／台灣廣廈有聲圖書有限公司
　　　　　　地址：新北市235中和區中山路二段359巷7號2樓
　　　　　　電話：（886）2-2225-5777・傳真：（886）2-2225-8052

代理印務・全球總經銷／知遠文化事業有限公司
　　　　　　地址：新北市222深坑區北深路三段155巷25號5樓
　　　　　　電話：（886）2-2664-8800・傳真：（886）2-2664-8801
郵 政 劃 撥／劃撥帳號：18836722
　　　　　　劃撥戶名：知遠文化事業有限公司（※ 單次購書金額未滿1000元需另付郵資70元。）

■ 出版日期：2021年6月　　　　ISBN：978-986-454-158-4
　　　　　　2023年12月6刷　　版權所有，未經同意不得重製、轉載、翻印。